"Cozy readers will savor c_____
tery. Ms. Furlong's turn o_____
ters are endearing, and _____
guessing until the very en_____
are loaded with Southern c_____ _____ characters, and tan-
talizing recipes—a pure delight!"

—Ellery Adams, *New York Times* bestselling author

"Georgia belles can handle anything—including murder—
as Susan Furlong proves in this sweet and juicy series
debut." —Sheila Connolly, *New York Times* bestselling author

Fallen peaches aren't the only things on the grounds of the Harpers' orchard . . .

I kept on reminiscing as I snatched napkins off the branches
and filled my bag. I was working my way through a row of
late-harvest trees, mostly freestones, meaning they peeled
away from the pit easily. My favorite was the O'Henry peach.
As a kid, I used to climb the branches and eat them until
my stomach hurt. I thought of how good a sweet, sun-warmed
peach would taste about now, especially since I'd passed on
the muffins earlier.

My stomach grumbled as I finished one row and cut
through to the next. I reached up and plucked another napkin
from a branch and surveyed the rest of the row. Down a ways,
I spied someone sitting on the ground, propped against one
of the trees. Obviously one of last night's guests had had too
much to drink and was sleeping it off. Well, of all things!

"Hey," I called out, ducking under a couple more branches
and heading toward the lazy drunkard. I had a thing or two
to tell this guy. Only, halfway there, I stopped in my tracks.
I recognized a man from the party. But he wasn't sleeping
it off. His blue-tinged, open-eyed face was slumped to one
side with my sister's brightly colored scarf cinched around
his neck . . .

Peaches and Scream

SUSAN FURLONG

BERKLEY PRIME CRIME, NEW YORK

BERKLEY
PRIME
CRIME

An imprint of Penguin Random House LLC
375 Hudson Street, New York, New York 10014

PEACHES AND SCREAM

A Berkley Prime Crime Book / published by arrangement with the author

ISBN: 978-0-425-27838-3

PUBLISHING HISTORY
Berkley Prime Crime mass-market edition / July 2015

PRINTED IN THE UNITED STATES OF AMERICA

10 9 8 7 6 5 4 3 2 1

Cover illustration by Erika LeBarre.
Cover design by Sarah Oberrender.
Interior text design by Laura K. Corless.
Interior map copyright © by Nurul Akmal Markani.

Penguin
Random
House

For my mother.
Your advice has always served me well.
Thank you.

Acknowledgments

The making of a book is a team effort and I'm fortunate to be part of an awesome team of people. A huge thank-you to my amazing agent, Jessica Faust, of BookEnds Literary Agency; and my editor, Kate Seaver, and her assistant editor, Katherine Pelz. Thanks also to Danielle Dill, publicist extraordinaire, and all the hardworking people behind the scenes at Berkley Prime Crime.

A special thank-you to my editing friend, beta reader, and best pair of second eyes around, Sandra Haven. Your advice and support are indispensable. Also, to Nurul Akmal Markani, who created an awesome map of the fictional town of Cays Mill, Georgia.

I depended on a whole host of experts including the fine folks at Dickey Peach Farms, Jaemor Farms, and Lane Southern Orchards. A special shout-out to the staff at Lane Southern Orchards who took time from their schedules to show me the complexities of a peach packing operation. Thank you also to Sergeant Bruce Ramseyer, who patiently answered my police-type questions. All these people are experts in their fields. Any mistakes you find within these pages are mine and mine alone.

A special thank-you to Patty and the staff of the historic New Perry Hotel, Perry, Georgia. Your warmth and graciousness epitomize the term "southern hospitality."

Finally, to my wonderful husband, Nyle. I'm so very grateful for your encouragement and steadfast support. And big hugs all around to our children: Patrick, Quinn, Regan, and Fiona—the best cheerleaders a mom could ever hope to have.

All my life, no matter where I travel or what adventure I'm living, I hear my mama's voice in my head, repeating over and over lessons she instilled in me during my youth. Lessons about what it means to be a proper Southern woman—feminine, sweet, charming . . . and most of all, strong. A handbook, of sorts. She calls these little gems of advice her Georgia Belle Facts—little bits of southern know-how passed down from Southern mothers to their daughters for generations. (Of course, she's put her own peculiar spin on a few of these southern tenets.) But overall, these facts are about living life to the fullest, with class, dignity and a sense of responsibility to care for our neighbors. Most important, though, her tidbits of wisdom have taught me that the Georgia Belle attitude isn't really about a particular region of the country. Nor is it about a person's heritage or financial status. In fact, because of my mama's tried-and-true advice, I've come to learn that the essence of southern spirit is for everyone—no matter who they are or where they live.

—NOLA MAE HARPER

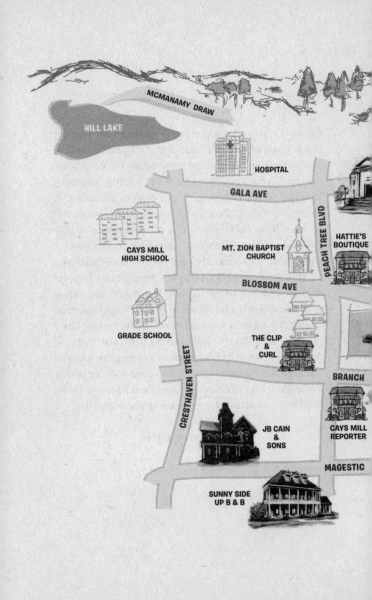

CAYS MILL, GEORGIA

HONKY TONK

TO THE HIGHWAY

CAYS MILL
BANK & TRUST

WAKEFIELD
LUMBER

PISTIL PETE'S
FLOWER SHOP

SUGAR'S
BAKERY

SHERIFF'S
OFFICE

TOWN SQUARE

MERCANTILE

ORCHARD LANE

EARL'S
BARBER SHOP

STREET

O'HENRY AVE

RED'S
DINER

CHURCH

BLVD

JOE PUCKETT'S CABIN

HARPER
PEACH FARM

Chapter 1

Georgia Belle Fact #027: In the South, we greet one another with bits of juicy gossip, not some ol' boring Yankee-like salutation.

I was idling on the corner of Blossom Street and Orchard, when the words came sailing through my open car window. "My word! Is that Nola Mae Harper I see?"

I snapped my head and squinted to the sidewalk where I spied the Crawford sisters sauntering along. I hadn't heard my full name, let alone that drawl I'd taken for granted in childhood, for a long time. I shot them a quick smile and waggled my fingers before moving down the road. As I continued, I noticed more than just a few of the locals rubbernecked as I passed, the sight of me eliciting curious stares and sudden whispers. I could imagine the return of the Harper family black sheep was going to crank the village's local rumor mill into full gear. Gee, it was good to be back.

They may have dubbed Georgia as the "Peach State," but what they weren't saying was my hometown of Cays Mill was the pit. I should know; I was born and raised in this two-stoplight town and had spent most of my adult life trying to shake its loamy soil from my boots. That's why I surprised myself when home was the first place I thought of when my work situation took a turn for the worse. Then I *really* surprised myself when I agreed to spend time at home watching over the family's one hundred–plus acres of peach farm while Mama and Daddy took their dream trip. But I guess I did owe them. Or so I'd been told—or had it implied in Mama's southern sweet talk—often enough.

Truth be known, they had been the world's best parents; and I, well . . . I hadn't always been the best daughter. At least that was what my older sister, Ida Jean, kept telling me. Of course, maybe she had a point. She'd stuck around Cays Mill, married the banker's son and was busy adding little twigs to the Harper family tree, a set of twins so far and another baby on the way. I, on the other hand, headed north of the Piedmont the first chance I got, took a job with a humanitarian organization and had been traipsing from one country to another for the last fifteen years or so, seeing the world or, perhaps more accurately, escaping from my own world. Heaven knows, if I hadn't left Cays Mill when I did, hard telling what type of shame I'd have brought to the Harper family name.

Anyhow, it'd been almost three years since I was home last and it looked like not much had changed in town. The city building, still the most formidable structure in the area, occupied most of the town green and acted as an unsurpassable anchor for Cays Mill's business section. Not that there were many businesses around these days. Like many small towns, the recession had hit our village hard. As I drove about the square, I saw more than a few vacant buildings, their empty windows only partially obscured under the bright awnings that served to protect the storefronts from the scorching Georgia heat. However, I was happy to see Red's Diner was still going strong. A line was formed outside the door, probably the after-church crowd, heading in for Red's famous breakfast hash, served with grits and a side of toast with—what else?—peach preserves.

At the next stoplight I stole a quick glance in the rearview mirror and swiped a short piece of cropped hair from my forehead, before gripping the wheel and turning off the square. I traveled southeast, winding my way a mile or so out of town, heading for the family farm.

If I had to describe Georgia, I'd say it was like a handmade quilt, tossed out all lumpy-like over the bed. The northern part of the state would be the biggest bumps, where the Appalachian hills offered a beautiful blue hue and the winding rivers ran through like errant stitching. Then came the Piedmont, with big cities like Atlanta and Columbus acting as the nubby knots holding the fabric and the batting in place. Next, the Fall Line, where the rivers made a showy descent like colorful fabric bargellos, cascading over rocks and flowing to the smooth coastal planes where scenic towns like Savannah provided a decorative binding, sealing the quilt's overall beauty. My family's little block of the fabric was located on the Fall Line, where the northern rivers dumped their sandy deposits, making soil conditions just right for growing peaches, which my family had done for as many generations as I could count.

Heading down the road out of town plunged me into the orchard area, where the sullenness of the weathered town stood in sharp contrast to the peach trees, standing row on row, like sturdy soldiers, their green uniforms shining in the Georgia sun, holding guard over this community. Even the late-August sun couldn't extinguish the bristling green of the leaves, whispering their welcome to me in the light breeze.

Even though I'd all but had my fill of peaches during my youth, I had to admit my heart kicked up a beat in anticipation as I neared home. It'd been so long since I'd been back, and I was craving a little time at home with my family. So much so that by the time I passed under the gate that marked the entrance to Harper Peach Farm, I was practically giddy with excitement. Or sick with nerves; I wasn't sure which. I couldn't believe I'd agreed to take over the family farm for three whole weeks. Even though the last of the peaches had been picked, packed and transported out, taking care of the farm was a huge responsibility. Still, it was going to be good to be home for a while. At least until I figured out what to do about my job. I'd been beside myself ever since my boss told me they were downsizing and I'd been allocated to a desk job in Atlanta. A desk job! After all these years of fieldwork, they expected me to be satisfied twiddling my thumbs behind a desk. Not this girl. No way.

"Nola Mae Harper!" I heard my daddy yell from the deep porch of our two-story farmhouse. Seconds later, the slamming of the screen storm door yielded a stream of ebullient Harpers.

"Whoa! One at a time." I laughed, embracing them warmly until I got to my sister, Ida Jean. Her hug felt stiff compared to the others. "Hello, Ida. You're looking good." I patted her expanding belly before turning to the oldest Harper child, my big brother, Raymond Junior—Ray to me, Bud to my parents and Raymond Harper II to his colleagues at the law firm. "I've missed you, Ray!" I buried my head in his chest, coming up for air to greet my sister's twin girls, who danced about our legs. In true southern fashion, they were properly named Savannah and Charlotte. Although I could never tell which was which. In the three years since I'd seen them, with only occasional photos for reference, I was astounded by how big they'd grown.

"Your hair sure is short," one of them said, gripping my legs, her eyes wide. I ran a hand through my dark cropped hair and chuckled. Both the girls were towheads—a combination of my brother-in-law's blond hair and my sister's light blue eyes. Typical little belles, they sported long curls that suited their sleeveless butter yellow sundresses and white sandals. By contrast, my khaki-colored utility shorts and black tank top, walking boots and knee-high socks— which all served me well in jungle situations—seemed apparently exotic to my nieces as their sparkling eyes took it all in. They possessed equal amounts of devilish energy that would be expected from any six-year-old, the problem being that with twins, the trouble was always times two.

Managing to break away, I headed straight for my parents, embracing Mama first. "Good to have you home, honey," she said against my shoulder. I swear, she'd shrunk another half inch. Although the whole county knew better than to let my mother's petite stature fool them. Della Wilkes Harper may be tiny, but she was a force to reckon with.

On the other hand, there was nothing small about my father. Daddy always loomed larger than life. Right then, he was hanging back, watching us with a grin spread wide over his face. I turned to him and held out my arms. He skipped forward, scooping me off my feet into a giant bear hug. "I can't believe you're finally home, darlin'. Now the party can get started!"

I peered over the top of his wide shoulders, ignoring the look of disgust on Ida's face, and let my eyes roam the orchard line, where a white tent had been set up to accommodate at least two hundred guests. In my quick glance at the tent, it almost appeared as if miniature peach trees held up each corner, but before I could figure it out, Daddy had released me from his hug for a close-up look at my tanned face and short hair. With a tousle of my hair he gave a laugh, loving me in his own way, always accepting of me, no matter what. I felt tears start to well and knew coming home had been the right choice.

Besides, this trip was extra special. My parents were celebrating their fiftieth wedding anniversary and this "dream trip" of theirs was really a second honeymoon, or first honeymoon, since they never got to go on a trip after their wedding. Anyway, this evening's party was sure to be a wingding. The trip had actually been a prize Mama had won for her peach chutney recipe in the National Condiments Competition, with the timing for the cruise set by the competition. Because no way would they have left at this time of year otherwise—the

Peach Harvest Festival was only a couple weeks away. Since our parents had never, ever missed a festival, Ida had decided to give their anniversary celebration a peach festival flair, so they were technically not missing this year's festivities either. I was anxious to see what she'd come up with. Knowing Ida, it'd be perfect.

Speaking of whom, as soon as Daddy swung me around to head for the porch, Ida started in. "It's just like you to show up for the fun. Never mind all the work it took to get ready for this party."

Aw . . . so that was it. "Sorry, Ida. I got tied up in traffic outside Atlanta. But I'll do double the work cleaning up after the party. I promise."

She harrumphed and stormed ahead, heading straight for the house. Mama waved away the bad air left in her wake. "Don't pay any attention to her. She's just exhausted. Hollis has been working long hours and the kids are wearing her out." My mother had been making excuses for Ida's behavior since we were children. I knew, on the other hand, that my behavior was always open for discussion. As if to prove that point, she looped her arm in mine and said, "Come sit awhile. I've made some tea; we'll get caught up on all your latest adventures." Which translated to: *Come in and sit with me so I can pick apart your life and remind you that you should be settled down, married and having children by now.*

I sent a pleading look Daddy's way, hoping he'd rescue me from the pending lecture. Instead, he patted my back and shot me a half-apologetic look. "Go on ahead. Bud and I have a few details to tend to. We'll have time to get caught up tonight."

"Yes, come on, dear," Mama insisted. "And don't worry about your bags. Your brother will put them in your room. Won't you, Bud?" She continued walking, not waiting for a response from Ray. Mama's questions were never really questions, but orders laid out with the type of charm that only a true Southern lady could pull off. "We've kept your room the same," she continued. "Even though you hardly ever come home anymore. Oh, and Hattie called. She's so excited you're back. Said she might stop by early to visit before the party."

The thought of seeing Hattie again thrilled me. Her family used to live just down the road and she'd been my best friend all through school. There was a time when she, Cade—her older brother—and I were inseparable. A smile tugged at my lips as I remembered the trouble we'd get into and how much fun we had annoying Ida and her friends. Of course, thinking back to the scowl Ida had greeted me with, I figured I still annoyed her.

I opened the screen door for Mama and followed her in. "Are you excited for the party tonight, Mama?" I asked, glancing around with a happy feeling. Our house was exactly the same as when I left, right down to a lingering smell of fried chicken mixed with the faint scent of Daddy's cigars. Today, there was also a little fruity smell mixed in. Ida must've been cooking up something peachy in the kitchen.

Mama nodded, motioning for me to sit at the dining room table as she headed for the kitchen. "Yes, I can hardly wait," she said over her shoulder. After a few seconds, she came back through the swinging kitchen door with a couple glasses of sweet tea. "Your sister has really put herself out getting everything ready." She took a sip of tea and swiped a napkin under her sweating glass before placing it back on the table. "I hope she's not working too hard, with the baby so close and all."

I looked away, feeling guiltier than ever for not coming home earlier and helping more with the party. I'd begged off on coming home a week earlier, claiming, correctly, that I had things to tie up at the Helping Hands International headquarters before I could leave. What I had to tie up was every string I could find to keep me out of a desk job—but to no avail in the end anyway. In retrospect it might have been more pleasant blowing up balloons with Ida. "I'm sure she's happy to do it. Fifty years, Mama." I patted her hand. "That's something to celebrate."

"Yes, it is!" she said, although I noticed her smile didn't seem to reach her eyes.

"Are you worried about the farm, because I'm sure I can handle—"

"Oh heavens no! I know you'll take good care of things around here."

I studied her for a moment. Something was off. "Are you sad to miss the harvest festival? I know it means so much to you." She and Daddy first met at the peach festival, and they'd never missed a single one in the fifty years they'd been married.

She tilted her head back and chuckled. My mama had a deep, raspy laugh that seemed too big for her tiny frame, but I never tired of hearing it. "How could I be sad when your sister has practically re-created the whole festival for tonight?" She leaned forward, eyes twinkling. "Oh, Nola. Wait till you see what's she's come up with. Why, the decorations, the flowers, the food . . . It's all just divine."

Boy, I owed my sister big-time. "I'm so glad, Mama. And I can't wait to see Hattie. When did she get back?"

"A few months ago when her father took ill. He's in the convalescent home east of town. Alzheimer's, I think. That family's had its share of trouble—that's for sure."

I dipped my eyes, running my hand over the marred top of our family table. Poor Hattie. I never understood how some people had to bear so much sadness while others seemed to breeze through life without a care. Maybe that was why I'd loved my job so much. It gave me a chance to try to right the off-balanced nature of life. Something I knew wasn't going to be possible from behind a desk.

"You know, she's started a dress shop down on the square," Mama added, bringing relief to the downturn in the conversation.

My mood lightened. "A dress shop! Hattie?" Although I shouldn't have been surprised. Hattie was always the epitome of southern fashion. "How about Cade?" I asked, wondering if he was still around.

"Cade McKenna? He's still here. He started his own contracting business."

"Really? He always did like building things. Do you remember that old fort we made over by the Hole?" The Harper farm included more than a hundred acres of land, most of which were planted in peach trees. The other part was wooded, with a branch of the Ocmulgee River cascading over large rocks and forming a deep, cool pool at the bottom. Growing up, we'd called it the Hole, short for the swimming hole. I'd spent many a hot afternoon cooling off there.

"Yes, you kids were always up to something." She paused and took a long sip of her tea. I could hear Ida knocking around in the kitchen and wondered if she would join us soon. Mama swiped her napkin around the sweating glass again and continued, "You three were a menace. I had to keep a constant eye on you. Heaven only knows all the trouble you got into."

I smiled, thinking she didn't know the half of it. And, never would, if I could help it. "I wonder if Cade will show up tonight."

She leveled her gaze on me, her blue eyes twinkling. "Of course he's coming, dear. *Everyone's* going to be here."

My mother wasn't exaggerating. In fact, the crowd started arriving early. It was only a little before five when I heard the first set of tires crunching on our gravel drive. Ray was already in position outside to direct the parking of the cars to strategically avoid a complete block-up of the property. Ida was no doubt directing everything downstairs. I was still in my room trying to decide between my only formal attire—a black halter-top dress, great for hot tropical climates, or a deep blue silk dress with long sleeves for countries with modesty codes—when a knock sounded on the door.

"Nola?"

I looked up to see Hattie standing in the doorway. "Hattie!" I screamed, running to hug her. "You haven't changed a bit." She hadn't, either. Hattie always looked like she'd just stepped out of the pages of a southern fashion magazine. Tonight was no different. She was wearing a cute little flowered sundress that barely glanced her knees and mid-calf rhinestone-studded cowboy boots. She even had her dark hair done up big, with a glitzy barrette holding back one side. I glanced down at the bed where I'd laid out my choices. Suddenly, neither dress seemed right. I was going to stick out like a sore thumb at the party.

"This suits you," she said, reaching out and fingering my hair.

"You think? I cut it earlier when I went to Darfur. Long hair just didn't work in the refugee camps."

She sighed. "Well, bless your heart. I can't even imagine. How long have you been gone this time? Three years?" she asked.

"At least. I don't think I've seen you since your mama . . ." I let my words trail off. A few years ago, Hattie lost her mother to cancer. I came back to support her during that awful time, but since then, I'd let our friendship slip. "Hattie, I'm sorry I haven't called more often. I haven't been a good friend to you."

She clasped my hands, squeezing tightly. "It's just as much my fault. The phone line runs both ways, you know? And you *were* here for me when I needed it most. It's just that after Mama passed, I lost my bearings." Her eyes grew moist. "You know, Nola Mae, there's just nothing better than a mama that's always there for you. You remember that, okay?"

I swallowed hard, trying to understand her sorrow, yet not wanting to think too much about the day I might not have my own mother. I just couldn't face the possibility of such significant grief. I reached out and hugged her again. This time when I pulled back she wore a happier look on her face.

"Well, let's not dwell on all that," she said. "What's important is that we're here now and are about to celebrate a happy occasion." She glanced down at the bed. "Having trouble picking your dress?"

I fingered the silk dress. "I bought this on a whim at an Indonesian market a few months back, but haven't worn it yet."

"For heaven's sake, why not? It's gorgeous! The color is perfect for your blue eyes."

"Really?" I stood and carried the dress to the mirror and held it in front of me. I wasn't sure. I'd never really considered such things. Most of my time was spent doing things like roaming field sites in search of water supplies, teaching English to slum orphans and searching rubble for earthquake survivors—strictly jeans and T-shirt type of stuff. I was out of practice when it came to dressing up. Usually, I just applied sunscreen, threw on a baseball cap and got busy. "You really think this one looks good?"

Hattie slid into the mirror next to me. She fingered the fine silk embroidery of songbirds in gold thread that edged the sleeves and matched the flowered trim around the scooped neckline. "Yes, I do," she said, brushing aside a piece of my wispy bangs. "Especially after I fix your hair and makeup for you."

I giggled. "The last time you said that was right before senior prom. I had a date with . . . Oh, what was that guy's name?" I'd stripped down to my skivvies and was pulling the dress over my head.

"Danny Hicks."

"Oh, that's right. Was that night ever a disaster! Especially when"—I choked on even saying his name, as that night flooded back on me—"you-know-who showed up. He's not still around here, is he?" I had a horrible vision of running into him at the party.

Hattie wheeled me around and started working the dress's buttons. "Last I heard he was somewhere up by Macon. I haven't seen him since I've been back, though."

"Good." I let the image of that night, the wonder of it at the time, the horror of it later, pass by. I'd left that behind me, I reminded myself. Forever.

"Well, don't worry," she assured me. "All that's in the past now. And tonight's not going to be anything like our senior prom. Fifty years of marriage! Can you imagine? What could possibly go wrong when we're celebrating something so wonderful?"

I turned back to the mirror and smiled at my image. At the moment, everything did seem right with the world. My parents were celebrating their marriage and embarking on an adventure, I had three weeks to hang at home, rest and catch up with my best friend . . . and the dress did look darn good on me. "You're right," I echoed her sentiments. "What could possibly go wrong?"

Chapter 2

Georgia Belle Fact #012: The reason Georgia women have such big hair is because all the gossip and secrets overflowing from their heads has to go somewhere!

I had to admit, Ida had done a wonderful job planning our parents' party. The atmosphere did remind me of the peach festival, only slightly more refined. The most stunning feature was the columns that held up the massive tent. I'd been right at my first glance—they did look like miniature trees but with gigantic clumps of peaches topping each one, right under the tent's white canopy. Each tent post had been wrapped in an oversized tube of cardboard that had been covered with crumpled tissue paper and painted brown to resemble the rough bark of a tree trunk. As I stepped closer, each peach cluster at the top seemed even larger, all fuzzy and blushed like the most perfect watermelon-sized peaches ever grown.

"Auntie Nola!" I heard the stereo echo of Savannah and Charlotte. "Aren't they *wooonderful*?" Their giggles spoke of their participation in creating this miracle. As I inspected the "fruit," the girls quickly related every step in the process of blowing up balloons, banding them with a string just tight enough to create a peach crease, flocking them with a fuzzy craft spray and then airbrushing them into the peachy hues with a sun-kissed blush. Mischievous laughs and twinkling eyes belied some trouble in getting the sprayed flock off their skin and off who knew what else. Yes, Ida, accomplished mother and craftsperson, had certainly outdone herself, especially considering the "helpers" she'd had on hand!

In the next heartbeat, the two scampered off, calling out to someone else, leaving me in their wake. I shook my head—the decorations were, in fact, *wooonderful*, but these little Southern belle nieces of mine were marvels. A moment of melancholy that I'd missed out on seeing them grow up, or on having any little ones of my own, prickled my skin. I rubbed my arms; I'd simply chosen another path.

I quickly glanced around at the rest of the affair. Ida had picked a beautiful, peach-inspired palette for the decorations, from deep crimson red-orange to pale yellow. I felt like I'd just stepped into the orchard at harvest time. I was glad she'd chosen to celebrate at the farm and not at the church hall or the local VFW. I was sure it cost a fortune to rent the three-tiered frame tent from as far away as Macon and the two hundred–plus chairs. But as I stood watching the sun set over the rolling peach grove, I knew there was no better place to celebrate this milestone than where my parents had built their life together.

"Nola Mae?"

I turned at the familiar sound of his voice. "Cade?" It'd been so long, I was caught off guard by his appearance. The three years since I'd seen him at his mother's funeral had caught up to Cade McKenna. He still looked a lot like his sister: the same dark hair, chiseled features and large solemn eyes. Only his were dark brown, almost black, while Hattie's were an unsettling blue-gray color. Now, though, his dark hair was prematurely tinged with gray and his eyes lined at the corners. I self-consciously touched my own cheek, wondering if the telltale signs of a decade and half since our high school days were visible on my face as well.

"You haven't changed a bit," he remarked, as if reading my mind. "Except your hair's lot shorter."

I chuckled and reached out with a hug, then quickly backed away. For some reason, our reunion felt awkward. Strange, because with Hattie it was as if we picked up where we'd left off. "It's been a while, hasn't it?"

"I'd say. Not since my mother's funeral. But I'm glad you're back, Nola." He shoved his hands into the pockets of his jeans, his gaze moving to the ground, obviously feeling as awkward as I did.

I ducked my chin, trying to make eye contact. "Mama says you've started a contracting business."

He nodded. "Yeah. Mostly remodels and repair work. There's not much need for new builds in this area. But I'm doing okay. And what about you? Guess you're still traveling and helping people."

I had to smile at the way he simplified my job. Cade had always spoken in a direct, straightforward way. He had an easygoing manner about him. Just the opposite of Hattie, who was more of a little ball of energy. "Yup. I've spent most of my time traveling. Haiti, then a few months in Indonesia, plus a little time in Sudan . . . and if you think the summers are hot here in Georgia . . ." I rambled on. Cade nodded politely, but I knew I was probably boring him to death. I couldn't help it; I loved my job. Well, at least the job I used to have.

"That's great," he jumped in when I finally came up for air. "How long are you going to stick around here, then?"

I hesitated. The day before I left headquarters up in Atlanta, I found out that I'd been reallocated from fieldwork to a position as an operations coordinator—with no chance of changing the minds of the bosses. Which meant I'd be stuck behind a desk planning relief efforts instead of actually providing hands-on help. I hated the idea of a desk job.

"Just until my parents return," I finally answered, not wanting to go into too many details about my current dilemma. "I'll be looking over the place for them while they travel." My eyes swept over the view to where the land rolled away in a series of ridges and then eventually turned into the dense green wooded areas along the river bottom. I'd seen a lot of the world since leaving the farm, places and scenery that Cade could never imagine. Still, the fruit-filled hills of our farm always held a special place in my heart.

Cade moved to my side, his dark eyes also taking in the countryside. The conversation died away and we fell into an uncomfortable silence, punctuated by waves of clicking tree frogs as they got in the last word before the sun dipped below the horizon. I couldn't quite put my finger on it, but for some reason, Cade and I no longer shared the same easy banter that we'd enjoyed as kids. Something was different about him. I stole a glance at his profile, trying to figure it out.

"What?" he asked, when he caught me looking.

"Nothing. I mean, is everything okay? You seem . . ."

He turned and faced me head-on. "I seem what? And what would you know about how I seem? We haven't seen each other for three years. And you barely spoke to me at my mother's funeral."

I took a half step back and shook my head. *Where is this coming from?* "It didn't seem like a good time to be all social, with your mama just passing and all."

"Was that really it?"

I shrugged. I actually kept to myself whenever I came back to Cays Mill because I didn't want to stir up questions. Questions about why I'd left so quickly right after high school. Of course, Hattie knew. But she'd never betray my secret, not even to her own brother.

He went on, "How come you don't ever come home anymore?"

None of your business. "Oh, don't be silly," I finessed. "I'd come home more if I could. My work just keeps me busy, that's all." I held up my hands, palms out. "I'm home now, aren't I?"

He studied me closely. "Yes, and I'm glad you're back."

Really? You don't sound like it.

Behind us, clanking dishes signaled that people were heading to the buffet line. Not knowing what else to say, I started glancing about and noticed Ida glaring at me from across the room. She caught my eye and waved me over. I turned to Cade and touched his arm. "Duty calls. I'll be sitting with my family for dinner, but I hope we can catch up some more."

He laughed. "Don't worry. Hattie is making enough plans to fill your social calendar for the next three weeks. Then there's the Peach Harvest Festival." I apparently had a blink-blink reaction at that, because he asked, "You're not leaving before the festival, are you?"

I knew someone would ask me sooner or later about the festival. I needed to make up my mind if I was going or not. It wasn't that I didn't love our annual tradition, because I did. I had tons of fond festival memories. There was always a kids' carnival, booths with folk art displays, great music and plenty of peachy food. My mouth watered just thinking about Harley Corbin's famous funnel cakes topped with homemade peach sauce. Or the veterans' local booth where they scooped hand-cranked peach ice cream. The festival was the biggest thing happening around these parts. That was the problem. *Everyone* would be there. Maybe even . . . Oh well, if I decided not to go, I could always fake some sort of illness. I put on my best smile. "Of course I'll be there. I wouldn't miss it for the world."

He exhaled and grinned. "Good. Then I guess we'll probably be seeing a lot of each other over the next few weeks."

I met his eyes again. Whatever attitude he'd had earlier was gone. He seemed back to normal, almost like the old Cade I used to know. "I'll be looking forward to that," I said, thinking that the idea of seeing more of Cade McKenna might be fun after all.

"You've done a great job with this party. It's unbelievable," I told Ida after we'd settled around the table with our food. I glanced at the couple dozen tables covered in white linen and set with simple but exquisite place settings. Ida had designed the centerpieces with low arrangements of flowers in striking shades of peach: dark peach gerbera and pink-tinged carnations alternated with spiky peach-colored delphinium. She'd even used cotton bolls and bits of fig branches from the farm as fill-in. Next to each arrangement she'd placed framed photos of our parents' wedding day, the old black-and-white images sharply contrasting with the colorful flowers. Above us, yellow paper lanterns cast a warm hue over the guests. I watched as Mama and Daddy mingled from table to table, practically glowing themselves as they worked the room and visited with their friends.

"Well, it *was* a lot of work," she replied.

I was feeling entirely plagued with guilt. "I'm sure it was. I'm sorry I wasn't here to be more of a help. I arranged to come back as soon as I could get away."

"I understand. I really do." She sighed. "It's just that things have been stressful around here." She pushed at her food, moving it from one side of her plate to the other, seemingly preoccupied.

I studied her more closely, my eyes sliding down to her pregnant belly. "Is it the baby? Is everything okay?"

"Oh, yes. The baby's fine." She leaned in closer. "It's a boy," she whispered. "But don't tell anyone. Hollis wants to keep it a secret."

I grinned, happy for her. With twin girls already, a boy would be a great addition. I glanced around. "Where is Hollis? I haven't seen him." *Not that I had actually been looking.*

She looked about nervously and tugged at the colorful scarf around her neck. I'd always admired my sister's ability to pull together an outfit. Even seven months pregnant she looked great in a simple black dress paired with a hand-painted silk scarf. She must have been to the Clip & Curl recently, too; her hair was tinged with honey-colored highlights. "It's hard telling," she said, her face falling. "He's been preoccupied with a big bank deal lately."

"Oh, I see," I said, understanding where the stress was coming from. No wonder my sister had come on so cold earlier. This party, her twins, the pregnancy . . . All that and Hollis had been busy with work and unable to help. Of course, the same thing could be said about me. I placed my hand on hers. "I'm sorry again. I should have come home earlier. It's not fair that you've had to take on all this on your own."

She looked up from her plate and squinted toward our parents, who were engaged in a lively discussion with Reverend Jones and his wife. "No, it's more than that," she started, but was interrupted by Hollis's arrival.

He plunked down next to her and slid his plate onto the table. "Good food, honey," he commented, placing a half-empty glass next to his heaping plate. He was probably drinking Peach Jack, a well-loved peach-flavored whiskey distilled right in our own county. I never really liked the stuff, but Daddy and Hollis seemed to have a taste for it. We seldom had a party without a bottle or two.

"Good to see you again, Nola," he said, but I didn't believe him. Hollis and I had never been on friendly terms—not since he made a pass at me the night before he married my sister.

"Hello, Hollis," I replied, trying to inject a bit of friendliness into my tone. I searched the room for Ray, wishing he'd hurry up and join us. It was going to be awkward with just Ida, Hollis and me.

Not seeing him, I turned my attention back to my own plate. Ida really had gone all out with the food. With help from Ginny at Red's Diner, she'd put together a scrumptious buffet: fresh greens with grilled peaches and a tangy peach vinaigrette, slow-roasted pork with the famous Harper Farm peach chutney on the side, and a yummy vegetable Napoleon made with fresh picks from Snyder's farm down the road. Even Ezra, the owner of the local bakery, had risen to the occasion. He'd donated the most delicately decorated peach ruffle cake with tiny white sugar blossoms. It was almost too beautiful to cut.

That was how it was in small communities. Everyone came together for happy events, just like one big family. I'd seen that in villages in Africa too, and had admired it in places where sharing water became a life-sustaining gift. Guess I'd never really appreciated that same principle in my own hometown.

I'd just started on my salad, when a series of high-pitched giggles made me look up from my plate. Hollis was playing with Ida's scarf, wrapping it around his hands suggestively while she tried to wrestle it back from him. "I think I'll just hang on to this for later tonight," he teased, sliding it into his pocket and shooting me a wink. I about gagged.

Thank goodness Ray showed up. "Hey, Hollis. Ben Wakefield is looking for you." He sat down, digging into his plate of food like he hadn't eaten for a month.

Ida groaned. "More business, Hollis? Can't it wait until tomorrow?"

He gave her a quick kiss, grabbed his glass and stood. "Not if the bank wants to keep Wakefield's newest deal. Don't worry, though. I'll be back in a jiff."

No hurry, I thought, watching him disappear into the crowd.

Ida absently moved her hand to her bare neck. "Oh shoot, he still has my scarf," she said, realizing her perfect outfit had been jeopardized.

Ray and I exchanged a half smile; Ida had always prided herself on being properly "put together." Ray said, "Don't worry, sis; he said he'd be right back. What type of deal is he working with Ben Wakefield, anyway?"

"Some sort of lumber deal," Ida explained. "Ben Wakefield's company has contracted with a developer in Atlanta and he's trying to strike a bargain with a few local landowners to purchase their properties' timber rights. Wakefield Lumber is using his bank to finance the deal. Hollis is expecting to be able to get a huge rate of return on the loan, plus a share in the whole thing."

"You mean, like a profit share?" Ray asked between bites.

Ida shrugged. "Yeah, something like that." She sighed heavily. "I don't really understand all that's involved. Only that it's taking all of Hollis's time these days. I'm sick of it. Actually, I'm sick of everything." She stabbed at her pork, sending splatters of peach chutney in every direction. "Especially peaches!" she cried, then covered her mouth in shock. I could see tears threatening at the edges of her eyes. "Oh, I'm so sorry. Excuse me. I need to use the restroom."

She stood abruptly, almost knocking over her chair. I also stood, meaning to go after her.

"Don't," Ray said, stopping me. "Let her have a little time alone. She's upset, but she'll get over it."

I sat back down. Out of the corner of my eye, I saw Mama and Daddy winding their way toward us. "I don't get it, Ray. What's going on around here?"

Upon seeing our parents, he plastered a smile on his face. "I'll tell you all about it later. Now's not the time."

His words not only piqued my curiosity, but gave me a little shiver of dread. Although both feelings faded as the evening wore on and the party picked up with lively tunes from a local bluegrass band. Couples zigzagged their way toward a portable dance floor set up at the back of the tent. Ray joined in the parade, asking a family friend for a dance. I kicked back and watched them, breathing in the cool night breeze blowing through the open-walled tent. I saw my parents take center stage on the dance floor, starting things off with "Kentucky Waltz." After a few refrains, other couples joined in the fun.

"How romantic." Hattie sighed, taking over Ray's abandoned seat. She was sipping on sweet peach tea, but knowing Hattie, it was probably laced with something a bit stronger.

"I know. I'm so happy for them," I agreed. "And to think, in another hour or so they'll be leaving for their cruise." The plan was that Ray would drive them to Macon, where they'd catch the red-eye for Miami. From there, they were off for three weeks in the Caribbean.

Hattie started picking at a piece of untouched cake Ray had left behind. "Mmm . . . yummy."

"Hey, there, Nola Mae." We both looked up to see a few of the local gals. They passed by in a breeze of flowery cologne, dramatically flipping their well-worked tresses over their shoulders and looking down their noses at me.

Hattie wiggled her fingers and plastered a toothy smile on her face. "Hey, all!" Then to me she whispered, "Lawd, if that Laney Burns keeps teasing her hair like that, it's gonna get pissed."

I laughed, then sobered as I touched my own short crop. "I don't quite fit in around here anymore, do I?"

"Like fitting in around here is all it's cracked up to be. Don't pay attention to those girls. They're jealous because you've been somewhere. I had the same thing when I got back from the city."

I nodded, still feeling a little deflated.

She patted my shoulder and changed the subject. "So, are your parents all packed and ready to go?"

I nodded. "I think they've had their bags packed for a week. Mama's so excited. She's always wanted to go on a cruise. They never had an official honeymoon, so I think this is her way of making up for lost time." I looked around. "Where's Cade?" I was secretly hoping he'd ask me to dance.

Hattie scanned the crowd. "There he is."

I glanced to where she was pointing and saw Cade deep in conversation with another man. "Hey, who's that guy he's talking to?"

Hattie's voice took on an annoyed tone. "That's Ben Wakefield. He owns Wakefield Lumber Mill."

I watched as Cade waved his fist in Wakefield's face. Behind him, Hollis was watching the argument with furrowed brows. "Cade seems angry about something."

Hattie pulled out a pink monogrammed hanky out of her bag, dabbed at her décolletage and sighed. "Oh, it's a long story. I'll fill you in later; now's not really a good time."

That was the second time that night I'd heard those words. First from Ray and now from Hattie. Something was definitely going on and I was eager to find out what. But before I could ask any more questions, a Hispanic-looking man swooped in and grabbed ahold of Hattie's arm.

"Come dance with me," he said, speaking with a slight accent.

Hattie popped up, wrapped her arms around his neck and planted a playful kiss on his cheek. "Nola, this is Pete Sanchez. Pete, Nola Mae Harper."

Pete smiled down at me. "My pleasure, Nola."

I simply stared, entranced by his devastatingly dark good looks, or maybe just taken aback by the way Hattie seemed to light up in his presence. She shoved him ahead and leaned down toward me, her eyes dancing wickedly as she mockingly fanned herself. "Oh my, I feel some serious sin comin' on tonight."

"I won't wait around for you," I said, laughing as I watched her catch up to Pete. The band was kicking things up a notch with a lively Hank Williams Jr. tune and couples were spinning crazy-like on the floor—most of them half-snookered by now. I looked back to where I'd seen Cade, but he was already gone. I sighed. Guess I wasn't going to get that dance after all.

Before I knew it, the evening was nothing more than a fuzzy memory Ray and I were rehashing over our Monday morning coffee. "So, Mama and Daddy got on their flight okay?" I asked. We were standing in the kitchen, a plate of spiced peach muffins on the counter between us. Mama had cooked up a storm before she left. There was enough food stored in the freezer to feed me and probably half the county for the next three weeks.

Ray blew steam off the top of his mug. "You bet. You should have seen them when I dropped them off. They were acting like newlyweds."

"Good for them. Have you talked to Ida yet this morning?" Ida and Hollis had taken the girls home early the night before. We'd made plans to start cleanup first thing this morning. The rental company was coming at nine to pick up the tent.

"No. I bet she's exhausted, though." He reached for a muffin.

Especially if she and Hollis played around with the scarf after the party. My stomach practically rolled at the thought. I pushed the muffins closer to Ray. Suddenly they didn't look so appetizing. "I'm sure she is tired," I agreed, rinsing my mug and putting it in the sink. "Hey, I'm going to get started on things outside. Maybe we can get a good bit finished before she gets here. I feel like I owe her for all the work she's done."

He shoved in his last bite and answered with a full mouth. "Sure. I'll be out in a bit. I've got a few business calls to make."

Ray was an attorney. A while back, he'd left a large firm in Atlanta and hung his own shingle in Perry, a town not far from Cays Mill. "Fine with me. Take your time, but later I want to talk to you about something you mentioned last night."

He nodded, his shoulders slumping and a dark look crossing his face. Noticing his reaction, another sense of dread settled over me. I pushed it to the back of my mind as I headed out to the yard to get started on my to-do list.

I glanced around. What had looked so pretty the night before was simply an ugly mess this morning: dirty dishes, turned-over chairs, empty beer bottles . . . Worst of all, a strong breeze had blown in overnight, scattering debris throughout the orchards, and half of the oversized peach balloons had deflated into dehydrated versions of themselves. The wind must have caught the pile of paper napkins off the cake table. Branches, as far as I could see, were covered with bits of peach-colored paper. It looked like a group of errant teens had TP'd us with off-colored toilet tissue.

I groaned and headed back into the house, coming out a few seconds later with a handful of garbage bags and heading straight for the orchard. I figured I better get the litter that was the farthest out first before it wandered any more. The morning haze was just burning off as I started down the hill. Since peaches grew best in well-drained soil, our house sat on the highest point of our acreage, with the peach trees running in straight lines from every side of the house.

When I was young, I once tried to draw a picture of our house. I was disgusted when Ray teased me, saying it looked like a scared, pink-haired witch. Although, looking back on it now, that was exactly what it looked like. I'd drawn the house in the middle of the paper, with its high-peaked roof, which must have resembled a witch's hat, and black windows—her menacing eyes, and the rows of pink-blossoming trees emitting from every angle like hair standing on end. I laughed, wondering if Mama had hung on to my artwork. If I got some time, I'd look through the boxes in the attic.

I kept on reminiscing as I snatched napkins off the branches and filled my bag. I was working my way through a row of late-harvest trees, mostly freestones, meaning they peeled away from the pit easily. My favorite was the O'Henry peach. As a kid, I used to climb the branches and eat them until my stomach hurt. I thought of how good a sweet, sun-warmed peach would taste about now, especially since I'd passed on the muffins earlier.

My stomach grumbled as I finished one row and cut through to the next. I reached up and plucked another napkin from a branch and surveyed the rest of the row. Down a ways, I spied someone sitting on the ground, propped against one of the trees. Obviously one of last night's guests had had too much to drink and was sleeping it off. Well, of all things!

"Hey," I called out, ducking under a couple more branches and heading toward the lazy drunkard. I had a thing or two to tell this guy. Only, halfway there, I stopped in my tracks. I recognized the man from the party. It was Ben Wakefield. But he wasn't sleeping it off. His blue-tinged, open-eyed face was slumped to one side with my sister's brightly colored scarf cinched around his neck.

Chapter 3

Georgia Belle Fact #048: Down here, we can tell how classy a woman is by the height of her hair and the thinness of her brow.

Twenty minutes later, Sheriff Maudeen Payne's cruiser came rumbling down our drive, gravel flying out behind her back fender like buckshot out of Daddy's twelve-gauge shotgun. Ray and I were standing on the front porch, warily awaiting her arrival. "Just keep your cool," he told me as she came to a screeching halt in front of our house.

I swallowed hard, watching Maudy throw open the cruiser's door and step out with an air of pundit authority that practically made my toes shrivel. "Should we tell her about the scarf?"

Ray grabbed my elbow and leaned in toward my ear. "If she asks you, tell her the truth. Don't try to distort anything in order to protect Hollis or Ida—do you understand?"

I nodded. He was right, of course. Still, I couldn't imagine throwing Ida's husband under the bus. As much as I disliked Hollis, I couldn't see the man strangling someone to death with a scarf. There just had to be some other explanation.

"Hello, Maudy," Ray greeted.

She nodded in reply and turned her head toward me. "Heard you were back in town," she said, adjusting her Stetson over her brown, boyish-cut hair. I'd known Maudy since grade school and she never was one for makeup or fussy hairstyles. As Mama always used to say, Maudy Payne just wasn't in touch with her feminine side. Of course, most people probably said the same about me. "Someone call in a murder?" she asked.

"Yes. He's in the orchard." I stepped off the porch and started to lead her toward the tree line. Ray hung close, neither one of us offering any more comments as we crossed the yard. We'd just made it to the first row when another sheriff's car roared down the driveway.

Maudy paused and held up her hand for us to do the same. "Hold up. That's my deputy." She took off her Stetson and waved it in the air as the deputy stepped out of his car and headed for the house. "We're over here, Travis," she shouted, then stuck two fingers in her mouth and let out a shrill whistle when he couldn't seem to locate us.

Travis's head snapped our way and he gave a little wave before breaking into a jog across the yard, keeping one hand on his rattling utility belt. "Hey, Sheriff. Hear we got a murder on our hands." He seemed almost excited at the prospect. "Should we call in the county crime scene guys?"

Maudy shook her head. "Thought I'd see what we've got first." She took off her hat and swiped at her brow with the back of her hand. "Well, let's have at it, folks. I'd like to get the body out of here before it gets much hotter. Lawd knows, the heat we've been having lately could about melt the skin off a person."

I cringed at her wording and continued down the path, retracing my steps through the rows until I came to the right spot in the orchard. I pointed at the body and hung back while the others moved in for a closer inspection. Seeing it once was enough for me.

The deputy removed his hat right away, exposing a head

of thin brown hair cut close in the front with longer pieces curling over the back of his collar. "I'll be! That's Ben Wakefield."

"Sure is," Maudy agreed. She ripped off her sunglasses, revealing a brow bushy enough to be mistaken for a woolly worm, and started circling the body. She finally stooped down carefully, peering into Ben's glazed eyes, and put a couple fingers where his carotid artery should be—used to be—pulsing. "Well, someone finally did in the old bastard," she mumbled. "Travis, why don't you call ahead to the county CSI unit and tell them to get their butts over here? Then give ol' Doc Harris a call and tell him we'll be needing an autopsy."

Travis nodded enthusiastically. "Sure thing. I'll get right on it." He whipped out his phone and started punching numbers.

Maudy creased her brow and gave the overeager deputy an impatient look. "Also," she added with a long sigh, "give J. B. Cain and Sons a call and tell them we'll need a transport once the crime scene guys are done. Doc can do the examination down at the funeral home. I think it's going to be pretty straightforward." Housed in a prominent federal-styled home a block off the square, J. B. Cain & Sons was the only funeral home in Cays Mill. It was said that mostly everyone within a thirty-mile radius of town passed through J.B.'s hands on their way upward. And, when they did, J.B. gave them a proper send-off, complete with a satin-lined bed and a limo-escorted parade in their honor. Everyone, whether they knew the deceased or not, gathered from far and wide to pay their respects. Yes, here in the South, we love a good funeral. I silently wondered whether the funeral home was big enough to handle the crowd this service was sure to draw.

Travis stepped aside to make his calls as Maudy slipped some plastic gloves on and squatted down to examine the body. Curiosity overriding my queasiness, I moved in a little closer myself and watched as she lifted each hand and examined his nails. "He's got a knot on his head the size of a watermelon," she commented before leaning in and giving a quick sniff around his face. "Whew! Peach Jack and a whole lot of it. I don't think he was in much condition to put up a fight."

"He had a drink in his hand most of the night," Ray commented. "Must have been tying one on."

Maudy nodded and fingered the scarf. "Belongs to a woman." Standing, she eyed Ray and me. "Did you happen to see a gal wearing this scarf last night?"

I rubbed my palms on the sides of my shorts and glanced at Ray, who seemed to be studying the ground with intense interest. We knew this question was coming, but still, neither one of us seemed able to form an answer. "It belongs to our sister, Ida," I finally managed.

Maudy ran her tongue along her lips. "Is that so? I reckon it does look like something Ida Jean would wear. She being the type that goes for frilly stuff and all."

I shuddered, realizing what Ida was up against. Maudy always did seem a bit prejudiced toward the pretty types. I glanced toward Ray for some support, but he remained silent. I was just debating whether or not to tell Maudy about Hollis when I heard the sound of a car door off in the distance.

"Go see who that is," Maudy ordered her deputy with a nod toward the driveway. Travis took off through the trees, still talking into his cell as he headed back toward the house.

"It's probably Ida," I blurted. "She's supposed to be coming over to help with the cleanup."

Maudy faced me head-on, widening her stance and placing her hands over the center of her gun belt. "Perfect timing, if you ask me."

Again, I shot a look toward Ray, wondering why he was being so quiet. Didn't he want to come to Ida's defense? We both knew Hollis was the last person to have the scarf. Why wasn't he saying anything? Maybe I should've kept my mouth shut, too.

We all stood in awkward silence until the rustling of

underbrush announced Travis's return. Ida was close behind, picking her way carefully over the uneven ground, one hand holding her sun hat in place, the other protectively resting on her protruding belly. "Travis Hanes, you'd better tell me right now what's going on," she was saying. Then, looking up, she stopped short, seeing Ray, Maudy and me standing before her. Before she could say anything, her eyes took in the body behind us and a loud scream escaped her lips. "That's Ben Wakefield!" She pointed a shaky finger toward the gruesome scene before us. "And my scarf!"

Ray moved in quickly. "Ida, I advise you not to say another word."

But Ida blathered on, her eyes wide with shock and her voice becoming shriller by the second. "How could he? How could he have killed him?" she shrieked over and over.

I ran to her side, wrapping my arms around her shoulders. "Hush up, Ida," I warned her.

It was too late. With two quick steps, Maudy closed in on us. She placed her thick hand on Ida's arm and wheeled her around in an about-face. "Exactly who are you talking about, Ida Jean?" Maudy's chest puffed out as she took in my sister with a look that reminded me of a hungry dog.

Finally coming to her senses, Ida clamped her mouth shut, her eyes darting between Ray and me with indecisive panic.

Maudy narrowed her eyes. "How about we go inside where it's a bit cooler, so we can have a nice long talk." Glancing over her shoulder, she said to Travis, "Secure the crime scene until the crime scene guys get here. Make sure everything stays just as it is." Keeping her hand on Ida's elbow, she motioned with her other hand. "The rest of you, come with me."

As soon as Maudy turned her back, Ray snatched my arm and hissed into my ear, "As soon as you can, get ahold of Hollis. Tell him to stay put, don't do anything stupid and, above all, don't say a word to anyone about anything until I'm there to represent him. Got it?"

I nodded. "Sure, but maybe we should call Daddy and—"

"No!" Ray snapped back. Then he softened his tone a bit and added, "I mean, let's not bother them until we know more about what's going on."

Back in the house, Ida and the sheriff, with Ray close behind, headed for the privacy of Daddy's den. As soon as the door shut behind them, I scurried to the kitchen, rummaged through one of the drawers for the telephone directory and snuck up the stairs to my bedroom. Cell phone in hand, I dove onto my unmade bed, landing between the rumpled pink coverlet and my wadded-up blue silk dress from the night before. It seemed like an eternity ago that I'd ripped off the dress, barely able to pull my old Bulldogs jersey over my head before collapsing into bed, contentedly exhausted from the party. Incredible how much things can change in just one day.

I punched in Ida's house number, just in case Hollis was still at home sleeping it off. Not receiving an answer, I paged through the directory until I found the bank's number. After a few rings, a woman answered, "Cays Mill Bank and Trust. Candace speaking."

I scrunched my face and sighed. It would be Candace who answered. "Hello, Candace. Is Hollis there?"

"Well, I'll be darned. Nola Mae Harper? I'd heard you were back in town. What's it been?"

"Uh, a few years, I guess."

"Bet your mama's glad you're back. Oh, but she's on her cruise now, isn't she? Bless their hearts, your mama and daddy sure do deserve a trip like that. I was gonna come out to y'all's party last night and help celebrate, but my bunion's been acting up so bad, I just couldn't bear to put on a pair of dress shoes."

I sighed. "I'm sorry to hear that."

"Oh, don't be. I spent the evening soaking them and they're feeling much better now."

"So, is Hollis in?"

"Hollis? Why, no, he's not. I wonder where he's at? He's usually in by now. You want me to leave a message for him?"

I glanced at my watch. Almost nine. *Where is he?* "No, that's okay. Thanks, Candace."

"Well, come up to the house sometime. I got a great crop of zucchini this summer. I'll fry you up some. Course, with my back being the way it is, I don't know if I can get it picked or not. Doc says I've got—"

"I'll try back later, Candace. Thank you." I hung up before she launched into another one of her illnesses. Over the years, Candace had been afflicted with almost every ailment known to mankind. By now, Hollis had probably given her enough sick-time pay to cover the cost of two secretaries.

Shoot. Where is he, anyway? I got up and started pacing the floor. I could try down at Red's Diner. Maybe he stopped in for coffee to clear the fuzz, or perhaps he was down at the barbershop getting a trim; he could have used one before the party, I'd noticed last night. I threw up my hands and heaved a sigh. He could be anywhere. Heck, for all I knew, he was on the lam, running from the police. I shook my head. No, I wouldn't allow myself to go down that path. There just had to be some other explanation for why that scarf was cinched around Ben Wakefield's neck.

The screen porch door creaked and I moved across the room to look out my window. Pushing aside my lace curtains, I glanced down and saw Maudy Payne crossing the yard toward the orchard. A couple more official-looking cars had gathered in our driveway, including a hearse from J. B. Cain & Sons. Seeing that she was out of the house, I ran back downstairs to find Ray and Ida. They were still in the den: Ray at the desk, hunched over with his face buried in his hands, Ida balled up in one of Daddy's oversized club chairs. I went directly to her, kneeling down by her side.

"What's going on, Ida?" I gently asked, noticing her tear-streaked face and puffy eyes.

Her eyes took on a slightly madcap look. "Maudy Payne's just sure Hollis killed that man. But I know better than that. Hollis isn't capable of murder," she bit out.

Of course, her words when she saw the body belied that statement, but that might have been just the shock of seeing a dead body with her scarf. Whatever the reason for her initial outburst, she'd changed her tune now.

I patted her arm and stood, moving to the comfort of the other chair. The stiff leather made a loud sighing sound as I collapsed into it. Ray looked up, added his own sigh and said, "Why don't you ask her where Hollis is now?"

I looked from Ray to Ida, who was now sitting ramrod straight, with a look of defiance on her face. "Ida?" I prompted, but she just sat there, chewing on her bottom lip. I continued, "I just tried calling the bank and he's not in yet. He wasn't at your house, either. . . ."

She turned toward me with blazing eyes and threw up her hands. "Okay. So, I don't know where he is. He didn't come home last night. But that doesn't mean he killed that man."

"Yes, but it sure doesn't look good for him," Ray pointed out.

I nodded. "I agree. You have to admit, Hollis has a lot stacked against him." I held up my hand and started ticking a list off my fingers. "He was the last person seen with your scarf. We know he left our table to find Wakefield and discuss something with him. And now he's missing the morning after Wakefield is murdered."

Ida shrugged. "There's not really anything that suspicious about Hollis being gone. There's been plenty of nights lately where he hasn't come home."

Both Ray and I did a double take. "He's done this before?" Ray asked.

Ida nodded and began rubbing her belly again. "The drinking has become a problem. It's not Hollis's fault, mind you. There's just so much stress lately at the bank. He can't help himself."

I narrowed my eyes at my sister. *When did she become such a doormat?*

"It's all this stuff with that timber deal," she added.

Ray leaned forward. "The Wakefield Lumber deal?"

"Yes." Ida lowered her chin and started fussing with her blouse. "I don't understand all of Hollis's business, but something went bad with the deal last week. Like I said, I don't know what. I was so busy decorating for Mama and Daddy's party, I'm afraid I didn't really pay much attention to anything else."

"Was Hollis upset or something?" I asked.

Ida's head bobbed up and down. "I'd say. He came home one day after work and locked himself in his office with a bunch of papers and a bottle of Peach Jack. I could hear him screaming on the phone at someone. I finally had to take the girls down to the Tasty Freeze for a dip cone just so they wouldn't hear all those ugly words."

Ray was scribbling a few notes on a legal pad. "But you don't know what it was about?" he asked.

"No. Like I said, I've been so busy I've hardly had time to breathe, let alone sit down and talk things over with Hollis. Then there's all this stuff with Daddy." As soon as she'd said it, Ida's hand flew to her mouth. She let out a little gasp, looking like someone who'd just let the cat out of the bag.

I sat a little straighter. "What do you mean? What's going on with Daddy?"

Ray shot Ida a look and sucked in his breath. "He's having financial trouble. Things haven't been going so well around here lately. We had a warm spell late winter and a lot of the trees blossomed out. Then a late frost hit." He shrugged. "Well, you know how it goes."

I nodded. So much of fruit farming relies on Mother Nature's cooperation. One bad frost can wipe out an entire crop. Still, we'd weathered through many a bad growing season and come out just fine. "Sure, but Daddy always has money in reserve for the bad seasons, right?"

Ida squirmed a bit in the chair, readjusting her body and pulling her legs up to one side.

Ray continued, "It's just that there's been so many things going wrong lately. The price of fertilizer and pesticide has almost doubled in the last couple of years. Then we had to replace one of the trucks and redo some of the irrigation lines. So, the reserve has dwindled."

This was all news to me. "Why is this the first time I'm hearing all this?"

Ida let out a long sigh and rubbed her temples.

Ray squinted her way before responding, "Mama and Daddy didn't want to worry you. Besides, Hollis was bringing them in on the Wakefield deal. Daddy was leasing the rights to the timber on the back twenty. He stood to make good money off it. Things were looking up." He paused for a second as if considering his words. "It's just that all this financial stress has been hard on him. You should probably know that he's been having some health issues."

"Health issues?" I about fell out of my chair. "Like what?"

Ida cleared her throat and sighed impatiently.

"Just a little trouble with his heart," Ray continued. "Palpitations, that's all. Nothing real serious. Doc Harris said this trip would be good for him. A little time away from all the stress is just what he needs."

Ah, so that's why Ray was so adamant that we not call our parents. He was trying to shield Daddy from any additional stress. Which made me wonder just how bad things really were. Did Ray know more than he was saying? Was he trying to protect me, too?

"Listen to you two!" Ida, who'd grown more restless by the second, blurted out. "Daddy's stress? What about me? What about Hollis? I know it looks bad for him, but there's just no way he killed that man. But that dim-witted Maudy Payne is out there right now, hot on Hollis's trail, like a hound on a coon. Lawd knows what she'll do once she catches up to him.

And what if she throws him in jail? What will I do then?" She looked toward Ray and me, her eyes filled with worry. "I've got the baby coming, and the girls to think of. . . ." Her voice broke away into a fresh round of hysterics.

"I'll do everything I can to help Hollis," Ray was quick to promise. "First, though, we need to find him. I'd like to have a chance to talk to him before Sheriff Payne gets ahold of him. Especially if he hasn't sobered up yet. Hard telling what he'll blab." He leveled his gaze on Ida. "Any idea where we should start?"

She shook her head. "No, no idea. The last I saw him was when we were leaving the party. The girls were getting tired, so we decided to leave around ten. We drove separate cars, so I said good-bye to Mama and Daddy and took the girls on back to the house. I just assumed Hollis was right behind me, but he never showed up."

"You weren't worried about him driving? He'd been drinking quite a bit last night," I said.

She shrugged. "He'd started laying off the liquor a couple hours earlier. The last I talked to him, he seemed pretty sober." Her eyes suddenly widened with worry. "Why? Do you think he's been in an accident?" She unfolded her legs and abruptly stood, faltering a bit and reaching toward the desk to catch her balance.

I sprung up to help steady her. "Let's not jump to any conclusions. Like you said, there's been a lot of nights he hasn't come home." I hedged a bit, unsure of how to ask the next question. Finally I decided to just come out with it. "Is it possible there's another woman?"

"No!" Ida snapped, shaking off my hand. "Hollis isn't like that. He's a devoted husband and father."

Except for the time he made a pass at me. But I didn't say that. I'd actually never told a soul about what happened the night before Ida's wedding, excusing it as just another one of Hollis's drunken blunders and afraid Ida would call off the whole marriage. Nothing like it had ever happened again, thank goodness! I just wished I could forget about it altogether, but truth was, some things were just downright unforgettable.

"Okay, okay," Ray said, holding up his hands. "Ida, why don't you head home and wait for Hollis there. Nola and I will start looking around town. Maybe we can get to him before the sheriff does."

Chapter 4

Georgia Belle Fact #097: A smart Georgia Belle never drinks too much; she just sips a lot.

Ray's words stuck in my head long after Ida left. How bad was Daddy's "little trouble with his heart"? Apparently bad enough that neither Ray nor Ida nor our parents had told me about it. Could all this business about Hollis and murder be enough to put Daddy over the edge, plunging to the other side? The seriousness of it all grabbed ahold of me and squeezed at my own heart: Daddy's health, the farm's financial trouble, and now Hollis. Worst of all, a teeny tiny part of me wondered whether Hollis didn't strangle Ben Wakefield, and if he did, where would that leave my sister? A single mom raising three children on her own? I could hardly bear the thought of it. And my poor nieces. You could say what you wanted about Hollis Shackleford. You could rightly call him a greedy, drunken, skirt-chasing, no-good pig, but you could never say he wasn't a good father. In fact, those sweet little girls worshiped the ground their daddy walked on and he treated them like little princesses. Damn that man! How could he get mixed up in all this?

"Nola?" Ray's voice brought me back into focus. "Were you listening to me?"

I nodded. "Sure. You want to split up and look for Hollis."

"Yeah. You hit the diner and the businesses off the square. I'll head out toward the county line. Maybe he went to the Honky Tonk after the party. He could still be there in the lot, uh . . . recuperating."

"Sounds like a good plan," I said, but my insides went wiggly at the mere mention of the Honky Tonk Bar. I so hated the place that I hadn't ventured back since the night before Ida's wedding, almost eight years ago now. After the rehearsal dinner, Ida went back home to get her beauty sleep while the rest of us headed out to the Honky Tonk to check out the band. We were just planning to kick back a little, do some line dancing and maybe take a spin on Bodacious, their mechanical bull. Only, halfway through the evening, a snookered Hollis corralled me on the way back from the loo and tried to grope me. Of course, I set him straight, but to this day, I couldn't look at the guy without thinking of a line from that old Georgia Satellites song: "Don't hand me no lines and keep your hands to yourself."

I shook off the memory of it all and retreated to my bedroom, two steps at a time, where I grabbed my cell and some extra cash and did a quick check in the mirror. Before I'd even made it down the porch steps, the sound of Maudy's gruff voice stopped me in my tracks.

"I said this tent isn't going anywhere. This is a crime scene, you idiot."

Shoot. I forgot about the tent people! I glanced over toward the tree line. Sure enough, the people from the rental company had arrived and were caught up in a tug-of-war involving one of the peach tree poles and Sheriff Payne. It was two against one, but it looked like the sheriff was winning. Something about her broad-stanced posture and the gun on her hip gave her a certain edge.

"This tent is part of a crime scene, and if you take it down, I'll arrest you for tampering with evidence," Maudy barked as a crepe paper peach fell and knocked her on the shoulder.

The tent guy threw up his hands. "If you say so, but my boss ain't going to like this. We'll have to charge these people extra."

Charge us extra? I skipped down the porch steps. "Do you really need the whole tent?" I asked the sheriff.

Maudy folded her arms across her chest and nodded. "Yup. And the tables and chairs and everything else. It all stays exactly how it is until I say so."

My jaw dropped. "But that could cost us a fortune in rental fees."

The sheriff shrugged. "Well, I'd advise that next time you throw a party, you make sure none of your guests are murdered."

I opened my mouth to retort, but shut it again. It wouldn't do to get on the sheriff's bad side. Besides, I knew what her real problem was and it wasn't about preserving the crime scene. No, the real problem was as plain as day. Maudy was ticked about not being invited to the party. I could see her point of view—it's never fun to be excluded—but then again, why would Ida invite her old high school nemesis? And while no one remembered exactly what had started the tension between my sister and Maudy Payne, everyone sure as heck remembered their infamous catfight behind the football bleachers. I was sure it still stuck in Maudy's craw that my sister bested her that day. But I didn't have time to soothe Maudy's rumpled feathers. I was on a mission. "Okay, then." I shrugged and turned to the rental guys. "I'll call when the sheriff is done with the tent. I wouldn't think it would take more than a day or so extra," I added, glancing Maudy's way, before heading toward my vehicle. She met my look with an icy stare.

On the spur of the moment, I decided to take a back-road shortcut into town. Boy, was I glad Helping Hands International rented a four-wheel-drive Jeep for me to use during my time stateside; any other vehicle would have bottomed out on this road. Nonetheless, about twenty minutes of butt-busting bumps later, my not-so-much-of-a-shortcut finally got me to Cays Mill. I worked my way around the square until I found a parking spot just down from Red's Diner.

Walking through the door, I found the place was filled to the hilt with local farmers sipping coffee and shooting the bull. Bits and pieces of peach-farming conversation floated through the air as I made my way to the counter. Ginny spied me at once. "Hey, there, Nola. Great party last night. I had a ton of fun." She gave a nod to the coffeepot in her hand. "Maybe too much fun," she went on. "Can't seem to get enough of this stuff to clear my head. I've already messed up a couple orders. Gave Frank there scrambled eggs instead of over easy."

A burly man at the counter jerked his head up. "And you forgot to butter my grits."

"Now, Frank, you didn't say buttered when you ordered those grits," Ginny countered.

"Aw, now, don't give me any grief, Ginny. How many years have I been coming in here and ordering my grits buttered and you went and left it off the ticket today." He looked at me with a wink. "She's no good for nothin' today."

Ginny shook her head and laughed good-naturedly. Reaching under the counter, she snatched a mug and flipped it right side up in front of me. "Bet you need a little of this, don't ya, sweetie?"

I waved it away. "Actually, I just stopped by to see if you've seen Hollis?"

"Hollis? Not since last night." She tucked one of her reddish curls behind her ear and leaned in close, a conspiratorial gleam in her eye. "Why?"

"Uh . . ." I struggled for the right words. If I wasn't careful, I'd start the rumor train chugging full force down the track. And by full force, I meant fast! No doubt, if you went around examining the mouths on the people around here, you'd discover racing stripes painted right down the middles of their tongues.

"Order up," a booming voice announced as two heaping plates appeared on the ledge behind Ginny. She reached around and grabbed the plates, then turned back to me. "Don't go anywhere. Let me get these out and I'll be right back."

I shifted impatiently on the stool and glanced around the place. It was good to see Red's Diner was still the same—a throwback to simpler times. Well, not exactly a throwback. In reality, Red's was caught up in a mid-century time warp with speckled Formica tabletops, steel-framed chairs and vinyl-covered booths. A silver napkin dispenser and a handled basket with ketchup, mustard, hot sauce, and salt and pepper rested atop each table. Actually, looking a little closer, I decided not a thing had changed since Ginny's folks opened the place way back when.

True to her word, Ginny hurried back to her position behind the counter. She stuck a ticket on a silver spindle and gave it a spin. "Make that bacon crisp, Sam," she yelled through the window. "And give Nola Mae a holler, why don't you?"

A hand shot through the window and waved. "Hey, Nola. Great party last night."

"Hey, Sam," I returned. Sam and Ginny had been several years ahead of me in high school, Sam being a football player and Ginny part of the cheer squad. They'd gotten married straightaway after graduation and started running the diner. I used to wonder if they'd stay together. Sometimes marrying too young led to disappointment later on, but Sam and Ginny always seemed happy together.

I slid off the stool, making my excuses. "I've really got to get going, Ginny. I'll stop back by later and we can catch up, okay?"

She lurched forward and grabbed my forearm. "No, you don't. Tell me what's happened to Hollis first. Has he gone missing?"

I glanced around, but no one seemed to be listening. "He didn't come home last night and Ida's worried, that's all," I whispered.

"Really? I hear he does that a lot. What's got her so worked up this time?"

Squirming in place, I shot a wishful glance at the door.

I really needed to get a move on; there was still a lot of ground to cover. "Who knows? Probably just pregnancy hormones. You must know how it is."

"Do I ever!" she exclaimed, her eyes taking on a faraway look. "Doesn't seem all that long ago that we were having babies. Of course, we started so early, you know." Ginny and Sam were not that much older than Ida, but they'd jumped the gun in the baby department, so to speak. Both their kids must practically be grown now. I'd love to ask if Emily, their youngest, had been presented to society as a debutante—a wonderfully old-fashioned southern tradition that I, sadly enough, skipped during my rebellious period—but there wasn't enough time for that whole conversation at the moment. Unfortunately, Ginny was oblivious to my need to hurry. She kept rambling on. "You know our Jake's a sophomore now at the University of Georgia and Emily's a high school senior and is—"

"Can I get some more coffee over here, Ginny," someone called out.

I took the opportunity to make a break for it. "We'll catch up some more later," I told her. "But if you see Hollis, tell him to give me a call."

I was just about to leave when the buttered-grits Frank touched my arm. "Try down at the barbershop. If he's not there or at the bank, there's only one other place to look."

"Where's that, sir?"

"Up at McManamy Draw out by the lake. He parks up there sometimes to sleep it off. I've seen him there when I'm out fishing."

I patted the old man's arm, thanking him for the information.

Leaving the diner, I headed toward the twisting barber's pole around the corner. Maybe Hollis had headed in for a shave and a trim. He *was* looking a little long around the collar the night before.

"Hey, there," I said, as the door jingled shut behind me. Earl, the bald-headed owner, had the buzzers out and was going to town on a young man. A waiting customer stood in the corner by the watercooler with a cup in hand, his gaze fixated on a small television mounted on the wall. One of the popular morning news shows was playing.

"Hey, there, Nola," Earl said, turning off the buzzer and reaching for a large white-bristled brush. He started whapping it against the guy's neck, sending bits and pieces of hair flying into the air like a snowstorm.

"Have you seen Hollis this morning?" I asked.

"No, not this morning. Hey!" he called out to the guy by the watercooler. "You seen Hollis Shackleford this morning?"

"What's that?" the guy asked, peeling his eyes from the television and spitting a mouthful of chewed sunflower shells into his cup. "Hollis Shackleford?"

I nodded.

"Can't say I have. He's not at the bank?"

"No. I already called there."

"Did you check at the diner?"

I nodded again.

"How 'bout up the Draw? He sometimes goes out there to . . ." He paused, his eyes shifting to the side. "To commune with nature."

The guys all chuckled at that. I chuckled too, but only halfheartedly. I was actually wondering why the whole town knew so much about Hollis's habits. First Ginny and Frank at the diner, now these guys. I was beginning to think Hollis was the laughingstock of the town. My poor sister. Ida was always so prim and proper, Hollis's ill-gained reputation was probably hard on her. And I knew better than anyone how hard it could be to escape the wrath of Cays Mill's gossipmongers. There was a time when a few of my youthful indiscretions wreaked havoc on the Harpers' good name. Not to mention that one horrible thing, the granddaddy of all indiscretions, which sent me packing before word got out and a plight worse than peach-eating fruit moths befell my family. Hopefully, we could find Hollis and get to the bottom of this mess before things got that far out of hand.

I let out another nonchalant chuckle and quickly thanked the gentlemen for their help. Back outside, I shielded my eyes against the late-morning sun and glanced around the square. Already heat was blazing off the walks, causing the petunias in the baskets hanging from the light poles to droop and shrivel. Even the courthouse flag was lying flat against the pole, nary a breeze in sight to make it wave. Scanning the sidewalks for a sign of Hollis, my eyes hit on the Clip & Curl, Hattie's Boutique and Pistil Pete's Flower Shop before wandering over a few vacant storefronts and back up the opposite side to the hardware store. Finally my gaze landed on Sugar's Bakery— the sight of which made me pause, my mouth watering for a slice of Ezra Sugar's famous lemon chess pie. I was standing there, momentarily distracted by my sweet tooth, when my cell rang. It was Ida.

"The sheriff's got Hollis," she sobbed into the phone.

I felt my shoulders sag. "Where'd they find him?"

"I don't know where he's been. He'd just pulled into the driveway when they nabbed him." Ida blew her nose and sniffed a couple times before continuing. "They've taken him in for questioning."

I nodded into the phone, thinking they must have been watching the house. "Don't worry, Ida. I'll get ahold of Ray right away. He'll take care of things."

She sobbed even louder. "There's more."

"More?" *Pray tell, what more could there possibly be?* I steeled myself for what she'd say next.

"That nosy woman from the newspaper showed up just as they were dragging him away."

"Frances Simms?"

"Yeees!" The word wailed over the line, causing me to pull the phone away from my ear. When I put it back, she was blabbing on like a fool. "I just know his picture's going to be plastered all over the front page of the *Cays Mill Reporter*. How will the family ever live this down? We'll be ruined. Absolutely ruined!"

Chapter 5

Sure enough, first thing Tuesday morning, Ray passed the paper across the counter toward me and right there, smack-dab on the front page, was Hollis's ugly mug. "What are we going to do now?" I asked Ray, who was leaning against the counter finishing his second bowl of Crispy Flakes.

"I've already called the office. My docket's not too full, so I should be able to split my time between here and my office in Perry. Hollis is going to need all the help he can get."

I spread a dollop of Mama's homemade peach preserves on my English muffin. "You talked to him yesterday?"

"Yes, briefly."

"What'd he have to say for himself?"

Ray rinsed his bowl and set it in the sink. "Seems he and Ben Wakefield had a few words at the party. Apparently, Wakefield hadn't made any payments on his loan."

I brushed some crumbs off my shirt and nodded. "I'm sure Hollis has been pressuring him for payment. But he deals with slackers every day. He would've received the money, one way or the other." *Hopefully "one way or the other" didn't include murder.*

"If only that was all there was to it," Ray replied, shaking his head. "When they arrested Hollis, they found an audit report in his pocket from some investigation firm in Macon. Hollis's bank hired a forensic auditor to investigate Wakefield Lumber's assets."

"Let me guess. The investigation didn't turn up good news."

Ray nodded and reached for the coffeepot, topping off his mug. "That's right. The report confirmed what Hollis had started to suspect: Wakefield Lumber is in big trouble financially."

"Didn't Hollis check into all that before putting up the bank's money?" I refilled my own mug and leaned against the counter, mulling over this new information. "I mean, certainly he didn't just loan money without collateral."

"Apparently Wakefield falsified his collateral claims. Something they wouldn't normally question until Hollis got suspicious. The proof was in the audit report Hollis got from the investigation firm."

"How big of a loan are we talking about?" I asked.

"A little over a million."

I blew out a stream of air. "You're kidding?"

"Afraid not. And a million bucks looks like a whole lot of motive for Hollis. Plus, he'd sunk not only most of the bank's assets into this investment, but some of his own personal money too, hoping to share in the profits." Ray drained his mug and piled it on top of the other dishes in the sink. "I believe Hollis when he says he didn't kill Ben Wakefield, but things look bad for him. The sheriff has enough evidence to make the charge stick. He'll be arraigned on Wednesday or Thursday, but I'm not sure Ida will even be able to put up bond money. And I'm not in any financial position to help them out."

"Me, either. But he can't just sit in jail!"

"Why the heck not? It's probably the best place for him right now. He needs to stay sober and out of trouble."

Ray had a point, but I couldn't stand to think about Ida going at it alone while Hollis sat in jail. She needed her husband and those little girls needed their daddy. "Yeah, but what about Ida and the kids? And his position at the bank? It's his livelihood."

Ray raised his shoulders and stretched his arms out, palms up. "I'm doing all I can, Nola," he snapped.

I blinked slowly a couple times. I really hadn't stopped to think how stressful this was for Ray. He was stuck in an impossible position. Representing his sister's husband, for probably no pay and against impossible odds. Plus, if he failed to get Hollis out of this mess . . . well, he'd have to carry the guilt with him for the rest of his life.

Crossing the room, I offered him a quick hug. "Ida and Hollis are so lucky to have you on their side, Ray. We all are."

He pulled back and ran his hands through his hair, before shoving them into the pockets of his jeans. "If you say so. But if I can't save him, Ida will never forgive me."

I mirrored his frown. He was right. And there was really nothing I could say to make the severity of the situation any better. Poor Ray. He had a huge burden to carry.

"Anyway," he continued with a sigh, "I'm heading back to Perry now. I've got to get some things lined up at my office, so I can get back here and help Hollis." He grabbed his cell off the counter and shoved it in the back pocket of his jeans. "What will you be doing today?"

"There's a long list of things to keep me busy: a broken door out in the barn, painting the equipment shed. . . ." I waved off the rest. "Mostly just light maintenance stuff."

"What about the irrigation lines that run along the south ridge?"

I squinted. "The irrigation lines?"

"Daddy didn't mention that? The lines haven't been working for almost a month now. The pump could be bad and most of the line needs to be replaced. With this heat we're having, it better get done soon."

"Why hasn't it been fixed?"

Ray shook his head. "Money, probably. I don't know for sure. Everyone around here has been tight-lipped lately. I'm just assuming it has to do with money, or the lack of it. I've offered to take a look at the books, but . . ." He shrugged off the rest.

Ray hadn't said the words, but I knew what he was thinking. Daddy and Ray didn't quite see eye to eye when it came to business. Which was the main reason Ray went to law school instead of taking on the farm.

"And there's another problem, too," he continued. "The tractor is broken. It's been sitting out in the west orchard for a couple weeks now."

"The tractor, too?" *Unbelievable.* We needed it to keep weeds down in the orchard, or they'd rob the trees of valuable water and nutrients. "You know, I talked with both Mama and Daddy before they left. They didn't mention any of these things."

Ray nodded. "Like I said, no one's talking about it. Almost as if they just ignore it, it'll go away." He homed his gaze in on me. "But you and I both know that's not how things really work."

Yes, I knew perhaps better than anyone that problems didn't just go away—I'd learned that early on the hard way. I'd then chosen a career where I'd been trained to face problems straight on, find solutions and, in the process, save lives. I'd been doing that very type of thing for the past fifteen years. Things like finding sources of clean drinking water, reuniting families separated by tsunamis and earthquakes . . . You name it, I'd done it. I'd always been proud of my work, but now I was feeling a little ashamed. Ashamed that I'd been busy saving families in faraway lands, while right here at home, my own family had been suffering.

I said good-bye to Ray and turned back to the sink to rinse my own cup. I stood there, sighing over the mess of dishes that'd accumulated over the last couple of days while my mind reeled with worry. Perhaps a little mundane house-work would help calm me.

Glancing around the kitchen, I spotted Mama's old Czar radio on top of the fridge. Perfect! I brought it down and set it on the counter, tuned in to Gladys Knight and her Pips croon-ing "Midnight Train to Georgia" and started scrubbing, rinsing and stacking dishes. The mistress of soul's soothing lyrics eased the monotony of washing dishes and helped me regroup some of the thoughts running wild in my mind. Foremost in those thoughts was Hollis's situation. I'd have to stop by later and check on Ida. Maybe I'd ask her if she wanted to come out to the house and stay. That way, I could help her with the girls while she waited for Hollis to be released. If, of course, he was released. I cringed at the thought, but I had no idea what I could do to help. On the other hand, the family's finan-cial problem was something I might be able to help solve.

As I placed the last dish in the drying rack, I decided it was time to see the problems plaguing the farm for myself. I grabbed my hat off the hook by the back door, laced up my field boots and headed out to survey the orchards.

Outside, I stopped short. The leftover party mess hit me like a slap upside the head. After sitting for two nights and being exposed to the morning dew, everything left over from the party had a soggy, dirty look. I silently cursed Maudy Payne. Crime scene, my foot! She was possibly the bitterest woman I'd ever known. All this because Ida snubbed her? And was she going to allow an old grievance to interfere with her current-day investigation? Knowing Maudy, prob-ably. Well, she and this droopy, dirty mess of a tent were starting to get on my very last nerve.

I wheeled around, turning my back on it all, and headed for the south orchards, my pace strong and determined. Trekking along the tree line, I eyed the tall grass growing between the rows. We'd always maintained weed-free strips directly under the trees, usually about ten feet wide, because wild vegetation will compete with the tree for water and zap

the soil of nutrients. Between the rows, however, we kept
an equally wide strip of turf, which cut down on erosion and
provided an area for our machines and picking crews. Judging by the current height of the grass, it looked as if things
hadn't been mowed for weeks.

As I cut through, the overgrown blades tickled my legs
while the brushy weeds underneath shed their sticky cockleburs along the edges of my boots. I pushed on, though,
fighting the overgrowth until I eventually arrived at my favorite spot in the orchard—the royal palace. I giggled, recalling
my childhood fascination with this spot of the orchard. Looking back, it was easy to see how peach names like Ruby
Prince, Majestic, Fire Prince and even Summer Lady inspired
my youthful mind to imagine a full court of royals, dressed
in their finest peach-colored attire, coming out at night for a
starlit ball. I fingered the curled leaves one of the mature Fire
Prince trees. This normally beautiful, robust tree yielded the
most gorgeous red-blushed peaches perfectly ripe for the
plucking in mid-August, this year's crop already picked and
shipped away. If the tree continued to be deprived of water,
however, it may never produce again.

I sighed and continued on until I finally spied the top of
the irrigation pump. I veered toward it, weaving through
more tall grass and ducking under branches of wilting leaves
until I came to it. The old diesel-powered pump backed up
to a holding pond where it drew water to disperse through
hose lines running along the base of each row of trees. Well,
usually that was how it worked. A few pushes of the starter
button yielded nothing more than a dry whining noise as
the engine ground down, refusing to start. The gauge on the
tank said full, so I knew gas wasn't the problem. I walked
around the pump, wiggling lines and thumping it here and
there, hoping for an easy fix, but nothing I did seemed to
make the darn thing work again. I swiped my damp hair off
my face and mumbled a few bad words. I had no idea what
to try next. But maybe . . . I looked up and squinted across

the pond. I knew someone who might know what to do—Joe Puckett. And his place was only a stone's throw away.

I followed a well-worn footpath until I spotted the low slope of the cabin's roof nestled along the edge of the woods that formed a border between Harper land and the neighbor's farm. No one knew the real reason, but the story was that back in the early 1900s, my great-granddaddy sold a couple acres of our land to the original Puckett for pennies on the dollar. The Pucketts had owned the land ever since, living a peaceful, almost hermit-like life tucked away in the obscurity of the tall pines. I hadn't been to his place since I was a teen and, quite honestly, if it weren't for the pump, I probably wouldn't venture there alone—the place always gave me the willies.

A little ways farther, I finally broke through the woods to the clearing where the cabin stood. Joe had let the place go since last time I'd seen it. All that remained was a skeletal portion of what was once a multiroom cabin. Now only one room was still intact, while the rest of the slatted-board structure leaned precariously to one side. The only thing keeping the whole cabin from falling over was an overgrowth of vines that engulfed the dilapidated building like a supportive hand.

"Joe! Joe Puckett!" I called out. The only response was the babbling of the nearby creek and the low call of forest birds echoing through the trees. "Joe?" I tried again, moving closer to the structure.

The outside of the cabin was littered with everything from splintered barrels and rusty buckets, to an old metal bedframe wrapped tight in creeping Jenny weed. Looking at the state of the place, I started to think I'd made a mistake coming here. If Joe had let his own place go into such bad repair, there was probably nothing he could do for me.

I was about to turn away when I heard the metallic *chung, chung* of a shotgun pump. Instinctively, my hands shot into the air.

"Lookin' for somethin'?" came a gravelly voice from behind me.

I slowly turned and faced Joe straight on. To my relief, he immediately lowered the gun, a flicker of recognition showing in his sky-blue eyes. "Aren't you one of the Harper girls?"

"Yes, sir," I replied, slowly lowering my hands.

A toothy grin spread across his face. Joe had wrinkles on top of wrinkles and I could see that his skin was stretched thinly over his wiry arms, every inch covered by brown spots. What I remembered as a full head of hair had dwindled down over the years to a few patches of white tufts that encircled his head, making him look like an unruly version of Friar Tuck.

"You've grown up some," he observed.

"Yes, sir," I said again. My parents had taught me to always "ma'am" and "sir" my elders. Failure to do so would result in a quick swat on the rump. I'd been swatted enough in my youth that such terms of respect now came naturally.

He dipped the shotgun toward an old bench by the front door. "Won't you sit a spell?"

I nodded and crossed to the bench, careful of where I sat. Most of the bench was either splintered or splattered with who knew what. Joe, not quite as cautious, plopped down on the far end and leaned the shotgun up against the doorjamb. Just as soon as he settled, he jumped back up again. "Where are my manners? Let me get you some refreshment."

I held up my hand to protest, but he was already halfway inside the cabin. Kicking at the boards below my feet, I thought back to the first time I'd met Joe Puckett. I was a young teen, helping the hands during harvest, when I caught sight of him carrying off a bucket of our peaches. Caught up in being a Harper and all, I ran right over to him, accused him of being a thief and demanded he give back the peaches.

Was I ever surprised when I got back to the house that evening and caught heck from my father. Daddy apparently knew all about Joe and his family taking fruit from the trees along the back acreage. I thought he was crazy for allowing such a thing; I even told him so, but he corrected me, saying that men like Joe Puckett—men who lived from the land and followed the old ways—were a part of the South that should be honored and cherished. "A dying breed," he'd said. "Besides, we've got plenty of peaches to spare." To this day, my face still turned red when I thought about my father dragging me up to the Pucketts' cabin with a basket of peaches and making me apologize for being so disrespectful.

Of course, what Daddy didn't tell me at the time was that he and Joe had long ago worked out a deal, a trade of sorts. Many years later I learned the *real* reason Daddy tolerated Joe's "pilfering": Joe distilled some of the finest moonshine in all of Georgia. My father must have been partial to the stuff, because over the years the Pucketts had been helping themselves not only to peaches, but to half the vegetables in Mama's garden. I can't think of how many evenings I'd looked out my window to see Joe's son, Tucker, out in our vegetable patch, his pockets stuffed full.

"Here," Joe said, coming out with a couple jars of clear liquid in hand. "Some of my finest."

I thanked him and took a cautious sip. So nasty! It felt like I was swallowing fire, but I tried not to let on. I'd been offered many unpalatable cultural treats during my travels. Things like crispy fried tarantula—a rare and prized delicacy in Cambodian refugee camps—and chewy ant larvae, generously offered from a food-poor South American mother with several children to feed. All heartfelt gifts offered with the same kind, giving spirit in which Joe offered me his specialty. So, I bravely drank on, and offered my praise. "That's good stuff," I choked out, swiping at the perspiration forming on my upper lip. I managed another enthusiastic sip before getting down to business. "I came by to ask you if you know anything about engines."

He swiped at his brow with his big paw of a hand and shrugged. "A bit, I reckon. I worked on Jeeps and such in Nam."

"There seems to be something wrong with the engine on our irrigation pump. I wonder if you'd have a look at it. I'd be willing to pay you for your time, of course."

He nodded, but remained silent, taking occasional sips from his jar and staring out at the woods.

I continued, "But if I can't get it running, we're likely to lose some of the trees. They're already showing signs of stress. I'll also be needing someone to help me place new drip lines. Some of ours are in bad shape."

"Where's your daddy?"

"He and Mama are on a trip. They left me in charge while they're gone."

He shifted his weight and heaved a sigh. "Your daddy and I never dealt much in cash. We usually bartered. Maybe that's been a mistake."

I cocked my head to study him. He was still staring off, his eyes darting from tree to tree, but the rest of his body seemed calm and relaxed. I knew what was next. He was going to want me to pay him in cash. Problem was I didn't have hardly any to offer. "I have to be honest, sir. I don't really have any cash to offer. Our family is going through tough financial times."

He stood up, kicking at a few pebbles with the worn toe of his boot, and hitching his thumbs in his suspenders. "Aren't we all?"

I also stood, trying to make eye contact, although his eyes continued to look everywhere but at me. I recognized the signs from remote villagers uncomfortable with strangers; Joe just wasn't used to holding conversation with folks. "Is there any way you'd be willing to barter with me?"

He shrugged. "If you don't have no cash, then I guess I'll have to."

I nodded. "What do you need, then?"

His eyes roamed up to the roof of his cabin. I followed his gaze, noticing the airy patchwork of shake shingles.

"A roof?" I asked, my heart sinking when he nodded. He extended his hand toward me, and before thinking, I grasped his callused hand and shook. The second his keen eyes met mine, I felt instant regret. *A roof!* It was a small roof, being that his cabin was only a little bigger than the average supply shed, but still, I had no idea how I was going to own up to my end of this bargain.

"Our tractor is also broken," I said as an afterthought, hoping to at least sweeten my end of the hasty bargain. *What have I done?* I knew Daddy had left some cash for miscellaneous expenses, but certainly not enough to cover roofing supplies. Or a roofer, for that matter.

He spat off to the side and bobbed his head up and down. "You payin' for all the parts?"

"Yes, sir," I quickly replied.

"I'll take a look at it, then."

Just like that, the deal was sealed.

Chapter 6

Georgia Belle Fact #072: No one should have to grieve on an empty stomach. So, when someone dies, the first thing we do is start cookin' for their loved ones.

Back at the house, I found Cade McKenna standing on the front porch. "I was just getting ready to leave," he said as I approached. "Thought I missed you."

"Well, I'm glad you didn't," I replied, marching up the steps. My hand involuntarily flew to my head. My hair must've looked terrible, not to mention my scratched-up legs and the mess of cockleburs clinging to my socks and boots. "What brings you out here, anyway?"

He shoved a foil-covered pan my way. "Food. Ginny at the diner made a casserole for you. On account of the death and all." A strange look must have crossed my face because he went on to explain. "Ben Wakefield's death. You know how it is around here. The ladies like to cook up a storm whenever someone passes."

I nodded. "Yeah, but why are you bringing this to me?"

Cade shrugged. "Seems Wakefield didn't have any family in the area. As far as we all know, he just lived by himself in that old Colonial out on Gala Avenue. So, since he died at your place, I guess Ginny figures you might be needing some comforting. You'd better get used to it; the story was all over this morning's paper. There will probably be more casseroles coming your way soon."

"Well, isn't that . . . thoughtful," I replied, thinking the real person who needed comforting was Ida; it was her husband in jail. Balancing the dish in one hand, I pulled open the screen door with the other. "Why don't you come in for a while and help me eat some of this?"

He hesitated, his dark eyes sliding down to his shoes. "I should really be getting back to work. I was just on my way to the Pearsons' place down the road. They have me re-siding one of their outbuildings."

"Well, you need to eat, don't you? Besides, I won't keep you long. I just need to run something by you, get your advice."

He shrugged and followed me inside to the kitchen. I glanced around at the tidy butcher-block countertops and freshly scrubbed soapstone sink and was secretly glad I'd taken the time to clean up this morning. Uncovering the casserole, I placed it in the microwave and starting pulling out plates. "There's glasses up there," I said, thumbing toward the cabinet. "Pour us some tea, why don't you? We can eat in the other room at the table."

"How's Ida doing?" he asked a few minutes later, after we'd settled at the table with two steaming plates of a crust-topped, creamy chicken casserole set between us. "This must be so hard on her."

I nodded. "It is hard on her and the girls, too. Ray is going to represent Hollis," I added.

"He's a good lawyer; he'll be able to help, I'm sure."

I shoved the casserole around my plate, but didn't take a bite.

Cade looked up from his own plate and commented, "Not hungry?"

"Just thinking about Ida. She needs comfort food much

more than me. It's her husband in jail. She's all alone at home with those kids and all. I'm thinking of asking her to come out here and stay."

"Good idea. She'll need your support through all this. Especially if Hollis is convicted."

I shot a look at him. "Why would he be convicted? He didn't do it." I narrowed my eyes, fully realizing the implication of his statement. "You don't think he killed Wakefield, do you?"

Cade's brows shot up. "I don't want to think that; but I have to tell you, there's been a big change come over Hollis since you were here last. He's been drinking hard. Folks are saying things, like that he's stepped out on Ida."

Folks are saying things! Gossipmongers was all they were, as I knew all too well. True or not, those *folks* made things all the worse. I squeezed my eyes shut, trying to control my anger. "That's because the people around here have nothing better to do than spread gossip. I'm surprised at you, Cade McKenna. I thought you were better than that."

He held up his hand. "Whoa! I'm just telling you what he's up against, that's all. And don't expect any help from Maudy Payne. It's a well-known fact that there's no love lost between her and Ida. Nothing would probably please the sheriff more than to lock Ida's husband away for good."

I nodded. "Don't I know it! She won't even finish up with the crime scene. I'm going to have to pay a couple extra nights' rent on that mess outside."

He shook his head and went back to eating.

I sat there watching him, trying to figure a way to bring up something that had been niggling at my mind ever since I discovered Ben Wakefield's body in the orchard. "Cade," I started, "this is silly, but I've just got to ask."

He looked up, shuffled his fork to his other hand and reached for a gulp of tea. "What?"

"I saw you arguing with Ben Wakefield the night of the party."

He slowly put down his glass, his lips tightening. "Yeah? So

I shrugged. "I just thought I'd ask what the argument w
about."

His brows furrowed. "Just about some business dealin
we have. Why?"

"Just wondered. You seemed so angry, that's all."

He tipped his head back and let out a nervous laugh. The
leveling his eyes on me, he said, "You don't think I kill
him, do you? Because that's what this is sounding like."

"No! I would never think such a thing!" I said with
much guile as I could muster, before pressing on in n
sweetest voice. "But if even someone like you has disagre
ments with Wakefield, others with really bad tempers mig
have had similar or worse troubles with him. What was t
argument about exactly?"

He gave me an uncertain once-over and shook his hea
"All it was about was a load of lumber I paid for but did
get. Wakefield was holding out on me and it ticked me o
That's all." He went back to eating, indicating the subje
was closed. I paused, watching him shovel in the casserol
For some reason, the sight of him wholeheartedly enjoyin
his food did more to put my mind at ease than anythin
Certainly, a man with a guilty conscious couldn't go aft
his food with such gusto.

I picked up my own fork and took my first bite, the
stopped mid-chew and studied the concoction on my pla
with renewed interest. It was good. Really good. Sort of lil
a chicken potpie, but better: creamy with all the right seaso
ings and a hint of wine in the sauce. It was the flaky, butte
sourdough topping, however, that really made it scrumptio
Still, as good as it was, I didn't feel much like eating. So
put my fork down again, letting out a long sigh and foldi
my hands on the table in front of me. "I need your advice.

He kept on eating, nodding for me to continue.

"Harper Peach Farm is in financial trouble."

He briefly looked up, swallowed, then reached for son

tea to wash it down before replying. "The whole area is in financial trouble. We had a bad season last year; people are hurting all over."

I shook my head. "No, I mean, we're in serious financial trouble. There's not even enough cash to keep up with the basics. I was just out at the south orchards this morning and the irrigation pump has been down for . . . for I don't know how long. The trees are stressed."

He scraped the last bite from his plate to his mouth and sat back, regarding me with a serious look. "You know, you haven't been around for a while. Maybe things aren't really as bad as you think. All the farmers in the area have been cutting corners where they can. That's just how it is these days."

"I see what you're saying and I wish that were the case. But things around here are more serious than that." I reached for his plate. "More?"

His hand shot out and covered mine, stopping me from removing the plate. "No, I'm fine. But thanks."

My eyes shot to his and a spark passed between us. Shocked, I jerked my hand away, accidently bumping his glass and causing tea to slosh over the rim. "Oops. Sorry," I mumbled, dabbing at the spill with my napkin.

We both laughed a little trying to cover the awkward moment. "So," he said, exhaling. "Your family's pulled through a lot of difficult seasons over the years. What makes you think things are so bad this time around?"

"Just what I've gathered from talking to Ida and Ray." I looked down at my uneaten food. I really did need to see if I could access the business accounts, check out the bottom line for myself. "Daddy's been under so much stress that his health is starting to suffer."

"I'm sorry to hear that."

Cade's voice was genuine. I didn't dare look him in the face, worried that the compassion I'd see in his eyes would send more sparks flying. I had enough going on without mixing romance into things.

He continued, "I'll do anything I can to help; you know that."

"I appreciate that. Thing is, I made a barter this morning with Joe Puckett."

"The old moonshiner?"

I glanced across the table and chuckled. "Yeah. He's going to try to fix the irrigation pump and one of the mowers, too. Seems he knows a little something about engines."

Cade smiled. "I imagine he would. Sounds like a good plan."

"Only . . . I promised him a new roof in exchange."

His smile faded as he sat back in his chair and regarded me with a curious expression mixed with perhaps a little irritation. "And how do you plan on accomplishing that?"

I toyed with my plate, rotating it this way and that, trying to think of a good way to impose on our friendship. If Mama were here, she'd certainly know how to handle this situation; a couple sweetly put words and a few bats of her lashes, and most men were putty in her hands. She once told me that a true Southern woman never did anything she could charm someone else into doing. I'd never really warmed up to that philosophy, always more of the do-it-yourself type of gal—at least until now. Roofs were not my forte.

I cleared my throat. "Well, you do own a construction business," I started in a sugary tone, throwing in a wink for good measure.

He scrunched his face and shot me a weird look.

I sighed. Although I'd witnessed the fine art of womanly wheedling from the master—whose cunning wiles never ceased to amaze—somehow over the years, I never picked up the ability to employ my own feminine charms. I decided I'd better just take a straightforward approach. I sat up taller and continued, "I was thinking you'd be able to help me with the roof. I'd pay for the cost of supplies, of course. And it's just a tiny roof. Not much bigger than this room," I added, waving my hand around the confines of the room to emphasize my point.

He didn't respond.

I started in again. "As for your time, maybe there's something *we* could barter for. Is there anything you'd want from me?"

His expression quickly changed from irritation to . . . to something else. I watched in horror, realizing too late my unfortunate choice of wording. The crinkles around his eyes deepened as a slow grin formed on his mouth. The look he was giving me made me blush, all the way down to my toes.

I laughed nervously. "Would you stop?"

He raised one brow, his grin widening. "Stop what?"

"You know darn well what I'm talking about, Cade Mc-Kenna," I bantered back. "I'm serious."

"So am I."

My heart was beating so hard, I was sure he could hear it across the table. I touched my fingertip to my hot cheek, half-afraid it was going to erupt into flames any second.

He broke into raucous laughter, stood and gathered his plate and glass. "No need to get all worked up. I'll help," he said. "And you don't even have to worry about keeping your virtue intact. All I was going to ask for was a date to the Peach Festival."

"I wasn't worried about my virtue," I said, completely avoiding his mention of the Peach Festival.

He chuckled again and headed to the kitchen. I grabbed my still-full plate and followed. "So you'll help?" I asked, a little confused about what sort of agreement we'd struck. Seemed I was having a day of deals, none of which was quite in my control.

"I said I would." He rinsed his plate and set it in the sink. "My schedule is packed, but I'll figure out a way to make it work. Just let me think on it." He pushed past me on his way to the door. "We can discuss it more over dinner," he added, over his shoulder.

I placed my plate on the counter before it slid out of my suddenly moist palms. "Dinner?" I scurried after him. "When?"

Out on the porch, he turned back and looked down at me

with another sly smile. "Tomorrow night. At the house. Hattie asked me to invite you over. You know how it is with the ladies around here."

I smiled. "Food equals comfort."

"That's right. She wants you to stop by the boutique around five, right before she closes." He leaned in and winked. "Probably wants to show off her new place of business."

"Absolutely. I've been wanting to see her shop anyway."

He wheeled around and skipped down the porch steps. "It's a date, then," he said, with a final wave and another round of teasing laughter.

Food does equal comfort, I thought, watching his truck rumble back down the drive. And I knew someone who could use a little comfort. I marched right back inside, snatched up the casserole and headed straight for Ida's house.

"Auntie Nola!" Charlotte and Savannah chimed in unison, before latching their arms around my legs. I shuffle-stepped into the house, dragging them through the front room while making low, gravelly monster noises. "Where's your mama?" I finally asked, out of breath.

One of them pointed a chubby finger toward the kitchen while the other picked a doll off the floor. "Look! I got a new doll. She's a cheerleader!" She held up the plush doll by its yellow yarn hair for my inspection.

"Cute. Does she know any cheers?"

"No, but I do!" Savannah said, snapping to attention, arms straight at her sides and a mischievous grin playing on her face. Her sister took the doll, clutched it against her chest and stared on with worried blue eyes. "Hit it!" Savannah yelled, before breaking stance and beginning to chant, "Bulldogs . . . Bulldogs . . . we've got class! Bulldogs . . . bulldogs . . . we'll kick your—"

"Savannah Harper Shackleford!" Ida seem to appear out of nowhere, sending the girls scurrying for cover amid an echo of shrieks and giggles. "I swear, I don't know what's gotten into that girl. She's been acting up something terrible."

"You look horrible," I blurted, before I could stop the words from tumbling out. But I was caught off guard by her puffy eyes, bedraggled hair and lack of makeup. I hadn't seen my sister look this bad since high school when she slipped into a funk after losing the title for Miss Peach Queen.

"Thanks," she retorted. "Did you just come over here to insult me or is there something you wanted?"

I bit my lip and shoved the casserole dish her way. "I brought some food."

She lifted the foil, peered inside and scowled. "It's half-eaten."

"Yeah . . . well, I had some. Ginny from the diner sent it over to me, but I thought I'd share."

She looked bug-eyed at me, her mouth opening and shutting a few times. "She sent it to *you*? What in heavens for? I'm the one with the husband . . ." She clamped her mouth shut, her eyes glancing around for any sign of the girls, before putting the dish down with a thud on her coffee table. Then with both hands on her hips, she started in again. "It's just like that Ginny Wiggins to use a hot dish to snub me. The women in this town are so classless. Why, they've pretty much excluded me from everything these days. They don't even call me to play Bunko anymore."

I plunked down on her davenport. This was going to take a while. "Hey, now. You're not making a bit of sense. Sit down and let's talk through this."

She plopped next to me, jerking up quickly to pull a stray Barbie from between the cushions before settling back down. I repositioned myself, rotating my body and tucking my legs up underneath me. "So, what's all this about the ladies in town?"

"Oh, Nola. It's been awful. Just awful. Ever since Hollis started drinking heavily, rumors have been flying."

I'd figured as much. I forced back the sigh inside me as I innocently asked, "Rumors?"

She nodded. "I was hesitant to speak of it around Ray yesterday, but it's true. Awful rumors. Like that he's too drunk to keep track of things at the bank. It's even getting around that he's been stepping out. Can you imagine?"

Yes, I can. But I kept my mouth shut and instead shook my head sympathetically. "I'm sure all this has been hard on you. What about the girls? How are they doing?"

She waved it off. "They don't have a clue. I've been able to keep it all from them. They just think their daddy's been busy with work."

"Are you sure they think that, Ida? You said yourself that they've been acting up lately. Maybe they're more aware of things than you realize."

Her shoulders slumped and she started wringing her hands. "I don't know. Maybe."

"What are you going to tell them now that he's in jail?" I kept my voice low, whispering the last part just in case little ears were lurking about.

Ida's eyes started to tear up again, so I quickly changed the topic. "Ida, do you have any idea how that scarf would have ended up around Ben Wakefield's neck? I mean, Hollis was the last person I saw with it. Have you had a chance to ask him? Did he drop it? Give it to someone else?"

"No, I haven't been able to talk to him. They plucked him right off my front yard and hauled him off to jail. I tried calling last night, but they wouldn't let me talk to him."

I thought back to how Hollis had suggestively taunted Ida with the scarf. If he'd make such classless innuendos at the dinner table, hard telling what he might do when no one was looking. Especially knowing how he couldn't keep his eyes off pretty girls.

I studied my sister, thinking she might be giving her husband just a little too much credit when it came to his fidelity. But, instead of bringing up Hollis's philandering tendencies, I'd need to turn things around if I wanted to get any information out of her. "Hollis is such a catch," I started. "I bet there's always women clamoring after him."

Her expression shifted from self-pity to indignation. "You bet there is."

"How about at the party. Anyone flirting with him there?"

Her eyes rolled upward as she considered my question. "No, not really. Well . . . Laney Burns, but she's always chasing after Hollis."

"Big-haired Laney Burns?" I croaked.

Ida scrunched her nose in disgust. "Yes, that's the one. But Hollis doesn't pay her any attention." She leaned in and whispered, "He would never be attracted to such low-rent trash."

And she was off telling me all the gossip on Laney, complete with sly looks and whispered tidbits, none of which pertained to what I needed to know, and my mind zoned out as all I could think of was how much this community thrived on—and died with—its gossip in full swing.

Chapter 7

Georgia Belle Fact #092: A true Georgia Belle cooks like Paula Deen, drives like Danica Patrick and dresses like Daisy Duke.

Laney Burns wasn't my favorite person, that's for sure, but for Ida's sake, I thought I'd drop by and pay her a little visit. At the very least, if Laney had been following Hollis around at the party, she might have seen something helpful. Unfortunately, knowing Hollis the way I did, there was a good chance Laney was the reason he was late getting home that night. In that case, she was his alibi. At any rate, it would be worth seeing if I could learn anything at all. Ray was already stressed out working on other angles, and I wasn't too sure I wanted Loose Laney sidling up to Ray anyway. Plus, heaven knew, if I handed these possibilities over to the police, there was no way our barber-cut Maudy would get a thing out of the coiffed Laney!

By the time I made my way to the Clip & Curl, it was almost closing time. Nonetheless, there were still a couple gals with their heads under the dryers, leafing through magazines and sipping colas. Doris Whortlebe, the owner, was busy putting the final touches on a newly washed and set head of gray curls. At the sight of me, she stopped mid-spray,

put down her can of Aqua Net and held out her arms. "We
I'll be! Get over here and let me see you!" she ordered.

I obediently scurried over for my plushy, aerosol-infus
hug. I let out a little cough. "Hello, Doris."

"I heard you were back," she enthused, releasing her gr
and holding me at arm's length. But the delight left her eyes
she saw my short locks up close. "Oh Lawdy," was all she sa

My fingers flew to my head as everyone craned the
necks to get a glimpse of the oddball in the room of bi
haired heads. I cleared my throat. "I'm not here to get
haircut," I started.

"Thank you, sweet Jesus," Doris belted, throwing up l
hands in mock surrender. "Because if you're plannin' on goi
any *shorter*, you might as well head over to Earl's and let h
go at you with the buzzers." She turned her focus back to t
head of billowy curls in her chair and started in with the ha
spray again. "Well, if you're here for extensions, sweetie, i
a little late in the day, 'cuz I'm closing up in about a half hou

"No, ma'am," I responded, my eyes drawn to the brig
little orange balls that swung from her earlobes as s
moved about. They perfectly matched the coral-color
flowers stretching every which way against the black bac
ground of her blouse. "I came in to see if Laney was he
I'd like to get my nails done." I glanced around, not seei
Laney anywhere. "Is she already out for the day?"

"Naw. She's just out back taking a smoke break. Take
seat over there," she said, indicating one of the waiting cha
and giving a cursory—and disapproving—glance at my wo
battered nails. "I'm sure she can fit you in before closing."

I'd barely settled my bottom on the pink vinyl seat befc
the back door popped open and Laney sashayed into the roo
a cloud of nicotine wafting in behind her. Her bottle-blo
hair was teased higher than ever and secured into a mini-po
with a jeweled clip. She wobbled toward me in poured-
jeans and impossibly high stilettos that clacked against t
linoleum floor until she spied me and stopped in her track

"Hey, there, Nola Mae. What are you here for?" Her sugary sweet smile didn't quite reach her heavily lined eyes.

I stood, holding out my nails for her inspection. "Think you can do anything with these?"

She pursed her lips and wrinkled her nose at the sight of my jagged-edged nails. "Well, I suppose I could try. I charge twenty-five for a manicure; pay now and you won't smudge your polish afterwards."

I fished the bills out of my pocket and settled at her table where I perched on a small white chair and laid my hands atop a padded countertop. "Put your hand in here," she said, pushing a sudsy bowl of pink liquid my way before sliding her own perfectly manicured nails over a rack of polishes. She finally settled on the gaudiest shade of pink I'd ever seen.

"Maybe I should try something a little less . . ." I struggled for words. The shade she'd picked reminded me of Pepto Bismol. "It's just that I don't think I'm a pink type of gal."

"Don't be silly. Every girl loves pink," she assured me with a twisted little upturn of her highly glossed lips. "'A Knowing Blush'. Isn't that the cleverest name ever?"

"A Knowing Blush"? Why that particular shade? I wondered. Was she trying to tell me something? I narrowed my eyes as she bent over and started rummaging through her purse, pulling out a stick of gum and doubling it into her mouth before lifting my hand from the bowl and patting it dry. "Put your other hand in the bowl," she told me, wielding a torturous-looking instrument, which she used to snip at my cuticles, her drawn-on brows furrowed with concentration as she began prattling on about how long it had been since she'd seen me, how busy she'd been with learning her trade (which I avoided questioning) and other minutiae of her life I wouldn't recall later. None of which required any response other than my occasional nod.

"Did you have fun at the party the other night?" I injected, trying to steer the conversation my way.

She popped her gum and nodded. "Sure did. The food

was to die for and that band y'all had . . ." She fingered her hair and smiled. "I haven't twirled like that since I took my last spin on ol' Bodacious."

"Who did you get to dance with?" I tried slipping into the real reason I'd sat at her chair in the first place.

She shot me a nasty look and snipped extra hard.

"Hey, take it easy. That thing looks like it could be dangerous."

"Don't be a wuss, Nola Mae. I've got to get at these cuticles. I swear, I've never seen nails such a mess."

"Kind of hard to keep nice nails when you're scouring rubble for earthquake survivors or picking rocks to clear land for a life-sustaining vegetable plot," I shot back.

"Well, bless your heart. You have been a busy girl, haven't you?" She branded a nail file and, with a slight sneer, snatched back my hand so she could saw away at the tips of my nails. "I bet your sister sent you over here today, didn't she?"

"Ida? Why would she do that?" I hedged.

She eyed me suspiciously. "She didn't send you over here on a witch hunt?"

I gave her my most innocent look. "A witch hunt? What do you mean?"

She clenched the nail polish, shaking it until the little bead inside quit pinging. "No offense, but your sister has poor Hollis on a short leash. Hardly ever lets him out of her sight. She's paranoid, you know. Thinking every woman around is out to get that husband of hers"

I peeked at Laney's own nails. Long, clawlike nails, painted hussy red and sharpened for action. *Meooow!*

"Besides, all Hollis wants to do is have a little fun," she went on, straining to open the bottle of polish. "There's no harm in that, now, is there?"

Depends on what type of fun you're talking about. "No. No harm," I said, trying not to let my irritation show. I grabbed the polish and opened it for her. "So, did you get much of a chance to talk to Hollis at the party?"

She snatched my hand back again and started painting on the pink. "A little."

"Oh, yeah? What all did you guys talk about?" I asked, trying to stay focused despite the hideous color she'd started gliding over my nails. "Business and such?"

"Business? Oh no. Why would I care about such things? No, we just—oh heck. We didn't really talk about much. Just small stuff."

"Small stuff?"

She faltered and ran a pink smudge over the top of my thumb. "Oh, shoot!" Flustered, she drenched a cotton ball in polish remover and started scrubbing my finger. The chemical smell of acetone rose up and tickled my nostrils.

"The weather, perhaps," I pressed. "I'd forgotten how hot it can be around here."

She stopped polishing and fanned herself. "You ain't kiddin'." Glancing over her shoulder, she shouted out, "Is the air broke, Doris? It's hotter than Hades in here."

"No. Don't think so. I don't feel hot. Any of y'all feel hot?" she asked around the room.

A chorus of no's rang out.

I swiveled my gaze back to Laney. She'd moved my first hand aside and started the whole process again with my other hand. I kept staring until I could see her start to crack. She glanced nervously around the room before leaning in and hissing, "For Pete's sake, Nola. What're you trying to do, ruin my reputation?"

I fought hard not to laugh out loud. "No, Laney. Nothing like that. I was just wondering if you happened to see Hollis with a scarf that night."

"Ida's scarf, you mean?" Her eyes took on a mischievous look. "Well, perhaps I did. Hollis and I were playing a little game of keep-away with it out in the orchard behind the tent. Just for laughs, you know? Nothing came of it."

Not for a lack of trying, I bet. "Where did the scarf end up?"

She hesitated a beat. "I don't rightly know. The last I

remember, it was caught up in a tree branch. Is that what this is all about? Did Ida send you over here looking for that scarf?"

I shrugged and she continued, talking in between cuticle snips. "Well, tell her that I didn't take her ugly scarf. It's not my style."

No, but trying to take her husband is just your style. Ida's words—"low-rent trash"—popped back to mind. I shook it off, trying to stay on track.

Laney chomped hard on her gum a couple times and went on, "Anyway, Hollis was too drunk for much fun, so I got bored and went back to the party. I never would have left him if I'd known what would happen."

"What do you mean if you'd 'known what would happen'?"

"I mean"—she moved her hand over her heart—"if I'd known he was going to strangle Ben Wakefield, I never would have left him out there. Especially since he'd been drinking so much Peach Jack."

I felt my jaw go slack. "You think Hollis actually did it? I thought you two were so friendly and all."

My line of questioning must have been frustrating her, because I noticed she'd skipped a couple of steps and went right to applying polish. Not too neatly, either. "I just know what I read in the paper. I can't believe Hollis strangled that man with his bare hands. He never seemed like the violent type. He's just a big ol' teddy bear, you know."

Bare hands? I tried to think back to what the paper article had said about the actual death. Did it mention the scarf? Maybe Maudy hadn't made that information public yet? I needed to tread carefully. I kept quiet for a few minutes, mulling over the scarf bit, while Laney slicked on the rest of the polish. Finally she finished my last nail and sat back to admire her handiwork. "There. That pink looks so pretty." I looked at my nails and shrugged. They did look kind of pretty. It'd been years since I'd worn polish.

Laney started cleaning up her workstation, while I stood and made my way toward the door. "Hey, wait a minute," she called after me. "Why all the questions about that stupid scarf?" Then her eyes lit up like a bulb as she put two and two together. "Oh my goodness. That's how it happened, isn't it? Hollis strangled that poor man with Ida's scarf!"

A southern-fried explicative sounded from across the room as Doris dropped a comb. She stared at me wide-eyed, her mouth agape and earrings still swinging from a whiplash head snap.

Uh-oh. Now I've done it. I ducked out the door before they could corner me for more information. It wouldn't be good if that little detail hit the Cays Mill rumor hotline. Heck, who was I kidding? *If?* Gossip spread so fast in our town, the telephone company practically had to install speed bumps on all the lines. Now that I'd let the cat out of the bag, it'd be only a matter time before everyone in town knew it had been Ida's scarf wrapped around Wakefield's neck. *What have I done?* Ida was going to kill me. That was if she got to me before Maudy Payne.

My only consolation was learning that Hollis didn't have possession of the scarf the whole evening. And if it wasn't with him the whole time, there was a chance someone else got ahold of it and strangled Wakefield. A slim chance, sure, but hope often comes in small packages.

Back at the house, I found a brown paper grocery bag on our front porch. I peered inside to find another covered casserole dish. I didn't even have to lift the foil to know it was tuna noodle this time.

I carried the bag into the kitchen where I removed the container and found a notecard from Candace, Hollis's secretary at the bank. In addition to instructing me to heat the casserole at 350 degrees until warmed through, she let me know just how sorry she was that Hollis turned to violence and landed himself in jail. But not to worry; she'd hold down the fort until the bank could find a new president.

For crying out loud, I thought. Did this whole town think Hollis was guilty? I wadded up the note and threw it into the garbage can. My pride didn't extend to the casserole, however. After all, I was starving, and I just happened to know, from years of attending potlucks, that Candace made a killer tuna noodle casserole with tastes of sour cream and scallions mixed in and finished with a topping of crushed potato chips.

While I waited for it to heat, I called Ida to see if she wanted to bring the girls over and join me for dinner. I held the phone against my shoulder while mixing one of my mama's zipped baggies of corn bread makings she'd left for me.

"Ida?" I asked. Her voice was so low I wasn't sure if it was her or one of the girls that answered.

"Yes, it's me," she said a little louder. "Sorry, but the phone's been ringing off the hook."

"People calling to see if you're okay?" I was hopeful that some of the townspeople had finally decided to show Ida some neighborly love.

"No. That pesky Frances Simms. She's called me three times already."

Uh-oh. "Frances? What did she want?" I innocently asked. It probably wasn't a good time to tell Ida about my conversation with Laney. Although I'd found a bit of news that might shine a little light in Hollis's favor, it was tainted with bad news. Namely, that Hollis and Laney were flirting around with each other after the party.

Ida went on, "Somehow she found out Wakefield was strangled with my scarf. Or at least she's heard a rumor to that effect. She's trying to get me to confirm her suspicions. Now, how do you suppose she found out? The paper didn't say anything about the scarf."

Hmm . . . Yet another reason not to mention my conversation with Laney. "Oh, you know how this town is. Nothing's a secret for long." I readjusted the phone between my ear and shoulder and started beating the heck out of the corn bread mix, taking out my frustration on a couple eggs rather than the blabbermouths that occupied this town.

"What's that noise?" Ida asked.

"I'm making corn bread," I replied, jumping at the chance to change the topic. "Candace dropped off a casserole—"

"What! She didn't bring *me* a casserole."

Oh, no. Here we go with that casserole-snubbing bit again. "I'm sure she just assumed you were staying here at the house."

"Well, if the whole town is so into my business that they can figure out it was my scarf wrapped around that poor man's neck, certainly they can figure out that I'm still in my own home."

She had a point.

I could hear Ida huffing over the line, working herself into a real frenzy. She started up again. "Why, that—"

"Say what you want about Candace," I interrupted, trying to redirect her agitation. "But she makes a mean tuna noodle casserole. Why don't you and the girls come over and have dinner with me. Ray's supposed to be home tonight."

"No, thanks. Frances Simms has been driving by all day. The second I set foot out this door, she'll accost me with her pen and notepad. I'm just not up for all that right now."

I told her I understood and promised to come by for a visit tomorrow. After hanging up, I poured the batter into a cast-iron skillet and slid it into the oven next to the heating casserole. I'd just shut the oven door when I heard the sound of tires on gravel outside. I glanced through the kitchen window to see Ray's SUV pulling down the drive.

"Just in time," I greeted from the porch. "I've got a casserole and a skillet of corn bread heating in the oven."

He pulled out his briefcase and a small bag and started for the house. "Perfect. I'm starved."

"You didn't bring a very big bag," I commented, noticing his duffel was only half-full at most.

"That's because I'm only staying tonight. I've got to get back to Perry tomorrow afternoon to see about another client."

I held the door for him. "Really? I was hoping you'd be here for a while."

He dumped his bags by the door and headed straight for the kitchen and started washing his hands at the sink. "Don't worry. I've got the situation covered. Let me get something in my stomach and I'll tell you all about it."

"Pink?" Ray commented a few minutes later as I pulled the corn bread from the oven. "That's surprising."

I squinted down at my freshly painted nails. "Surprising?"

"Not really your color, that's all. You seem more the camo green type. You know, something you'd wear while warding off vicious lions in the African bush."

"I've never chased lions!" I laughed. *Poachers, maybe, but never any sort of vicious animal.* In fact, I remembered my first night in a tent positioned outside a remote Somalian health center, where we assisted refugees who'd escaped the genocide. The night sounds had terrified me. Especially the skittish cries of innocent zebras as they were snatched from their herds by hungry lions, while yipping jackals stood by to lick up the leftovers. Suddenly, an ugly scene flashed through my mind of Hollis being snatched from his family by the vicious lioness Maudy Payne, while the townspeople stood by jeering and heckling.

I forced the awful image from my mind and glanced back at Ray, who was making quick work of the casserole, and told him about my visit with Laney Burns. "But I'm afraid I might have messed things up."

"Oh yeah? Why's that?" he asked between bites.

"I asked her if she saw the scarf at the party. In a round-about way," I quickly added. "But she put it all together and broadcasted to the whole salon that Hollis strangled Wakefield with Ida's scarf."

Ray's grip tightened around his fork. "What! Why would you even ask her about such a thing in the first place?"

"It was stupid of me. I'm sorry." I swallowed down a lump in my throat. "It's just that I went by Ida's and she mentioned that Laney was flirting with Hollis at the party . . . and, well, I hated to think it, but I wondered if maybe Hollis and Laney might have gotten together after the party. You know how he is. Especially when he drinks. I just wanted to find out if she'd seen the scarf."

He put down his fork and started rubbing his temples. "Oh no. Of all places to go asking questions like that. The Clip and Curl is gossip central around here." He drew in a deep breath, held it for a few seconds and slowly let it out. "Listen, I know you're just trying to help Ida, but you need to let me handle this. Plus, if Maudy gets wind of it, she'll be furious. That's not going to help Hollis."

I closed my eyes and pinched my nose. "Sorry," I whispered.

"What's done is done."

I sighed and raised my eyes. "Don't you want to hear what she said?"

"Might as well, I guess." He abandoned his fork and leaned back in his chair, folding his arms across his chest.

"She admitted to fooling around with Hollis out in the orchard right after Ida left the party. Apparently, Hollis was too drunk to be much fun, so Laney left him there."

"And the scarf?"

"It was tangled up in a tree branch. Not in Hollis's hands."

Ray shrugged. "That doesn't mean anything. Hollis could have got it later and still used it to strangle Wakefield."

I held up my finger. "Yes, but so could someone else. The thing is, we now know that's a possibility. If you had to, you could put Laney on the stand, right? And if she testified about the scarf, it could create reasonable doubt, couldn't it?"

He unfolded his arms and pressed his fingertips together, contemplating my words for a second before shaking his head. "Let's just hope it doesn't come down to a trial."

"You don't feel confident?"

"I'd just prefer to find the real killer and get Hollis off the hook. But I can't count on the local law enforcement to look much further than Hollis. I'll pass this latest on to

Sheriff Payne, but don't expect much. She already thinks she's got her man."

"And she's only more than happy to stick it to Ida," I added.

"That's why I've decided to bring in a private investigator. As soon as he's finished some other work in Macon, he'll come down here. I'm hoping it'll be in the next day or two."

I felt so much relief knowing help was on its way, even though I secretly wondered how Ray was going to pay for the expense of a private investigator. We ate in silence for a while before I finally asked, "When will you be back?"

"Friday, for the arraignment. Until then, don't discuss Hollis with anyone else. Okay?"

"Cross my heart. Besides, I'm going to be busy with stuff around here." I filled him in on my deal with Joe Puckett and how I'd convinced Cade to help with the roof repair. "The only problem is I'm not even sure we have enough money in the accounts to cover the cost of repairing the roof, not to mention the parts for the pump and tractor."

"And laying new irrigation lines," he added.

I rubbed at a kink in my neck. "Yeah, it doesn't look good for the farm. I can't believe things are this bad."

Ray reached across the table, touching my arm. "Hey, don't give up. You're one of the most resourceful people I know. You'll think of something; I'm sure of it."

I managed a halfhearted smile in return, wishing I felt as confident as Ray. Dealing with the plights of refugees, orphans, the diseased and the displaced was much easier than dealing with my own family's problems. With other people's issues, I could approach objectively. The problems I now faced with Hollis and the farm cut a little too close to the heart. The stakes were personal and so was my fear of failure.

Chapter 8

Georgia Belle Fact #073: When life gives you lemons, put them in your sweet tea and take a nice long sip.

Just after sunrise the next morning, I stood on the porch, coffee mug in hand, admiring the tiny diamond-like sparkles of dew on the front lawn and making my plans for the day. Ray had risen even earlier, eating a quick breakfast before leaving with his duffel bag slung over his shoulder. He'd planned to stop by the jail and visit with Hollis before heading back to the work awaiting him at his office in Perry. As for me, I'd awakened with a new attitude. Fear of failure had never stood in my way before and I wasn't about to let it stop me now. I was determined to save my family's livelihood.

I willed myself to look past the crime scene tape and disastrous remnants from the party, and really study the orchard. My eyes roamed from early spring producers like Flavorich to the late-season O'Henry and Summer Lady peaches. We'd planted enough strains to maximize our picking time, knowing that diversification was the key to a bountiful harvest. I wondered if it was time for the Harpers to look toward other forms of diversification. After all, change was inevitable. The last century alone brought with it new technologies and new markets. Daddy hadn't really ridden the wave of change. Instead, he'd sort of come along kicking and screaming, clinging to the old ways and hoping for miracles. But we'd moved beyond that point now. What we really needed to do was make our own miracle.

I swilled the last of my coffee and sighed. I'd just turned to head back inside for another cup when Joe sauntered around the corner of the house. "Mornin'."

"Morning, Joe. You're up and at it early." I noticed his eyes were drawn to the crime scene tape.

"Don't mind that mess. What can I do for you?"

"Been out lookin' at your equipment."

I tipped my empty mug his way. "Why don't you come in so we can talk about it? I've got coffee on."

He nodded, removing his hat and clambering up the steps. He hesitated inside the doorway. "What's wrong, Joe?" I asked, turning back from my way to the kitchen.

"This is a fine house you have." His bright eyes took in every square inch of the front room, from our ancient uphol-stered sofa to Mama's collection of Depression glass dis-played on the window ledges. While everything seemed outdated to me, I tried to imagine how impressive it must seem to Joe, who'd spent most of his life living in not much more than a shack.

"Thank you, Joe, but won't you come on back to the kitchen? The coffee's still hot and I think there's some corn bread left over from last night's supper."

His face lit up as he followed me the rest of the way through the house and settled in one of the chairs at the kitchen counter. I cut an extra big slice of corn bread and poured him a cup of coffee. "Why's all that yellow tape out in your yard?" he asked.

"The sheriff put that up. Ben Wakefield was murdered out in our orchard the other night. She's investigating it."

Joe started eating. "Is that so?"

"Yes. I'm surprised you haven't heard."

"Don't get much news up my way."

I nodded. "Well, she's arrested my brother-in-law, Hollis. Half the town thinks he did it." I slid a jar of Mama's peach preserves and a spoon his way.

"You don't?"

"No, I sure don't." A question popped to mind as I watched him spread a dollop of the preserves on his corn bread. "Did you know Ben Wakefield?"

He shrugged. "My son used to work for him up at the mill."

"Your son worked for him?" My mind flashed back to a young, shy boy from my youth who loved nothing better than fishing down at the Hole or running his coon dogs at night. I hadn't thought of him for a long time. "His name's Tucker, isn't it?"

"Was. He's dead."

"Oh, Joe. I'm sorry."

He glanced up from his food and nodded.

After a long, uncomfortable silence, I dared to speak up again. "So, tell me what we're up against with the equipment." I cut him another slice of bread and topped off our coffees.

"It weren't too bad after all," he surmised. "Think I can have it all back up and runnin' with just a few parts and a little know-how."

"Wonderful! That's the best news I've had all week."

He nodded, dipping his spoon again for more peach preserves as I collected a notepad and pencil from next to the telephone. I jotted down a list of parts as he rattled them off between bites. "I can stop in and order these today. They'll probably arrive in a day or two."

He finished up and pushed his plate aside, making a little sighing sound and patting his belly. "Thank you for the breakfast."

We both stood. "Glad you enjoyed it."

He gathered his hat and repositioned it on his head. "Le[t] see. What day is this?"

"Wednesday."

"Then I'll be by Friday mornin' to see if you've got t[he] parts." He glanced back toward the floor and shuffled h[is] feet. "I'd noticed your daddy let all his help go."

"That's right. Times have been tight. He let them go rig[ht] after harvest."

"Well, I'm figurin' you might want some help mowi[n'.] It's a big job."

My antenna flew up. Another deal coming and I need[ed] to be careful this time. I didn't have any resources left fo[r] barter. "Yes, sir, it is a big job, but I think I'm up to it."

His gaze briefly met mine with a little twinkle befo[re] darting away again. "I'm sure you can. But I'm thinkin' y[ou] may need time to tend to other things. I'd be willin' to ta[ke] care of it for a fair trade."

I shook my head and chuckled. No way was I going [to] get caught up in another deal with him. "I don't believe [I] have anything left to trade."

"Not true, missy." He nodded toward our open pant[ry] door, where rows of golden fruit–filled jars lined the shelve[s.] "I'd be happy to work for enough preserves to get r[e] through the winter."

"Mama's peach preserves?" I couldn't believe someo[ne] would trade all that work for a few jars of jelly. Althoug[h] there wasn't much in the world that compared to the goo[d-] ness of Mama's preserves.

He nodded. "Yup. As far as I'm concerned, your mam[a's] peach preserves are as good as gold."

Once again, I shook hands with the wily old gentlema[n.] I fetched a box and fixed him up with a dozen jars of p[re]serves before sending him on his way. A smile played on [my] lips as I watched him descend the porch steps, the box [of] preserves clenched to his chest. "As good as gold," he'd sa[id.]

He was right. The answer to our problems had been right under my nose the whole time. If only I could make it work.

The whole town was hopping today, people moving in and out of shops carrying bags of goodies. I parked my car in one of the few open spots on the square and cut across the courthouse lawn on my way to the Cays Mill Mercantile, pausing for a second to admire the colorful mass of flowers at the base of General Lee's statue. Red, white and blue petunias surrounded a plaque that read, *In Memory of Our Confederate Dead.* I looked up at the formidable figure of Lee mounted on his horse, thinking back to the time in high school when Hattie and I climbed up and draped Laney's black lace push-up bra across his chest. How Hattie had gotten ahold of Laney's bra, I never knew. But to this day, I couldn't look at the statue without remembering our little stunt.

A bell jingled overhead as I entered the mercantile, garnering a wide smile from the woman behind the counter. "Nola Mae Harper! I—"

I held up my hand, stopping her mid-sentence. "Bet you heard I was back in town," I quipped.

"Why, yes! Welcome home, sweetie. It's good to see you."

"You, too, Sally Jo." Sally Jo had been manning the front counter of the mercantile since I was an itsy-bitsy thing. In all that time, I don't think I'd seen her in anything other than Levi's and a chamois shirt. Still, her utilitarian choice of clothing and short, bobbed gray hair suited her personality. Sally Jo was a hardworking, honest gal with a sweet disposition and a willingness to help anyone in need. We were similar in that regard, always willing to lend a helping hand. Come to think of it, we were alike as far as fashion went, too.

"What can I do you for?" she asked.

I handed over my list and started to explain: "Just a few things for around the farm. Here's a list of parts. How long do you think it'll take for them to come in?" The Cays Mill

Mercantile carried everything from hardware to small farm needs and even had a small clothing section in the back stocked with outdoor apparel—which was probably where Sally picked up all those chamois shirts. Anything they didn't carry, like engine parts, Sally Jo could special order.

She lifted a pair of readers that dangled from a chain around her neck and placed them on her nose. "These parts won't take long. Let's see. I'd say Friday, for sure." She paused, perusing the rest of my list. "I see you also have mason jars on this list. Getting ready to do some canning?"

"Just thought I'd experiment with a few of Mama's recipes."

She smiled at me over the rim of her glasses. "Is that so? Well, isn't that sweet? I do love her chutney. She always gives me a few jars at Christmastime, you know." She pointed to one of the aisles. "Jars, rings and lids are down that aisle. If there's anything you need help with, just holler."

I spent a few minutes gathering everything on my list and was just turning to head back to the cash register when a ruckus arose from the front of the store. "I told you I don't want any of those darn things in my window!" Sally Jo belted out.

Hurrying up front, I placed my items on the checkout counter and watched the scene unfold.

"But we have to stop Wakefield from cutting trees."

"Not all my customers agree with your position on the matter, Mr. Reeves. Lumbering is an honorable profession. Just how do you suppose we get wood for building homes and making furniture? Why, even that paper you're trying to put up in my window is made from trees."

"This paper is recycled."

Sally placed her hands on her hips and let out a loud harrumph. "Well, it originally came from a tree! Listen, young man, I'm sick of this smear campaign you're running against Wakefield Lumber. Have you no decency? The man was just killed, you know?"

Her words didn't seem to faze the guy. I watched as he flipped a strand of blond hair out of his face and squared his gaze on Sally. The vehemence in his eyes was scary. "So what? I'm glad he's dead. The world is better off without people like him."

My mouth dropped. Where was Maudy Payne now? Here was a man with enough motive, and definitely enough twisted logic, to kill Ben Wakefield. A prime suspect if I'd ever seen one!

"Out!" Sally ordered, pointing a shaky hand toward the door. After the fellow finally shuffled away, Sally returned to the register and started ringing up my order. "Sorry you had to witness that ugly scene," she told me. "That young man is a menace."

"Is he from around here?"

She started bagging my stuff. "I don't believe so. His name's Floyd Reeves. He showed up here last month and started putting up flyers and such. No one paid much attention to him at first. He was sort of a lone renegade. But lately, he's been recruiting some of the local high school kids. He's got a regular little posse now."

I handed over my credit card. "What's his beef with lumbering?"

"Who knows?" She gave me the slip to sign. "He's just against it, it seems."

"But why? He's worried about illegal lumbering or protecting endangered animal species?"

Sally shook her head. "Now, something like that might make sense. I could sort of understand if he had a reasonable cause he was supporting. It seems, though, that he just doesn't want any trees cut down. No matter that they're cut to regulation and replanted." She exhaled and shrugged. "You know how kids that age can be. They're always looking for a reason to rebel. Sometimes it doesn't matter what the cause; they just have to protest something."

I agreed. My own misguided youth was filled with

enough rebelling to keep child psychologists busy filling medical journals for a lifetime. Still, could this kid be enough of a head case to actually kill someone to promote his cause? "You've heard, I'm sure, that the sheriff's arrested Hollis for Wakefield's murder."

Her mouth drooped. "Yes, I've heard. I've been thinking about your sister and those precious girls of hers. So sad, really."

I bristled. "What's sad is that he's been wrongly accused. Hollis says he's innocent and I believe him."

I was about to add the possibility of the murderer being the anti-lumbering Floyd Reeves when she slid my purchases across the counter with a mollifying smile. "Well, bless your heart. That's the right attitude. You just go on being loyal to your family . . . no matter what they've done."

I left the mercantile so mad, I could hardly see straight. It was no wonder I ran smack into Frances Simms from the *Cays Mill Reporter*. "There you are, Nola! I was just out at your farm."

I readjusted my grip on the cumbersome case of mason jars. "You were? Why?"

Her birdlike features homed in on me with an exacting expression. "Just hoping to get a statement from you about Ben Wakefield's murder."

"I don't have a statement. Sorry." Shuffling past her, I made a beeline for my Jeep.

She followed close on my heels. "But I heard you were the one to find the body. I also heard a scarf might have been used to asphyxiate him. Can you confirm that report?"

Uh-oh. Ray was right. My little fiasco at the Clip & Curl was getting ready to explode in my face. If Frances knew about the scarf, it was only a matter of time before Maudy Payne caught on that I was the one who told. "No comment." I picked up my pace.

Frances pursued me across the square and right up to the

back of my Jeep. "The people of Cays Mill have the right to be informed," she pressed.

Trying to ignore her, I placed my purchases on the ground next to my back bumper, pulled out my key fob and clicked open the locks. I slid everything into the cargo space and turned to make my escape. Unfortunately, Frances blocked my way.

"Excuse me, Ms. Simms," I said, trying to nudge her out of the way. For being such a frail-looking woman, Frances was sure hard to budge.

She pressed closer. "Has Hollis ever discussed with you the fact that he risked all of the bank's assets on one of Ben Wakefield's trumped-up Ponzi schemes?"

"No!"

"You mean the bank wasn't backing Wakefield's latest lumber venture?"

"No, I mean I'm not answering any of your questions," I bit out. "Now move out of my way!"

I squeezed past her, flinching as my arms scraped against the sunbaked metal of my Jeep.

"Just one more thing," she called after me. "Was it really Ida's scarf wrapped around Ben Wakefield's neck?"

Chapter 9

Georgia Belle Fact #034: Deep fat-fried chicken pairs perfectly with crispy gossip.

I kept going, breaking into a jog until I reached Hattie's Boutique.

"You're early," she said, looking up from the front counter as I burst inside. Her look of surprise quickly turned to alarm as she noticed my state of panic.

"Hide me!" I stood in the middle of her store, out of breath and frantically searching for a suitable hiding spot. I spied a set of dressing rooms. Dashing across the floor, I dove into the nearest stall and slammed the door shut. Not more than a second later, I heard the shop's door open.

"Did Nola Harper happen to come in here?" It was Frances.

"Frances! I'm glad you're here. I've been wanting to talk to you about the ad I placed for this week. I'm just not sure if you've quoted me correctly—"

"Not right now," Frances cut her off. "I'm hot on a story."

The door shut again and Hattie sniggered and called out, "The coast is clear."

Easing the door open, I took a cautionary peek before coming all the way out. "Frances Simms has more than a

little paparazzi in her. You should see how she pursued me
around the square."

"Oh, I know. She's all worked into a tizzy. Wakefield's
murder is probably the biggest story Cays Mill has seen, unless
you're counting last year's debacle at the debutante ball."

My ears perked up. "Last year's what?" I asked, heading
toward a display of handbags that caught my eye.

Hattie chuckled. "Two of the debs got into it over a young
man. They ended up smearing cake in each other's faces."
She laughed some more. "You should have seen the picture
in the paper."

I picked up a black leather bag, fingering the soft leather
and fine stitching. "That doesn't compare at all to murder."

"Oh my goodness, Nola. You've been away for too long.
Have you forgotten how seriously people take the debutante
ball? Why, those poor girls haven't shown their faces around
here since that horrible incident." She paused for a beat. "Do
you like that bag?"

Glancing up, I saw the insecurity in her expression. "Like
it?" I waved my hands around the room. "Hattie, I like everything in here. The whole place is gorgeous! I'm so impressed
with what you've done." The wide-planked pine floors and
walls painted in subdued hues of mauve with white oak mold-
ings gave the place an uptown feel, but still it somehow managed to seem feminine and homey. Perhaps it was the
comfortable seating area with a chintz sofa and coordinating
flower-print chairs, or the children's nook, tucked away in the
corner and painted with a fairy-tale-themed mural that made
it seem so inviting. "It's absolutely amazing, Hattie!"

She blew out her breath, her shoulders notably relaxing.
"I'm so glad you like it. Cade spent practically every weekend for six months helping me put it all together. Do you
remember what this building used to be?"

I scanned my brain, trying to remember as I ran my hand
along a row of dresses. Her inventory was just the right
mixture of classic and more modern styles. I wasn't sure

how, with such a small shop, she'd managed to carry something to suit almost every type of woman's taste. "No, I don't remember. What was it?"

"The old video shop. Don't you remember coming down here Friday afternoons and picking up movies for the weekend?"

"That's right!" I twirled around, getting my bearings. "Horror was there." I pointed at the far wall. "Family movies in the middle . . ."

"And romance, right here," Hattie finished, pointing double fingers down at her counter.

We both giggled. "Romance was our favorite. But, if I remember correctly, you only wanted to watch movies with Julia Roberts, like *My Best Friend's Wedding*, *Pretty Woman*. . . . Oh my gosh! How many times did we watch *Pretty Woman*?"

"And why wouldn't I? She's a hometown girl."

"She was born over in Smyrna. Almost an hour away."

Hattie nodded. A mischievous grin crossed her face. "I had the previous owner throw in all the romance movies as part of the deal when I bought this place. We can watch *Pretty Woman* after dinner tonight, if you want?"

"For old times' sake, I think we should."

"For old times' sake," she agreed. "Just let me finish up a few things and I'll be ready to close down for the day."

I was about to ask what I could do to help when the door opened.

"Hey, there! Can I help you?" Hattie asked. Then Hattie blinked double time, pulling my attention to the woman as well. I had to make a conscious effort to shut my mouth.

"I don't know," the woman slowly said, walking up to the nearest rack and pulling out a dress. She gave it a snide once-over before hanging it back up. "I'm not sure if you have anything to suit my taste."

She reminded me of a cross between Dolly Parton and Lady Gaga. Sort of a Dolly Gaga, I guess. She was wearing a skintight pink pantsuit showing all her abundant curves, with a bold zipper that was unzipped low enough to reveal her ample cleavage.

Her black, spiked stilettos added an extra four inches to her already impossibly long legs, while her hair, salon red and teased to the max, rose at least another inch above her crown in a perfectly puffy bump and then fell around her face in wavy tendrils, softening the telltale age lines around her eyes. I couldn't help but wonder how long it took her to put that look together every morning and just how much cosmetic surgery it took to pull it off. The thing was, it suited her. I couldn't quite figure out why, but somehow, on this woman, what would have normally been considered trashy, looked good, in a weird sort of way.

"Is this the only boutique in town?" the woman asked.

"Yes, it is. There's more shopping in Perry, of course, but it's a little ways away. There's always Macon, but—"

"Never mind." The woman cut her short. "This will have to do." She started snatching blouses off the racks. With a tip of her chin, she called me over and shoved a dozen or so garments at me. "Be a dear and run these over to a dressing room, won't ya? And, let's see, do y'all have any spandex leggings?"

Hattie stole a glance at her watch and shot a quizzical look my way. I knew what she was thinking. By the looks of things, it was going to be a late dinner.

I passed by the counter on the way to the dressing room and leaned in to whisper, "How about I help you here and then we'll grab some quick takeout afterwards. Maybe some burgers from the Honky Tonk."

The corners of Hattie's mouth tipped upward. "I can do better than that. Let me call Cade and tell him we'll be late. He can start fixin' dinner and have it ready for us when we get up to the house. He won't mind a bit. He thinks he's a better cook than me anyway."

I agreed and trudged the rest of the way to the dressing room with my load. As soon as I returned, the woman had another pile waiting for me. This went on for a while, but just when I thought my arms were going to give out, she finally declared she was ready to try on. After forty-five minutes of squirming and shimmying, and turning the air blue with cusswords, the woman finally emerged from the dressing room and made her way to the counter with a stack of outfits. Shoving a bejeweled hand into her purse, she rummaged around and pulled out a credit card.

Hattie glanced at the card and gasped. "Millicent Wakefield? Oh, I had no idea. Were you related to Ben Wakefield?"

"That depends if you call being his wife related," the woman answered.

Hattie offered a little gasp. "Oh, I'm so sorry."

Millicent seemed unfazed. "Well, it would have been ex-wife if he hadn't gone and gotten himself murdered. And don't be sorry; he was a lousy husband anyway. I might have killed him myself if Hollis Shackleford hadn't beat me to it." She reached in her purse and pulled out a pack of mints, offering one to each of us as we stood slack-jawed. We declined and she tossed a few into her mouth, clacking them against her teeth a couple times before chomping down with a loud crunch.

Hattie and I exchanged a look. "That's a strong statement," I said.

She waved it off. "Aw, don't take me seriously. I would never do something that might land me in prison. I don't look good in stripes." She tipped her head back and let a low, raspy laugh. "Ah, heck. I shouldn't be laughing. Benny and I had some good times together early on in our marriage. But then he got all caught up in his work and it all got so dull. We just kind of went our separate ways."

Hattie passed the slip across the counter for her signature. "I'm sorry, but I didn't even know Mr. Wakefield was married."

No one must have known, I thought. One thing was for sure, though: when word of this got out, it'd spur a casserole-baking frenzy. The well-meaning gals in town surely wouldn't let a widow go hungry during her time of grief.

Millicent laughed some more. "Well, now. It was no secret. But I can see how people might not know about us. We married young and have been separated for years. I live up in Macon.

We have a second home up there and, well . . ." Her eyes skimmed over the shop. "I do prefer the shopping up there."

Hattie frowned.

Not me, though. Things were looking better all the time for Hollis. I could hardly wait to tell Ray about these new suspects. First, Floyd Reeves—the kid with a chip on his shoulder—and now an almost ex-wife nobody knew anything about. One who maybe wasn't getting the deal she wanted in a divorce? "It sounds like you two had an arrangement all worked out. What happened?"

Millicent grabbed her bags and looked at us with what I assumed was genuine shock, though I couldn't be sure from the well-drawn-on eyebrow arches whether she'd really raised them or not. "Why, I'm surprised y'all don't already know. I just assumed in a town this size that word would have gotten around already."

"About what?" Hattie and I asked in unison.

"Benny was trading me in for a newer model. He'd met some young hussy from around here and wanted to make it permanent."

"From around here?" Hattie asked.

"Yes, some young thing that works at the salon, of all places." She rolled her eyes, hefted her purchases and flounced out the door.

It was a while after Millicent left before Hattie and I even moved, both of us rooted in shock. Finally Hattie spoke up. "Do you suppose she means Laney Burns?"

"Well, she sure as heck isn't talking about Mrs. Whortlebe!" I glanced down at my nails noticing little pieces of polish were already starting to chip off around the edges. "A Knowing Blush," Laney said it was called. Now I wondered if she'd chosen this particular shade as some sort of twisted little play on words. Maybe she knew a lot more than she originally told me.

I shook my head. I was being paranoid. Besides, this whole thing about Laney and Ben Wakefield didn't make sense. The whole time I talked to her, Laney never once showed any emotion over Wakefield's death. If she was involved with him, she'd certainly be grieving his passing. Instead, she gave me the impression she had her heart set on Hollis. Which . . . maybe she did . . . and Wakefield found out? And he confronted Hollis and . . .

"What is it, Nola? You look like you've seen a ghost."

I glanced from my nails to Hattie and then bit my lip. If Millicent was right, and Laney was caught up in some sort of weird lovers' triangle with Hollis and Ben Wakefield, Hollis just gained another motive for murdering Wakefield. "Nothing. Nothing at all," I replied. "What do you say we finish here and head up to your place for dinner? I'm half-starved."

"You know what I think," Hattie was saying a little later as she locked the boutique's door. I'd helped her rush through her closing chores: rehanging clothes, vacuuming and counting the day's receipts. "I think Maudy Payne better get her thumb out of her butt and start considering some other suspects. Millicent, for starters. That woman seemed off to me. Did she seem off to you?"

"Way off. But Millicent isn't the only suspect Maudy's missed or refused to consider. She's got it out for Ida, you know? Probably hoping Hollis is guilty just so she can stick it to her."

"Really?" Hattie pocketed her key and pointed up the street. "Come on—you can fill me in on the way. It's not too far. We'll just walk from here." I was glad I was wearing my low-heeled boots since we were walking, although I noticed Hattie didn't seem to have any trouble maneuvering in her own three-inch strappy sandals, which went perfectly with her fresh-looking yellow-and-white-checked sundress and chunky white jewelry. Completing the look, she had her long dark hair done up in a Jackie-like French roll. I fingered my own hair, whimsically thinking back to my longer-haired days. I was never into fancy updos, but liked the ease of pulling it all back in a ponytail.

I looped my arm in hers as we started up the street in a

companionable silence for a bit. Up until a couple years ago, the McKennas and Harpers had always been neighbors. But after Hattie's mother passed and her father became ill, she and Cade decided to sell their peach farm and buy a house in town together. The majority of the sale proceeds went to pay for their father's care, but as Ray had told me earlier, each was able to use a small portion to start their own small businesses. By the looks of it, Hattie had made good use of her share of the money. I hoped Cade's construction business was doing as well as her boutique.

"How is your father doing?" I asked. In all my excitement over this Hollis stuff, I'd forgotten to ask about her father. Apparently, I needed to brush up on my friendship skills.

She sighed. "He has good days and bad. More good than bad so far, so that's a blessing. He'd love to see you, if you get the chance."

"I'd like that," I agreed.

We'd started to pass the flower shop when Pete came out the door holding a large watering can. "Have a good dinner, *mi querida*," he said with a slight accent. He started pouring water over a colorful window box of trailing petunias, pausing for a second as Hattie strolled by, his dark eyes taking in every inch of that perky sundress and bare legs. "Perhaps I'll see you later?"

Hattie shot him a sizzling-hot look. "Promise to whisper sweet Spanish nothings in my ear?"

Pete's grin widened. "Anything you want, *amorcita*."

"Oh stop, you two! You're making me jealous." I playfully tugged at Hattie's arm, pulling her farther down the walk.

"Hey!" she protested. "You're ruining my fun." She gave a little finger wave to Pete as we walked away.

I chuckled. "Something tells me that you and Pete have plenty of fun together. Is it serious?"

"You mean more serious than sweet nothings and a lot of hot, spicy . . ." She let the words hang, laughing at my expression. "I was going to say 'food.'"

"Yeah, right."

"No, seriously. He makes the best chili rellenos ever!"

"So *that's* what you call it!" I countered.

We turned the corner, still laughing, and started up Orchard Lane.

"So, how's Ida been doing?" she asked, bringing me back to the present situation.

"Not so great. Worried for Hollis. Ray's sending an investigator to help out. He should be here tomorrow."

"An investigator? Well, good. Seems our sheriff's got a one-track mind."

"Well, admittedly, Hollis looks really guilty." I went on to explain how Hollis hired a firm to investigate Wakefield Lumber and found that he'd loaned more than a million dollars based on fraudulent collateral. "They found the investigation report in Hollis's pocket when they arrested him."

"So, Maudy thinks Hollis found out about the fraud, confronted Wakefield and things escalated."

I nodded. "Apparently, that's enough of a motive for her. She thinks she's got her man. Except I believe she's being too narrow-minded."

Hattie glanced my way. "I'd say. Like I said before, Millicent seems kind of suspicious to me."

"Yes. And a young man named Floyd Reeves. I saw him today at the Mercantile."

Hattie nodded. "I know who you're talking about. He's been organizing protests against Wakefield Lumber. He's got a real nasty attitude, but do you think he'd really be stupid enough to kill someone? I mean, it doesn't make sense. Just because Wakefield's dead, it doesn't mean timbering is going to suddenly stop."

"You're right. It doesn't make sense." My mind flashed back to the angry young man I'd seen earlier that day, and I shrugged. "Who knows? Hopefully Ray's investigator will look into it all."

We'd reached a small, quaint house covered in dark green shakes. It had a wide porch and white-trimmed dormer windows. "This is it," she said, waving her hand in front of the house. Everything about it was well kept, especially the yard, which reminded me of a meditation garden with little artsy statuettes hidden near bushes and wide patches of purple, yellow and white flowers adding colorful accents to the abundance of shady flora. A white picket fence seemed to bring it together into an inviting space that made me want to linger outside with a cup of tea and a good book.

"The house is beautiful and . . . your garden. It's magical!"

Her lips curved upward. "I can't take all the credit. Pete helped me. He's a talented landscape artist," she said, moving up the wide steps and motioning me inside before I could ask what other talents he might have. The screen door shut with a bang behind us. "Cade!" Hattie called out. "We're here."

The divine smell hit me as soon as I walked through the door. "What is that?" I asked, following Hattie through the cozy family room to the kitchen at the back of the house.

She inhaled deeply. "I'd say my big brother has made his specialty."

We'd come into the kitchen where Cade was bent over the stove, lifting what looked like thick brown pancakes from a large cast iron skillet. He glanced up. "Perfect timing; the fritters are almost done."

If I was in my right mind, I would have found the sight of him in a flowered apron that was at least three sizes too small for his well-developed physique humorous, but instead my breath caught. I stood, momentarily frozen in place, mesmerized by the sight of his muscled biceps under his rolled-up T-shirt, the sheen of sweat on his forehead, the sparkle of his eyes as he worked. I was completely caught off guard by the flips in my stomach.

A nudge from behind pulled me back to reality. "Hey, I was asking you if you want some wine."

Heat rose to my cheeks. "That'd be great; thanks." I willed myself to settle down the flutters as I eased around the island and stood next to Cade. "It smells wonderful. What are you fixing?"

"Ribs on the grill and fried corn fritters are coming out of the pan."

"Wait until you taste Cade's ribs," Hattie said, setting wineglasses down in front of each of us. "He makes the best sauce in the county."

"Really?" I was fascinated. "I didn't even know you could cook."

Cade had finished plating the fritters and passed the plate to me before grabbing a clean, larger platter with tongs on it. "It's just something I picked up over the years. Here, take this, too." He handed me a bowl of freshly chopped coleslaw. "I thought we'd eat on the deck." He started for the door, calling over his shoulder, "Hey, sis, bring our glasses and the wine bottle out, will you?"

I followed him out, placing the fritters and slaw on the deck table before joining him at the grill. I watched as he slathered a rich-looking sauce over the top of a couple racks of baby ribs. I inhaled the rich, smoky tomato smell and sighed in anticipation. "I can hardly wait to taste it," I commented, my mouth watering.

"If you think that looks good," Hattie chimed in as she joined us on the deck, "wait until you have these fried corn fritters. I swear, I could eat these every night." She cast a grateful glance Cade's way, broke a piece of fritter off and popped it into her mouth with an appreciative eye roll.

"Hey, if I didn't know how to cook, I'd starve around here."

"What? I can cook," Hattie protested, topping off our wineglasses.

"Only if you count boxed mac-n-cheese as cooking," Cade teased, pulling the ribs from the grill and stacking them on the big platter.

"Speaking of cooking," I said, as we settled around the table. "I have something I wanted to pass by you guys." I scooped up a load of slaw while Hattie put a couple of fritters on my plate. Cade followed up with a generous cut of meaty ribs. I took a second to use my fork to pull some meat from the bone, spearing it with a piece of fritter and a running it through the slaw. I closed my eyes as I bit into the scrumptious combination. The perfectly spiced meat combined with the salty, crispy corn fritter and the tangy coleslaw was a bite of heaven.

"What's that?" Cade was asking.

I opened my eyes, trying to remember what I was saying before my first bite. "Oh, my. This is so good."

Cade beamed with pride.

"You were saying something about cooking," Hattie reminded me.

"That's right. Sorry," I said, setting up my next bite while I started to explain. "I was telling Cade yesterday that Harper Peach Farm isn't doing too well financially."

Hattie's smile faded. "I know; he told me. I'm sorry. Seems your family is having such a difficult time right now."

I nodded. "Well, I was thinking about how a lot of the farms up north sell specialty items like peach preserves, peach candies . . . stuff like that. There seems to be a demand for those types of things, especially around the holidays." I took another bite, chewing slowly so I could enjoy all the flavors.

Hattie spoke up. "Oh, most definitely!" She glanced at Cade. "You remember that gift box of jellies we ordered for Aunt Connie last Christmas? That came from that peach farm up around Musella—what's its name? I can't remember offhand, but they sell everything: preserves, syrup, peach candy and even little knickknacky things like peach Christmas ornaments and stuff. Anyway, Aunt Connie just loved it."

I swallowed. "Exactly! Why couldn't we do the same thing? You know all those recipes my mama has for peach this and peach that. They've been handed down through my family for generations."

Cade reached for the roll of paper towels in the middle of the table and piped up, "And isn't your mama always winning prizes for her recipes?" He went to work on wiping the sticky sauce off his hands.

"That's right. Actually, that's how they won this cruise

they're on right now for her peach chutney recipe. And she's placed several times at the State Fair for her jellies. And just this morning, Joe Puckett traded about two days' worth of mowing for a dozen jars of her peach preserves."

Cade raised his brows and laughed. "Really? Too bad it couldn't have been that easy for the last deal you struck with him."

I laughed and agreed, feeling more enthusiastic about my ideas by the minute. "Anyway, I thought I'd start simple. Maybe just chutney and preserves. Of course, I'll want to test the market."

"What do you mean?" Hattie asked.

"I need to see if people will actually buy the stuff. Mama has a surplus of canned peach preserves stored away in our pantry. I thought I'd try to sell a few dozen jars at the Peach Festival next weekend. I'm going to try to duplicate a few of her recipes, too. Just to get an idea of how things might come together for the business. There's so many things to think about. I know there's a lot of regulations when it comes to selling food products." Not to mention everything I'd need to do just to sell a few jars next week. My mind reeled with details: I'd need a catchy sign—something to really draw customers to my booth—and maybe some professionally printed labels for the jars and . . . Oh, I'd need a slogan, a logo, or at least some sort of business name. *Hmm . . . what would that be?*

"But you don't have a booth," Cade pointed out.

My shoulders fell. "You're right. And it's probably too late to get one."

Hattie poured me some more wine. "Not necessarily. You could set up right outside my shop. All you'll need is a table and a sign of some sort. You could run it by the planning committee tomorrow night. We're having a meeting over at the diner after it closes."

I sipped at my wine, mulling over her suggestion. "You know, that might just work. I wouldn't be with the main vendors, but I'd get all the foot traffic from people going in and out of the shops on the square."

"That's right," Hattie agreed. "Last year was the first festival for my boutique, but I made pretty good sales. We get people from all over the county, you know."

Cade shook his head. "So, let's say you are successful this weekend. Then what?"

"Then I set up a website and we start selling our peach products online. Plus a few of the festivals around the area."

"We? You're only here for a couple more weeks, remember? Then you'll be traipsing off to some foreign country to do your own thing."

"Cade!" Hattie interjected. "That's not nice."

He glared across the table at his sister. "Maybe not, but it's the truth. She hasn't been home for how long? Now she's just planning to waltz in here and save the day with a few peach recipes? Then leave the work behind for others to pick up."

I flinched at the severity of his words, heat rising to my cheeks. He was right. Who was I to show up and play hero? Still, why so vehement? I'd seen traces of this irritation with me ever since I'd arrived. What was he so angry about?

Hattie started in, trying to cover the awkwardness. "Cade, I don't think—"

"No, it's okay, Hattie," I said, standing and clearing my plate. "How about I help you get these dishes done, okay? I should be going soon."

Her face fell. "But I thought we were going to watch a movie—"

"Maybe another time, okay?"

She shot out of her chair and snatched up Cade's plate with hers. "Please don't bother with these dishes. Cade will be happy to do them after he gets back from walking you to your car." She shot him a murderous look. "That'll give him a chance to apologize for being such a jerk."

Chapter 10

Georgia Belle Fact #035: "Y'all ever heard that song, 'The Devil Went Down to Georgia?' Well, every Georgia Belle knows it's true . . . so watch your back, you hear."

"So, you don't seem too thrilled with my ideas," I finally said to Cade as we approached my Jeep. I'd just endured the longest, most awkward three blocks ever and was determined not to let the evening end on a bitter note.

"No, your ideas are fine. They might even work. I'm just surprised, I guess." He was walking next to me with his hands in his jeans, eyes glued to the sidewalk. The sun was just starting to set, bringing a little relief from the afternoon heat. A nearby mockingbird was ratcheting up his night call, echoing the sounds of his chatty feathered friends.

"Surprised that I'd want to help my family?" His nonchalant shrug set my blood a-boiling. "Okay, that does it. What gives, Cade? Ever since I arrived, you've been acting like I've done something wrong. What? You don't like my job?"

"Not your job, exactly. I mean, I'm sure it's exciting and all. At least more exciting than this Podunk town."

Oh, so that's it. Jealousy. "Hey, if you don't like it here, why don't you go somewhere else?" *Like straight to . . .*

His head snapped up. "Who says I don't like it here?"

"You. You just said it's boring."

"Yeah, but I happen to like boring."

"Well, that's your problem, not mine. I just happen to like my job." Even though I knew that job I liked so well no longer existed.

He sighed. "That's great. But you and I both know there's more to it than that. You're . . . Oops!" He reached out to steady me after my toe caught in a crack along the walk. "Careful!"

I mumbled, "Thank you," and quickly shook off his hand. "I really have no idea what you're talking about. More to it? Like what?"

We'd reached my car door. While I searched through my purse for the key, he put his hand on the doorframe and leaned in, his voice low. "You ran out of this town like a coon being tracked by a pack of hounds, Nola."

I shimmied around and glared up at his face. "Oh, lovely comparison. That sure makes me feel good."

"You know what I mean. You ran from something and you've kept running all these years. You hardly ever come back, and when you do come back for a quick visit, you avoid everyone."

"Well, I'm not avoiding people now. I've been all over town. I'm even going to the Peach Festival. Isn't that what you've been on me about? Going to the Peach Festival?"

He frowned. "It's great you're trying to help your family, Nola. But as soon as your parents get back, you'll be off and running again." His eyes searched mine. "We used to be such good friends: you, me and Hattie. Yet you never told me what drove you away. Something happened. And I thought we were friends enough that you'd tell me."

I sucked in my breath. He was right; I never told him and I never would. Cade was a good guy, the solid-morals type of guy who could never understand what I did all those years ago.

I exhaled and rolled my eyes, giving him a playful little

shove. "Oh, come on! Stop with all the drama already. Nothing happened. I'd just outgrown Cays Mill, that's all. Not everyone's cut out for small-town living, you know."

His lips pressed into a thin line and I caught a flash of anger cross his face. But instead of pushing it further, he let it drop. We stood there, suspended in awkward silence as his eyes lingered on mine. After a half beat too long, I looked away. No, Cade must never know my secret. If he ever found out, I'd lose his friendship, tenuous as it already was, forever.

An ear-busting, roaring sound jarred me awake first thing that Thursday morning. I lurched out of bed, grabbed for my robe, swinging it on as I ran down the steps as fast as my sluggish legs would carry me, and peered out the front window. My breath caught. A helmeted man, dressed in all black leather, was parking a motorcycle. I was deliberating whether or not I should go for Daddy's shotgun, when he reached up and removed his helmet.

My jaw dropped. Then my heart. It was him. I huddled there, mouth open, completely and utterly gobsmacked. The secret I'd been trying to outrun all these years had just returned . . . and was standing in my own front yard, looking as wickedly hot as ever—too hot for even the Devil to handle. The idea of Daddy's shotgun seemed suddenly all too appealing.

Dragging my feet, I made my way to the front door, pausing for a quick glimpse in the hallway mirror before opening it.

"Hey, Nola," he said as if we'd just seen each other a couple days ago. "Wow, you cut your hair."

My hand flew to my head, then back to my gaping robe as I watched him hang the helmet on the handlebars and reach around to a large black saddlebag, pulling out one of the tiniest basset hounds I'd ever seen. "This is Roscoe," he announced, setting the puppy on the ground. It wrinkled its forehead and cast a large brown-eyed look my way before moseying over to Mama's petunia bed and lifting its leg. "Well, aren't you going to invite us in?"

"In the house?" I croaked, cinching my robe tighter.

"Well, yeah. Why? You got something against dogs in the house?"

Four-legged dogs, no. Two-legged ones are another story. But before I could formulate a decent answer, one worthy of my gracious southern upbringing, he snatched up the dog and started for the porch.

"Didn't Ray tell you I was coming?" he said, stopping inches from me. A familiar, fresh-soap scent rushed to my nose, unleashing a whole slew of unwanted memories. I struggled to maintain my ground when what I really wanted to do was turn heel and run back inside. "Is it Roscoe?" he asked, readjusting the pooch squirming in his arms. "He's no trouble really. Ray said you wouldn't mind if he stayed."

"Here?" *No way is Dane Hawkins and his mutt staying in this house.* "I'm afraid that's impossible, Dane."

"I'm going by Hawk now. It's more suiting for a private investigator."

This is our private investigator? I was going to kill Ray. "You staying here wouldn't be appropriate."

Hawk stopped short, cocked his head and shot me a strange look. "Appropriate?" Then a gleam of understanding showed in his blue eyes and he started laughing. Not just some run-of-the-mill laugh, either, but a deep, husky laugh that took me back fifteen years or more to a starlit summer's night down by the river. We'd shared a lot of laughter that night, and other things, too.

"What's so funny?" I asked, wishing my voice didn't sound so weak.

He finally stopped laughing and leveled his gaze on me. "I'm not staying here, just Roscoe. So don't worry, darlin'. I'm here on business." He pushed past me, his boots making a determined clomping sound as he opened the screen door and walked into the house.

Inside the living room, he set the dog on the davenport and started pacing around. "Well, after all these years, I finally get to see the inside of the Harper farmhouse. Interesting."

"I'm sure it is." I shooed the dog onto the floor. "Ray hired you to look into Hollis's case?"

"Yup. I'm your man."

No, you're not. Nor will you ever be. "I see. Well, if you're not staying here"—*and you're definitely not*—"then where?"

"Someplace called the Sunny Side Up." He laughed a little more. "Sissy-sounding name, huh? Anyway, they don't take dogs." He grinned down at the tiny ball of brown and white fur.

I hated this man, this situation, this darn dog—well, maybe not the dog per se—but the facts were that Hollis and my family needed help and I had to forget the past, grow past my personal feelings and move on. I cinched the belt of my robe tighter. "Look, if Ray thinks you're the right man for the job, then so be it."

He looked at me with a mix of surprise and indignation, as if confused that anyone would question his abilities. I just shook my head. Ego just never grows up.

He started for the back of the house, his hands swinging confidently at his sides while his eyes took in his surroundings. I followed, becoming more irritated by the second. "Your daddy's room, I bet," he commented, stepping inside the distinctly masculine den and running his hand along the top of the desk. "I always envisioned myself sitting across from your daddy in a room like this, talking with him, man to man."

I closed my eyes for a second, took another deep breath and opened them again. "There's some things you should know about Hollis and his case. But, we're not discussing it in here. This is Daddy's private study." I pointed a rigid finger toward the hallway. "We'll talk in the kitchen."

He waved his hand toward the door, indicating that I should lead the way. I shuffled ahead, back through the living room and down the hall that led to the kitchen, distinctly aware of how big my heavy chenille robe must make my hips look. "Coffee?" I asked, once we'd reached the kitchen.

"Black."

I worked my way through the motions of measuring the coffee and filling the maker, feeling his eyes on my back the whole time.

"Why'd you cut your hair?"

"Long hair didn't suit my work." Not wanting to continue this conversation any longer than necessary, I slid a mug under the stream as soon as the liquid starting dripping. Then another for me, cringing when the hot liquid hit the burner and sent up an acrid-smelling puff of burnt coffee. "Here you go," I said, placing his mug down before settling in across from him, gripping my own mug between my cold palms, hoping the hot porcelain would calm my trembling fingers.

"Ray told me about your work. Is it the travel you like or helping people?" he asked, shedding his leather jacket on the back side of his chair. I quickly averted my eyes from his tautly stretched T-shirt.

I nodded. "Both. And you? You're a private investigator?"

"Hey, it's more lucrative than my old job." I must have looked confused because he went on to explain, "I used to be a cop. Up in Atlanta."

"I see." I focused on drinking my coffee. I'd never kept tabs on Dane, or Hawk as he called himself now, but it didn't surprise me to find out he'd gone into law enforcement. He was always a take-charge type of guy.

"I'm good at what I do," he assured me. "That's why your brother hired me. He says Hollis's chances will be slim if it goes to trial. Ray wants me to find something before that happens."

I nodded, glad the conversation was on point now. Nothing really mattered, I told myself, except helping Hollis, and Ray was right—we really had to come up with something solid before any trail. "I've picked up a few things that may help." I went on to tell him about Floyd Reeves, the overenthusiastic protester, and my encounter with Millicent Wakefield at Hattie's Boutique. He pulled a notepad and pencil out from his leather jacket pocket to take notes as I talked. "There's something else, too. Hollis is. . . ." I rolled my eyes up toward the ceiling, trying to think of the right way to put it. "Well, he's sort of a womanizer."

Hawk leaned forward. "Is that so? Thought he was married to your sister?"

Unfortunately, he is. I nodded. "That's true. But I've been hearing things about him around town."

He gave me a scrunched-face look. "Substantiated 'things' or the typical gossip stuff?"

I sighed. "Just hear me out, will ya? There's this gal that works at the salon, Laney Burns. She was messing around with Hollis after the party, right before the murder supposedly happened. And that's not gossip; I got it straight from her own lips." *Highly glossed, sneering lips, but still . . .* "Anyway, she saw the scarf—the one used to strangle Wakefield— tangled up in a tree branch. It was still there when she left Hollis that night, half-drunk, she said, in the orchard."

"Okay. So, it could have been picked up by someone else later." He shrugged. "Or not."

"Okay, so that's not much," I admitted. "But there's something else."

The chair creaked as he shifted his weight. "What?"

"This isn't something we'd want to necessarily get out, but I think maybe Laney was also seeing Ben Wakefield." I explained to him what Millicent told Hattie and me.

A flicker of understanding crossed his face. "Uh-oh."

"Yeah, that's what I thought. It'll look bad for Hollis if

it comes out that he was caught up in a love triangle with Laney Burns and Ben Wakefield."

Hawk nodded. "It sure will." He stretched his arms above his head and yawned. "Anything else I should know?"

I shook my head, a little surprised at his nonchalant attitude. He didn't seem to be feeling the same anxious urgency that I did. Maybe because he handled this type of stuff all the time, or, more than likely, because the stakes weren't as high for him. After all, it wasn't *his* sister's husband facing down a murder charge.

Hawk stood and rubbed at the back of his neck. "Thanks for the coffee. I'm going to get settled at the B and B for a little rest. I've ridden half the night." He started for the door.

"Rest?" I followed on his heels. "Aren't you going to get started?"

"I'll work better after I get some sleep." He bent down and started running his fingers over Roscoe's flappy ears. "Be good, fella," he said to the dog, who I noticed was back up on the sofa again. He looked over at me and winked. "I'll be in touch, Nola."

As soon as the screen door slammed shut, I gently lifted the dog back down to the floor and plopped down in his place on the sofa. Not more than a half second later, he stood and placed his little stubby legs on mine, raising himself up and letting out a long, soulful croon at the sound of Hawk's motorcycle pulling away. "It's going to be okay, boy," I said, lifting him up to my lap. As I stroked his soft puppy fur, he cocked his head, raising one ear slightly and staring up at me with his solemn brown eyes, endearing me with his puppy-dog gaze. Unable to resist, I drew him to my chest and nuzzled my chin along the smooth warm bridge of his nose. "It's going to be okay," I repeated. Although I wasn't so sure. Things had just gone from bad to downright crappy: Hollis in jail, the farm failing, and now Hawk. It was like I was stuck in a horrible nightmare.

After a few soothing minutes cuddling the dog, I took a

hot shower and quickly changed into a pair of shorts and a T-shirt. Sitting down with another cup of coffee, I gave Ida a call. Just as I suspected, she was holed up in the house, still hiding from the world. "Aren't you going to the arraignment today?" I asked her.

"I want to go, but I'm not sure what to do with the girls."

"I'll come by and watch them for you. Let's see," I said, glancing at the wall clock. "The hearing isn't until two o'clock. Why don't you let me bring by some lunch beforehand."

"Don't bother. I don't have much of an appetite."

"You have to eat. You need to keep up your strength. Besides, I want to talk through a couple things with you."

A long sigh sounded over the line.

"I'll be by a little before one," I pressed.

She sighed again, but by the time I hung up, she'd reluctantly agreed to lunch. With that done, I started in on the next thing on my list: experimenting with some of Mama's recipes.

Mama kept her recipes alphabetized in a wooden box in the back of the pantry. I pulled out the box, fingered my way over every type of peach recipe imaginable—peach salsa, peach cider pound cake, peach seared pancakes, sweet peach ice cream, on and on—until . . . bingo! I located the one for her peach preserves. As I fingered the well-worn recipe card, written in my grandmother's precise script and covered with sticky pink blotches, my mind wandered to childhood days spent in the kitchen watching Mama and Nana stirring up family gossip as fast as they stirred the bubbling pots of sweet peach liquid. Always the tomboy, I'd never bothered to pay much attention to the whole preserve-making process, only hanging out in order to steal a quick lick of the sweet goo, or get first dibs on any excess preserves that didn't make it into the pressure canner. Now I wished I'd paid closer attention. I mentally shrugged. No matter. How hard could it really be?

I glanced over the recipe again and began assembling all the ingredients. Since I didn't have any fresh peaches, I planned to use some of the peaches Mama had stored in the freezer. I took out several bags and stuck them under a stream of hot water. As soon as they thawed enough, I'd put them in a pot and finish heating them.

Next, I filled a large stockpot with water and set it on the stove to boil. I'd need to sterilize all my equipment before I could start cooking. As I worked, I thought back to what Cade was saying the night before. He'd made me angry with the little doses of reality he'd thrown my way, but he was right. After getting home, I'd stayed up half the night researching what it would take to really operate a peach product business on the side. There was much more to it than I'd imagined. Things like inspections, permits and licenses, product labeling . . . And what was more—who was going to do all this? Daddy wasn't one to try new things. Come to think of it, Mama wasn't too keen on change, either, and Ray was out of the question. He was busy with his own career and had practically abandoned anything to do with the farm. Ida had the girls and her own life, and who knew what that would be like if Hollis was convicted and sent to jail. My shoulders sagged. The only chance this had of really working was if I stayed and saw it through. Was that something I really wanted to do?

After boiling and setting the jars to dry on a clean white cotton towel, I read the recipe again. Then, as I worked through each step, I could almost hear Nana's deep southern drawl: *Measure and set aside your sugar. Measure out your fruit into a big pot and add a smidgen of lemon juice. Start heatin' the mixture and put in a package of pectin. Stir it until it reaches a hard boil, one that can't be stirred down. Add the sugar and stir until it boils again. Ladle your hot liquid into clean jars.*

I tuned in the old Czar radio to break the monotony as I stirred. Roscoe must have been a music aficionado, because as soon as he heard the radio playing, he wandered into the kitchen and settled at my feet. "Hey, there, Roscoe. You like Buddy Holly?" The dog answered by whapping his tail in beat to a stanza from "Peggy Sue." We worked on together, his little body warming my feet as music and sweet peach smells filled the kitchen. Finally, the liquid reached a rolling boil, so I dumped in the sugar and stirred some more. When it came back up to a full boil again, I excitedly removed the pot from the heat and began filling and sealing the jars.

Only, my preserves didn't look like preserves. Instead they looked like syrup, or, more accurately, like an off-colored fruit punch with floating chunks of peaches.

"What went wrong?" I asked out loud. Roscoe stood and let out a little whine. Stepping back, I stared at the mason jars wondering if they would jell up after they cooled. Hopeful, I left the jars to sit while I got ready for lunch with Ida.

"Dane Hawkins?" Ida asked. "Why does that name sound familiar?" She was pushing a pile of half-eaten potatoes au gratin around her plate. I'd stopped by the diner on the way over and picked up a couple of the daily lunch specials to go: fried grouper, cheesy potatoes au gratin and a slice of pecan pie for just under seven bucks. I was having no trouble finishing mine, which I'd ordered with a side of butter beans and an iced tea.

"He used to live around here. His daddy ran the mechanics garage down in Cordele." We were sitting at Ida's kitchen bar, takeout bags spread around us, while the girls, long finished with their meals, watched a movie in the family room.

"Cordele, huh? Then I guess we didn't go to school with him. I wonder why his name sounds so . . . Oh my goodness. Is he that hoodlum that you dated a couple times? The one Mama had a conniption fit over?"

I slowly nodded my head. "She forbade me to see him."

Ida went on, "Aren't you glad listened to her? Can you imagine what things would have been like if you'd ended up married to a private investigator?" She said "private investigator" like her mouth was full of vinegar.

Ida's holier-than-thou attitude was wearing thin. "Well,

that *private investigator* is the one helping your husband, *the banker*, who is facing down a life sentence for murder." *Not to mention that he's usually drunker than Cooter Brown. And chases anything in a skirt.*

Of course, I didn't say that last part out loud. Thank goodness. Because Ida's eyes instantly grew wide, tearing around the edges. I put down my fork and reached across the table, patting her trembling hand and trying to soften my words. "I'm sorry, Ida. It's going to be okay." I'd uttered those same words to Roscoe just that morning. And I still didn't believe them myself.

She shook her head and pulled her hand back, shriveling into herself. "I'm nervous about the hearing today," she whispered. "What if the judge sets an outrageous bail? Or what if they keep him locked up until the trial . . . or forever." She turned away, rubbing her belly and looking out the kitchen window. I followed her gaze, noticing for the first time just how straggly their yard was looking. I bit the inside of my lip, worrying about what would happen if Hollis never returned. Would Ida move back home with the girls and the new baby, or try to go at it alone? I stared across the table at my sister, my eyes settling on her pregnant belly, worrying about the unseen effects of all this stress and cursing myself again for my harsh words. I shoved her plate a little closer. "You haven't eaten much."

She kept her gaze fixed out the window.

I went on, "Ray will be there. He'll make sure Hollis gets a fair shake. Maybe he'll even get him released on his own recognizance," I said, grasping at straws and knowing darn well recognizance was unlikely with a murder charge. Not to mention Hollis's recognizance would be a detriment, not an asset. At least locked up, he was sober. "Look, getting back to Dane Hawkins. I know you don't think much of the guy. To tell the truth, he was the last person I wanted to see, but he must be good at what he does. Ray's trusting him to prove Hollis's innocence." I exhaled and picked at my own food for a second before adding, "He's already got a few leads."

She turned back, her face brightening a little, so I went on to explain about Floyd Reeves and Millicent Wakefield. "So, you see," I finished, "that's why we need someone like Hawk looking into things. Heaven knows Maudy Payne won't bother herself with these other suspects."

"Hawk?"

I nodded. "That's his professional name."

She smirked, a little more of the priggish Ida returning, but I didn't care. At this point, I much preferred Ida's pompous attitude over her drama queen misery. I glanced at the kitchen clock. It was nearing two o'clock already. "You best get going, I guess."

She nodded, slowly pushed back her chair and stood.

"We'll get through this, Ida. Just have faith," I said, standing with her.

"It's hard to have faith, Nola, when the whole town thinks he's guilty."

"I don't. And neither does Ray. Just hold on to that. And know that Ray's doing everything possible to help you. We both are."

In a rare moment of sisterly tenderness, Ida came toward me with her arms outstretched. I pulled her in as far as her baby bump would allow and gave her a little extra squeeze for reassurance, making her promise to call later.

I walked her to the door, watching her hug the girls goodbye while spelling out last-minute warnings of consequences for bad behavior just to turn around and temper those same warnings with extra loving pecks on their rosy cheeks. My sister was a good mama.

I shot her one last reassuring smile before she left, but deep down, I hoped Ray wasn't making a mistake by putting so much trust in Dane Hawkins. So far, I wasn't all that impressed.

Chapter 11

Georgia Belle Fact #042: A Georgia Belle never gets upset when she sees her ex with someone else. After all, our parents taught us to be charitable with our castoffs.

It was becoming a habit to sip my morning coffee on the front porch while watching the sun rise over the treetops. This morning's sunrise seemed unusually bright, especially since I knew Hollis was back home with Ida and the girls. The judge had set bail and Ida had readily paid it. Later, I'd dragged it out of her that she'd paid the bond with rainy-day money she'd squirreled away over the years. Lucky for Hollis that she had, or he'd be sitting in jail for a while, awaiting his trial. Of course, keeping him locked up and dry might have been the better option. Nonetheless, I knew Ida felt relieved to have him home, and I was happy for her.

During my babysitting gig the day before, I'd munched my way through a bag of popcorn and a dozen cookies while watching *The Parent Trap* and enduring a makeover that left me looking like a spiky-haired clown, before Ida finally returned home with a bedraggled Hollis in tow. Even so, the extra calories and "new look" were a fair trade-off for the opportunity to witness the sweetest homecoming ever.

Because nothing, not even Hollis's scruffy face, stale-smelling clothes and sullen expression, could deter my nieces from giving their daddy the world's most enthusiastic welcoming. I still smiled when I thought back to their chorus of shrieks and the way they threw themselves at him, smothering him with hugs and covering him with tiny kisses.

This morning coffee was especially satisfying because, in addition to the glorious sunrise, I was also watching Deputy Travis Hanes pull down the crime scene tape. Apparently, Maudy had finally come to her senses. Either that or she was overly confident that she had all the evidence she needed to put Hollis away. Nonetheless, as soon as Deputy Travis finished, I swilled down the rest my coffee, scooped up Roscoe, who was napping at my feet, and headed straight for Daddy's den, where I phoned the rental place. Despite the short notice, I managed to get them to agree to come out later that afternoon to remove the tent. I certainly didn't want to pay for an extra day's rental. Ida, Ray and I had long ago agreed to split the cost of Mama and Daddy's party, but as things were, I'd probably just put the extra rental fee on my own card and ask Ray to ante up his portion. It didn't seem right to approach Ida about such things, especially with everything she was going through.

Feeling good about checking off that item, I took a small break to play with Roscoe before moving on to the other tasks on my list. I hated to admit it, but I was growing fond of the little fellow. Especially in the evening, when every single creak and groan of the old house seemed to spook me. "You'd protect me, wouldn't you, sweetie?" I said out loud, taking the slight raise of his floppy ears as a yes. On impulse, I took his long basset ears, pulled them to the top of his head and tied them in a loose knot. "There!" I laughed at his solemn expression. "I must say, Roscoe, not even the gals at the Clip and Curl could give you a better updo than that." He let out a playful *woo-woo* sound and shook his head until the ears flopped apart. He shot me an indignant look; then, incident forgotten, he tooled off to his food bowl, in case some morsel might remain. I, in turn, got back to more pressing matters. I added a couple more tasks to my list: I needed to do a quick once-over of the yard and orchard again. Most of the debris had blown from the orchard by now, but there was still a lot of litter inside the tent that needed to be cleaned up. But I'd save that task for a little later in the day. First, it was off to town. In addition to picking up parts at the Mercantile and attending the planning committee meeting that evening, I wanted to run a jar of my failed preserves over to the diner and see if Ginny had any idea what might have gone wrong.

Next, I opened Daddy's desk drawer and pulled out the petty cash envelope he'd left to cover any minor expenses, like the engine parts. With the envelope came the scent of Daddy's cigars, which he stored in the same drawer. I inhaled and smiled. The smell always took me back to one particular fall day during my childhood. We'd gone up to Atlanta for the State Fair. Mama had entered her peach chutney in the homemakers' exhibit—and won, too! We were all so happy, riding home that night in Daddy's Oldsmobile: Ida, Ray and I crammed in the backseat with our souvenirs clutched in our sticky, cotton-candy fingers and Mama in the front seat with her blue ribbon and the prettiest smile on her face. I remember sometime on the way home, rain started pouring down and I fell asleep to the rhythm of the wipers, tucked in safely between my siblings and covered in Daddy's old Muskegon jacket—the rough material laced with the scent of bourbon and spent cigars. I don't think I'd ever felt safer or happier than that night.

Those were the good old days, filled with hard work and plenty of fun, too. Before life got complicated and before I'd made a few bad choices that sent me running from home. Funny how things changed. Coming back to Cays Mill the other day, the biggest thing on my mind was keeping a low profile to avoid stirring up the town's gossipmongers while

I took care of the farm and figured out my job situation.
Now I was facing down not one but two major family crises:
losing the family business and a brother-in-law charged with
murder. And, if that wasn't enough, my past—wearing tight
jeans and looking better than ever, no less—had come back
to haunt me.

It was all enough to make me want to lay down my head
and have a good long cry, but instead I sucked it up and
turned my focus to the things I could control. Like getting
the tractor and irrigation pump back up and running. I
counted out the bills in the envelope, which turned out to
be barely enough, if *even* enough, to pay for the parts I'd
ordered at the Mercantile and Joe Puckett's roofing supplies.
Hopefully Cade could scrounge together enough supplies
from his surplus stock to cut down on the overall cost. I
tucked the bills into my shoulder bag along with a jar of peach
goo, checked to make sure Roscoe had plenty of food and
water, and headed for town.

"Did you follow the recipe?" Ginny was tipping my jar of
runny preserves from side to side, observing the liquid as it
sloshed about. I'd already run by the Mercantile and picked
up parts and a few other supplies before stopping by the
diner, so most of the lunch crowd had already dispersed,
leaving only a few stragglers behind, sipping coffee and
chatting over an extra slice of pie.

"To a T," I declared.

"And it was your mama's recipe, right?"

"Right." I took another spoonful of chili. Despite the
stifling heat, Sam's spicy chili hit the spot. "I was hoping
you could tell me where I went wrong."

She swiped a red curl off her face. "Did you measure the
fruit and sugar exactly like the recipe said?"

"Yup."

"Used pectin?"

"Uh-huh."

"Brought it up to a full rolling boil before adding the sugar?"

"Yes, I did all those things and it still turned out like that."

"Well, how should I know, then? I'm no expert jelly maker."

"Yes, but you've made it before, right?"

"Sure, but just here and there. Nothing like your mama does. Maybe you ought to wait until she gets home and ask her where you went wrong."

I shook my head and explained my plan to start marketing and selling some of my family's recipes. "You see, I think we could sell some of this stuff online. It seems to work for the bigger orchards up north. And we could use a little extra side income. But first I need to figure out how to make the stuff. Mama always makes it look so easy."

"It's not that hard, really. Just takes practice." She swiped at the counter with a wet rag while she considered my dilemma. "I'll tell you what," she finally said. "Why don't you bring your ingredients by one day and we'll give it another try. In my kitchen this time. That way, maybe I can see what you're doing wrong." She lifted a huge tray of silverware and started rolling them into napkins. "You coming to the meeting tonight? It starts at six and I reckon it'll wrap up sometime around seven thirty." Red's Diner only served breakfast and lunch, closing down every day at four o'clock. The schedule had worked well for Ginny and Sam over the years, allowing them to spend evenings at home as a family. Of course, they were always willing to open back up for special events like the occasional party or tonight's Peach Festival planning meeting.

"Yeah, I'll be there." I explained to her my plans for testing the market at the Peach Festival. "There's already enough jars stored up in our pantry for this weekend, but I'd love to be able to crank out a few more." *Especially since Mama wouldn't take well to coming home to an empty pantry.*

She seemed pleased. "Well, like I said, I'll be glad to help."

She paused for a second and then added, "Does this mean you're planning on sticking around a little longer this time? 'Cuz we'd sure love to have you back in Cays Mill, you know."

It was a valid question, one I'd been tossing around in my own mind, but I didn't have an answer yet. Deep down, I knew this plan for selling peach products wouldn't be successful unless I stayed and saw it through. After all, there was no one else in the family who had the time or the ambition to take on a project this big. But was I ready to give up my job, however unappealing it now seemed, and stay in Cays Mill? I hadn't decided. Truth be told, I couldn't even make that decision until I had more information. For starters, was anyone even interested in buying Harper Peach Preserves?

I looked up from my chili, realizing Ginny was still waiting for my response. Luckily, the bells over the door jingled, momentarily distracting her. "Just take a seat anywhere. I'll be right with ya," she called out, leaving me to my lunch while she grabbed some menus and scurried over to a couple of well-dressed ladies.

Just then, the doorbells jingled again, and in walked Hawk with none other than the tittering, gum-chomping Laney Burns hanging on his arm. Catching sight of me, she dragged him over for an introduction. "Hey, there, Nola. This is Hawk," she purred, looking quite proud of herself. "Isn't he just something?" Hawk was rolling his eyes and grinning as if agreeing to Laney's assessment.

My eyes darted from her to Hawk, and back again, getting sidetracked by her candy-red claws tracing circles on his biceps, which he flexed in response. *Unbelievable! Is there no limit to his ego?* "Yeah, he's something," I mumbled.

She giggled and batted her clumpy lashes his way. "Hawk is just taking me out for a bite. Ain't that sweet?"

"Depends on who might get bitten, I guess."

Hawk smirked, but my comment seemed to fly right over Laney's head. She licked her lips and continued, "Hawk's just in town for a few days on business." She shimmied in a little closer to him. "But I'm thinking I might find a way to convince him to stay on longer."

That did it. I abandoned the rest of my chili and stood abruptly. "I'm sure you will," I said through a forced smile. I tossed a couple bills down and made a quick break for the door. Was this what he called an investigation, philandering with one of the main suspects? How dared he waste my brother's good money! And that blasted Laney Burns. Was there any man she didn't try to catch with those claws of hers? Of course, I could expect that type of thing from Laney. It was Hawk that surprised me—Mr. Studly Detective. All biceps and no brain—that was what he was.

I burst outside and stopped on the sidewalk, my heart pounding and fists clenched, momentarily disoriented in my own haze of anger. I was searching the square, trying to remember where I'd parked, when I spied Frances Simms making her way toward me. My anger turned to panic and I started considering escape routes. Before I could make a break for it, though, she was upon me.

"Hello, Frances," I said, bracing myself.

She shot me a curt nod and breezed past me on her way into Red's. I blinked in confusion. Just the day before she was on me like white on rice; today she barely gave me a second look. What was up with that? Had she already gotten the story she wanted? If so, from whom? Thank goodness the *Cays Mill Reporter* only came out on Tuesdays and Saturdays. Although, with all the days between issues, it meant that Frances had more time to build up her story. I cringed. Tomorrow's headline was probably going to be a real eyepopper.

There's a reason "stressed" equals the word "desserts" spelled backward. Because as my stress levels ratcheted, my eyes were naturally drawn to Sugar's Bakery. Suddenly, nothing sounded more soothing than a sweet, sugary, sinfully scrumptious cupcake.

Ezra Sugar's head snapped up the moment the door opened. "Nola Mae! I was hoping to see more of you. Great party last weekend." He patted his ample belly. "Really enjoyed the buffet," he added, flashing a toothy grin. Ezra was a hulk of a man, nearly six and a half feet tall with dark brown skin and a bald head that reminded me of a twelve-pound bowling ball resting on top of his humongous rack of shoulders. If you saw him on the street, you'd think he was a linebacker, not a baker. But his desserts were magical. Already the yeasty smell of dough and warm sugar had relaxed my shoulders and calmed my heart rate.

"Well, thank you again for the cake you made for Mama and Daddy. That was so generous of you. Everyone raved about it."

He waved off the compliment. "Glad to do it. I think the world of your parents." He lowered his eyes and took a more serious tone. "I was so sorry to hear about the trouble Hollis got himself into. Too bad for Ida and those little girls of theirs."

I winced. Again it was "the trouble that Hollis got himself into," with the immediate assumption of the guilt on Hollis's part. I nodded. "Yes, but my brother, Ray, is working the case and we're hopeful the *real* killer will be brought to justice."

Ezra grimaced. "If you say so, Nola. Anyway, I was glad to see Hollis back at work today."

"He's at the bank?" I was surprised. I would have thought he'd spend a couple days at home catching up with Ida and the girls.

"Yes, ma'am. Saw him there this morning when I went in to make a deposit. He looked bad, real worn-out. But working is probably the best thing for him right now. Keep his mind off the trouble he's got. Although, it made me wonder how long they'll allow him to keep that job. It doesn't seem right for a bank to let their folks' money be handled by a criminal."

"He's not a criminal," I started, but stopped myself and sighed. I realized it was useless to try to defend Hollis when everyone already seemed to have their minds made up, so I let the topic drop. Instead, I scanned the case, trying to decide between the lemon with buttercream frosting or the death-by-chocolate cupcake.

"Ya know, speaking of Ben Wakefield," Ezra continued, "something strange happened just before you got here."

I looked up. "Oh yeah? What was that?"

"A woman came in. A real looker. Shoot, I'd never seen anyone so dolled up in my life. She said she was Ben Wakefield's widow. I didn't know he was married. Did you? Heck, that man had been coming in here at least twice a week for a couple months to buy coffee and a treat." He paused and tapped on his case. "He had a thing for my smart tart. Ordered it every time. It's my healthy take on the normal tart, made with honeyed yogurt instead of sugar and cream."

That's not the only tart Ben Wakefield had a thing for, I thought. But, instead of actually saying that, I just nodded and smiled, hoping he'd get on with the story.

Ezra adjusted his apron straps and continued, "Anyway, like I was saying, I had no idea he was married. Don't you think that's strange?"

"It is sort of strange, isn't it?" I agreed. Come to think of it, in a town like Cays Mill it was hard to figure how such a basic detail would have escaped detection. Still, Millicent had explained it away as a logistical coincidence. I shrugged, my eyes wandering to the raspberry-filled cupcakes. *Decisions, decisions.* "Millicent told me she lived mostly in Macon. Didn't like it down here in Cays Mill. Not enough shopping," I added, as if that explained everything.

"Oh, I didn't realize you knew the woman." My head snapped up from the case and, seeing his wide-eyed expression, I realized he'd misinterpreted me. I started to explain that Millicent and I weren't friends, but he cut me off before I could get the words out. "Don't get me wrong. She seemed like a nice enough lady," he said, backtracking. "Just not the usual type from around here."

I almost laughed. This coming from a man who really stood out in a crowd. "Well, I'm sure after she tastes your baking, she'll be back for more."

He blushed.

"I'll take one lemon and one chocolate," I finally ordered, giving up on choosing.

Using a piece of tissue paper, he reached into the case and plucked my choices off the shelf. "Hope you're right. I'd like to see her come back to my shop. She's a big spender."

"A big spender? What do you mean?"

"Made a big order. 'Bout cleaned out all my bagels and scones first thing morning."

"Really?" That seemed strange. When we spoke at the boutique, I'd gotten the impression she didn't know anyone in the area. Why would she need such a big order? "Did she happen to mention why she needed so many?"

He'd bagged my purchase and starting ringing up my order. "I think she said something about a staff meeting up at the lumber mill."

The lumber mill? Of course! Why didn't I think of that angle before? Next to peach farming, the mill had been one of the leading industries in the area, employing hundreds of people and sustaining the town through many economic slumps. Despite rumors of financial trouble, if Millicent gained possession of the mill, she could probably close the place down and sell off the company's assets: machinery, buildings, inventory and maybe even land holdings. I wondered what assets the mill still owned and if they would amount to a motive for murder. Did ownership transfer to Millicent after Ben Wakefield's death? If so, and if there was money to be made, Millicent may have had just as much motive as anyone for wanting Wakefield dead, especially since it looked like her marriage was in trouble. But before I jumped to conclusions, I needed to find out who actually acquired the mill after Wakefield's death. I knew just who to ask, too.

"Nola?" Ezra's voice cut through my thoughts. I realized he must have been waiting for me to pay for my order. Blinking a few times to clear the fog, I apologized and quickly fished some money out of my shoulder bag. After collecting my change and thanking him again, I left Sugar's Bakery and marched down the street toward the bank.

The Cays Mill Bank & Trust was situated about two blocks north of the square on Gala Avenue, creating a transition between the business section of town and a quieter residential neighborhood. The bank itself stood out like a sore thumb among the surrounding bungalows and well-kept one-story ranches. Wanting to give the appearance of well-heeled stability, the town's founders constructed the bank to look like a scaled-down version of Mount Vernon, complete with white pillars and a red roof. The entrance was flanked by two large urns filled with ferns and colorful annuals. I paused to admire some trailing petunias before entering through the large double doors.

I bypassed the tellers and headed toward the back of the bank to Hollis's office, where I found Candace perched at the secretary's desk. She stopped typing the moment she saw me. "Nola Mae! Oh my goodness, what's this?" she asked, pointing to my bag. "Sugar's Bakery? Well, you shouldn't have. But what a sweet way to thank me for the casserole." She laughed. "Get it? A 'sweet' way to thank me."

I glanced from the bag still clutched in my hands to her outstretched ones and sighed. "Of course, Candace. Thank you so much for the casserole. It was delicious." I reluctantly handed over the bag, craning my neck for a glimpse toward Hollis's office. "I think I'll just pop in and check on Hollis," I said, scurrying around her desk while she was still distracted by the contents of the bakery bag.

"Oh, my favorites," I heard her exclaim as I stepped over the threshold into Hollis's office.

He looked up from a pile of paperwork and smiled. "How nice to see you, Nola." Although his tone was slightly subdued, his smile seemed genuine.

"How you holding up?" I asked, sliding into one of his guest chairs, my gaze drawn toward a shot glass next to his desk blotter. A little amber liquid remained in the bottom.

He sighed and tossed down the file he was holding. "Okay, I guess." Then he shook his head. "That's not true. You're family, so I might as well say it straight. I'm scared, Nola. Real scared. Those few days in the county jail were the worst days of my life. I can't even imagine what the state pen would be like."

I shuddered, mental images of bars, stainless steel cots and large ugly men with piercings and gang tattoos forming in my mind. "Let's hope it doesn't come to that."

Hollis leaned back and clasped his hands behind his head. "Let's hope not. Ray's a good lawyer, but he's up against a lot of damning evidence."

"Like the report they found in your pocket when they arrested you? The one investigating all of Wakefield's assets."

"Yeah, that; plus lots of people saw me with the murder weapon. And they pretty much confiscated everything to do with the bank's deal with Wakefield Lumber. It looks bad."

I bobbed my head in agreement. No sense denying the obvious.

"Truth is," he continued, "I really did want to kill Ben Wakefield. He'd scammed me big-time. But you know me better than that, right? You know I could never kill someone."

He seemed relieved when I nodded. "I'm glad," he went on. "Because most of the town thinks I'm guilty. Hell, even my own secretary thinks I did it. Everyone's looking at me like I'm a criminal."

I pointed toward the shot glass. "You may not be a killer, Hollis, but you're not giving people a lot of reason to believe in you these days."

Snatching up the glass, he drained its contents. "Just a little something to calm my nerves," he explained, opening a desk drawer and stashing the glass inside. "Can't blame me for tipping a little back now and then. I've been under a lot of stress."

"Well, like you said, we're family so we might as well say it straight." I leaned in to emphasize my point. "Your drinking is getting out of hand, Hollis. It's hurting your family and your business. And drinking's not going to do anything to help this mess of trouble you've got yourself into. In fact, it'll probably make it worse."

He scowled and started tapping his pen on his desktop. "What exactly is it that you came in here for, Nola? To harass me? Or is there something else you needed to talk to me about?"

I sat back, lowering my chin to my chest and studying my hands. I should have known better than to take such a direct approach with Hollis and his drinking. I'd seen this type of thing over and over in my work. You can't just scold away someone's addiction. Hollis needed professional help, but still, what a louse! Ida and the girls deserved better than this. I rotated the kinks out of my neck and took a few calming breaths before continuing. "I actually came in here to ask about Wakefield Lumber."

"What about it?"

"Who takes over now that Ben Wakefield is dead?"

"It was a sole proprietorship, so his heirs inherit, just the same as they would any other assets, like a home or a car." He waved the last part off. "Well, it's obviously more complicated, but that's essentially how it works. Why do you ask?"

"Did you know Ben had a wife?"

Hollis lurched forward. "Ben Wakefield was married?"

"Yes. Didn't Ray tell you? The thing is, I just found out that she apparently held a meeting up at the lumber mill this morning."

Hollis's eyes darted back and forth. "I had no idea. That means she could have had motive to want Wakefield dead. I need to call Ray about this right away." He started reaching for the phone.

"Hold on," I quickly interjected, a little surprised with how quickly he pounced on this Millicent Wakefield thing.

Of course, Hollis was probably desperate for any way out of his current situation. I should have thought this whole thing through before questioning him about the mill's new ownership. After seeing his desperation up close and personal, I decided not to bring up my other theory about Floyd Reeves. Hollis might just go renegade with anything I gave him. No, best to just hand over any new information directly to the professionals: Ray and, heaven help me, Hawk. "Ray will be back in town tomorrow," I said, trying to distract him. "You can talk to him then. Have you met with Dane Hawkins, the investigator?"

"Yes, Ray introduced us." He rolled his eyes.

"What?"

"I didn't have a good first impression. He doesn't seem all that . . . capable to me."

I shrugged. True enough. With his tight jeans and leather, Hawk came off more like someone running from the law, not someone aiding it. But I tried to stay positive. "Ray believes he's the best person for the job."

Hollis didn't look convinced, so I switched gears again. "I wanted to ask you about something else."

He must have sensed another loaded question, because he started tapping again with the pen. "What?"

"Laney Burns."

"Laney? What about her?"

"Do you have a thing going on with her?"

"A thing? You mean an affair? No!" He stopped tapping and tossed the pen aside. "Okay, so she's fun to flirt around with, but it never goes further than that."

Fun to flirt with? This coming from a guy who made a pass at me the night before his own wedding? What a lecher! My shoulders tightened as I began to fume. "Are you sure, Hollis?"

"What do you mean? Of course I'm sure!"

I held his gaze for a moment, then felt myself begin to soften a bit. He seemed sincere, but still, he'd been drinking so much lately. Maybe he didn't realize what he did in his drunken stupors. "She said she was messing around with you in the orchard after the party."

"You didn't go telling all this to Ida, did you?"

I squinted across the desk. "No, but I will if it comes to that. I'm not going to let my sister be played for a fool, Hollis." Of course, my younger, less confident self never had the heart, or the nerve, to tell her what happened the night before her wedding. To this day, I wasn't even sure Hollis remembered what he did that night, or any time he drank heavily. Regret overcame me. If I had told her, or at least talked to her about my suspicions that he had a drinking problem, maybe I wouldn't be sitting here right now, trying to come up with something to save her sorry excuse for a husband from a murder conviction.

He shook his head, his hand hovering by the desk drawer where he stashed his liquor. He must have had second thoughts, though, because he took a deep breath and folded them on top of his desk instead. "Look. I already explained all this to Ray."

"Good. It shouldn't be too hard to explain it to me, then."

He sighed. "There's nothing to explain. She was coming on to me that night, that's all. She's like that, you know. Always flirting around with men. I had just helped Ida get the girls settled into the car and was heading back to my vehicle when, out of nowhere, Laney showed up. She saw the scarf hanging out of my pocket and grabbed it, teasing me with a game of keep-away. All I could think was how ticked Ida would be if I didn't get that scarf back."

"So you played along?"

"I tried to get it from her, but she ran into the trees. I chased after her for a while, then gave up. I don't know what happened to the scarf after that. Well, not until I found out how it was used, anyway."

"That's not the story Laney is telling. She said you guys messed around together in the orchard, but you were too drunk for much fun, so she left you there alone."

"She's lying. Ask Ida. I'd been drinking that night, but I'd sobered up before it was time to leave."

I mulled this over, remembering that Ida did say something about Hollis being sober enough to drive home that night. But could I really believe anything Hollis said? And what reason would Laney have to lie about such a thing? Was she covering up something else? "So, why'd you get home so late?"

"I'd been expecting a fax from that investigative firm I hired to look into Wakefield Lumber."

"The report the cops found in your pocket."

"Exactly. I came by here, to my office. I knew Wakefield was up to something. He was late with his payments. In fact, I questioned him at the party about it and things got heated between us. But when I saw that report . . . well, it confirmed everything I suspected. Wakefield had scammed me out of a boatload of money."

"So you were upset."

"To put it mildly."

"Did you go back to the party looking for Wakefield?"

"No!" He slapped the top of his desk. "I swear that's not what happened. And I'm getting sick and tired of retelling this story."

I ignored his antics. "Where'd you go then?" I pressed.

He leaned forward, elbows on the desk and head buried in his hands. "I couldn't go home after that. I needed to get my head together before I went home and told Ida. . . . I mean, I'd just found out we were ruined financially, and mostly due to my negligence. So I went by the liquor store and got a bottle of Jack and headed out to this spot I like to go to."

"Up McManamy Draw by Hill Lake?"

He looked up. "You know about that?"

I nodded. "This is Cays Mill. No one has secrets around here." Well, maybe a few, like Wakefield having a wife, but still . . . I stood and shouldered my bag. That was when one of the files on his desk caught my eye. "What's this?" I said, pointing at a file marked with a familiar name. "Is that Puckett, like in Joe Puckett?"

Hollis shrugged and tidied up the pile, Joe's file disappearing into it. "It is, just normal banking stuff." He looked at the door as his other hand moved toward the desk's side, where his liquor drawer awaited.

"Sure. I understand." Still, I was surprised to see Joe's name attached to anything to do with the bank. As far as I knew, the old fellow rarely came to town. Especially not to use the bank. I imagined what money he had, he kept hidden away under his mattress. But I didn't push the issue any further. By the looks of Hollis, he'd had enough interrogating for one day. Judging by the haggard look in his eyes, as soon as I left, he'd more than likely be back into his liquor drawer again. So I told him good-bye and turned on my heel. On the way out, I passed by Candace, who waggled a set of sticky-lemon fingers my way and wished me a good day.

Right. Like there's anything good about this day so far.

Chapter 12

Georgia Belle Fact #071: In a Georgia Belle's eyes, any man who plays the banjo is simply divine.

"Nola, over here!" Ginny called, waving at me from the other side of the room full of festival participants. Red's Diner was put up neat, so to say. Everything polished to a T with stainless steel glimmering, the floor sparkling, and even the red vinyl glistening with cleanliness.

I made my way across the room to where Ginny, Sam and Hattie were huddled together. "Glad you made it," Hattie said, squeezing my arm. I was glad, too. After the day dealing with messes—Hollis and then the leftover party mess—it was good to be around friends.

"Me, too," Ginny added, leaning in front of Hattie. "I'm so excited you'll be selling your jams at the festival this year. You'll have to talk to Margie Price before the meeting is over. She's in charge of organizing this year's vendors."

"Sure. Where is she?" But I'd no sooner asked than a booming voice cut through the crowd, telling us all to take a seat. I settled at one of the tables next to Ginny and Sam; Hattie sat across from us with Pete taking the chair next to

her. The room was packed, but I recognized a few in atten-
dance: Ezra Sugar, Sally Jo from the Cays Mill Mercantile,
Mrs. Whortlebe from the Clip & Curl, and Frances Simms.
It stood to reason that most of the town's business owners
would be there. It was probably one of their biggest sale
days of the year.

After everyone found a seat, a wiry man with a tattered
hat jammed atop his head moved to the head of the room.
"Who's that?" I asked Hattie, eyeing his handlebar mustache
and long braid trailing down the back of his T-shirt.

She giggled and whispered back, "Don't you recognize
Wade Marshall? He's our mayor now."

That's Wade Marshall! You could have knocked me over
with a feather. But this was what happened after being away
for several years. People I knew in my youthful prime
changed, while I, at least in my own mind, stayed the same.
I'd noticed quite a few examples of this since I'd returned.
Small things, like Mrs. Whortlebe, bless her heart, who had
put on at least fifteen extra pounds and changed her hair
color from mousy brown to a shocking black. Despite the
changes, though, she was still recognizable. Wade Marshall,
on the other hand, had undergone more than just a little
change. The once-upon-a-time baby-faced, nerdy boy, who
took the 4-H blue ribbon every year for his bug collections,
had morphed into a . . . a . . .

"He looks like one of those Hell's Angels, doesn't he?"
Ginny leaned in from the other side.

That's it. A Hell's Angel.

She went on to explain, "But he's done a great job as
mayor. He's working on bringing the town back to life."

I sat back, trying to keep an open mind as Wade began his
spiel. Not about his looks, mind you. I'd been raised to value
people for their actions, not their appearances. No, I needed
to keep an open mind because I just couldn't imagine Wade
Marshall as anyone other than a pesky seventh grader who

terrorized me in science class by dangling a hairy-legged spider in front of my face. How in the world did he ever get elected as mayor?

"It looks like we're going to have a record turnout for this year's festival," Wade was saying. "We'll have artists and vendors attending from around the county. I'm also pleased to announce that we've been able to secure a carousel for this year's kiddie carnival."

An enthusiastic round of applause erupted.

He cleared his throat and continued. "It'll be set up on the courthouse green along with the other children's activities." He pointed to a crude map, drawn on foam board and propped up on an easel. "Both Blossom and Orchard streets will be blocked for vendor booths, with food stands here, and a stage here." He turned back to the table with a glint of pride in his eye. "I'm happy to announce that my bluegrass band, the Peach Pickers, will be playing on the stage Saturday night. Hope y'all stop by for a listen!"

"He's in a band?" I hissed in Hattie's ear.

"Yup. Banjo," she confirmed. A sense of awe suddenly overcame us. To a Southern gal, the banjo was the end-all of instruments. Why, a guy could be the homeliest man alive, but if he played a banjo . . . Well, what more need I say?

"And more good news, folks," Wade continued. "Judging by the booth fees we've collected already, we should be right on track with our budget."

Another round of clapping started up, but abruptly ceased when the diner door flew open and Maudy Payne stepped inside with her bad attitude preceding her by a couple steps. She briefly caught my eyes, her lips twitching upward in a snarly grin. I shuddered and turned away, focusing again on Wade, who was now droning on about revenue and budgets. He finally wrapped things up with a nod toward Maudy. "Again, a huge thank-you to Sam and Ginny for providing the meeting place and refreshments this evening. Now I'm turning the podium over to Sheriff Payne, who'll be discussing this weekend's security concerns."

Wade settled back into his chair as Maudy sauntered over to take his place. While she went on about various security rules, I found myself thinking about my own festival projects. I had a lot of work left if I was going to get my preserves ready in time. Starting with making them palatable! I leaned toward Ginny. "Are you still available to help me with my recipes?"

"Sure. How about Sunday? We close early right after the church crowd finishes up, so say around four o'clock? That'll give me time to get the kitchen cleaned up and ready."

"Perfect," I agreed, grateful that she could spare the time. As the meeting wore on with topics such as volunteer coordination and shuttle buses for visitors, I considered more personal tasks, like labels for my jars and a sign for my booth. By the time the last speaker wrapped up, I'd assembled my own mental to-do list.

"I'm so glad I came tonight," I told my group as we made our way over to the counter where Ginny and Sam had placed a large urn of coffee and several plates of cookies.

"Are you Nola Harper?" a voice came from behind. I turned to find a pleasant-looking woman wearing a flowered blouse, straight gray skirt and a classy strand of pearls. Her blond hair was cut into a crisp bob angled toward her large dark eyes and high cheekbones. She held out her hand. "I'm Margie Price. I own Sunny Side Up."

I abandoned my quest for coffee and took her hand. "A pleasure. I was hoping to run into you this evening."

She nodded. "Hattie mentioned you planned on starting a home-based business."

"Yes, that's right. My family owns one of the local peach farms. I'm expanding our business by selling jams and preserves, and a few other things. I'm hoping to put a few jars on a table outside Hattie's Boutique next weekend. Just to see how they sell."

"Wonderful idea! We'll have food vendors from all around, but something local like that is sure to be a hit."

I smiled. "I hope so."

"And as soon as you get your business up and running, give me a jingle. I'll be one of your first customers. I'd love to offer my out-of-town guests a taste of local fare."

"Really? Thank you!" I gushed. I could hardly believe my ears. A customer already and I hadn't even started.

My enthusiasm, however, was quickly squelched by Maudy's sudden appearance. "I need to talk to you," she insisted, rudely interrupting our discussion. She motioned for me to step aside, so I turned to Margie with an apologetic look and excused myself. Maudy and I navigated our way around several conversational groups before settling on a quiet corner of the diner where we faced off, each of us assuming a defensive posture.

"So, this Hawk guy paid me a courtesy visit yesterday," she started.

Uh-oh.

She stood with her arms crossed over her chest. "Ray thought he needed to bring in an investigator, huh?"

"Well . . ." I hesitated, trying to find my tact. "He's just hoping to locate the real killer, that's all."

She pressed her lips tight and scrunched her brow. "I've already found the real killer. There's no doubt about it. Your brother-in-law had motive, means and opportunity, and I've got the evidence to prove it. Any jury would convict him."

"You're right, Maudy. The facts are stacked against Hollis, but we still think he's innocent."

"You're biased."

I crossed my own arms, sucked in my cheeks and lowered my gaze. "Do you know who Millicent Wakefield is?" I threw out, not giving her time to respond before spouting off some more. "She's Ben Wakefield's widow—that's who. And it's possible that his death saved her from a nasty divorce battle and earned her control of Wakefield Lumber. Have you looked into her? Or any other suspects, for that matter?"

She rocked onto her toes and stared down her nose at me. "As a matter of fact, I have. Which brings up something else I wanted to tell you." She slid her eyes across the room and nodded at Frances Simms, who was ogling us from behind her heavy black-rimmed glasses. "I don't appreciate you spouting facts about my case all over town."

I felt my shoulders crumple. "What do you mean?" But I knew darn well what she meant. She'd found out that I blabbed about the scarf. I took a step backward, my back pressing against the wall.

Maudy stepped forward and shook her finger my way. "If I find you're going around causing trouble for my investigation, I'll throw you in a cell and leave you there."

"Sheriff Payne!" It was Ginny, carrying a white foam takeout box and sidestepping in front of me, cutting off Maudy's direct attack. "Thank you for coming to the meeting tonight. Bless your heart. I know how busy you are trying to keep our streets safe, so we wouldn't want to keep you any longer. But here." She handed Maudy the box. "A little something for you to munch on back at your office."

Well, give the dog a bone. Ginny's ploy worked! Maudy's hard gaze left me with a glance at the box already being placed in her hand. Then her eyes instantly softened and I saw her tongue give a quick swipe of her lower lip. She gratefully accepted the box and excused herself, obviously eager to partake in Ginny's notoriously good food.

"You okay?" Ginny asked, after Maudy left. "I swear, I wish someone else would come along and run for her position." She giggled. "Last election, someone went around with a marker and added the words 'in the ass' on all her campaign signs. It was hilarious." She swiped her hand through the air as if spelling it out for me. "Vote Maudy Payne *in the ass* for Sheriff!"

We both laughed. Leave it to Ginny to know just the right

thing to do and say. I reached out and gave her a quick hug. "Thank you."

She waved it off. "Heck, that's what friends are for!"

Her words stuck with me as I left the diner. Friends. Since returning, I'd realized I had more friends in town than I thought. Sure, Cays Mill had its share of naysayers and gossipmongers, but I'd also been surprised by a few true acts of friendship since I'd arrived: Hattie, so willing to take back up with our best-friend status despite the fact that I'd neglected our friendship all these years; Cade, coming to my rescue with Joe Puckett's roof; and Ginny, willing to take time from her family and business responsibilities to help me with Mama's recipes. Come to think of it, the locals here weren't all that different from the people of the small villages I'd traveled to, with their petty squabbles and vicious rumors . . . and yet still with hearts that forgave and hands willing to help in times of trouble. It made me wonder whether things might have been different if I'd stayed all those years ago instead of running from my secret. A twinge of regret that I'd abandoned my family, all for nothing, pricked at my conscience. I shook it off; I'd done my best with the hand fate had dealt me.

I left my Jeep parked on the square, deciding to walk to the Sunny Side Up. I was determined to find Hawk and report my latest findings. As far as I was concerned, he was wasting his time hanging out with Laney Burns. Millicent Wakefield was the new prime suspect.

Walking along Branch Street, I passed the *Cays Mill Reporter* building before turning the corner and heading down to Majestic Boulevard. Majestic boasted some of our town's most beautiful homes, from large Colonials with black shutters and red doors to impressive Italianates with deep-set arched windows and scrolled accents. The Sunny Side Up Bed & Breakfast, however, was the only home in the neighborhood loyal to its heritage. Built in true Southern Antebellum style, the impressive three-story with a deep pillared porch stood proud among its immigrant-styled neighbors.

I'd been dying to see the inside of the bed-and-breakfast, but as I neared the place, I started to lose my nerve. Did I really want to just show up at the place Hawk was staying? Was that even appropriate behavior? Then it occurred to me: What if someone from town saw me? What was I thinking? This was just the type of behavior that could ignite a whole explosion of rumors.

Just as I was about to turn on my heel, Hawk's motorcycle roared to the curb. He dismounted and came right over, a perplexed look on his face, and, I noticed, a few lipstick stains, too. "Looking for me?"

"Yes." I squinted at the smudges on his jawline. Crimson red, a perfect match to the bloodred claws I'd noticed on Laney Burns earlier that week. I suddenly thought of my own chipped pink nails and instinctively curled my finger-tips into my palms.

"You look mad." He was looking at my clenched fists.

I shook my head and relaxed my hands a little. "No. Uh . . ."

"You want to go for a drink or something?" He indicated toward his bike.

"No! No, thank you." I pointed toward the porch. "I just have a couple things I wanted to tell you about."

We chose a pair of rattan chairs, covered with pretty flower-patterned cushions, and sat back like two friends getting ready to catch up on old times. Only I knew the old times Dane Hawkins and I shared were better off left not discussed.

No one spoke at first; the only sound between us was the whirring of the large fans above our heads as they circulated the air, bringing little relief to the heat and humidity that lin-gered even as the sun sat low in the sky. From somewhere down the street, I could hear happy sounds of children trying to cram a little more playtime into the last minutes of daylight.

"So, what's up?" he finally asked.

I brushed away a lock of hair stuck to my forehead. "I found out something today that might be important to the case."

He leaned back, crossing a booted foot over his knee. "I'm all ears."

I glanced out toward the yard, wondering how much time I had before the owner, Margie Price, finished at the meeting and returned. Running into her so soon again might prove awkward. "I think Millicent Wakefield has inherited control of Wakefield Lumber."

"Is that so?"

"Yes. She had a meeting at the mill this morning. Probably meeting with employees and assessing the situation."

He nodded. "Interesting. I'll check into the status of the company."

"Good. What have *you* been able to find out?"

He drew in his breath. "Well, I've been working a different angle than you."

Judging from the lipstick smudges on your face, probably the horizontal angle.

"But what I've learned also points to Millicent."

I leaned forward. "Really? Like what?"

He picked at the sole of his boot, dislodging tiny pebbles from the tread. "After a little finessing, Laney confided in me about her affair with Ben Wakefield. She knew about his wife all along, but Wakefield led her to believe he was getting a divorce. Seems she had her heart set on marrying the guy. But, earlier in the day, she'd seen him driving around town with another woman. She said they looked cozy."

"Another woman?"

Hawk waggled his brows. "A well-dressed blonde, as she put it, with lots of bling."

"Oh my goodness! Millicent! But that would mean she was down here at the time of the murder."

"Exactly. But hear me out."

I sat back and took a deep breath.

"When Laney found out it was Wakefield's wife, she became furious."

"And killed him!"

"No; sorry. Laney's not the murdering type. She's more of the . . ."

His face took on a faraway look as he searched for the right way to describe Laney. Obviously, Hawk had lost his objectivity when it came to her. He looked like a smitten schoolboy.

"So . . ." I prompted, quickly losing my patience. "She decided to make him jealous by flirting with Hollis at the party," I finished for him.

"Yeah. Something like that."

I turned these new facts over in my mind, trying to imagine the complete scenario. Something nagged at me. "You know what? I didn't get any of this when I spoke to Laney the other day. In fact, the more I learn about Laney, the more I realize she never really tells the real story. Have you noticed that?"

"What do you mean?"

"I mean, it's possible she's playing you."

"Playing me? How's that?"

"She knows you're here to investigate Wakefield's murder, right?"

He nodded.

"And she knew Millicent was here at the time of the murder. Isn't it possible she killed Wakefield in a fit of scorned jealousy and is trying to frame Millicent? I mean, don't you think it's weird she's giving you this information out of the blue? When she talked to me, she was happy to give a story about Hollis being so very drunk at the time, something I've now heard may not be that true. Maybe she made that up to further imply Hollis's guilt, and since Hollis was already arrested, she thought that was enough. But now, knowing there is an investigator here to help Hollis, maybe she's just making up other stories to throw suspicion onto Millicent. Any story that throws suspicion on anyone other than herself might be her defense mechanism."

"Yeah, okay. It crossed my mind. Still, at least evidence is building toward other suspects. If anything, there's enough here to create reasonable doubt about Hollis's guilt." He stood and motioned toward the porch steps. "Well, I've got an early morning tomorrow. Can I give you a lift back to your car?"

"No, thanks." I stood and headed for the steps, turning back at the last minute, unable to resist a little jab. "A little finessing, huh? You might want to scrub all those kissy marks off your face," I said, leaving him wide-eyed and rubbing at his jawline. Not a thing had changed about Dane Hawkins.

By the time Cade's truck pulled into my drive first thing Saturday morning, I was up and dressed, and had already packed a hearty lunch. I grabbed the cooler and the box of parts Joe needed and ran outside to meet Cade. I was surprised to see two other trucks pull in behind his.

"What's all this?" I asked, setting my stuff on the ground.

"Just some friends," he explained, hopping out of the truck. "They decided they could spare a few hours to help a neighbor. I'll introduce you to them once we're at Joe's." He loaded my things into the bed of the truck alongside some boards and several boxes of shingles. "We're expecting rain later this afternoon," he said. "So we need to get a move on. Hop in."

"Hold on a minute," I said, running back to the house. I grabbed lunch meats, a jar of mayo, pickles and a loaf of bread, then threw it all in a bag. I found Roscoe in his usual spot on the sofa. "Come on, boy. You're going for a ride."

"A dog?" Cade asked when I reappeared with Roscoe in my arms.

"Just a puppy, actually. You don't mind if he rides along, do you? I'm watching him for . . . for a friend."

Cade shrugged. "Sure." He glanced back at the house. "Is Ray coming?"

"He's not due back until later today," I explained, moving aside several stacks of paperwork as I climbed into the passenger side. It looked as if Cade's truck doubled as an office. Roscoe let out a little whimper so I placed him on my lap and stroked his fur, trying to calm his nerves. I was surprised he was so jittery, especially considering he usually rode on the back of a Harley.

"Just like old times, huh? Minus Hattie," I commented, once we were on the move. I was referring back to our high school days when we spent many a Saturday afternoon tooling off to town in their daddy's Chevy.

"She wanted to come help, but Saturday's her busiest day at the shop." He reached over and turned down the radio. "Speaking of the old days, remember that time we all went mudding down by the Hole? I about tore the axle off Daddy's truck trying to get pulled out of that mess. Man, was he ticked."

I started to laugh just as we hit a bump in the road. Roscoe reacted by digging his claws into my bare legs. "Ouch! Calm down, Roscoe!" I brushed him off my lap and scooted closer to the middle, giving him his own space by the window. I looked back at Cade. "Hope these paths aren't too much for everyone's vehicles." Since there weren't any roads leading directly to Joe's cabin, we were navigating the orchard's access roads, hoping to get near enough to his cabin that we didn't have to carry supplies too far.

Cade tapped the dash. "Are you kidding? No problem."

I turned and glanced out the back window, hoping the other guys felt the same. "Sure nice of your friends to help out."

"They're good guys. Besides, they all owe me. The thing about being a contractor is your friends are always asking for favors—help with this and that, borrowing tools; you know how it is."

I nodded. "Still, thanks for cashing in your favors on me. And it looks like you've got plenty of supplies."

He glanced my way. "Yup, but a lot of the stuff was left over from other jobs. The shingles won't match, but I doubt Joe will care. Anyway, I was able to keep your supply cost down. I'll just send a bill your way, once I get it all tallied up."

I smiled. "Perfect." After everything that had gone wrong this week, it was good to finally have something go right for a change.

After a rough-and-tumble ten-minute ride, we finally pulled up to the edge of the woods by Joe's cabin. He was waiting for us, standing with his hands in his pockets and his hat pulled low over his head. As soon as I opened my door, Roscoe shot to the ground and started sniffing. I pulled out a plastic bowl and water bottle I'd brought to give him a drink but he was too busy sniffing to take a break.

"Who's this?" Joe asked, reaching down and swiping his weathered hand over the dog's back. "Got yourself a coon dog, do ya?"

"Not exactly," I started, but Joe had already moved on, walking around the bed of the truck, eyeing the supplies. "Looks like your word's as good as your daddy's. And extra help, too," he added with a nod toward the guys who had gathered around.

Quick introductions were made before everyone jumped in and began carrying supplies along the trail leading to Joe's cabin. That was when I realized how impossible this job would be without the extra help. Even though we'd pulled up to the edge of the woods, it was still another thirty yards over a rocky, rooty trail to reach Joe's cabin. Then reality really set in, when I realized the actual physical strength it took to tear off and replace the rotted roof decking and roll out and attach the large bundles of black felting paper. I left the heavy work to the guys, acting as their gofer by fetching nails, small tools and anything else they needed. Joe did his part keeping the guys going with an endless supply of liquid refreshment. Halfway through the job, I decided we'd better break for some solid food, before all the hooch went to the guys' heads. I retrieved the cooler and my extra bag of food and slapped a few more sandwiches together.

"How about some sandwiches?" I called out. After the guys were settled on the porch and happily eating, I took my own food to a nearby stump, so I could keep an eye on Roscoe, who was shuffling between trees, his nose to the ground as it had been all morning.

I'd just started eating when Joe moseyed over. "You'd think their sniffers would wear out," he joked.

I made room for him on the edge of the stump. "I guess it's a good thing he's got a good nose. His owner's a detective. That nose might come in handy one day."

Joe raised a brow. "A detective, eh? The sheriff still don't have her man?"

"She thinks she does, but I'm not so sure."

"Is that so?" he grunted, balancing a mason jar of moonshine between his knees and tearing into his sandwich. "Good fixin's," he said, licking his fingers between bites.

I motioned toward the cooler. "There's more where that came from."

We ate in silence for a while, batting at the flies that'd started buzzing around our heads. Joe took a long swig of his drink and coughed a little. "When the flies swarm like this, it means a storm's a-brewin'."

I shielded my eyes against the sun and peered through the trees. The sky was a clear blue, not a storm cloud in sight. "That's what they're saying, but it's hard to believe. The sky's so clear."

"One's comin'. Mark my word."

I looked his way. "At least you'll have a solid roof over your head tonight."

He tipped his jar my way and smiled. "That's right. I've been wanting to get this roof fixed for a long time now. Never could afford it, though." He squinted up at the roof where the guys were at it again. They'd started on the shingles, passing them hand over hand to one of the guys, who drove a single nail to hold each in place. Another guy followed up behind him, pounding in a couple more nails, making sure each shingle was securely attached. "I know it don't seem like much to you, but this old cabin has made a good home for me and mine."

"I'm sure it has." I glanced his way, wanting to tell him that I'd seen much worse living conditions. People living in mud huts, with no source of clean water. Or the slums I'd seen in Guatemala where entire neighborhoods consisted of homes built with scavenged cardboard and scrap sheets of metal propped up and held together with nothing but sticks and rope. But then I realized Joe must have been feeling some of the same desperation that I'd witnessed in those faraway lands. Desperation and the desire to simply meet the basic needs of food and shelter. At least now I figured out why I'd seen that file on Hollis's desk. More than likely, Joe had gone to the bank for a loan to fix his roof. Of course, Hollis had probably denied the loan. After all, Joe had no collateral. That also explained why Joe was anxious to make a deal with me that included a new roof.

"Yes, sirree." He started up again, bringing my thoughts back to the present. "This has been a fine home. We had ourselves some good times here. At least back in the day before the missus went sick. She died when Tucker was just thirteen. It was hard on the boy."

I looked away, avoiding the raw pain that showed on his face. "I'm sorry, Joe."

"Yup, they're all gone." He drew my attention back by spreading his hand through the air. "This land is all I have now." Raising his jar again, he let out a dry chuckle and added, "And this." After tipping back the rest of the liquid, he righted himself and swiped the back of his hand across his lips. "Guess we'd best be gettin' back to work before that storm rolls in," he said, standing and starting toward the cabin. I stayed put for a second, watching him amble back across the yard, his shoulders bent forward as if he was walking against the wind.

Finally, I stood and brushed off the back of my shorts, the irony of it all hitting me again. All these years, I'd traveled so far away to help people around the world when my neighbor, even my own family, needed my help. Not that I'd go back and change the last fifteen years of my life. The thing was, what had first started out as my desire to run from home had helped me actually find my place in this world—and not geographically speaking. Rather, over the years, my work as a humanitarian helped me find a purpose. Something I probably wouldn't have been able to do if I'd stayed around here, working on the farm. But, since returning home, something had shifted. I'd found not only purpose, but a type of warmth and neighborly love that I hadn't even realized I'd been missing. Maybe . . . just maybe, Cays Mill wasn't so bad after all.

Chapter 13

Georgia Belle Fact #052: In the South, we not only love our neighbors, of course, but even for the questionable among them we make sure they never go hungry.

"I asked Hattie to join us," Ginny said as I walked into the diner's kitchen. I plunked down the heavy box of ingredients I was carrying and reached for the glass of iced tea she was holding out. "By the way, Reverend Jones was asking about you this morning. Wondering why you weren't at services."

Ah, yes, welcome back to the fold. "I overslept, I guess," I lied. But as soon as the words were out, I started squirming. I was raised to believe Sundays were for churchgoing, period. The real truth was that I hadn't overslept, but opted for the soft comfort of my own bed over one of Reverend's hard-edged sermons because . . . well, I just wasn't ready to face down the guilt I felt over my own past sins.

Ginny eyed me strangely, but thankfully let the topic drop. Instead, she pulled a plate from the microwave and passed it my way. "Here. Try this. We can't make preserves on an empty stomach." Knowing that we wouldn't be able to use the kitchen until the last of the after-church crowd had cleared out and the place was cleaned and prepared for the next business day, I'd spent most of the day taking care of chores around the house. I'd been so busy I hadn't even taken a break for lunch. Now it was already late afternoon and getting close to my usual dinnertime, so I was ever so grateful she'd thought to have something for us to eat.

"It's a new recipe: hash brown casserole with beef," she continued, handing me a fork. I took the plate and sat at the end of the stainless steel work counter. "I threw in some sweet corn, too."

I took a bite and raised my brows in appreciation. "Mmm. This is wonderful." The textures were amazing. Crispy and creamy at the same time, with a little extra crunch from the kernels of sweet corn. "Is that sour cream I taste?"

Ginny beamed. "Yes. Glad you like it. I made one for Ben Wakefield's widow. Still can't believe I never knew that man was married. Anyway, thought I'd run the casserole by their house this afternoon."

My ears perked up. "Really. Mind if I go with you?"

Ginny shrugged. "Sure. Why not?" She sat across from me with her own plate and had just started in when Hattie pushed her way through the hinged door that separated the diner and kitchen.

"Hey, all!" she called out before stopping short and staring down at our plates. "Oh, my!" I could see her nose twitching. "That smells divine."

Ginny started to stand. "I'll heat some up for you."

Hattie stopped her. "Don't bother getting up. I can get it. You forget that I've worked your kitchen before. I know where you keep everything."

"Hattie fills in sometimes in a pinch," Ginny explained.

"And Ginny's helped over at my place, too," Hattie replied, scooping out a generous portion of casserole on a plate. "Speaking of helping, how'd it go at Joe Puckett's yesterday?"

"Great. Thanks to Cade and a few of his friends, Joe's got a new roof."

"I'm so glad to hear it," Ginny said between bites. "That poor man's had his share of heartache. First his wife, then his only child killed in that terrible mill accident."

I gasped and set down my fork. "What? Joe's son was killed at the mill?"

"Didn't you know that?" Hattie asked with a half-full mouth. She swallowed and dabbed at her lips with a napkin. "When was that, Gin? Do you remember?"

"Just last year. April, I think." Ginny shuddered. "It was horrible. He was operating the chipper . . . and . . . well, it killed him instantly. Joe was so distraught over Tucker's death, he locked himself in that cabin of his most of the summer. I sent Sam over several times with food. I was afraid the poor man wasn't eating."

I abandoned the last couple of bites and pushed aside my plate. "That's awful." It was also a good reason to feel a lot of hatred toward Ben Wakefield. Enough to kill over? I immediately dismissed the idea. No way. More than likely the conniving Millicent, or the scorned Laney Burns, or even the bitter Floyd Reeves, was responsible for Wakefield's murder. Not Joe. Joe was simply an old man who wanted to live the rest of his life in his peaceful patch of woods making moonshine and reveling in the memories of happier days with his wife and son.

Hattie's sigh interrupted my train of thought. "Enough of this sad talk," she said, tapping my arm. "What do you say we get busy making some peach preserves?"

And so we did. For the next couple hours, we measured, stirred and poured until we'd filled a couple dozen jars of beautifully set peach preserves. Ginny even taught me a neat little trick for thawing my peaches. She macerated them in sugar while they thawed. She told me this was to soften the fruit and ensure that I didn't end up with hard bits of fruit floating in a mess of juice. Which was exactly what I had the first time I attempted to make preserves with Mama's frozen peaches. Now, after pulling one perfect jar after another out of the canner, I felt confident I could do it on my own next time. "Thank you again for using your day off to help me figure this out," I told them, as we dried the last pot and prepared to call it a successful day. "I think I've got the hang of it now."

I was instantly sandwiched in a group hug. "We're just so glad you're here, Nola." Hattie gushed into my right ear.

"And we'd do 'bout anything to get you to stay," Ginny added from the other side. "Even if it meant we had to spend every weekend helping you make peach products for your new business."

"Hey, speak for yourself, you old married woman," Hattie joked. "I, for one, have better things to do with my weekends. And it has nothing to do with making peach stuff."

"Making something else?" Ginny shot back.

The corners of Hattie's mouth turned upward, but before she could expand on the thought I jumped in. "Making spicy Mexican food. Hattie told me she and Pete are really fond of making—what did you call it? Chili rellenos together, I do believe. Isn't that right, Hattie?"

"Uh-huh. That's right. Pete likes to stuff his—"

"Enough!" Ginny playfully covered her ears.

"You started it," Hattie protested.

Ginny pointed to the door, barely able to contain her laughter. "Go on. Get out of here, you wicked harlot."

Hattie tipped her head back and laughed as she sashayed her way across the room with a little extra wiggle. Right before exiting, she licked her finger and touched it to her bum and made an exaggerated sizzling sound.

Ginny and I were still laughing a few minutes later as we made our way out the door with the casserole and onto the walk. "Your car or mine?" she asked me. "The Wakefield place is about a half mile out of town, on the same road as the lumber mill."

I was about to suggest we take my Jeep, when a familiar blond head caught my attention. "That's her right over there."

Looking back at Ginny, I noticed her eyes were wide in wonderment. "Will you check out that outfit?" she said. "I could never pull that off."

"Me, either," I agreed. In fact, I would have thought mixing so many animal prints would be some sort of fashion faux pas, but on Millicent, the zebra print leggings, black-and-white leopard print vest over an all-black super-short dress, and supersized crocodile bag swinging from her shoulder seemed to work. I pulled on Ginny's arm. "Come on, let's catch up to her."

We darted across the street and cut through the corner of the courthouse lawn just in time to see her duck into the alley between the Clip & Curl and the VFW hall. "Where is she headed?" Ginny asked, juggling the foil-covered dish from one arm to the other as we scurried down the sidewalk.

"I have no idea, but let's see if we can catch up to her." We dashed into the alley and stopped short. Millicent was nowhere to be seen. "Where'd she go?"

Ginny nodded toward the back door of the Clip & Curl. "Maybe in there."

We crossed over to the door and were about to enter when we heard voices from down the alley. It sounded like Millicent and a man. Squinting, I caught a glimpse of Millicent's backside around the edge of one of the large blue Dumpsters that lined the alley. She was standing in the VFW's service doorway holding a heated discussion with someone. I was almost a hundred percent sure it was Floyd Reeves, but a stack of wood pallets was blocking my view.

Turning to Ginny, I held my finger to my mouth, indicating that we should continue as quietly as possible. Crouching, I shuffled toward one of the Dumpsters and took refuge behind it, Ginny following close on my heels. "Are you nuts? What are you doing?" I heard her make gagging noises. "Lawdy! It smells like a thousand cats used this thing as their litter box."

"Shh! I think she's talking to Floyd Reeves."

"The kid who hates lumbering?" The foil on the dish made crinkling noises as Ginny struggled to stay crouched.

"Yes," I hissed. "Shh! I want to hear what they're saying." But their words were inaudible over the buzzing air-conditioning units that lined the alleyway, noisily pumping cool air into the adjacent businesses. Staying in my crouched position, I duckwalked along the lower edge of the Dumpster, hoping to be able to hear better. Just then, the back door to the Clip & Curl swung open and Laney Burns came bouncing out, a cigarette in one hand and her lighter in the other. She lifted the cigarette to her lips and paused. "Nola Mae? Is that you? What in heaven's name are you doing down there?" Cooling units or not, Laney's voice came in loud and clear. Reacting quickly, I jumped up and glanced down the alley, just in time to see Millicent shove an envelope into the hands of Floyd Reeves.

At the sound of Laney's voice, both Millicent and Floyd turned toward us. A brief flash of terror crossed Floyd's face as he reeled and dashed out the back side of the alley. Millicent, on the other hand, leveled a determined look our way and started toward us, heels clicking against the concrete. As she drew closer, facts started racing through my mind: Ben Wakefield was divorcing her; upon his death, she inherited the mill; she'd been spotted in town at the time of the murder; and just now she was handing something to an overzealous, hateful man who'd already stated that he was happy Ben Wakefield was dead.

One thing for sure: I was staring into the well-made-up face of my new number-one suspect in the murder of Ben Wakefield. And she was staring back with a sugary sweet smile that didn't quite meet her eyes. "Is there something I can do for y'all?"

Behind me, I heard the rustling of aluminum foil. Ginny stepped out from behind the Dumpster. "Actually, yes. I was getting ready to bring this up to your house when we spotted you from across the street. Thought we'd save a trip and just give it to you in person."

"Well, isn't this sweet?" Millicent took the dish and turned her attention back to where Laney and I were standing. That was when, all of a sudden, another fact flew to mind. Probably the most important one of all: I was standing between Millicent and her dead husband's mistress.

Unfortunately, this realization must have already dawned on Millicent. She smiled tightly at Laney and asked, "Are you the gal that does nails here at the Clip and Curl?"

Laney calmly placed her cigarette between her lips and flicked the lighter with her signature red-lacquered nails. After lighting up, she took a long drag and blew out the smoke with a wry smile. "Why, yes, I am."

Millicent stepped a little closer and gave her an up-and-down, her lips stretching even farther over her already taut face. "Well, ain't this something," she said, removing the foil the rest of the way from the top of the dish. "But it seems to me that you might need this casserole more than me." With one smooth move, she hoisted the dish in the air and dumped its contents over Laney's head.

Hours later, back at the house, I was still laughing as I told Ray about the incident. The image of Laney standing there, eyes wide and cig dangling from her lips as gooey pieces of hash browns dripped down her head, would forever be burned into my mind.

"Guess she got hers." Ray chuckled, then sobered again as his lawyerly mind took over. "Hawk told me that Laney saw Millicent in town the day Ben Wakefield was murdered. And now you saw her hand something to Floyd Reeves?"

"That's right. An envelope. Thick like it was stuffed full of something. Could have been money." We were out on the front porch watching the storm clouds roll in while sucking on chicken wings and sipping beer that Ray had picked up at the Honky Tonk. Roscoe had planted himself smack-dab between us, ogling the chicken while thumping his tail against the porch floorboards. "There's something else, too," I added, reaching for the roll of paper towels set between us. I hesitated a second before telling him what I'd learned about Joe Puckett's son being killed in a milling accident. It almost felt like I was speaking ill of a friend. "But, as grief-stricken, even as angry as he must be, I can't see Joe committing murder. Can you?"

He shook his head. "I'd hate to think of Joe as a suspect, but his son's death does make for a strong motive. Come to think of it, I should have Hawk check into the mill. Maybe safety issues are a problem there. If that's the case, there might be more people angry with Wakefield and the way he was running his operation." He leaned back, wiping his hands as he mulled over this new information. After a long swill of his beer, he drew in his breath and started up again. "This mill thing aside, I'm still more inclined to think Millicent Wakefield is our killer. We'll just need to prove that she was in town the day of the murder. Then we'll have motive and means. I'll get Hawk working on it tomorrow." Ray shrugged and picked up another chicken wing, tearing a piece from the bone and tossing it over to Roscoe, who gobbled it up and immediately begged for more.

"Don't do that, Ray! You're going to ruin him. Dogs aren't supposed to eat people food."

"Oh, okay. Don't go getting your knickers all in a twist." He wiped his fingers on a towel and stood. Reaching down, he scooped up another beer and twisted the top off. "I'm going to head inside to make a couple calls. I need to fill Hawk in on this thing with Reeves, and I suppose I should call the sheriff, too. She needs to know what you and Ginny saw in the alley today. She'll probably want to pick up Floyd Reeves for questioning."

"Don't bet on it," I mumbled as the screen door slammed

shut behind him. Maudy Payne was dead set on Hollis as the killer, and nothing short of a confession from the real murderer was going to convince her otherwise.

Early Monday morning, I laced up my field boots and headed out to the orchards, Roscoe with his clumsy paws pummeling behind me, his nose to the ground and long ears flopping about. At one point, I heard a sharp yelp from behind and turned to find the poor fellow desperately trying to pull his head from the ground. "For Pete's sake, Roscoe! What have you gotten yourself into now?" I stooped down, expecting to find his nose tangled in the weeds, but instead discovered he was standing with his front paws on his own long ears. "For crying out loud!" I exclaimed, rescuing him from his own demise. "I wish you'd let me tie those pesky things in a knot on top of your head before you hurt yourself."

I swear he looked annoyed with the suggestion.

Laughing, I released him back to his sniffing and we continued on our way. The previous night's rain had tempered the humidity and brought a fresh crispness to the air. Perfect conditions for a long, mind-clearing walk. I made my way past our barn and toward the south ridge, the highest point of our land. From here I knew I'd have one of the best views of our orchards.

As I moved along, I suddenly got an antsy feeling—a feeling I remembered well from growing up on the farm. I'd felt it nearly every spring. Especially after a long winter when the orchard lay dormant and chores dwindled, making my muscles hunger for physical labor and my mind crave the feeling of accomplishment that came with putting in a full day's work. Which made me realize that even though I hadn't always appreciated it, growing up in a hardworking farming family was a blessing. My experiences in my youth had served me well in my career as a humanitarian. No matter the crisis, I could always hold my own. That very same grit and determination was just the thing my family needed to carry them through this current crisis.

In the spring, the abundance of pink blossoms would make the south ridge vista breathtaking, but even now as I worked my way to the top and took in the rolling green acres with their rows of sharply pruned trees, I was caught off guard by its beauty. A sense of pride overcame me. This was my family's land. Land my great-grandparents purchased with nothing more than borrowed money and a prayer for a better life. I couldn't begin to imagine the resolve and courage it took to break through the spring sod and plant an orchard that wouldn't even produce its first fruit for three to five years. Or the toil and sweat compiled by the next three generations who tended the trees with passion, hope and sometimes even despair.

I inhaled deeply, the smell of warm earth flowing through my nostrils and bringing back memories of seasons past. Whether I wanted to admit it or not, my heart was entrenched in this land. "I'm staying," I whispered, reaffirming out loud what I'd already subconsciously known for the last few days—I'd do just about whatever it took to make sure this farm remained in the family for generations to come.

At the sound of my voice, Roscoe came over and stood next to me, whapping his tail in the dirt. I looked down and he rolled over for a belly rub. *Silly pup!* I quickly squatted down and, suddenly, a sharp crack rang through the air. A gunshot? Instinctively I crouched lower, covering my head while Roscoe pressed against me, whimpering. Was someone shooting at me?

We huddled there for a few seconds before another shot rang out. Then another. This time, I could tell the sounds were coming from across the orchard. Slowly unwinding, I dared a peek over the fields. In the distance, I saw a cloud of blue smoke, heard another loud crack, and finally recognized it as the sound of backfire. Then I heard the rumbling of an engine cranking to life. I took off down the hill, the smell of burnt fuel stinging my nostrils as I neared the old irrigation pump.

"Hey, there, young lady!" Joe called out. He was standing by the holding pond watching to see if the pump was extracting water. "I think I've got it goin' again. Yup," he added, running around the pump house to examine the first stretch of drip lines. "It's pumpin'."

I joined him under a row of trees, bending over to get a closer look at the long line of black hose running along the base of each tree. When working properly, our system delivered intermittent drips of water that provided a slow but steady supply of moisture directly to the root zone. Looking around now, I could see where several of the damaged lines were allowing too much water to pass through. "We'll have to turn off the flow to a few of these lines until I can get them replaced," I told Joe.

He looked up from petting Roscoe and nodded. We started walking the rows together, Roscoe tagging close to Joe's heels as we turned off specific pressure valves, cutting the water to the damaged lines. By the time we were done, my back and legs ached from trudging along the rows. Even my well-worn boots chaffed along the back of my heel. "Thanks for your help, Joe." I shifted uncomfortably, my damp shirt sticking to my back. I scanned the area for Roscoe, and noticed him lapping at some water that'd gathered under one of the lines.

"How 'bout you?" Joe asked, eyeing the dog and then me. "Need a little somethin' to cool you down?" He motioned across the pond toward his cabin. Despite the heat and hard work, Joe, I noticed, was looking no worse for wear.

My mouth felt like cotton, but I wasn't sure what Joe was offering would fix that. What sounded good was a whopping big glass of iced tea. "Think I'll pass this time. I have a few things to do up at the house." His face fell, making me feel bad for declining his offer. Surely it was lonely for him living out here by himself. I thought back to what Hattie had told me and that little niggle of suspicion came back. "Joe?" I started, unsure of how he'd take my prodding. "I heard what happened to Tucker. I hadn't realized he was killed up at the mill."

Joe turned away, his body seeming to shrink as he gazed out over the fields. Instantly, I regretted the pain I'd brought by opening old wounds. I started trying to soothe things over. "I'm sorry, Joe. I shouldn't have asked."

He flicked a glance my way and shook his head. "No. It's true. My boy was killed up at the mill last year." He pulled a hanky from his overalls and wiped down his forehead. Finally meeting my eyes, he went on to explain. "An accident with one of the machines."

My heart went out to him and I reached over to touch his shoulder. "When accidents like that happen, there's usually an investigation. Sometimes the court awards the family compensation."

His bobbed his head. "They looked into it. Said my boy was at fault."

"Tucker? But how?"

"Drinkin', they said. But I don't believe it for a minute. Sure, he liked to partake a little, but never before work. Tucker was a good boy." He wiped at his face again. "Just twenty-two when I lost him." This time his voice caught and he turned away, lifting his hand to indicate the conversation was done. "Gonna head back to my place for a spell. I'll check on that tractor this afternoon."

Chapter 14

Georgia Belle Fact #024: Sweating is for our sweet tea glasses; we Southern Belles glisten.

By the time Roscoe and I made our way back to the house, my hair was plastered to my head and my T-shirt clung to me for dear life. I could hardly wait to get inside and shower, but as I approached the porch, I noticed Hawk's bike parked off to the side of the house, under the shade of a large magnolia. *Shoot!* All I wanted was a hot shower at the moment. Probably, he was in the den talking to Ray. If I was quiet, perhaps I could sneak in and get in a quick shower before having to face them.

I scooped up Roscoe and cradled him close to my chest. "Shh," I told him. "Not a peep!" Tiptoeing, I took the porch steps as quietly as I could, hopping over the third one, because I knew it would creak under my weight—a lesson I'd learned the hard way during my teen years after trying to sneak back into the house after breaking curfew. However, even though I'd successfully avoided the creak, the problem of the squeaky screen door loomed before me. So, as slowly as possible, I opened it just enough to slip between the screen door and the frame. Successful, and cradling Roscoe closely, I then started inching open the main door.

"Hey! I've been looking for you."

I started and looked up to see Ray watching me from inside the front room. Sighing, I pushed the door open the rest of the way and stepped inside, a wonderful rush of cold air greeting me.

His hound nose kicking in, Roscoe sensed his master, howled and dug his claws into my arms. "Ouch! Easy, boy!" I bent over and released him, watching him take off in a sniffing frenzy. Then, turning back to Ray, I asked, "Hey, Ray. Thought you were heading back to Perry today. Something up?"

"I decided to stay an extra day. Probably have to head back tomorrow, though." He motioned toward the den. "You might as well hear the latest news on the case. Hawk's back there. I'm just heading into the kitchen for some drinks. Looks like you could use something. You're glistening."

I laughed at his use of one of Mama's terms. Contrary to all theories of human science, my mama had never sweated a day in her life. Me, on the other hand . . . Well, I didn't glisten, sparkle or even get dewy. I got downright sweaty. I sighed. Just one more thing that set me apart from my true Southern Belle roots. "Sure, I'll take an iced tea." I trudged toward the den, tugging and shaking my shirt dry on the way. "Hello, Hawk," I said, plopping down with a thud in the chair next to him. Roscoe was already prancing on top of his lap, planting big, sloppy puppy kisses all over his cheeks. I folded my arms across my chest to ward off a sudden chill brought on by the combination of my damp clothes and the fan circulating overhead, and watched as master and dog got reacquainted.

Ray finally came in with the drinks. "You were up and out early this morning," he commented, handing me my tea.

I guzzled down half the glass before speaking. "Joe got the pump up and running in the south orchard, but a lot of the drip lines are bad, so we spent half the morning shutting off valves."

Ray seemed pleased. "At least the pump is running again.

That's a major accomplishment." He paused, handing Hawk his drink before settling behind the desk. "We've made some progress, too."

"That's right," Hawk started. He lowered Roscoe to the floor and told him to sit. I scowled as the little scamp obeyed Hawk with grateful eyes but had failed to sit even once on my command. "We met with the sheriff this morning and found out a few things."

"Like what?"

Ray spoke up. "For starters, the lab wasn't able to find any prints on the scarf. Looked like it'd been wiped clean."

"No prints? Not even Ida's prints?"

"None," Hawk said. "But the real news is that the sheriff's finally looking into other possible suspects."

"Finally! Who'd she add to her suspect list?" Leaning over, I snatched a piece of junk mail to set my glass on, then leaned back and rubbed at the goose bumps forming on my arms.

Ray folded his hands on the desk blotter. "Hawk checked into the mill. It seems Millicent Wakefield does take over now that her husband's out of the picture. So, you were right."

"Did you tell Maudy about the payoff in the alley yesterday?" I asked, noticing a smirk lurking on Hawk's face. "What?"

"A payoff?"

My eyes darted between Ray and Hawk. "Well, what else would you call it?"

Ray cleared his throat. "We can't really call it anything without further proof. It's hard telling what might have been in that envelope."

I stood, a bit tired of the conversation and really needing a hot shower. "I see. But you did mention it to her, right?"

Ray nodded. "Yes, we did. She said she'd look into it. But, before you take off, there's something else you should know."

I could sense it was something bad, by the way Ray's back stiffened. I glanced toward Hawk, who seemed to be studying the floor. "What is it?"

Ray let out a long breath and started running his hands

through his hair until it stood on end. "Someone vandalized Millicent Wakefield's car last night."

"A Mercedes," Hawk threw out. "An expensive one."

The first thing that jumped to mind was Laney Burns and retaliation for the casserole dump. I started to tell Ray, but his next revelation stopped me short.

"A bottle of Peach Jack was opened and dumped inside the vehicle," he added.

My mind whiplashed back to Hollis. Peach Jack: his drink of choice. "Oh, no! Prints?"

Hawk shook his head. "Wiped clean."

"Is Maudy going to arrest him?" I thought of Ida. This was going to put her over the edge.

"Fortunately, there's not enough evidence," Ray said. "Without prints, she really can't tie the bottle to Hollis. But it does look bad. Just one more thing stacked against him."

I didn't want to believe that Hollis would be that stupid. Then again, there was that empty bottle of Peach Jack. Had Hollis transferred his anger from Ben Wakefield to Millicent, the new owner of the mill? "Do you think maybe he . . ." I started.

Ray held up his hand. "Already talked to him about it. He says he didn't have a thing to do with it. Still . . ." He shrugged.

I finished his thought out loud. "Still, he's been drinking a lot lately." After accomplishing so much out in the orchard that morning, I'd come back to the house feeling encouraged and full of hope. With this latest news, it felt as if that hope was being sucked right out of me. I really couldn't stand to hear any more, so I excused myself, thinking a hot shower might restore my positive perspective.

A half hour later, I bounced back downstairs feeling refreshed but hungry. I was planning on running to the diner for some dunch—my term for late lunch and early dinner—and to grab the jars of preserves I'd left behind the day before in the wake of the casserole fiasco. Only my bounce fell flat when I reached the bottom of the steps and saw Hawk sprawled out on the front room floor, roughhousing with Roscoe.

"Hey," he said from the floor. "I forgot to thank you for taking such good care of my buddy."

"You're welcome." I looked around. "Where's Ray?"

"He went into town. Something about checking on Ida."

"Good." I hesitated, not really wanting to get involved in much more conversation. I was starving and really needed to get to the diner before it closed. "I'm heading into town myself to run a few errands," I hedged, glancing suggestively toward the door.

Taking the hint, he stood and brushed off his jeans. After bending back over to give Roscoe one last scratch behind the ears, he walked toward the door and held it open for me. I adjusted my shoulder bag and motioned for him to go ahead, so I could lock up the place.

He started down the porch first, stopping on the top step. When he turned back toward me, his head was level with mine. "You know," he started in his easy drawl. "Hollis is lucky to have you as a sister-in-law."

I was taken aback, a little flattered and confused all at the same time. I'd never really thought of myself as a good sister-in-law to Hollis. We'd more or less tolerated each other over the years. Still, it was a nice thing for Hawk to say. Actually, put the compliment together with the fact that we were standing not more than a foot apart, his blue eyes boring into mine, the whole moment was more than nice; it was unnerving. I gulped. "You think so? Why's that?"

He continued, his attitude nonchalant although his intense gaze never left my face. "Despite the fact that everyone in town is against him, you're still on his side. Both you and Ray. I envy that."

Did he say 'envy'? Everything in my life was a mess; what was there to envy? I scrunched my brow. "I don't understand."

"That's just the point. You don't even understand what there is to envy. All this comes so naturally to you and your siblings."

I shook my head, still not getting it. "All what?"

"Loyalty. Your loyalty to each other," he explained. "It's rare to find people so willing to go to bat for you in a time of crisis. Especially given the fact that Hollis hasn't always made the best decisions." He started ticking off points. "You know what I'm talking about. The drinking, womanizing, gambling the family's nest egg . . . Most people would give up on the guy. Actually, they'd probably be glad to see him go to prison just so they could get him out of their lives. But not you and Ray. Y'all just keep on doing whatever you can to help him."

I'd never thought of things quite that way. And the fact that Hawk did left me quite speechless. Maybe I'd misjudged him. Did he actually have a sensitive side buried under all that tight denim and leather? It made me wonder what might have happened all those years ago if I'd just told him about the—

"Why are you looking like that?" he asked.

I could feel my eyes widen. Mama always did say I should never play poker. "Like what?"

"I don't know. You suddenly had an odd look on your face. Is there something going on with your family I should know about?"

I immediately cleared my expression. Mama was right. I was an open book. "No. Nothing at all." The sound of crunching gravel interrupted us. I looked over Hawk's shoulder, surprised to see Cade's truck coming down the driveway.

"Looks like you've got company. I'll catch up with you later." He skipped down the steps. By the time Cade parked his truck, Hawk had already crossed to the magnolia tree and kick-started his bike. From inside the house, Roscoe let out a long, mournful bay.

Cade slowly walked my way, one eye on Hawk as he thundered down the drive. "Who was that?"

"The investigator Ray hired. Dane Hawkins. Calls himself Hawk. I would have introduced you, but as you can see, he's not much on manners."

Cade came up the steps and stood by me. "That's the investigator?" He stared after the gravel dust left behind from Hawk's bike. "He rides a motorcycle?"

I exhaled. "Yup. Guess he likes to stay inconspicuous." I glanced at Cade, but he seemed to have missed my sarcasm.

Instead, he stared longingly down the drive, watching the last specks of dust dissipate from Hawk's quick retreat. "I've always wanted one of those. Asked for a dirt bike for Christmas once."

"Oh really? Didn't you get it?"

"Heck no! Are you kidding? My folks thought it'd be too dangerous. Said I'd probably kill myself." He hesitated for a second, obviously searching his memories. "That's okay, though. They got me a really nice shotgun instead."

I did a double take, chuckling at the irony of his statement, then realized he wasn't joking. Of course, once I reconsidered what he was saying, it did make sense. Around these parts, most kids learned how to shoot right along with reading and writing. "It's good to see you, but what brings you all the way out here?" I asked.

He held up his hand. "Hold on." He jogged back to his truck and extracted a heavy box. "To bring these by," he said, struggling to balance the box as he ascended the porch steps. "Your preserves. Get the door, will ya?"

I skipped ahead and held the door open. "My preserves?"

"Yeah. Went into the diner for some coffee first thing this morning and Ginny said you'd left them there. I knew I was going to be out this way, so thought I'd bring them by for you."

I followed him through the house and to the kitchen where he slid the box onto the counter. "Well, that's so sweet of you. Thank you, Cade."

He turned back to me. "No problem. Hope they didn't

get too hot in my truck. I had to run a load of supplies to a
new job I'm doing down the road." He reached down and
scratched between Roscoe's ears. "Hello there, boy."

I peered over the side of the box, a sense of pride welling
inside me. Silly that I'd feel so happy about a few jars of
preserves. "I'm sure they're fine. Speaking of jobs, how
much do I owe you for the roofing supplies?"

He tapped the back pocket of his jeans. "I've got the list
right here, just haven't had time to tally it up yet. I'm about
starved, though, so what you say we head to the diner and
discuss it there. I'll buy."

His proposition flung me into an immediate eternal
debate. Was it really a good idea to go to lunch with Cade?
Something had shifted with us since I returned: sly looks,
little sparks, bated innuendos and even some heated emotions. Truth was, there'd been more than just a little innocent
flirting going back and forth between us, but so far that was
simply all it had been, just flirting. I sensed, however, that
Cade wanted more to come of it. Was he thinking of this
lunch as a date? And, if I said yes, would I be giving the
impression that I was ready to take things to the next level?

He cleared his throat, bringing me back to focus. "Make
up your mind, Nola." He glanced at his watch. "I'm about
starved, and the diner closes at four, remember?"

My rational voice kicked in, along with my growling
stomach, and overpowered my doubts. Certainly, if we were
going to discuss business, it really wasn't a date. "Sure." I
shrugged. "Why not? But I'll buy my own," I added.

"Suit yourself," he replied, a temporary flash of triumph
showing in his eyes. He motioned for me to lead the way. "We'll
take my truck. I've got to head back this way anyway."

Asking him to wait, I ran back inside to make sure Roscoe
had enough food and water before heading out to the truck.
Once again, I found myself removing a stack of papers from
the passenger seat. "Is this your truck or your office?" I teased.

"A mess, isn't it?" He pulled from our drive and onto the

main road, one hand up on the dash keeping a clipboard of papers from sliding to the floor.

"You always were a slob." I'd remembered visiting the McKennas' house as a kid, always amazed at the contrast between Hattie's ultra-organized room and Cade's room, which usually looked like a tornado had just hit.

He laughed, his eyes sliding across the cab to me. "What can I say? Old habits die hard."

"Yes, they do," I agreed, gazing out the window. I was watching peach orchards and pecan groves roll by, paired together like siblings: the looming pecans, standing straight and tall, towering over the smaller, burgeoning peach trees, which, if not sharply pruned and restrained, would grow rampantly wild. Sort of like me and my own siblings. And it was pretty easy to guess which one of us would be considered the wild-growing peach tree. Especially if they knew about *all* the things I'd done that summer before leaving. "Joe got the pump up and running," I commented, trying to keep my mind off the past and on more important, present-day matters. "He's supposed to be working on the tractor this afternoon."

"Your daddy will be happy about that."

"Yup. I wonder if he'll be happy about my plans for selling peach products."

I kept my gaze averted, but I could feel Cade glancing my way as he spoke. "I'm sure he's always proud of you, Nola. No matter what you're doing. But don't expect him to be enthusiastic about coming back to a new enterprise loaded onto him. He's got his hands full, just trying to keep up with the farm. Like I was telling you before, I can't see him adding an Internet business to the mix."

He was sure right about that. My daddy wouldn't take well to an Internet business. He still kept most of the farm's records in an old ledger book. "You know," I went on, "Margie Price over at the Sunny Side Up wants to buy our preserves for her guests. And Ginny said she'd carry them, too." I continued to explain my thoughts for marketing locally.

"I'm thinking there's small towns all around here that have places like the diner where we could pitch our products. Really, if you think about it, Macon's not all that far and there's tons of opportunities up there."

"I agree. Just don't go getting your hopes up that your parents are going to be able to keep up with all that. Making the product is only the start. Then there's the initial contacts to make and constant resupplying afterwards."

We were passing by several white clapboard houses that bordered the edge of town. An old man sitting on a lawn chair under the branches of a shade tree raised his hand and tossed us a slow wave. Cade was right. I'd known all along that my parents wouldn't—couldn't—do what it took to get our farm back on firm financial grounds. What was it they said about teaching new tricks to . . . Well, perhaps that wasn't the best saying for this particular situation. But I'd already realized there was only one way this would work: if I stayed on to see this thing through. It had been admitting it, and then committing to it, that was the hard part. "I thought I'd stay. See to it myself," I blurted out.

"What?" Cade glanced over his shoulder and swerved to the side of the road. Hitting the brakes and throwing the truck into neutral, he turned in his seat and faced me. "Did you just say you're staying in Cays Mill?"

The look on his face made me laugh. "Yup. That's what I'm saying."

He tipped his head back and let out a little whoop. "That's great!" Then, calming a little, he turned back to his serious self. "But what about your job? And I thought you couldn't stand it here. Too boring and backwards for you."

I held up my hand, still laughing. "That's not exactly what I said! It was your interpretation. And about my job . . ." I sighed. "Well, it's a long story." I pointed back to the road. "Let's get to the diner and talk about it over lunch. I'll tell you all about it, but I swear, I'm going to pass out if I don't get something in my stomach soon."

"Sure thing!" His head bobbed up and down as he maneuvered back onto the road. "Have you told Hattie? She's going to be—" His voice was cut off by the sound of sirens screaming up behind us. Cursing, he swerved back to the side of the road again, making room for the sheriff's car. "Holy crud! We almost got creamed!"

Taking a deep breath, I tried to quiet the squall of adrenaline from the near miss. "That looked like Travis," I said, staring after the cruiser, which had already become just a white speck on the horizon. The sirens from the first vehicle had barely faded when we heard a second set coming from behind. The intensity of the wailing increased until finally another sheriff's cruiser appeared and whizzed past us so quickly that the sides of the truck shook. "And that was the sheriff."

"Both of them? Something big must be going on." Checking over his shoulder, he wrenched the truck back onto the road and punched the accelerator. I grabbed the little handle above the door and braced myself as we sped after the cruisers.

"What could it be?" I asked, adjusting my seat belt, which had automatically cinched up on the first wild curb. Cade must have had a little NASCAR know-how buried in him, because he was keeping up well with the sheriff's car.

He clenched the wheel and shook his head. "No way of telling." We were headed away from town, toward the freeway.

Then I saw it. A black plume of smoke rising over the treetops. "Look!" I tapped my window. "It's coming from the direction of the mill."

My knees bounced nervously as he punched the gas and gained speed on a straight stretch of the road before whipping onto the mill turnoff. Then we slowed to navigate the twisty road leading uphill to the mill. As we grew nearer, the smoke grew thicker, and an acrid smell assaulted us.

"It must be bad," I said, but I had no idea how much of an understatement that was. As we turned onto the service road leading directly to the mill, large flames came into sight. Their peaks lashed out at the blue sky like angry lizard tongues. "Oh no!"

We parked back a ways and walked closer on foot. As we neared, I saw the blinking red lights of a couple fire engines through the smoke as yellow-clad volunteer firemen scurried with hoses. It also became apparent that things weren't as serious as we first thought. "It isn't the mill buildings. Looks like it's just a stockpile of wood on fire," I commented, my eyes scanning the bigger buildings for any sign of flames. Off to the right of the main building, a large group of workers was gathered. A middle-aged man with a clipboard scurried about, jotting down notes as he talked to several of the employees. "I hope no one's been hurt."

Cade nodded, craning his neck around as more cars pulled into the clearing behind us. After a few minutes, people ventured out of their vehicles and gathered to watch the spectacle, some on top of their car hoods, lying back and watching the scene as if it was Friday night at the drive-in movie.

I spied Ginny and hurried over to her, Cade right behind me. "Ginny!" I gave her a quick hug. "Can you believe this?"

She frowned. "No. I left Sam to finish up while I came up to see what was happening." She shook her head. "Thank heavens it isn't the mill itself!"

I turned my gaze back to the scene, watching as the firemen kept their hoses steady against the flames. A smaller crew of men was busy hosing down adjacent stacks of wood in hopes of preventing the fire from spreading. Fortunately, it looked like the responders were starting to get things under control.

I thought back to what Ray had said earlier that morning about someone vandalizing Millicent Wakefield's car. Could it be this fire was started on purpose, too? Did someone have it out for Wakefield Lumber? Of course, my mind instantly flashed to Floyd Reeves. Scanning the grounds again, I now paid more attention to faces in the crowd, searching for Floyd. He wasn't there. Who I *did* see, though, was Millicent.

Excusing myself, I broke away from Ginny and Cade and

pushed through the crowd until I reached Millicent. She was standing all alone, watching intently as the firemen worked.

"Millicent?" I said, approaching from behind. She turned and glanced my way, but didn't bother to answer. Instead she tightened her lips, folded her arms across her chest and turned back to watch the fire.

"I'm so sorry, Millicent," I persisted, coming up alongside her.

She shot me a cold look, but I continued. "You must be in shock. First Ben, then your car and now this . . ."

Her expression loosened a bit. "You heard about my car?"

"Yes, and I can't believe someone did that to you."

"Probably that crazy nail woman."

I didn't respond to that. Of course, Laney would be the first person that jumped to mind for her, and had been originally for me, too, but I knew the police suspected Hollis, so I thought it was best to just let the whole car vandalism issue drop.

Then the sound of applause arose from the crowd behind us, as the firemen successfully put out the last of the flames. She glanced back and scowled. "Sickos. Treating this like some sort of source of entertainment."

I nodded toward a group of employees that had gathered outside the mill. Frances Simms was buzzing about asking questions and taking pictures. "At least it looks like no one was hurt."

She brought both hands to her face and rubbed her cheeks. "That's true. Thank goodness no one was injured. Still, this is a nightmare. Like you said, someone doing all these terrible things to me."

I offered a sympathetic nod before her words fully sank in. I narrowed my eyes. Did she, too, think this mill fire might be deliberate? Or know it was?

I glanced back at the now-smoldering woodpile just in time to see one of the firemen poking at the ashes with a long-handled shovel. "Hey, Sheriff!" he called out, scooping something out of the ashes. "Take a look at this!" He raised the shovel in the air, revealing a burned-out metal gas can.

A gasp arose from the crowd, followed by the breakout of low murmuring. Frances Simms shot out of nowhere, camera clicking away. They all knew there was only one reason for a gas can to be in a woodpile—arson!

The exited buzz of the crowd died down momentarily until something else captured their attention. It was Maudy Payne, who'd been kicking at the ground around the burn site. Suddenly she bent down and picked up another item. "Well, I'll be," she declared, grasping it carefully with her handkerchief and raising it into the air for all to see, or perhaps for Frances to get a good shot for the next issue of the *Cays Mill Reporter*. "An empty Peach Jack bottle. Why, who might that belong to?"

Judging by the instantaneous bending of heads and excited whispering, the crowd thought they knew the answer to that question. By the looks of things, the rumor mill had just kicked into high gear. And, unfortunately, Hollis was going to be ground to pulp by its fiercely spinning axle.

Chapter 15

Georgia Belle Fact #004: Sisters are like two different flowers from the same garden. But Georgia Belle roots are always connected—try to uproot one and you'll have the other to contend with, too.

"Tell me again how you plan to use Mama's recipes to save our family farm?" Ida was sitting across from me at her kitchen table, Savannah and Charlotte flanking either side. We'd covered the table with an oilcloth and laid out every art medium possible: markers, crayons, colored pencils, even finger paints. The idea was to have the girls brainstorm a cute logo for Harper Farm's new line of peach products.

Biting my lip, I fought hard to keep my patience with Ida. I'd already explained my plans to her a couple of times, but her mind seemed to be elsewhere. "I told you all about it, Ida. Weren't you listening?"

She picked up a stack of scratch paper and began fanning herself. "Of course I was. I'm just a bit distracted, that's all." She glanced at the girls and drew in a deep breath, her eyes roaming over the tabletop. "Don't you think this peach business thing is a whole lot of trouble to put yourself through for something that might not even work?"

My shoulders sank. "I was hoping you'd believe in me, that's all. Maybe show some support."

She stopped fanning and stared at me for a couple beats. "Why, of course I believe in you! You're my sister, aren't ya?"

I smiled. "Good. Because your girls are the next generation of Harpers, after all. Don't you think it's worth trying something, anything at all, to preserve their heritage?"

The girls' heads popped up at the mention of their names. "Mama, what's a heritage?" Savannah asked, her blue eyes wide with question.

Ida brushed a strand of hair out of her daughter's eyes and tapped a finger on her freckled nose. "A heritage is like a big ol' present your parents and grandparents work their whole life to give to you."

Charlotte sat up a little straighter. "A present?"

Ida chuckled. "Yes, darlin'. And, if you ask me, you girls are lucky to have an auntie who's willing to work so hard to make sure you get that present one day." She cast a brief but warm smile my way and, just like that, I knew Ida was on board with my ideas. Still, I could tell something was eating away at her. Something she didn't want to bring up in front of the girls.

"Let's see what we've got here," I said, reaching across the table for a picture Charlotte had drawn. It was one of those classic kid pictures where the horizon cut straight down the middle of the paper, dividing the green grass and the blue sky. In the center was a very good copy of the farm's large red barn with a grinning sun, complete with sunglasses, hanging over its roof. "Well, isn't this the sweetest!" I said, fussing over her drawing.

"That ain't all that good," Savannah piped up, eyeing the picture from across the table.

"Isn't," Ida corrected.

"Isn't," Savannah echoed, sliding her own paper my way. "Look at mine."

I picked hers up—a simple drawing of a large, somewhat lopsided peach with a huge green leaf attached at the top—and gave it an equal amount of fussing. "Well, look at this. I don't think I've ever seen such a beautiful peach. Why, it looks good enough to eat." I pressed my lips to the paper and made gobbling sounds, bringing on a raucous round of giggles from the girls.

Charlotte's little voice cut across the table. "Do you like mine better?"

"Don't be silly," Savannah said, hushing her sister. "What does a barn have to do with peaches? Right, Auntie Nola?"

I paused, staring down at both pictures, feeling the heat of Ida's glare bearing down on me. My brilliant idea of the girls coming up with a cute little logo was looking less brilliant all the time. Suddenly, an idea struck me. "You know what, girls? I'm going to use both." I scrounged up my own crayon and paper and went to work sketching out my idea. When I finished, I held up a giant peach with a smiley face. "See? It's Savannah's peach with the smiley face from Charlotte's sun. It's perfect! When people see it, they'll feel so happy, they'll want to buy up tons of peachy things."

Whoops and cheers boomed out in stereo, until Ida threw up her hands, clasping her ears and shouting, "Enough! Settle down, now, ya hear."

The room fell into instant silence, my nieces looking stunned at their mama's outburst. It wasn't like Ida to lose her patience. I eyed her closely, noticing just how drawn and sallow her face looked. She'd gone back to fanning herself again. "I'm sorry." She shook her head. "I'm just having a bad day, that's all."

"Why don't you two run along and play in your rooms. Let your mama and I talk a little," I told the girls. But they stayed rooted, hesitant to leave their mother. "It's okay. Your mama just needs a little rest. Go on, now. Go play. I'll pick up this mess."

The idea of not having to clean up must have been enough of an enticement, because they jumped right out of their seats and scurried out of the kitchen. "What's going on?" I asked Ida as soon as they were out of sight.

Ida busied herself getting us some tea. "That pesky Frances Simms again. She called here this morning and was asking all sorts of questions."

"Questions? Like what?" I was trying to cram crayons back

into the box, ending up with about ten extra that didn't seem to fit. Why couldn't someone invent a better crayon box, anyway?

"All about that fire up at the mill. You know they found a bottle of Peach Jack in the weeds right by where the fire was started?"

I nodded but kept quiet. Of course I'd known. I'd seen the sheriff find it, but I was hoping Ida wouldn't hear of it so soon. Glancing over, I watched how slowly she moved about the kitchen, getting ice and pouring tea. All this stress couldn't be good for her. Or her baby.

"Then there's that car thing," she went on. "Ray told me all about it. You heard, right? Someone vandalized Millicent Wakefield's car."

Grabbing the dishcloth, I went to work on scrubbing marker off the tablecloth. "Yeah, I heard."

"Well, they found a bottle of Peach Jack there, too."

"That doesn't mean anything. Lots of people drink Peach Jack." Not as much as Hollis, but that was better off left unsaid.

"Well, anyway. That call from Frances got me all worked up again. Just when I was feeling better about things, too." She passed me a glass of tea and we both sat down again. "You don't suppose she's going to paint an ugly picture of all this in the paper, do you?"

I cringed. It was Tuesday. Time for another issue of the *Cays Mill Reporter.* "What can she say? There's no evidence linking Hollis to either one of those crimes." A ray of sun floated through the kitchen window and landed on the tablecloth, highlighting a few streaks of finger paint I'd missed. I went back to the sink for the dishrag, while Ida cleared the rest of the art supplies and picked up our empty tea glasses.

"Oh, you don't know Frances. She's got a way with words, you know. She may not say anything directly slanderous, but believe me, there will be some sort of innuendo. I swear, she has it out for Hollis." She started rinsing the glasses. "I wish she'd just stay out of our business for a couple days; I think Hollis would do much better. He's already come up with a plan to try to salvage some of the money he's lost on this lumber deal."

My muscles stiffened. "A plan? What type of plan?"

"Oh, I don't know." She hesitated, staring off to the side and chewing her lip as she tried to recall the details. "I think it had something to do with the same old lumber deal." She shrugged and pointed to the side of her head. "Sorry. When Hollis starts talking business, it just goes in one ear and out the other. I just know he was feeling better, kind of back in control again, if you know what I mean, and that's all I really gathered."

That was probably true. Ida was more in tune with the latest fashion magazines than she was her husband's business. Not that she wasn't smart enough to understand the banking business, but her priorities were aligned differently: family over finances, love over labor and, above all, femininity at all times. I reached over and gave her shoulders a quick squeeze. "Don't worry about it. I'm sure Hollis has everything figured out." Only I was worried plenty. What was Hollis up to now? And why, with all this going on, was he jumping right back into things? From what I'd heard around town, folks weren't too happy with him. Even if he was exonerated of all charges in Ben Wakefield's murder, the board of directors might still call for his resignation. And probably rightfully so. His drinking alone would be reasonable cause, not to mention putting the bank's life on the line with such a single and huge investment in a company whose bottom line was already suffering. Still, what a blow that would be to Ida and the girls.

I gathered up my pictures and headed for the door. "Girls, I'm leaving!" My call was answered with a sudden flurry of footsteps and an onslaught of hugs and kisses that quickly dissipated as Ida flipped on their favorite afternoon cartoon. I paused by the door and watched as she settled on the sofa, a girl nestled on either side, snuggling in for a mid-afternoon rest. Good, a little R & R was exactly what Ida needed.

• • •

Hoping to get the labels done by Friday, I drove straight to town and found a spot a few doors down from the print shop. Getting there meant I'd have to pass by the newspaper building and risk running into Frances Simms. So, as a precaution, I hunched my shoulders and hid my face behind my paperwork, sneaking as quickly as I could past Frances's office. I would have made it undetected, too, if it weren't for the man who came out carrying a large stack of newspapers. Curiosity made me stop. I dropped my guard and asked, "Is that today's edition?"

"Sure is. Hot off the press." He picked one off the top and handed it to me with a flourish. "Here. Be my guest. You'd best get one now; these are going to be hot sellers."

I thanked him and quickly unfolded the paper. The headline practically jumped off the page, "Hollis Shackleford Released on Bail." The article was accompanied by a picture of Hollis that must have been taken at a recent black-tie dinner because he was wearing a tuxedo and standing at the head of a table making a toast. On the table in front of him, as plain as day, was a bottle of Peach Jack. My eyes then landed on the headline of the article right below it: "Sheriff Seeks Peach Jack Drinker in Connection to New Crimes." I squeezed my eyes shut, so mad I could have kicked the brick wall in front of me. When I opened my eyes, I scanned that article, which cinched the noose over Hollis's neck as neatly as if mentioning him by name, describing how Peach Jack bottles were discovered at the scenes of Millicent's car vandalism and the fire at the mill.

All I could see was red, my pulse pounding. Even anyone who didn't know Hollis's drinking habits would now jump to the conclusion that he committed the other crimes. How dared Frances do this!

Storming into the newspaper office, I waved the crumpled newspaper in my hand. Immediately, Frances's head popped up from her desk. Her eyes—wide with surprise and magnified even wider by her heavy black-rimmed glasses—seemed grossly out of proportion with the rest of her birdlike features.

At the sight of her, my blood boiled even further. Frances must have been able to hear it bubbling because she immediately went into defensive mode. "Every word of those articles is factual, mind you. I take pride in delivering unbiased, impartial—"

"Impartial, my foot!" If I were brewing up a batch of Mama's peach preserves, I'd call my current state a full rolling boil. I pounded my fist on top of the paper. Frances about jumped out of her seat. "You know darn well that a picture is worth thousands of words. Slanderous, biased, *mean* words." I was so mad, I couldn't think straight. I gritted my teeth and let out a low growling sound, my southern upbringing preventing me from letting loose with the string of cusswords floating through my head.

I stood there growling, while she passively nodded, a little smirk tugging at the corners of her lips. "Well, as long as you're here," she started, reaching across her desk to realign a couple of pencils. "I have a few questions I'd like to ask."

My jaw dropped. The nerve of this woman!

"Like for starters," she continued. "Is it true that your brother-in-law ran an asset investigation on Wakefield Lumber? Because if he did, it's my theory that the results of that report are what sparked his anger and—"

"No comment!"

Frances's brow quirked above the rim of her glasses. "How about the rumors about the bank?"

"The bank?"

"That Hollis embezzled money."

"What! That's ridiculous!" I rubbed my suddenly aching temples. Yet another fine example of malarkey straight from the town's gossipmongers. I began reputing this latest rumor, but before I could get another word in, Frances went on firing questions like a Gatling gun, one right after another. Each question made me angrier than the one before, until finally, I'd had enough. "You know what your problem is, Frances? You've got a one-track mind."

Frances crossed her arms with a smug look. "Well, no one but Hollis had as much to lose by dealing with Wakefield."

I threw my arms in the air. "My point exactly! You never give a thought to who has the most to *gain*!"

Her smugness dissipated with a quiver of her brow, as if she might have missed something obvious. "Oh really. And who might that be?"

"Millicent Wakefield, that's who!"

Frances clamped her mouth shut.

I kept going. "After all, with her husband dead, she gains control of Wakefield Lumber. And good timing, too. Considering he was getting ready to divorce her. What's more, Laney Burns told me she saw Millicent in town the day Ben Wakefield was murdered!"

Frances leaned in, eyes gleaming. "Is that so?" She reached into her desk drawer and extracted a notepad and pen. Clicking the pen, she leaned forward again, headlines dancing in her eyes. "What else can you tell me?"

I bit my lip, regretting my outburst. That darned woman! She could get things out of me without even trying, it seemed. Knowing I had to tread carefully, or I'd end up in trouble for slander, or worse—arrested for interfering with Maudy Payne's case—I checked myself and chose my next words carefully. "All I was saying is that there's more than one way to look at this case and more than one suspect in it." I tried to backtrack.

Frances clicked her pen again and let it hover over the notepad. "Yes. Millicent Wakefield, to be exact. Are you saying she's got control of the mill now?"

I held up my hands. "*I'm* not saying it; that's pretty much a public fact."

"And Laney Burns saw her the day of the murder?"

I felt my knees weakening. "Did I say that?"

"Uh-huh."

Maudy Payne was going to throw me and my big mouth in jail—that was for sure. "That's just hearsay. Don't quote me on that." *Please don't quote me on that.*

Frances clicked her pen again and slapped the notebook closed, a gloating smile playing on her lips. "Well, thank you for stopping in, Nola. I do appreciate these new leads. You can be sure I'll put them to good use."

I'm sure you will.

Back outside, I stood stewing on the sidewalk, suspended between outrage and regret. Regret for my impulsive tirade, which was undoubtedly going to lead to trouble, and outrage that Frances had once again printed something that was going to harm my family's reputation. One look at today's headlines and everyone in town was going to dub Hollis as some sort of Jack of All Crimes. Peach Jack, that was. I tried to glom on to the slimmest sliver of hope that my unintentional feeding of this news shark might take her off Hollis's back. But from my experience with her so far, it was a false hope at best.

"You're looking fit to be tied." It was Hawk, who seemed to appear out of nowhere. Perhaps he was better at snooping than I first thought.

"Just got done talking to Frances Simms."

He squinted and cocked his head to one side.

"She runs the *Cays Mill Reporter*," I explained, shoving the crumpled paper his way. *Shoot, the man's here to investigate and isn't even aware who the culprit is that has the town so set against Hollis.* I took a deep breath, trying to calm myself down. After all, Hawk wasn't even from these parts. "Wait until you see this issue. The pictures she's printed practically string the noose right around Hollis's neck."

He glanced it over and gave a little shrug. Whether he expected it from any newspaper or expected Hollis deserved it, I couldn't tell. "You're right; that's pretty bad."

I shot him a withering look. "Yes, it is, and what exactly have you been doing to help his case? Anything?" *Besides gathering DNA samples from Laney Burns.*

His chin jutted out. "What? All of a sudden you have some sort of problem with the way I'm doing my job?"

No, not all of a sudden; all along, but I didn't say that. Instead I took a deep breath and held it for five counts before exhaling. "No, sorry. I'm just upset, that's all."

"Well, to answer your question, I was just in talking to the sheriff. Seems Floyd Reeves is nowhere to be found. The sheriff thinks he's headed back to Macon."

"Macon? That's where he's from?"

"According to Sheriff Payne, yes."

"Do you think his meeting with Millicent in the alley had anything to do with Ben's murder? Like maybe she paid Floyd to kill him?"

His gaze turned flat. "Could be. Or it could be nearly anything else. In the meantime, Payne is working on Hollis pretty heavy for that fire. A lot doesn't add up, though."

I could feel my brows furrow. "Like what?"

"What would Hollis have to gain by setting it? He's already under suspicion about the murder of the mill's owner, so arson at the mill only further points to him. He has nothing to gain."

Gain! Just like I'd pointed out to Frances, now much to my regret, there were other ways to look at things. "Millicent!"

"Huh?"

"Millicent has just taken over the mill and maybe found out it's in financial trouble. Maybe that payoff to Floyd was for him to set fire to the mill so she could collect insurance money. A woman like Millicent probably has no desire to run a mill, and this would be a perfect way to get her money out of it quick."

Again, Hawk offered no facial expression in response. I figured he was thinking it over, trying to ignore the fact that I'd come up with, once again, the kind of ideas that he should have been coming up with himself. Finally he said, "If it was arson, why start the fire during the middle of the day? Before the work shift was even over. When it would be easily detected. And a woodpile? That's not going to pay out anything."

I tilted my head and paused, mulling over his point. Okay, so maybe he was right. All those facts didn't add up to arson, at least not a smart plan for arson. Then again, I didn't have the impression that Floyd Reeves was overly smart. Another thought came to mind: maybe Millicent's motive wasn't to collect an insurance payout, but to frame Hollis for the murder she had Floyd commit for her in the first place. If that was the case, it would make sense to start the fire during the day, so it would be detected and put out before it spread too far and caused any real damage.

I was about to tell Hawk my new theory when I noticed him focusing on something over my shoulder. "Looks like your boyfriend's come looking for you again."

Glancing behind me, I saw Cade coming down the walk. I started to correct Hawk on the boyfriend reference, but he cut me off. "Catch ya later, Nola. I've got to hit the road. I'm heading up to Macon to try to track down Reeves. Ray thinks he's the key to Hollis's case. I should be back in a couple days." He turned and sauntered off just as Cade caught up to me.

"The investigator again?" he asked.

"Yup. He's leaving town for a couple days, chasing a lead." I detected a flash of some sort of emotion in Cade's eye. Relief? It was hard to tell and I really didn't want to put all that much thought into it anyway. I decided to change the topic. "So, what brings you into town?"

"Lunch, actually." We both turned our heads and glanced at the diner. I knew what was coming even before he asked, "Why don't you join me?" He swept his hand toward the diner and added, "We never did get there yesterday and we still need to discuss your bill."

"Sure, why not?" I relented as we took off across the square for Red's Diner.

• • •

The smell of hot meat and fried onions hit me as soon as we walked through the door. I surveyed the chalkboard inside the entrance. Today's special: panfried chicken, corn pone, field peas and lemon chess pie. A quick glance around at once told me the panfried chicken was popular. All the guys at the bar were gnawing on bones and racking up piles of crumpled napkins.

Ginny caught my eye and pointed us toward an empty booth in the back. We'd barely settled before she appeared and plunked two glasses of ice water in front of us. "Two specials?" she asked, turning the pages on her order pad and pulling a pen from behind her ear without even so much as a smile or a "hey y'all."

I hesitated, glancing over the menu.

"Don't bother with the menu," she snapped. "Just get the special. It's good. Look around. Everyone loves it." As if on cue, one of the men at the bar turned, waved a half-chewed bone my way and shot me a thumbs-up. Ginny put one hand on her hip and shook her shoulders at me. "See what I mean?"

I gulped. "Uh . . . okay, then. I'll have the special."

"Make that two specials and two iced teas," Cade added.

As soon as Ginny turned away, I leaned in and whispered, "Wonder why she's so cranky?"

"Beats me. Probably nothing." He shrugged and extracted a piece of folded paper from his back pocket and began scanning the columns of figures. Which just went to show how unobservant some men really were. Just watching Ginny as she maneuvered the diner, slopping coffee into cups and snatching up spent plates with a scowl, I could tell it wasn't "nothing." Something big was bothering her. I was double sure of it when she placed our order on the ticket spindle and spun it so hard I could feel the breeze halfway across the room. "I've tallied up the numbers for you," Cade was saying. "You made out pretty well, actually." He slid the paper across the table.

My eyes popped at the final figure. It was much lower than expected. "Are you sure? This doesn't seem like much."

"Most of the materials were scavenged from my leftover pile. I didn't have to purchase much."

"Yes, but your time."

He pointed toward the lower portion of the paper. "If you'll look at the bottom, you'll see I accounted for my labor separately."

My eyes scanned past the figures to the bottom of the paper, where I saw the words "Peach Festival" spelled out. I rolled my eyes and giggled. "Cade McKenna, you are insufferable!"

"That may be, but a deal's a deal." A slight upward turn of his lips hinted at the grin he was suppressing. But it soon faded when Ginny stomped back with our iced teas, slapping them down and turning on her heel without a word.

"Still think it's probably nothing?" I asked with raised brows as he mopped up the tea that'd sloshed over the table.

"Maybe something *is* bothering her."

"Ya think?" I rolled my eyes and scanned the room for a possible reason for Ginny's sour mood. A difficult customer? Overworked? I sipped at my tea and considered the possibilities. No, probably not anything work-related. Ginny had been waiting tables for years; she'd dealt with worse crowds than this with a smile on her face. It had to be something personal. Maybe a problem with one of their kids. Just having teenagers would be enough to send most people over the edge. Or problems with Sam? Naw. I'd never seen two people more suited for each other.

"What are you thinking?" Cade asked.

"I'm thinking I need to see what's going on with Ginny," I said, setting down my tea and excusing myself. Only I sat right back down when the door opened and Millicent walked in carrying a newspaper. She immediately homed in on the only open space—the booth right behind us.

Oh great. Who else has the paper already? Then it struck me that maybe the article was the reason behind Ginny's sudden shift in attitude? I glanced around nervously, wondering how quickly tongues would start wagging. I should probably call and warn Ida.

My eyes wandered back to Millicent as she passed by our booth. I tossed her a little wave as she passed by, but she barely looked my way. While she wasn't tuned in to her surroundings, her surroundings were definitely tuned in to her. Practically every head turned as she passed through the diner, her poured-on hot pink pants, fur-trimmed vest and metal-studded boots blazing a new trail in the Cays Mill fashion scene.

"Get ahold of that outfit," Cade commented, his eyes grazing her backside as she passed.

"Shh . . ." I pressed my fingers to my lips and fought to control a sudden onset of the giggles. I raised up on my tippy toes, risked a quick peek in her direction and saw her running her finger across the text of the paper's front-page article. Before I could glance to see Millicent's reaction, Ginny returned and plunked our plates down before us, her malevolent aura covering the area like a wet blanket on flames and pulling my attention away from Millicent altogether.

"Anything else?" she snarled, starting to turn away without waiting for a reply.

I reached out and snatched her hand, pulling her back. "Ginny, what is it? What's wrong?" *Did she read the headlines already? Maybe she decided she'd rather not associate with one of Hollis's family members?*

Her shoulders slumped. "What do you mean? Nothing's wrong."

I pressed for an answer. "Oh, come on. Something's going on. You're not yourself today."

She rotated her head and glanced around the room. When

she looked back I could see tears forming at the edges of her eyes. Her breath caught as she spoke. "You're right. Something has happened, but . . ." She swiped the back of her hand across her cheek. "Now's not a good time. I'll fill you in later." She offered a brave smile and headed over to take Millicent's order.

Cade immediately tore into his chicken, speaking between bites. "Wonder what that's all about. Seems like everyone's having their share of trouble lately."

"That's for sure," I agreed, feeling a bit better. It seemed her attitude had nothing to do with the newspaper headlines. Before I could even exhale with relief, however, my sense of solace was replaced with a sinking feeling. If not the article, then what? Ginny was one of the most upbeat, resilient people I knew. Something big must be happening for her to be so upset. And nothing could bring down my own mood faster than seeing a friend suffer. So, while the chicken was just the way I like it—tender-soaked in buttermilk and deep-fried in peanut oil until the perfectly seasoned skin crisped just right—I pushed it aside and opted for the immediate boost I knew the sugar-laden lemon chess pie would give.

Cade looked up, a corn pone between his fingers. "Dessert first?"

I filled my fork with a load of lemon filling and shrugged. "Why not? Life's short, right?" Pausing, I closed my eyes and let the smooth, cheese-like filling set on my tongue, the smidgen of sweet tartness giving me a familiar happy feeling. This was what I'd missed most during my travels—the down-home comfort that only true southern cooking could bring, like an elixir for the troubled soul. Forgetting myself, I let a little moan escaped through my lips.

"Good, huh?"

I opened my eyes to see Cade grinning from ear to ear. I swallowed hard, a hot blush stinging my cheeks. Luckily, Millicent's cell phone trilled from the next booth, cutting the embarrassing moment short.

"And why should I agree to meet with you?" she hissed over the phone. I strained to hear her side of the conversation over the constant din of clinking dishes and murmured conversation. "Oh yeah? What's in it for me? . . . Fine. . . . Yeah, I know the place. . . . Eight? Why so late?" She heaved an impatient sigh, listening intently to the other side of the conversation. Whoever she was talking to must have been convincing, because she finally relented. "Fine. I'll be there. But this better be good."

Cade and I exchanged a look, but with Millicent in earshot, we didn't risk commenting. Instead, Cade steered the conversation back to the Peach Festival, and after much bantering back and forth, he agreed to meet me first thing Saturday morning in front of Hattie's Boutique to help me get my booth set up. I, in turn, agreed to accompany him to the evening dance. As a long-standing tradition, the festival always concluded with a dance, held right out on the street in front of the stage—the same stage where the Peach Queen would be crowned and where our multitalented mayor, Wade Marshall, would be strumming along with his band, the Peach Pickers. I made a mental note to scrounge up my old cowboy boots and spend some time brushing up on my two-step.

The rest of our lunchtime conversation passed by with several awkward moments. Not because of our looming date—yes, I was willing to call it a date—but because my own reeling thoughts about the murder distracted me from the conversation. While Cade went on about some of his latest ideas for expanding his construction business, I kept thinking about the recent fire at the lumber mill and its connection to Ben Wakefield's murder. When he shifted the conversation to ask about things at the farm, I simply picked at my chicken and offered up a few short replies. Noticing my ambivalence, the poor guy even tried steering the conversation to more fun topics, like Hattie's newfound relationship with Pete Sanchez, but then my mind wandered to Millicent and Ben's marriage and whether or not their troubles might have contributed to his murder. Overhearing the suspicious snippets of Millicent's phone conversation had turned my mind back to the case and piqued my curiosity. Was something big coming up? Something related to the case? I knew just how to find out.

Chapter 16

Georgia Belle Fact #054: A Southern gal can never have too many pairs of cowboy boots.

"Tell me why we're here again?" Hattie and I were crammed into the front seat of her fuel-efficient compact, the most recent issue of the *Cays Mill Reporter* and a box of Moon-Pies between us. "Isn't this something your detective should be doing?"

"I told you already, he's out of town chasing down a suspect. And this is important. I overheard Millicent say she's meeting with someone tonight and I need to know who." We were parked in the shadows across the street from Millicent's front door. I swatted at mosquitoes as I spoke. It was stifling hot outside, but Hattie's car didn't have enough gas to close the windows and run the air. The Wakefield mansion, as it was known around town, was located on prime property overlooking the Ocmulgee River. Well, prime, that was, if you discounted the fact the often swampy river bottom was a like a breeding ground for hungry mosquitoes.

"And you based this on some phone conversation you overheard? Why, she could have been planning anything!"

She unwrapped her second MoonPie and used the wrapper to shoo the bugs away. "What if we're going to all this trouble just to find she was planning a surprise party for her mama or something?"

"Believe me, this is no surprise party. It's got something to do with Wakefield's murder; I'm sure of it."

Hattie scrunched her face and pointed at the paper. "Speaking of the murder. Could Frances have been any more obvious? Where'd she come up with that picture anyway?"

I shrugged. "I don't know. She must have had to dig deep to find it. I swear, Hattie, this town has Hollis tried and convicted already."

She patted my hand. "It'll all work out. It always does."

Spoken like a girl who's seen her own share of trouble.

She went on, changing the topic. "How are things at the farm?"

She'd hit on the one bright spot of the day. "Pretty good. Joe got the tractor fixed. He's going to start mowing the orchards tomorrow. Thought I'd head into the Mercantile tomorrow and order replacements for some of our irrigation lines. At this rate, things will be in tip-top shape by the time my parents return. And thanks to your wonderful brother, my bill for Joe Puckett's roof came in lower than I expected."

The corners of her lips turned upward at the mention of Cade. I could swear I saw a conniving gleam in her eye. "What are you wearing to the festival?"

My stomach flip-flopped. "I have no idea." Actually, I hadn't even given it a thought. My usual utility shorts and tank wouldn't quite pass muster with the Peach Festival crowd. "I'd been planning to stop by and pick out some more clothes, but with everything going on . . ."

"Don't mention it. I've got something in the shop that would be perfect. Just come by a little early and we'll get you fixed up." She snatched up my hand. "But don't count on me for fixing these nails. You'd better get over to the salon. You don't want to be countin' out bills with hands like these."

I frowned at my fingertips. She was right. My week-old manicure looked, well . . . a week old. Besides, ever since finding out about Millicent's car being vandalized, I'd been wanting to talk to Laney Burns again. Call it silly, but it just seemed like too much of a coincidence that the vandalism occurred directly after Millicent dumped a casserole over Laney's head. Knowing Laney, she wouldn't take well to someone mussing her hairdo. It must take a lot of effort to get it teased to that height.

"By the way," Hattie continued. "How's your sister holding up?" She pointed at the headline again. "All this can't be easy on her."

I hadn't been able to get ahold of Ida yet, but I could imagine the latest headlines, coupled with the damning photos, had sent her scurrying back to hermit status. A new sense of frustration enveloped me, as I thought about how stressed Ida looked last time we visited. All this couldn't be good for the baby. I started to express my worries to Hattie, when I became distracted by the Wakefields' garage door opening. A Mercedes-Benz, complete with custom-scratched pinstriping and a busted headlight, rolled down the drive. "There she is," I said, motioning for Hattie to follow.

"She's really bookin' it," Hattie replied, pulling away from the curve and punching the accelerator.

"Not too close. She'll see us," I warned, suddenly feeling like I was playing a part in a television detective show. "Wonder where she's heading?" Instead of making the turn toward town, Millicent turned onto the road leading toward the freeway.

"I don't know, but we may have to bail on this mission if she goes too far. My gas gauge needle's hit the red zone."

"Don't worry about it," I assured her. "This is one of those fuel-efficiency models, right?"

She mumbled something under her breath and made a sudden wild swerve. "Sorry; possum on the road," she explained as I peeled my death grip off the dashboard and swallowed a couple times to clear my heart out of my throat. We continued following Millicent's taillights for another couple miles until it dawned on me where we were heading—the Honky Tonk.

"Well, hey! This evening may turn out okay after all," Hattie surmised, after we'd watched Millicent disappear into the brightly lit roadhouse as we slowly cruised past her and found a parking spot.

I turned stiffly in my seat and watched Hattie tear through her pocketbook, searching for something. She seemed overly enthusiastic, considering the circumstances. The Honky Tonk? Certainly she remembered all the unfortunate events that'd transpired over the years at the rowdy roadhouse. There was that time in high school when we tried to pass on fake IDs and the bouncer called the cops—guess it wasn't too smart to use a Xeroxed copy of my mama's driver's license with my own picture transposed. The guy just couldn't believe I wasn't forty-two. Then there was the infamous wedding rehearsal party, when Handsy Hollis busted a move that would make every family get-together for decades seem unbearable. And . . . "You don't really want to go in there, do you?"

"What do you mean? Of course I do."

I shook my head. "Don't you recall what happened last time?"

She paused, one hand on the door handle, the other gripping a wad of one-dollar bills. She scrunched up her face. "No, I don't. What happened?"

I threw up my hands. "You ended up with a busted nose, that's what. Don't you remember? You were holding Bodacious's reins with one hand, your beer with the other, and had just let loose with an ear-shattering rebel yell when you slid over the bull's neck and ended up face-first in the sawdust?"

She rubbed at the tiny bump on the bridge of her nose and shook the bills my way. "Well, I'm not planning on getting on that bull again. This is for beer. Don't tell me you've forgotten about two-buck Tuesday? Besides, how we gonna know what Millicent is up to unless we venture inside? What better place than somewhere too crowded with people for her to notice us?"

She had a point, so I reluctantly clambered out of the car and followed her across the lot. Once inside, I wasn't sure what hit me first—the stale smell of beer and sweat or the ear-throbbing country lyrics booming from the jukebox. I practically had to yell to get Hattie to hear me. "Do you see where she went?"

She shrugged and headed toward the bar, her wad of bills clenched firmly in her hand. I stood my ground, scanning the crowd until I finally caught sight of a familiar blond head. Bingo. Millicent was in one of the back booths, deep in conversation, only I couldn't see who was sitting across from her. I moved toward the hall that led to the restrooms, where I hoped to get a better view and a little reprieve from the loud music.

"What are you doing here?"

I wheeled around to find myself staring into Laney Burns's raccoon-lined eyes. The extra eyeliner must have been what she considered her evening look. "Laney! How are you doing?" I couldn't stop my eyes from wandering upward toward her previously casserole-covered hair, a giggle rising in the back of my throat. Despite a poorly executed attempt to cover it with a cough, a couple of chuckles escaped.

"Y'all probably found that incident in the alley funny." She fingered her hair. "Let me tell you, it took forever to get those tiny chunks of beef out of my hair."

I bit my lip to keep from exploding into hysterics.

"Why, I've never been so mad in all my life," she went on. "The nerve of that woman. She must be unhinged to act that way. No wonder Ben couldn't live with her." We moved closer to the wall so that a couple of other ladies could pass around us. The bathrooms were always busiest on two-buck-beer night.

Squaring my shoulders, I maneuvered until I was directly in front of Laney. "I bet you were mad, Laney. Anyone would be. In fact, no one would blame you if it crossed your mind to get back at her . . . somehow."

"Get back at her? What do you mean?" I'd seen this act before from Laney. All dumb and innocent. But the sudden darting of her eyes and fidgeting with her blouse gave her away. I wasn't the only one who couldn't hide her reactions well. I continued to watch her closely, but didn't offer any further explanation. I'd learned long ago that sometimes the less said, the better. Lulls in the conversation often made people uneasy and they'd rush to fill the gaps. Especially a chitchatter like Laney.

"Are you talking about that car thing? Because that wasn't me. Don't you read the paper? That was Hollis that did that!"

"Is that so?" I pursed my lips and stared her down for a few more seconds. When she didn't crack, I decided to switch tactics. "Say, do you have time in your schedule tomorrow to work on my nails?"

She shook her head. "No, sorry. All booked up."

I held out my fingers for her inspection. "That's too bad. I got so many compliments on the last manicure you gave me, but I'm afraid it's about worn off."

She glanced at my nails and openly cringed. Still, she held her ground. "Nope. Too busy."

"Really? I'd be willing to throw in a little extra for working me in on such short notice."

She started to weaken. "How much extra?"

"Five bucks."

She raised a finely arched brow.

"Ten. But that's as high as I can go." Heck, it was higher than I could afford to go already. Still, the extra time to work the truth out of her would be worth it.

"Well, I suppose I can cut my lunch short. Fine. One o'clock, then."

Hattie sidled up next to us, two beers in hand. "Hey, there

you are!" She handed me a warm plastic cup and turned to Laney with a plastered-on smile. They exchanged a chorus of "hey alls" and looked each other up and down: Laney checking Hattie's hair, and Hattie surveying Laney's choice of outfit.

"Bless her heart," Hattie started as soon as Laney excused herself. "That girl should come into my shop. I'd fix her up with something decent to wear."

I looked over my own outfit—a pair of long khaki shorts and a white T-shirt—and back at Laney's getup—a mini that was so short it could have doubled as a belt, and a low-cut blouse. As Laney walked away, I recalled that Hattie had invited me in early Saturday for a little "fixing up." Obviously she wasn't lumping me into the same fashion category as Laney Burns, but it was as likely that in Hattie's eyes I'd fallen off the other side of the scale just as far.

"Can you believe the crowd that's here?" Hattie was saying. "Have you found Millicent yet?"

I pointed to the booth where she was sitting. "She would have to pick that booth. Unless I walk right over there and say hi, I'm not going to be able to see who she's talking to. I'd much rather get the information I need without her knowing I'm here."

"Think she'd recognize me?"

"Probably. We talked awhile when she was in your shop, remember? And we asked her some pretty pointed questions. That's why I'd prefer to stay incognito. Besides, who knows who's sitting across from her? What if it's someone we both know?" I took a quick sip of beer and gagged—warm, flat and really bitter . . . ick! No wonder it was so cheap. "Oh, well. Guess we can wait it out. Eventually they'll finish talking and get up to leave. We'll see who it is then."

"Wait it out? I don't have time for that. I told Pete I'd meet up with him later."

"Oh? You two cooking up something hot and spicy tonight?" I teased.

"Not if I'm here all night, we're not." Taking a long drag

on her beer, she studied the crowd before turning back to
me with a twisted smile and holding out her cup. "Here, hold
this. And don't ever say I don't make any sacrifices for you."

With a little extra wiggle in her step, she sashayed across
the room and, with a devilish grin, made her own selection
on the jukebox. Then she turned and made her way over to
some men sitting at a table cluttered with empty beer cups. I
didn't recognize the fellows, but judging by their soiled
T-shirts and steel-toed work boots, they were just a bunch of
good ol' boys kicking back after a hard day's work. Hattie
flipped her hair before leaning down to whisper in one of the
guys' ears. A wide grin broke over his face as he stood, wiped
his palms across his ratty jeans and snatched her eagerly by
the waist. In a flash, they were out on the dance floor, Hattie's
partner performing the most aggressive two-step I'd ever seen.
Not that Hattie couldn't keep up; I'd seen her cut loose a
number of times. Although I did suck in my breath at a couple
of their dizzying spins and one backbreaking dip. Soon, the
dance floor filled with couples, each doing their own version
of the boot-scootin' boogie. Still, Hattie's strategy didn't dawn
on me until, with a few well-placed spins, she and her partner
danced their way toward Millicent's booth. Then, with a curt
nod and a passing spark of conspiracy, her partner picked up
the tempo. With a couple quick steps and one long shuffle, he
guided her directly in front of the booth.

That was when the unthinkable happened. I wasn't sure
what she'd seen, but whatever it was caused Hattie's eyes to
pop and her muscles to tense. And, as everyone knows, two-
stepping with stiff muscles is like trying to herd cats—
downright impossible, dangerous even. Because the very
moment Hattie's muscles tensed, her partner decided to send
her spinning across the floor. Only instead of gracefully spinning like a top—a move I'd seen her do a thousand times
before—the heels of her calf-hugging cowboy boots collided
and she fell like a ton of bricks, smack-dab against another
dancer's elbow. Poor Hattie. It was possibly the first time in the

Honky Tonk's history that someone had busted their nose, not once but twice, from something other than a drunken brawl.

Blood spurted, she grabbed her face, the other dancers twirled on oblivious, and Hattie rushed from the dance floor, leaving her compatriot-in-crime in the dust. "Come on. Let's get out of here." She scurried past me toward the door, cupping her face in her hands.

I chased after her, snatching a clean rag from the bartender's hands as we passed by, hightailing it to the parking lot. We leaned against the hood of her car, pressing the rag against her face until the blood finally stemmed. "Let me have a look."

"No," she wailed. "It hurts like a son of . . ."

"Let me look," I insisted, pulling the rag away. I angled her, taking better advantage of the light streaming from a nearby lamppost. "Hey, it doesn't look all that bad. I don't think it's busted this time."

She pinched the bridge of her nose, giving it a tentative wiggle. "Are you sure?"

I got real close and squinted. "Well, it's a little swollen, and you'll probably have a shiner tomorrow, but it's definitely not broken."

"Sure hurts like the dickens." She started fishing through her pockets for the keys. "You'd better drive in case the bleeding starts again. I swear, the things you talk me into."

"Me? I was willing to kick back and wait it out. It was your idea to head out on the dance floor with Mr. Cotton-Eyed Joe." I paused for a beat, drawing in a deep breath. "I'm sorry, Hattie. I *do* appreciate you. What'd you find out anyway?"

She glanced back toward the bar just as a couple cowboys staggered out, blaring music following them through the open door. "Come on. I'll tell you on the way back to town."

Chapter 17

Georgia Belle Fact #082: A Georgia Belle knows
life isn't always perfect, but your nail polish sure
better be.

Although I'd only had half of a beer the night before, I awoke
Wednesday morning feeling like I'd been on a two-day
bender. Probably because the truth about who met with Millicent at the Honky Tonk kept me awake most of the night.
Well, that and the guilt of knowing I'd failed miserably in
the puppy-sitting department. When I'd arrived home from
the Honky Tonk, I discovered Roscoe had chewed the cushion on Mama's favorite armchair and left a yellow puddle
the size of Hill Lake by the front door. Guess I'd left him
alone for too long. Poor thing. Today, I was determined to
make it up to him with an extra-long early-morning walk
through the orchard. Besides, I needed to think through
what Hattie told me she'd seen at the bar the night before:
Hollis in the booth with Millicent.

I was afraid Hollis's meeting with Millicent had something
to do with that new plan Ida had mentioned. The one she said
Hollis had come up with to recoup the money he'd lost. Really,
though, could he actually be stupid enough to get involved with

Wakefield Lumber again? Or had his drinking simply muddled his senses? Or . . . I hated to think it, but was there possibly something going on with Hollis and Millicent? It gave me the shivers to think about either one of them in *that* way, let alone together. I shook my head. Too many thoughts to sort through at once. Especially without my usual morning caffeine fix.

So, after downing a couple cups of coffee, I grabbed Roscoe and headed out to the orchards to clear my mind and mull over this new twist of events. "Watch out for those ears!" I warned him, as we trudged along the southeast portion of our farm. As usual, his nose was to the ground, ears dragging, as he followed closely on my heels.

While moving between the rows, I found myself assessing the state of the orchard: ground moisture levels, leaf conditions and any telltale signs of crop-eating pests. I knew my father made these walks on almost a daily basis. He had to. Changes unfolded daily in the orchard and a good farmer took note of these changes, adjusting his strategy along the way. Now that I'd decided to stay and help out, I'd need to start looking at the orchard with a keener eye. I slowed my pace, moving my gaze to several trees where sucker growth shot up along the base of the trunks and some sort of invasive weed had settled in around the roots. In my mind, I made a to-do list of pruning, ground clearing, weed control . . . The tasks were endless, but since I'd committed to staying, the challenge excited me.

Still, despite my best efforts to clear my mind and focus on other things, Hollis and his meeting with Millicent remained in the forefront of my thoughts. I just couldn't shake the thought that he was getting himself back into the thick of things. I made a mental note to call Ray as soon as I got back to the house. Until then, I tried pushing those thoughts aside and kept walking, making my way out of the trees and down a steep hill bank to one of my favorite childhood stomping grounds. The Hole, as we'd always called it, was a spot where our little branch of the Ocmulgee tumbled down the rocky hillside, forming a deep pool of water before

flowing on through the countryside. An excited Roscoe ran
ahead, dipping his nose in the cool water while I stood under
a far-reaching live oak and fingered the frayed rope that
hung from one of its branches. As a kid, I'd delighted in
swinging Tarzan-like and dropping into the cool pool of
water. Lots of memories . . . good memories.

Then my eyes wandered down the river a bit, toward the
secluded spot where, years ago, I'd spent those few fateful
hours with Hawk. To this day, I wondered how different things
would have been if I hadn't left the dance early to steal away
on the back of his bike. At the time, I'd felt so free, so wickedly rebellious. But under the stars, with the sweet smell of
spring grasses and the night sounds of tree frogs to serenade
us, things went too far. Then, when I discovered . . . I sighed.
Best not to think too much about the past now. There were
too many other things, important things, to keep my thoughts
busy. Like Hollis and Millicent. What could they have been
meeting about? And why so late in the evening and at the
Honky Tonk? Of course, these days, mixing business and
pleasure was the standard mode of operation for Hollis.
According to Ida, and half the townsfolk, he spent most of
his evenings at the bar. He'd probably come to think of it as
his home away from home. Or, in this case, his second office.

Drawing in a deep breath, I shook my head and let it back
out with a low groan. Being back at my childhood hangout
wasn't bringing as much solace as I'd anticipated. I called
to Roscoe, who was poking his nose in a crawdad hole, and
started back to the house. My appointment with Laney was
only a few hours away, and with the festival quickly creeping
up, I had several other errands to run, including picking up
my jar labels from the print shop and getting enough supplies to make another batch of preserves. While there were
more than enough jars in Mama's pantry, I hated the thought
of her coming home and finding I'd stripped her cupboard
bare. Besides, I needed to figure the normal expenses for
this enterprise to determine my proper price structure.

Approaching the house, I was surprised to find Joe out by the barn, parking the tractor. "Joe! How's it going?"

"Just fine." He hopped down and pulled a hanky from the back of his overalls and began dabbing his brow. As he wiped, I noticed an angry red mark on the side of his arm.

"You've hurt yourself." I pointed at the blistering wound and wrinkled my brow with concern. "It looks painful, too."

He quickly pulled down his shirtsleeve, turning his gaze downward. "It's nothing. Just burned myself when I was repairing the tractor engine. Guess these old hands are out of practice. But I got everything mowed down. Took a while. The grass was gettin' pretty tall."

"Thank you, Joe. My daddy's going to be glad that job's marked off the list."

He raised his chin and puffed out his chest. "When's he comin' home?"

"A week from this Sunday."

He slid his eyes sideways, rolling his lips before spitting out the side of his mouth. "Is that so? Got more chores that need doin' before he gets back? I could use some extra cash."

I wanted to talk to him about helping me replace some of the irrigation lines, but knew better than to rush into any deal with the sly fellow. "Care to come in for something to drink?"

He grinned, reaching back into his pocket and handing Roscoe a nibble of something. "Don't mind if I do."

"What's that you're giving him?" I kept my tone in check, but I wished people would quit feeding Roscoe. He was going to get spoiled.

"Just a little bit of dried pork jerky. I keep some in my pocket while I work. Look, he's taken to it."

"I'd say." Roscoe was looking up, eyes wide and licking his chops, while his tail excitedly thumped in anticipation of more. I snatched him from the ground and headed for the door just as Joe was reaching back in his pocket. "Come on in, Joe. Looks like both you and Roscoe could use a little refreshment."

Inside, I turned Roscoe loose with fresh water and a bowl of puppy food and poured Joe an ice-packed glass of tea.

After a long drag, he sighed and swiped the back of his hand across his lips. "Boy, that hits the spot."

"Have a seat," I said, reaching up and flipped on the radio. The twangy lyrics of a popular country tune filled the kitchen as I glanced around for something to offer. I finally placed a couple slices of toast in the toaster. "How about some toast with a little peach jam."

"Sounds right nice, thank you." I turned to see him tapping the toe of his worn boots on the floor.

"You like this song?" I asked, waiting for the toast to pop up.

"It's a good tune. Heard it played at your folks' party, too."

I gathered the butter and a jar of preserves from the fridge and started to explain it was remix of an older song, but stopped mid-sentence when the full weight of his words hit me. "You were at the party? I didn't see you."

As I set the butter and preserves on the table, I saw him lean away. His eyes grew wide and he stopped tapping. "Just for a bit."

I heard the sound of the toast popping but his reaction made me pause.

Shrugging, he reached for another sip of tea, but his hand trembled and the ice clinked. He set it down and stood, wiping his hands on his overalls. "Think I'll pass on that toast. Best be gettin' back home. Got my own chores to tend to."

"Wait, Joe," I called after him as he took off through the mudroom and out the back door. Out in the yard, I caught up to him, maneuvering to cut him off before he could get any farther. "Joe, is there something you want to tell me?"

He rubbed his fingertips over the beads of sweat forming over his lip. "No, I don't reckon so." He reached into his pocket. "But here's the keys to the tractor."

When he reached out, his shirtsleeve crept up, revealing the wound again. "You should have Doc Harris take a look at that."

He shook his head. "Naw. Don't have much use for doctors. I'll just put some salve on it. Don't you worry none about me. I'll be fine."

Only I was worried plenty and not just about his injury, either. One thing was clear—Joe was nervous and hiding something. Had Joe seen something at the party, something that he didn't want to reveal about Wakefield's murder? Then another thought hit me: Watching him walk back across the yard and disappear into the orchard, all I could think was that this kind old man who I'd grown so fond of probably had more reason than anyone to want Ben Wakefield dead. His son's death at Wakefield Lumber weighed heavily on him even today. And now, knowing he had been at the party that night, I realized he'd had the opportunity to kill him, just like so many others. Then there was the burn on his arm. He'd said it came from working on the tractor, but . . . I rubbed at a kink forming in the back of my neck as it occurred to me that maybe I'd been looking at this whole thing wrong. Maybe Millicent hadn't paid Floyd to set fire to that woodpile. Maybe it was . . . No, it couldn't be Joe. I bit at my lip, fretting over this latest revelation. It just couldn't be Joe, could it? I bent down, scooping up Roscoe and pulling him close to steal a moment of comfort from his soft fur and warm little body before heading back into the house.

"You're late," Laney stated, rolling her eyes to the large clock that hung on the wall. From the sink across the room, Mrs. Whortlebe clucked her disapproval at my tardiness as she prepared the sink area for a client's shampooing. She paused for a second to send a sharp look my way. "About time ya got here, Nola Mae. Didn't your mama teach you the importance of being on time?"

"Yeah, you're fifteen minutes late," Laney complained. "And after I cut my lunch break short and all."

I lowered my head. "I'm sorry, Laney. I got tied up at the

Mercantile. Sally Jo needed my help with something." That was only partially true. Actually, after stopping by the print shop to pick up the labels for my preserves, I'd gone in to check on some drip lines to replace the faulty ones in the south orchard. When I walked in, I found Sally Jo behind the counter, crying her eyes out. She was terribly upset about something, but I never could coax out of her what it was. Still, I was hesitant to leave until I got her settled down.

I slid into the chair across from Laney and plunked my hands on top of the table, sending her a pleading look. "Do you think you still have time to work me in? I want to look my best for the festival."

Laney tapped the corner of the desk. "Pay up now. I don't want you smudging my work trying to fish money out of your pocket when I'm done."

Thanking her, I laid out the bills including an extra five on top of my already promised ten-dollar tip. This seemed to smooth her ruffled feathers. As she picked up the bills, I noticed she'd added tiny little gems to the tips of her own red nails. Probably a little extra bling for the weekend's festivities. As for my color, there was already a bottle set out along with a few of the same torturous tools she'd used last time. "That shade looks familiar. A Knowing Blush?" I asked, remembering the name of the polish she'd used before.

"A Knowing Blush? Why, heavens no!" The corners of her lips curled upward. "This one's called Double Trouble Pink."

I narrowed my eyes. The names of these polishes were sounding fishy to me. A Knowing Blush and now Double Trouble Pink? Like maybe trouble was coming my way, or, heaven forbid, Hollis was in for another round of trouble. Or perhaps it was Laney's subtle comment on the town's most recent stream of unfortunate events: murder and now arson. Then again, Laney wasn't really the subtle-comment type.

She got down to work, her mouth moving as quickly as her fingers as she jabbered on about the weekend's festivities, what she planned to wear to this event and that—reminding me that I promised Hattie I'd come early to her shop Saturday morning for own my fashion fix—and other trivial tidbits that passed in one ear and out the other until my attention was sidetracked by a low moan coming from across the room. "Oooh, please don't stop, Doris. This is the best shampoo I've ever had. I can just feel all my stress melting away."

Doris let out an irritated sigh. "Shoot fire, girl! If I keep this up, I'll scrub your hair right off. You wanna be bald?" For some reason her eyes slid my way with that comment, but she quickly caught herself, grabbed the extendable sprayer and started rinsing.

Laney pointed a nail file toward Doris and silently mouthed the word "cranky."

"Yeah, I sort of figured that," I whispered back, noticing Laney was bypassing the cuticle snipper this time. Thank goodness. "What's going on with her? She's usually so chipper."

Laney shrugged and popped her gum. "All I know is that brother-in-law of yours stopped by earlier this morning."

"Hollis?"

"That's right. And Doris has been upset ever since."

"Really?" *What is that all about?* Then I got to thinking that a lot of people seemed upset lately. First Ginny, then Sally Jo, and now Doris. All business owners and all suddenly upset. Was Hollis responsible for all this? Did it have something to do with his meeting with Millicent? A feeling of dread rolled through my stomach. "Do you know what he said to her?"

Laney shook her head. "No, sure don't. Whatever it was got her all worked up, though." She finished the polish on my first hand and removed my other from the soaking bowl. She leaned forward and, lowering her voice even more, added, "She's off her game today. Should have seen what she did to the Crawford sisters earlier."

"The Crawford sisters?" A mental image of the two elderly ladies with billows of snowy white curls flashed through my mind. "Do tell, Laney," I said, lifting my first hand and admiring my newly glossed pink nails. I could definitely get used to this manicure thing.

She continued to whisper. "Well, they came in for their weekly color rinse and set this morning. Only Doris messed up the color and instead of leaving with their usual color, Silver Lining . . . Well, let's just say they looked more like they'd been caught in a Purple Rain."

"Uh-oh."

Laney shook her head, her finely arched brows coming together as she concentrated on the fingertips of my second hand. For a while things grew quiet between us, until I broke the silence with another question. "Did you happen to run into Hollis last night at the Honky Tonk?"

Her head snapped up. "Yeah. So?" She sighed. "Did Ida send you over here to pump me about Hollis?"

"Ida? No. Why?"

She gave me a decisive once-over and shrugged before turning her focus back to my nails, carefully brushing the glass-like pink over each one. One thing about Laney, she took her work seriously.

I continued, "I just happened to see him there with Millicent and wondered what he was up to."

"Why don't you just ask him?"

I shrugged.

"Shoot!" She used her own nail to scrape a smudge of pink off my skin. "Hold still! You're making me mess up." She sighed and glanced impatiently at the clock. "If you want my opinion, they were just shootin' the breeze. Honestly, I don't think anything's going on between them." She looked up and winked. "Just in case Ida was wondering."

"Going on? Oh, Ida wasn't . . . I just happened to see him there and wondered what he was up to, that's all."

She looked up from my nails and rolled her eyes. "Well, duh. He was drinking. I hear tell that he's there every night, slammin' down the booze like it's nobody's business."

"Oh, I see." Deciding time was running short, I broached another topic on my mind. "I thought it was lousy what Millicent did to you with that casserole."

She chomped down hard on her gum, but didn't say anything.

"After all, you can't help it if Ben Wakefield found you attractive."

"That's right. I mean, if you got it, flaunt it, right?"

I nodded, thinking Laney had the flaunt part down pat. Across the room someone cried out and dropped a cussword. Laney and I both turned to see what the ruckus was about. It seemed Doris had the shampoo lady in her chair and was ripping through her hair with a comb. "Darn it, Doris. You're tearing my hair out with that thing," the lady was complaining.

"It's not my fault. You're the one who insisted on extra shampooing. Your curls have gone and tightened so much they're about too tight to slip a second through, let alone any comb."

Grimacing, I turned back to Laney and tried to steer things back to our own conversation. "By the way, did you happen to read the paper yesterday? All that business about the fire and the damage done to Millicent's car?"

"Sure did."

"Then you saw the bottles of Peach Jack in those pictures."

Laney recapped the polish and slid it back into the rack, declaring me done. "Yeah, and we both know who likes Peach Jack." She chuckled at her own cleverness.

I waved my hand in front of my mouth, blowing on my nails. "That's just the point, isn't it? Everyone in town knows about Hollis's preference for the stuff. Making it the ideal way to frame him."

Laney started to squirm with nervousness . . . or excitement, I couldn't decide which, but a telling flush suddenly tinged the apples of her cheeks. A Knowing Blush, one could say. I pressed my lips together, trying to suppress my smugness. I'd hit on a nerve. Was she was about to spill? Perhaps tell me how she'd taken out her anger over the casserole thing on Millicent's car?

My anticipation grew as she leaned over the table and cupped one hand to the side of her mouth. "That's exactly what I was thinking, Nola. Sure, Hollis likes his Jack, but he's not stupid. He wouldn't go and trash Millicent's car and then leave his bottle behind. I don't care how snookered he might have been." She sat back up and shrugged, bringing her voice back to its normal volume. "That's just my opinion, though. Everyone else in town is sure it's Hollis. Heard tell that he might lose his job over all this."

"I'd be all for that!" Doris chimed in. She was rolling giant pink curlers into her client's hair. "Why, they should have fired his sorry butt long ago. He's nothin' but a double-crossing, no-good, drunk . . ." She paused in the middle of her rant and looked my way. "Sorry, sweetie. I know he's family and all—"

"Through marriage, not blood," the woman in curlers piped up. "Which is a different matter altogether."

I did a double take. How'd this woman know so much about me? I didn't know her from Adam. But one thing I did know, this conversation was heading in the wrong direction. Deciding I'd better get out while I could, I snatched up my bag—ignoring Laney's warnings about my still-wet polish—and made a hasty retreat.

Back in my Jeep, the first thing I did was dial Ray's number on my cell phone. He wasn't due back into town until Friday afternoon, but I figured these latest developments warranted disrupting him at work. I needed to let him know what I'd learned about Joe. I also wanted to find out if there was any news on Floyd Reeves. Mostly, though, I wanted to inform him about Hollis's latest antics: his meeting with Millicent Wakefield and wreaking havoc with a few of the town's small business owners. I wasn't quite sure what Hollis was up to now, but I suspected it meant trouble. Double Trouble.

Chapter 18

Georgia Belle Fact #050: Finding a man is serious business. Dressing up your assets is just a wise business decision.

After speaking to Ray, who promised to look into this latest thing with Hollis, I pushed everything else to the back of my mind so I could spend the rest of the week focusing on getting ready for the festival and the debut of my family's new sideline business. I cooked and stirred and tested and steamed up the kitchen for hours on end the next couple of days to get the actual products lined up. My feet ached from so much standing and my hair plastered itself to my head, but, in the end, if they didn't sell, we'd have enough preserves to last us and half the town through the winter!

Between batches I had price tags to make and labels to affix. At the last minute, I decided to dress up my jars by adding a swatch of pretty fabric to each lid, tying it off with a decorative strip of raffia. Which turned out quite well, if I said so myself. Oh . . . then there was the sign for my booth. Borrowing inspiration from the chalkboard at Red's Diner, I sprayed a board with chalkboard spray, trimmed it out with rustic scrap wood I found out in the barn and carefully painted on the words: *Harper's Famous Peach Recipes* in white paint. The rest of the board I would complete with chalk, enabling me to change it depending on the product I'd be selling. Tomorrow, I'd only have the preserves to list. Hopefully, one day, I'd have several other products like Mama's famous peach chutney, or my nana's peach candy. . . . Maybe even sweetly spiced pickled peaches, a recipe one of my great-aunts perfected years ago. My mouth watered at the thought of that favorite fall treat of mine, which I loved to heat and eat over vanilla bean ice cream.

My enthusiasm grew as I wrapped up details and gathered my materials. Deciding I needed a practice run, I laid everything out on the dining room table. Stepping back, I was happy to see that the entire display, laid out on a blue gingham-covered table, exuded a feeling of down-home country goodness. Exactly the look I was going for.

However, as I quickly discovered first thing Saturday morning, all that down-home appeal added up to a lot to carry. Lucky for me, Ray, who'd rolled in late Friday night, was there to help me haul boxes from my parking spot two streets off the square, to Hattie's Boutique. It was a little before eight in the morning and, even though the festival wasn't due to open to the public until ten, the streets were already crowded with vendors setting up their wares and eager festheads mulling from booth to booth trying to catch a sneak preview of this year's offerings. I was just as eager and had already spied a gorgeous braided rug in subdued earthy tones that would be perfect for the mudroom off the back of our kitchen. I made a note to return to the booth later.

On the courthouse lawn, a giant Peach Harvest Festival banner flapped in the morning breeze, which carried the faint scent of flowers mixed with the hot cinnamon smell of candied pecans being fired up. For the kiddie fair, a large colorful carousel, with mirrors and wildly painted horses, was the main attraction, next to an inflatable jump house and large slide. An expanse of lawn was left open, however, where I knew the Jaycees would be hosting potato sack races and a giant tug-of-war match.

"Can you smell that?" Hattie asked, as I entered her shop with my first load of supplies. She inhaled again, her eyes turning upward with pleasure. "The church ladies have already started baking."

She was referring to our festival's claim to fame—the world's largest peach cobbler. The twelve-foot-by-six-foot culinary spectacular always took place down the street in the parking lot of the Mt. Zion Baptist Church. More than likely, preparations would have begun in the wee hours of the morning. It took several teams of people, working around the clock to mix the five-gallon buckets of ingredients, which were then placed in a pan, constructed of school bus floor panels, and stirred by giant boat oars. Throughout the day, the official baker would stoke the fires under the giant brick oven, sending up a wonderful aroma of hot peaches and buttery crust. Then, sometime around two in the afternoon, the church bells would ring, signaling that the first taste was ready.

"Yes," I enthused, momentarily closing my eyes as memories of hot peach cobbler topped with hand-cranked peach ice cream flooded my mind and aroused my taste buds. "I can hardly wait to get my bowl." Giant sized or not, in these parts, the Baptists were known for making the best cobbler around.

"Cute sign," Cade said, pausing for a second to regard my handiwork. He was in the middle of helping Hattie push a rack crammed with outfits outside. In addition to my table, Hattie planned on displaying a rack of discount dresses in hopes of enticing customers into her store. I noticed she'd also arranged a small table in the corner of the boutique, filled with covered trays of cookies and a large glass tea dispenser. "That a girl," I said, pointing to the treats. "Bait them with a discount and reel them in with cookies."

"It's all about the marketing." She laughed.

"Where do you want these?" Ray finally made his way into the boutique and was stumbling with the heavy box of preserves. I jumped in to help him maneuver the box to the counter. "I know two little girls who are going to love that carousel," he commented.

"Are they ever! What time did Ida say she'd show up today?" I was eager to show her my booth and what I'd accomplished with the preserves. And, of course, the twins would be so proud to see their artwork on the labels.

"She wasn't sure. Said it depended on what time Hollis could get away from work. The bank is open until eleven, I think." I knew from our conversation a couple days before that Ray was eager to talk to Hollis. I'd told him about seeing Hollis meet with Millicent and also what Laney had said about Hollis upsetting Doris. Ray was anxious to get to the bottom of these new developments, but so far, Hollis had succeeded in avoiding him. He'd even had Ida make some lame excuse about why he couldn't come to the phone last night.

"Maybe you can pin him down today," I suggested.

Ray shrugged. "That's the plan. But we'll see. He's definitely been avoiding me." He rubbed both hands along the scruff on his chin. A bit of anger welled inside me. Here Ray was killing himself to get Hollis out of trouble while keeping his own law business going in Perry, and Hollis wouldn't even take the time to answer his calls. What was wrong with that man? Made me wonder what new way he'd devised to land himself into trouble this time.

"What would you like me to do?" A dark-haired young man had entered the boutique, wearing jeans and a white T-shirt with this year's Peach Festival logo. I guessed him to be almost six feet tall and probably close to eighteen years old.

"Nash! You made it!" Hattie sidled up to the young man and made introductions. "Everyone, this is Nash Jones, the reverend's son. I've hired him to come in and help out today."

"Hello, Nash. I'm Nola." I extended my hand, which he shook with a firm grip. I was liking the kid already. "Are you a student?"

"Yes, ma'am. I'll be a senior at Cays Mill High."

"Really? Then you must know Emily Wiggins? Her folks own Red's Diner."

Nash dipped his chin and grinned. "Yes, ma'am. Sure do."

Hattie raised her brows and let out a little giggle. "Anyway," she said, after introductions were finished. "Nash is here to help with whatever we need."

Ray jiggled the keys to my Jeep. "How about helping me carry a few loads from the car, Nash?"

"Yes, sir."

"I'll help, too," Cade said, following them through the door.

As soon as they left, Hattie turned back to me and clapped her hands together. "Well, now that the boys are out of here, I have something to show you."

She hauled me to one of the dressing rooms and pointed to a dress hanging on the hook. "Go in there and put this on and hurry out."

I stammered for a response, but she cut me short with a little shove. "Hurry up, now. We don't have much time. I want to get you fixed up before the boys get back with the next load."

A few seconds later I emerged wearing the little peach lace sundress.

Hattie gasped, her hands flying to her mouth. "Why, if that isn't the cutest ever! Come over here so I can see you better."

Joining her in front of the mirror, I twirled around, sizing up my new look. Hattie was right. With little capped sleeves, a scooped neck and a fitted bodice, the dress gave a feminine feel to my slim, boyish physique. The color was good, too. It seemed to make my blue eyes pop.

"Perfect, perfect, perfect!" Hattie was carrying on. She clasped my hand and dragged me toward the countertop. "Let me just add a few special touches now."

I watched as she dug in her purse and pulled out a wicked-looking comb and a tube of something. She took to my short crop with the comb, teasing along my crown and then following up with a dollop of hair gel, pulling at pieces of my hair. "I'm just going to give this hair of yours a little zap of energy. Don't worry, now. It'll be fine."

Trying to take her word for it, I stood motionless while she worked her way around my head, teasing and pulling. Finally she finished with the hair, dipped back into her purse and pulled out her makeup bag. "Now, for a touch of glamour."

My hand shot up. "Oh, that's okay," I protested. "I'm not much for makeup."

"Relax, will ya? And hold still," she barked, a fully loaded mascara wand dancing preciously close to my eyeball.

The torture finished just as the shop bells jangled with the return of the guys. Snatching a pair of strappy sandals from atop the counter, she quickly stepped between me and the men. "Hurry, slip these on."

I obeyed, tapping her on the shoulder when I was done.

She cleared her throat, getting everyone's attention. "Excuse me, fellows. I want to introduce you to someone."

Behind her, I rolled my eyes. She was really taking this thing too far.

She stepped aside and held out her hands like a game show hostess. "The new Nola Mae Harper, businesswoman and friend extraordinaire!"

Letting out a chuckle, I took a little bow for my audience. But when I raised my head I was surprised to see everyone staring at me with shocked expressions. "What?" I scurried back to the mirror for another look, hardly recognizing the woman who stared back at me. Hattie had worked my short hair into wispy angles that complemented my features, pronouncing my cheekbones and making my eyes appear larger and my lips look full and pouty. Or maybe it wasn't the hair bringing out those features, but the way she'd accented my eyes and highlighted the angles of my face with makeup. Whatever it was, I liked the final result.

Apparently so did Cade. In the mirror, behind my own reflection, I noticed his eyes riveted on me. I stood motionless, my heart thudding as he took me in like a long drink of cool water.

Hattie stepped between us, breaking his trance. "Well, what do y'all think? Perfect for her big debut today, don't ya think?"

"Yeah, looks great, sis," Ray called out from across the room. He and Nash were busy trying to pull the base out on a portable table, oblivious to my transformation.

Cade, on the other hand, was anything but oblivious. "Perfect. Simply perfect," he mumbled in a low, husky voice.

Hattie glanced back and forth between us, a gleam in her eye. "Well, I never would have imagined such an enthusiastic reaction, but I'm glad you approve, big brother."

I felt my cheeks growing hotter and hotter and wondered if anyone else noticed they were about to burst into flames. I hastily moved toward the refreshment table, hoping some tea would cool me down.

"Is this your mama's recipe?" Candace from the bank was standing at my festival table, scrutinizing a jar of preserves.

"Yes, ma'am. The one and only."

"In that case, I'll take two. Although I really shouldn't on account of my blood sugar levels. Doc Harris said I should modify my eating habits." She waved away his suggestion like it was a pesky fly. "Where do you suppose he gets off telling me to modify my eating habits? Have you ever sat next to him at a potluck?"

Shrugging, I took the jars and quickly wrapped them in tissue paper, placing them inside a brown-handled bag, which I tied off with a piece of red gingham ribbon. Sales had been steady, but not spectacular, with locals for the first couple hours and then slowly more people arriving from out of town as well. "Here you are," I said, taking her money and dipping into my apron for change. "Are you having a nice time today?" I asked, trying to steer the conversation in a more positive direction, but wondering if I could try making a few jars of preserves with something sugar-free, like Stevia powder. Of course, I had to remind myself, I'd just barely gotten a grip on the regular recipe.

"Well, I would be, of course, if it weren't for my sciatica. Boy, it sure acts up when I walk on concrete. Doc told me I should get myself some thicker soled shoes, but I just can't find any pretty ones," she started whining.

"Was Hollis at the bank this morning?" I asked, cutting her short. I wasn't raised to be so rude, but Candace could go on about her ailments forever.

At the mention of Hollis, her eyes popped and her mouth pursed into a perfect little *O*.

"What is it, Candace? Is something going on with Hollis?"

She clamped her mouth shut and shook her head from side to side.

I narrowed my eyes. "I know he's your boss and I do admire your loyalty, Candace. But he's my sister's husband. He's family. If something's going on, I should know about it. Don't you think?"

"Your sister already knows. I made sure of it."

Now I was really curious. However, while Candace may freely tell you more than you'd ever want to know about her own personal medical conditions, she wasn't one to spout off about other people's business. She was discreet. A great quality for someone who worked in a bank and one of the main reasons Hollis had kept her on all these years.

"You know, Candace, Ida hasn't been herself these days, what with the baby and all." Grabbing an extra jar of preserves, I started carefully wrapping it in tissue. "Honestly, I've been quite worried about her."

"You have?"

"Uh-huh. All this going on with Hollis has taken a toll on her . . . and the baby."

Candace gasped, her hand flying to her lips. "Oh Lawdy, is the baby all right?"

I let her question hang. "The whole family is so worried. Especially Hollis. You know, say what you want about Hollis

Shackleford, but he's a good daddy. His children mean the world to him."

Candace's head bobbed up and down. "You got that right."

Reaching out, I took back her bag and slid the newly wrapped jar in alongside the others. "Here. A gift—"

"I couldn't." She started to hand it back.

"No, take it, please," I insisted, placing my hand on her arm, leveling my gaze on her. "For being such a good friend of the family."

She bit back a little whimper and started fidgeting with the ribbon on her package. A part of me felt guilty for putting her into such a moral dilemma. Another part of me said to heck with morals; this was Hollis we were talking about. If something was going on, I needed to know. For Ida's sake.

"He was drinking again," she started. I had to lean in and listen closely, as her voice was barely a whisper. "Locked himself in his office and drank himself silly."

"This morning?"

"I know. Awful. Absolutely awful. He kept mumbling something about not enough money."

"Really?" It didn't make any sense. Maybe Candace misunderstood.

"Oh, I feel so rotten for spreading this around. Yes, I do."

I steadied my hand on her arm. "You're only telling me because I'm family. And you know family has to look out for each other. Especially those precious young ones."

Her back straightened as resolve firmly rooted itself. "That's right. That's why I called Ida. We were getting ready to close down, and I was worried Hollis might try to drive in his condition. I called Ida to come and get him."

"Did she?"

Candace nodded her head. "She was so upset, but she made me promise not to tell anyone. Said she'd make arrangements to come get him soon. In the meantime, she told me to take his car keys and go ahead and lock up the bank."

I glanced at my cell. A little before noon. Hollis was

probably still in his office, sleeping it off; I doubted Ida had been able to get there yet. Looking back at Candace, I could tell she was regretting having said so much. Again I patted her arm. "You've done the right thing by telling me. Ida doesn't have any business trying to manhandle Hollis when he's in that type of condition. Think of the baby. I'll make sure she gets the help she needs. And discreetly," I added, offering her a quick wink, at which she gave a little sigh. I looked around for an opportunity to break away from my booth. Now I needed to call Ray and let him know where he could find the elusive Hollis; not to mention I did need a restroom break.

Finally my eyes landed on Nash, who was coming my way with a handful of money. "Excuse me," he said, nodding to Candace. "But Ms. McKenna is sending me over to the VFW stand to pick up a couple pulled pork sandwiches. Do you want me to get you something?"

My stomach rumbled in response. "That would be wonderful, Nash, but would you mind watching my booth for a couple minutes first?" I came out from behind the table and unstrapped my money apron, passing it to him. I was hoping to find a private spot where I could call Ray. "I just need to visit the restroom. Be right back." I excused myself and trotted into the shop.

Hattie looked up from helping a customer as I passed through. "If you're heading for the restroom, I'm afraid there's a line back there. Seems it's the most popular spot in the shop this morning."

"Uh-oh." I simply couldn't hold it for much longer. She mentioned the port-a-johns, with an apologetic look.

On the way back out the door, I stopped by my booth and gave Nash a quick run-down on selling preserves and made a beeline for the port-a-potties. At least the lines were short. I was able to get in and out in record time plus place a quick call to Ray, who said he'd meet Ida at the bank to help her with Hollis. Ray was good at that kind of thing. Finally I could relax a bit, quit eyeing the crowd for Hollis, and concentrate on my family's new enterprise.

The day was so nice, it was difficult not to tarry on the way back to the boutique. Glancing down Blossom Avenue, I saw a line was already forming in the church's parking lot with people eager for their taste of the mammoth cobbler. Perhaps a little later, I'd send Nash back out to scrounge up a bowl for me. On the yard in front of the city building, the potato sack races had just begun, cheers ringing out from the crowd as they encouraged their favorite participant. I paused for a second, remembering a few races from my own youth. I usually crossed the finish line neck and neck with Ida, each of us vying for first place. I sighed and shook my head at the memory—seemed we'd spent most of our child-hood competing over one thing or another.

With all the festivities, I found myself easily distracted as I weaved my way back through the booths. Everywhere I looked was awash in bright colors: banners hanging from the lightposts, children with brightly colored balloons and a rain-bow of booths dotting the side streets. The lively tunes of a popular local band, the Banjo Boys, floated in the breeze along with tempting smells of roasting peanuts, kettle corn and fun-nel cakes. I was heading into sensory overload! First I stopped to sniff a display of soy candles, then to admire a quilt stitched by the talented ladies of the St. Francis Altar Society and, of course, linger a bit at a booth with handsomely hand-carved fruit bowls that I knew would look perfect full of peaches and resting on Mama's dining room table. I was just about to pur-chase one when a familiar pair of tight jeans caught my eye.

"Hawk. You're back," I said, joining him by the lemonade stand.

He glanced down at me with a smile, then back at the woman taking his order. "Add one more lemonade, would ya, darlin'?"

I smiled. "Thanks."

Hawk paid her; then we stepped aside as she prepared our order, slicing fresh lemons. After that she'd press them through a custom squeezer that emptied the juice, lemons and all into tall plastic glasses brimming with ice along with spritzes of a sugary syrup.

Leaning against the stand, Hawk folded his arms and took in my new look. "New dress?"

"Hattie gave it to me," I explained, smoothing out a few wrinkles that'd accumulated while I sat all morning. "I'm test-selling my new line of products today. Guess she thought I'd better look the part."

"Well, you look real nice."

"Thanks." I cleared my throat and moved the conversation along. "So, Ray says you didn't have any luck up in Macon."

He nodded. "Seems Floyd Reeves is as slippery as a wet snake. Thought I had him pinned down at one point, but he eluded me. I'll pick up his trail again next week. Ray wanted me to come back down and look into some other things."

"Other things?"

"Here's your drinks," the woman behind the stand interrupted.

I turned to see her place three lemonades on the counter. "Three?"

As if to answer my question, Laney Burns sashayed onto the scene, her long red nails encircling the cup as she snatched it off the counter. My shocked gaze automatically wandered from her spiked heels to the top of her maxed-out head of hair, stopping for a second to ponder her latest shade of nail color. Tart Cherry, perhaps? Or Wanton Scarlett?

"Hey, there, Nola." She flashed her best sugary smile and wrapped her free hand possessively around Hawk's biceps. "Sweet of you to keep Hawk company while I powdered my nose, but I'm back now."

I attempted to match her fake smile, but it was difficult with my jaw hanging halfway down my neck. Instead, I mumbled something stupid, grabbed my drink and left before someone misinterpreted the weird expression on my face. I certainly didn't want Laney to think I was jealous. Because I wasn't. If anything, I was disgusted. Disgusted by the fact that my brother hired an idiot. If Hawk had really left his pursuit of a suspected arsonist to come back here pursuing other leads, then why was he wasting time messing around with Laney Burns? It was possible, of course, that his interest in Laney wasn't personal at all. Maybe Ray asked him to check into the possibility that Laney vandalized Millicent's car. Aw . . . I knew better than that. Hawk might be doing a little undercover work with Laney, but it wasn't the investigating type of undercover. It was just Hawk being . . . well, Hawk. Guess some things just never changed.

Once again, I started making my way back to my booth when a frantic voice cut through the crowd. "Nola! Nola!" Off in the distance, I could see Ida running toward me, one hand on her belly and the other excitedly waving her cell in the air. Breaking into a jog, I met her halfway. "What is it? What's wrong?"

Her wild eyes searched my face as she pointed to her phone. "It's Hollis. He's been hurt!"

"Hold on, now," I said, gripping her shoulders firmly. "He's safe. He's locked up inside the bank. Didn't Ray call you?"

"Yes, but he wasn't there. I came out here looking for him, but . . ." She pointed at the phone again, her fingers trembling so badly, I thought she was going to drop it.

"But what, Ida? What's happened?"

"He called me."

"And what did he say?"

Her hand flew to her cheek. "Oh, Nola. I could hardly make heads or tails out of what he was saying, he was so drunk. But he was moaning something awful. Like he was in pain. I just know there's been some sort of terrible accident. I told his secretary to take his keys, but he must have had a spare set somewhere."

"His car's not at the bank?"

She shook her head.

I scanned the crowd again, but the noise and the crush of the onlookers for the tug-of-war made locating Hollis next to impossible. "Where's Ray?"

"He met up with Cade and they're both out looking."

Hawk caught up to us, his own cell phone to his ear. "Okay. Will do," he said, disconnecting. "That was Ray. He told me what's going on. So far, no sign of Hollis."

Ida let out a short sob. Then another and another. She was working up to hysterics.

"Listen," I intervened. "I'm sure he's okay. He's probably just sick from drinking. Did you call him back?"

"Over and over again. But it just keeps going through to voice mail. Oh, I hope he's not lying dead somewhere along the side of the road," she wailed.

"Where are the girls?"

She pointed over her shoulder. "I left them with Hattie. I went to the shop looking for you and she said you came this way—" She paused, clenching her teeth and letting out a little moan.

I shot a worried look Hawk's way. "Ida! Are you having contractions?"

She waved it off. "Oh, just little ones. I always have these my last month."

"Are you sure?"

"Yes, I'm sure!" she snapped. "I've been through this before, you know."

"Okay, let's go back to the shop and get the girls. I'm taking you all back to the house for a rest."

She dug in her heels and shook her head. "No. I'm not leaving until I find Hollis."

Hawk stepped forward. "Look, Mrs. Shackleford. Why don't you let us guys do the searching? Besides, I'm trained for this type of thing."

Yeah. And you did such a good job tracking down Floyd Reeves. But I didn't say that. At this point, I wasn't all that concerned about Hollis. By now, his antics were wearing thin on my patience. What really concerned me was Ida's condition and what all this stress was doing to her. I shooed him off to go search and turned back to Ida. "Come on, sis. Let's get you back to Hattie's shop."

Chapter 19

Georgia Belle Fact #084: A Georgia Belle's most cherished possession is her family. That means everyone in the family—even the ones we'd rather not mention.

"I bet you wanna buy some of my nana's peach preserves, don't you?" We arrived back at the shop just in time to catch Savannah in full swing of things. "I promise you, ma'am, it's the best peach preservers you'll ever taste." She crossed two fingers over her heart and batted her lashes while her sister Charlotte, off to the side, was showing an attentive customer the great artwork on the labels. A chorus of *oh*s and *aw*s sounded from the line, which was about seven people deep, all with money out and waiting.

Nash, who stood behind the girls making change for the latest purchase, looked on with concern as we approached. "Everything okay, Ms. Harper?"

"Sort of. I'm so sorry I've been gone all this time."

Hattie appeared in the doorway. "Don't be silly, Nola. We're fine." Taking one look at Ida's condition, she jumped into action. "Let me help," she said, dashing to Ida's side and guiding her toward the shop.

Ida shrugged her off. "Stop with the fussing, will y'all? I'm fine."

"You're not fine, Ida. I'm taking you to the house where you can rest and I can keep an eye on you for a while. The guys will call as soon as they find Hollis."

"Good idea," Hattie agreed. "And let me keep the girls here with Nash and me."

Ida shook her head. "Oh, I don't know. I hate to impose. . . ."

"Please, Mama! Please!" they echoed from behind the booth. "We're having so much fun."

Ida gave in and agreed to let Hattie watch the girls while she and I made our way back to my Jeep. She was unusually quiet on the ride back to the farm. It wasn't until we'd reached the gate that she finally spoke. "I'm sorry to drag you away from the festival."

"Oh, believe me, those girls of yours have everything under control. They're much better saleswomen than me anyway."

She chuckled, then gritted her teeth again, her hand instinctively flying to her belly. I pulled up next to the house and put my Jeep in park and turned in the seat. "You're having more contractions, aren't you?"

"Yes, but they're not the real thing. Promise. They'll go away with a little rest. Besides, the due date isn't for a couple weeks yet."

Hopping out, I came around and helped her out of the car and up the porch steps. As soon as I opened the door, Roscoe shot out between our legs.

"My word! What was that?" Ida cried.

"Roscoe!" I shouted after him, but he tore off through the yard and was already halfway around the barn. "Well, shoot! Wonder what's gotten into him?" I'd given him a long outing this morning and left him plenty of food, but I sort of suspected he'd been spoiled. Ever since Ray started feeding him people food, then Joe with the jerky, the poor dog had gone nuts. He'd been constantly sniffing around for people food and only nosing at his own puppy kibble.

"That's Dane Hawkins's dog," I explained to Ida, who'd already spread out on the davenport. I went to cover her with the afghan, asking if she wanted something cool to drink.

"No, I'm fine. Have you checked your phone? Any messages from the guys?"

I took a quick peek and set it down on the coffee table in front of her. "Afraid not. But don't worry; they'll find Hollis soon. Ray knows where to look." I was thinking the first place they probably went was up McManamy Draw. That seemed to be Hollis's favorite haunt. If not there, maybe the Honky Tonk. I worried my bottom lip, remembering what Candace had said about Hollis's condition. If he really had been drinking as much as she said, he had no business driving anywhere. Hopefully, he hadn't driven off the road somewhere.

Trying to push the thought aside, I peered back out the front window, searching the yard for any signs of Roscoe. "Ida, will you be okay here for just a second? I should chase after Roscoe. I think he's heading for Joe Puckett's place."

"Joe's? Why? Does he have a taste for moonshine?"

"No. Jerky, I'm afraid. Joe gave him some and he's developed a taste for it. He turns his nose up at his real food now."

She waved me on. "Go on. I'll be just fine now that I've got my feet up."

I kicked off my sandals, slipped on my field boots, and took off across the yard, calling Roscoe's name as I searched around the barn. Somewhere off in the distance, I heard a little whimpering sound. It seemed to come from the orchard that led to Joe's property. Just as I thought. He was being led by his stomach. "That dog is so spoiled," I mumbled, trudging off toward the trees.

By the time I made my way through the orchard and had reached Joe's property line, I'd worked myself into a tizzy. I hadn't asked to have dogsitting in my basket of responsibilities at all. I needed to be back at the house taking care of Ida. And I would be, too, if Joe hadn't fed Roscoe those treats. I hated to be disrespectful, but I was going to have to set him straight on the matter.

"Roscoe! Roscoe!" I called, working my way over the path that led to Joe's cabin.

My calls were answered with a low baying sound rounded off with a series of tiny whimpers. I quickened my step. It sounded like Roscoe was upset about something.

"Roscoe!"

A sharp yelp sent me scurrying into the woods behind Joe's cabin. There I found Roscoe, pawing at the bottom edge of a small woodshed. "There you are, Roscoe!" Bending down, I lifted him to my chest and stroked his fur, but he kept whining and clawing to get back down. "What is it, boy?"

That was when I heard it. A thumping noise from within the shed, followed by a low moaning sound. "Joe?" I cried, suddenly worried for my friend's safety. Had someone beaten him and locked him in the shed? Who would do such a horrible thing to the kind old gentleman? "Joe?" I called again, bending down and throwing my weight against a heavy log that was propped against the door. As soon as the log budged, I grabbed the handle and threw open the door, its rusty hinges wheezing as it banged open. I rushed inside, Roscoe darting ahead of me, caught up in a sniffing frenzy punctuated with a series of high-pitched yaps. My eyes quickly scanned the dark shed, taking in the crude wooden shelves, each stacked with rows and rows of jugs and sealed mason jars. The place must have doubled as food storage, because I also spied a row of my mama's preserves along with a barrel of wild apples and a couple slabs of salt pork hanging from the rafters—which explained why Roscoe was so eager to get inside. Then suddenly, a slight movement from the dark corner of the shed caught my attention. "J—" I stopped short, my vision finally adjusting to the darkness of the shed. It wasn't Joe, but Hollis.

"Hollis!"

He was crumpled in a heap, an empty mason jar on the ground next to him.

"Nola? Is that you, Nola?" He let out a cough, which turned to a gagging sound and ended with a heave. I stepped back, covering my face as he vomited.

"What are you doing here, Hollis?" I asked, scooping up Roscoe and taking another step backward. "And how'd you get here?" I hadn't seen his car around anywhere.

"Took a ditch up the road a ways," he managed, regaining some control and starting to stand, only to slump back down again. "You need to leave now. It's Joe. Joe's the . . ." Hollis closed his eyes and let out a little snort.

"Don't you pass out on me, Hollis Shackleford!" I carefully circumvented the splatter zone and leaned down to tap Hollis's face with my free hand. "Hollis! Joe's the what, Hollis?"

"The killer." The words didn't come from Hollis, though. They came from Joe. I wheeled around to find him standing behind me, shotgun in hand. "I'm the one who killed Ben Wakefield."

I looked from his dazed face to the shotgun trembling in his hands and was dumbfounded. Even though I'd had a niggling of suspicion, hearing the words straight from his mouth was shocking. Of course, the signs were there all along—the motive of his son's death, his presence at the party the night Wakefield was killed. Only, I'd chosen to ignore them, pushing them to that remote place in the back of my mind where I put all the unpleasant thoughts and ugly truths I was unwilling to face. Only now there was no more denying it: Joe was a murderer. "Put down the gun, Joe. Let's talk about this."

He looked down at the gun, confusion registering on his face as if he was surprised he was holding it. "It was an accident, I swear." To my relief, he leaned the gun against the shed wall and stepped away. "I didn't mean it. . . ." He shook his head, raising his hands and staring incredulously at his own palms. "We were arguin' and . . . It was an accident. You believe me, right?"

I clenched Roscoe close and glanced from Joe to the shotgun, which was still only a few quick steps away from

where he stood. "I do believe you, Joe. But let's step outside
and talk some more. I'll help you. I promise."

He bobbed his head, turned slowly and made his way
back through the shed door with heavy steps. I glanced once
more at Hollis, who was slumped backward and snoring
loudly. A line of drool dribbled from his open mouth. I
sighed with disgust and quietly shut the shed door to keep
Roscoe from the salt pork. Then I joined Joe out at the same
stump where we'd sat and shared sandwiches the other day.
That seemed so long ago now.

As soon as I put Roscoe down, he started pawing at Joe's
pant legs for a treat. Joe reached down and scratched his
head. "Sorry, lil' fella. Don't have nothin' for ya right now."

"Tell me exactly what happened, Joe," I started, still keeping my distance. But as I watched his demeanor crumple—his
shoulders drooping and his arms retracting tightly around his
torso—my caution melted away and a feeling of sympathy
took over. Crossing to the stump, I placed a hand on his shoulder. "Go on, Joe. It's okay. Tell me what happened."

"That music y'all were playing that night. Mighty catchy.
I wanted to come closer so I could hear it better, maybe
watch people dancin'. . . ." His voice caught at he spoke.
"Anyways, I was back a ways, watchin' from the orchard,
when I saw him."

"Ben Wakefield?"

"Uh-huh. Mr. Wakefield." He clenched his midsection
tighter and shot me a long, searching look before breaking
eye contact again. Looking at the ground, he thumbed toward
the shed. "A while back, that man in there came 'round and
told me Mr. Wakefield was going to take my land."

"Hollis? He told you that?"

"Yup. He's your kinfolk, I suppose. He'd been up here at
my place with some fancy document. Said I hadn't paid my
taxes and Wakefield was going to take my trees. Why, these
trees are my livelihood."

For a second I was confused. His livelihood? Then, as I

watched his eyes scan the forest, it dawned on me that his moonshine still was probably hidden out there somewhere, camouflaged among the thick underbrush of the trees.

He went on. "Thought I was free and clear with Wakefield dead, but Hollis came back up here again today with those same fancy papers. Drunk as a skunk, too. I dunno how he even got here. . . ." He shook his head. "Anyway, said the new owner of the mill still wanted the trees. That he was going to buy my land for back taxes and sell it to the mill for profit. He was so lit up, I thought maybe if I locked him up for a while, let him dry out, maybe I could talk some sense into him."

"Back taxes? But you should have received some sort of notice. You should have an opportunity to pay them before your property goes into foreclosure."

Joe shrugged, his eyes rolling over the trees that surrounded us. "Some papers came. But I didn't understand them. That's why when I saw Mr. Wakefield, I thought I'd explain. I told him, 'I don't need to pay no money for this land. It was given to my granddaddy by the Harper granddaddy.' That's what I told Mr. Wakefield that night in the orchard. Only he wouldn't listen. He laughed and called me ignorant. And I—"

"You murdered him in cold blood!" We both startled, turning to see Hollis behind us, waving the shotgun in the air. "And tried to pin it on me."

"Put the gun down, Hollis. Before you hurt someone!"

"Step away, Nola. That man's a killer," Hollis cried out.

Part of me wanted to step between him and Joe and part wanted to step the other way, farther outside of his wavering aim. "You're drunk, Hollis. Put the gun down. We'll work this out."

Only he gripped the gun tighter, the barrel bobbing dangerously as he shouted, "Get out of here, Nola, before he kills you, too!"

I watched in horror as Hollis wobbled and gripped the gun tighter, his fingers precariously close to the trigger. "Put the gun down, Hollis; you're not thinking—" I started to plead, when suddenly a brown streak zipped past my feet and darted between Hollis's legs. Roscoe was running full charge toward the open shed door and straight for the smell of pork. Hollis startled, stumbled over the dog, lost his balance, and as he fell backward, a deafening shot rang through the air. Out of the corner of my eye, I saw the stump splinter and shards of wood fly in all directions. I also saw Joe fall to the ground.

"Joe!"

The old man was on the ground, clutching his side, blood seeping through his fingers. I gave him a quick once-over. He was bleeding badly, but still breathing. I looked over at Hollis, who was on the ground, looking dazed and confused, the shotgun safely in the grass a few feet away. "You shot him!" I accused.

"Shot him?" Panic crept over his features as he struggled to stand. "I did? Didn't mean to. I was just trying to scare him away from you."

"Well, you did!" I spied Joe's hanky hanging out of his pocket. Snatching it, I began pressing it against the wound.

In the meantime, Hollis stumbled over. "Is he going to die?"

I shook my head. "I don't know." Joe had lost consciousness and was lying motionless on the ground. His bleeding decreased with the pressure and his breath seemed steady. "We've got to get help. Where's your cell?" I asked Hollis.

"It's dead. I ran the battery out trying to call for help."

I chastised myself for leaving the house without mine. For a second, hopelessness overtook me. Then I pulled it back together, trying to stay calm and think through the situation. "Listen, Hollis. Are you sober enough to watch over him? Make sure he doesn't bleed out?"

Hollis's blurry eyes took in the scene before him, but he sucked it up and nodded. "Think so. What can I do?"

"Get down here and hold this against his wound. Keep pressing. We don't want it to start bleeding again. I'm going for help." I took off running through the trees heading for the orchard, tripping a couple times on roots that jutted out over the trail. Finally, I broke free of the forest and gained some speed on the newly mowed paths between the peach rows, the whole time my mind forming a plan. There wouldn't be time to call an ambulance. Besides, it would never make it over the orchard paths and back to Joe's property line. No, my best bet was to get my Jeep and transport him myself.

As I neared the house, though, I caught sight of an ambulance parked in the drive. An ambulance? My first thought was that Hollis got his phone working and already called for help. But that wasn't even rational. Not enough time had passed for that. Then it hit me. Oh, no! Ida!

I took the porch steps two at a time, bursting into the family room, and found Ray, Cade and Hawk standing by the door watching as two paramedics attended to Ida. It appeared they were getting her ready to be transported. "What's going on?" I demanded. "Is she okay?"

Ray steadied me by the shoulders. "Everything's fine, Nola. She's just in serious labor."

On cue, Ida gritted her teeth and let out a low moan. When the pain subsided, she looked my way, worry playing between her mask of pain. "Nola, they haven't found Hollis yet!" she managed, before stiffening with another contraction and letting out a series of quick breaths interspersed with hiccup-like sobs.

Hollis? My mind whiplashed back and forth for a second before I blurted out, "I found him, Ida. And he's okay." *Drunker than a skunk, but okay.* "He's at Joe Puckett's cabin. He . . . uh, he accidently shot Joe."

"What!" Ida cried, as the paramedics moved her to the gurney. "He shot Joe?"

There was a second of confusion in which everyone froze in place. Not a word was uttered, as the men and paramedics shot looks between Ida and me until another one of Ida's moans pierced the silence.

One of the paramedics jumped into action, grabbing his bag and pointing toward the door. "Let's get her loaded. You take her in," he told his partner, "and phone for another transport. I'll go with these folks to see about the shooting victim."

I grabbed my own bag off the foyer table, searching the side pocket for my keys as I followed them outside, explaining the situation as they loaded Ida into the ambulance. "There's no way an ambulance can make it up to the cabin. We'll have to take my Jeep and meet it back here at the house."

"Fine," the EMT replied, making sure Ida was secure. He started grabbing extra bandages and medical equipment, stuffing them into his bag at a frenzied pace. His hand hovered over a cache of bottles and syringes. "How old is the victim?"

"I'd say close to seventy."

"Where's the wound?"

"In his side."

"Left or right?"

Pausing, I strained my memory. "Le . . . no, right. Definitely right."

The paramedic shook his head and fired off a few more questions. Finally, he grabbed a few more items along with what appeared to be a soft stretcher and started for my Jeep.

"I'm going with you." I turned to find Hawk standing behind me. Cade and Ray were next to him.

"So am I. You'll need help getting him down that trail," Cade added.

Ray nodded. "Good. I'm going with Ida. Hattie's still got the girls at the shop, so they'll be fine."

That settled, we took off across the driveway, catching up with the paramedic. Right before climbing into the driver's side, something caused me to turn and look back. Ray caught my eye, sending me a reassuring nod and a tiny little wave before continuing his ascent into the ambulance. It was such a tiny gesture. But with that one single glance, I realized how right Hawk had been when he said my siblings and I shared a special bond. We did. Even without Mama and Daddy around, we could hold the family together.

Chapter 20

Georgia Belle Fact #101: It's not your money that counts or your smarts. Not even your looks. The only thing that really matters is the love in your heart.

The County Medical Center was bustling with noise: machines whirring, codes sounding over the intercom, rubber-soled shoes squeaking up and down the halls. I slouched in the hard-back chair of the emergency waiting room, my mind wandering back over the evening's events. After getting Joe out of the woods and into my Jeep, another ambulance was waiting at the house to transport him. Once he was loaded, Cade, Hawk, Hollis and I followed the ambulance to the hospital.

At the hospital, Hawk stayed in the emergency waiting room, to receive news on Joe's condition, while the rest of us made our way to the maternity wing where we caught up with Ray in the visitors' lounge and awaited the announcement of the newest Harper. While we waited, I filled everyone in on what had really happened at the cabin.

"Then Hollis is finally in the clear," Cade said, after I answered an onslaught of questions.

"Guess so." I noticed my tone didn't sound all that enthusiastic. Not that I wasn't happy that Hollis would finally be exonerated of Wakefield's murder; I just wished the real killer hadn't turned out to be Joe.

"Hollis may still have some trouble coming his way," Ray said.

My brows furrowed. "How's that?"

"He may face charges for shooting Joe. Especially since he was under the influence at the time." Ray stood and retrieved his phone from his back pocket. "I'll go call the sheriff now and fill her in on everything that's happened." Looking at me, he added with a sigh, "I'm sure she'll have plenty of questions for you and Hollis."

A while later, when a nurse came in with news that Ida had delivered a healthy boy, a chorus of whoops filled the air. Mother and baby were exhausted and resting, so visitors besides Hollis weren't recommended until tomorrow. Tapping together our cups of stale coffee, we offered a toast to the new baby and took turns guessing the name and birth weight. Our enthusiasm dimmed, though, when Hawk joined us in the lounge with news of Joe's condition. While most of the buckshot had passed through his side with minimal damage, some had lodged inside him. He'd lost a lot of blood in surgery and was still experiencing some shock. They wanted to keep him in ICU overnight to monitor his condition. Upon hearing the news, I sent everyone home for some rest, while I volunteered to wait it out at the hospital's emergency waiting room. For some reason, I felt the need to stay and wait for news on Joe. After all, he didn't have anyone else.

Early the next morning, I woke to find Ray standing over me, a steaming cup of coffee in his hands. Behind him were Cade and Hawk. My eyes were immediately drawn to a white bag in Cade's hands. "Sugar's Bakery?"

"Yup. Scones. Thought you might need some."

"Yes, definitely." I gratefully accepted his offerings. A little caffeine and sugar were just what I needed. He also handed me the keys for my Jeep, which they'd used to go to my house to crash last night. I glanced at the wall clock. Not even seven o'clock yet. After the gang left the evening before, the sheriff showed up with Deputy Travis in tow. I spent more than an hour fielding questions about Joe's murder confession and how he came to be shot by Hollis. By the time I'd satisfactorily answered all of Maudy's questions, or so I hoped, it was well after midnight.

I took a long drag from the coffee cup, trying to wake up my brain, while Ray made his way to the nurses' station. I'd munched my way through half a scone by the time he returned with some news. "The nurse said Joe's awake and doing okay. They're moving him out of ICU and into a room first thing this morning."

I sighed with relief. "Great news."

Ray nodded. "What do you say we head over and sneak a peek in the nursery? See if we can see our new little nephew," he suggested. We all agreed, making our way back once again to the maternity wing. Finding the nursery, we all four stood, our noses pressed against the glass searching the names on the bassinets.

"Hey, guys." It was Hollis. He was coming down the hall, a cup of coffee in hand, looking as proud as could be. "Here to see my boy?" He puffed out his chest and pointed down the hall. "He's in the room with Ida. Come on back and see him."

I started to protest, imagining the last thing Ida would want was a room full of men gawking at her in her hospital gown. Before I could head them off, though, they trotted down the hall after Hollis. Surprisingly, Ida didn't seem put out at all with the entourage of visitors. In fact, she looked quite happy to see us. "His first visitors." She beamed from across the room, holding the baby up for our inspection. "Everyone, meet Hollis Jr."

That stopped me in my tracks. *Hollis Jr.? Oh boy.*

"We're going to just call him Junior for a while," Hollis said, taking a seat next to Ida on the bed. His gestures were extra animated as he went on about his son. "Looks like a linebacker, don't y'all think? I mean, look at the way he's built."

"Oh, Hollis. Enough!" Ida bantered. "Maybe he won't even like football."

"Not like football?" Cade and Hawk said in unison. Which quickly prompted an all-out discussion on this year's SEC prospects.

I shook my head, pushed past Ray and the guys, and moved in closer, anxious to get ahold of the sweet little thing.

Cradling him securely in the crook of my arm, I reached down with my other hand and tickled his plumb cheek. "Well, hello, there, Junior. I'm your aunt Nola." He opened his mouth, quietly pursing his lips until they formed a sweet little *O* shape as his velvety blue gaze connected with mine. I fell instantly in love. "Oh, Ida." My voice caught. "He's absolutely perfect."

She beamed with happiness. "We think so, too."

My heart practically overflowed with joy as I held my nephew. Joy and a bit of regret. Regret because as I looked at him, I couldn't help but think of the child I'd lost so long ago. My stomach knotted as my gaze landed on Hawk. He'd never known our one reckless night had resulted in a pregnancy. For me, however, I'd replayed the sequence of horrible events over and over in my mind. Wondering if there wasn't something I could have done differently.

It was my senior prom and I'd gone with Danny Hicks. He wasn't my first choice for a date. Cade was. But in those days, Cade never noticed me as anything other than a friend. Poor Danny. My heart just wasn't into it, which was why when Hawk, a rebel from one county over, showed up and crashed the party, I was more than willing to ride off with him on the back of his motorcycle. I still remember how free it felt. Like I was riding miles away from Cays Mill, when in reality we ended up down by the river, not far from my house.

I was in way over my head with Dane Hawkins. And after a few laughs and more than a few sips of beer, we . . . Well, one thing led to another. I was mortified when I found out I was pregnant. Hattie was with me. We'd lifted the pregnancy test from the back aisle of the Pearson's Drugstore. I didn't know where to turn. Of course, in hindsight, I realized I should have gone to my mama, but at the time, I couldn't bear the disappointment I'd bring my family. I was overcome with shame. There wasn't a moment that went by that I didn't wish I could take it all back, make the baby go away, go back to living my carefree life.

Then I got my wish.

The cramping started one afternoon when I was working my summer job at the Tasty Freeze. Horrible waves of pain and nausea. One look at me after work and my mama rushed me to Doc Harris's office. That was where the bleeding started. It only took Doc a couple minutes to figure out what was going on: I was pregnant and losing the baby. All those silent prayers were answered. Just like that. Only I was devastated. Absolutely overwrought with guilt and remorse. Had I really prayed for the loss of human life? I knew, even now, as I looked back over the years, that guilt propelled me into a career of atonement. Even my colleagues marveled at my tireless efforts to save lives. It was because I was forever making up for the one life I'd lost. One precious little life . . .

"Nola?" My sister's voice brought me back to focus. I shook my head. How long had I been staring at Hawk? By the look on his face, too long. In fact, one quick glance told me that everyone in the room was looking at me with concern.

"Are you okay?" Ray asked.

"Just tired. Afraid the last couple of days have caught up with me." I gave the baby a quick squeeze and handed him back to Ida.

"Catching murderers and being shot at can do that to you," Cade said.

"I'm just grateful no one was seriously hurt." I cast a woeful look Hollis's way. "And at least now everyone will know who really killed Ben Wakefield." Even as I said the words, I could hardly believe it was true. Joe had killed Wakefield. It just didn't seem possible. Looking over at my brother, I asked, "What'll happen to Joe? It wasn't premeditated; he just lost control. I mean, the man was practically pushed over the edge. First his son, then Wakefield threatening to take his land."

Ida let out a snort. "I still can't believe you were involved in that, Hollis. Really, now. Taking an old man's land? That's low."

"He didn't pay his taxes, for cryin' out loud," Hollis protested. "It's just business, Ida. You know that."

I frowned at him. "I have the feeling you've been putting the squeeze on a few other people in town, too. Ginny and Sam? Maybe Sally Jo at the Mercantile and Doris at the Clip and Curl."

Hollis held up his hand. "I'm completely in my rights to do so. Each of their loan agreements contains an acceleration clause. It's completely legal, isn't it?" He looked toward Ray for help.

"Well." Ray cleared his throat. "Legal, yes. Good business? Well, that's another thing."

"I don't get it. What's this 'acceleration clause' about?" Hawk asked.

"Basically"—Ray took on his attorney persona and started to explain—"it's a mortgage clause that renders the loan contract null if the borrower misses a payment. At that point, the lender can call in the full amount of the loan. It's common in business loans. It protects the lender in case the borrower defaults. Assets can be seized or whatever it takes to pay the loan."

"So all these people defaulted on their loans?" Cade asked.

Hollis hemmed and hawed a little before our relentless stares forced him into an explanation. "Well, yes. Sort of. Sally Jo missed last month's payment. Claims she lost track of time. Ginny and Sam? Well, their son's college tuition has them strapped. They've only been making partial—"

"What?" It was Ida. I wasn't sure if her hormones were still on overdrive from the birth, or what, but by the way she was looking at Hollis, there was going to be another murder in town. "You're basically extorting our friends to raise money so you can buy some poor old man's land out from underneath him? Face it, Hollis. If you hadn't sunk so much money into the Wakefield Lumber scam, you wouldn't need to recoup your losses."

Hollis hung his head in shame. "You're right." Then he drew in his breath, lifted his chin. "But I never killed any-body. And we can put all this behind us now. The killer's been caught and my name's been cleared." Except for the fact that he shot Joe. One glance at Ray told me he was thinking the same thing, but neither of us brought it up. Now wasn't the time for that discussion.

"Anyway," Hollis continued. "Now maybe things can get back to normal." He reached over to pat Ida's shoulder, but she shifted away. Something told me that it'd be a while before things were normal again in the Shackleford home.

"Well, I for one am ready to call it a day." I stood and straightened my dress, which now sported a partially ripped seam and a coating of dust. Who knew, when I put it on the morning before, just how much wear and tear it would go through?

"I'll ride with you." Hawk started for the door.

Cade jumped up and started after him. "Me, too. I need to get back and help Hattie with the girls, anyway." Hattie had generously offered to keep the twins for the rest of the weekend, so Hollis and I could spend time at the hospital with Ida.

"Hold it, guys." I shot Ray a pleading look. "Would you mind giving them all a ride? There's something I need to do on the way out."

Luckily, Ray was more than happy to run the guys back to their places. He looked up at the clock on the wall. "I'll probably drop them by their places and then head to church before heading back over to Perry. I have some work to catch up on before tomorrow morning."

"Church?" Ida teased. "Haven't seen you there for a while."

He glanced my way and winked before looking back down at Ida and the baby. "Well, I ran into Reverend Jones, doing his rounds here last night while we were waiting for word on Ida. I wanted to thank him for his prayers. I figure I've got a lot to be thankful for." He ran a finger across Junior's cheek. "But don't worry, now. I'll be seeing you all next weekend after I pick Mama and Daddy up from the airport. Won't they be surprised to find out we've had an early visitor?"

After telling everyone good-bye, I headed back out for the nurses' station and inquired about Joe. A few minutes later, I ran into Deputy Travis lingering in the hall outside Joe's room.

"Nola."

"Hello, Travis. How's Joe?"

He fingered his Stetson in one hand, a coffee cup clutched in the other. "He's better. The doctors are going to keep him awhile for observation. Sheriff's coming back by soon to ask him a few questions."

"Is he awake?"

"Believe so."

I glanced toward the room. "Mind if I pop in for a minute?"

Travis mulled over my request for a couple seconds before finally shrugging. "Don't see why not. Sheriff didn't say he couldn't have visitors."

Joe was sitting up in bed, his eyes glued to a television

hanging from the wall. A popular reality show was playing. "How are you, Joe?"

He peeled his eyes away from the television and nodded. "Reck'n I'll be just fine."

"So glad to hear it. I've been worried about you." I took the chair next to his bed. "The deputy's outside the door, you know."

"Yup." His eyes wandered back to the screen.

"Has the sheriff been in yet to talk to you?"

"Nope. The deputy said she'd be comin' by later this morning. Wonder if they got television in prison?"

I swallowed hard and nodded.

A brief smile flashed across his face, then faded away. "I'll never see my land again."

His age-spotted hands fumbled with the bed linen, rubbing it between his fingers like a strand of worry beads. I drew in my breath. "What made you kill him, Joe? Why didn't you just walk away?"

His eyes bounced back to me, wide and scared. "I didn't mean to kill him. It just happened. I never meant for him to die."

Part of me felt bad for Joe, but strangling someone didn't happen just by accident. I shook my head. "I don't understand."

He worked his mouth back and forth a few times before finally speaking again. "I saw him leave the party and come out to the orchard. He was just standin' around, like he was waitin' for someone. That's when I decided to talk to him about my land."

He paused for a second, shifting uncomfortably in his bed. I stepped forward to readjust the pillows behind his back. "We got to arguin'," he continued. "He said all sorts of things about takin' my land. He called me stupid. Even said my boy was stupid for gettin' himself killed in the machinery like he did."

At the mention of his son, I could see a surge of emotions welling inside Joe. Emotions that were eating at him, needing to get out. I sat on the edge of his bed, resting my hand on his arm, right above his IV line. "Go on," I gently urged.

"Well, I got real angry when he said that. Didn't mean to, but I shoved him. I shoved him hard and he fell backwards and hit his head on one of the tree branches."

I nodded. "Then what?"

Joe scratched at his whiskers. "Couldn't believe what I'd done. That I'd killed him. I got scared and ran." He averted his gaze. "I'm ashamed. But that's what I did. I ran."

"You ran?" *Was I hearing him correctly?* No mention whatsoever of strangling Ben Wakefield? Or the scarf. Was he confused? Maybe his injuries had taken more from him than I thought. "Joe, news about Ben Wakefield's murder has been all over town. It was in the newspaper and everything."

A quick glance downward and a flush of his cheeks said it more clearly than any words—Joe couldn't read. No wonder he wasn't aware of the developments in the Wakefield murder or the pending foreclosure on his land. Still, his account of the argument seemed sincere to me. Could it really be that Joe had no idea Ben Wakefield was strangled to death? If so, that could only mean one thing: Joe wasn't the killer.

"Have you seen Deputy Travis?" I asked the nurse a few minutes later. Joe's account of his argument with Ben Wakefield had stirred up a mixture of emotions. For starters, I felt relieved that perhaps Joe wasn't a murderer after all. Confusion, because if Joe wasn't the killer, then who? Then, of course, I was worried because I knew as soon as Maudy became convinced that Joe wasn't the killer, she'd probably turn her focus right back to Hollis. Worse yet, she might even assume Hollis had tried to pin the whole thing on Joe and that shooting him was no accident. I shuddered. How awful would that be? Then I felt guilt. Guilt because instead of taking what I knew straight to the sheriff and perhaps getting

Joe off the hook for murder, I wanted to talk to Ray first. Get his opinion about Joe's story and figure out the best way to rally another defense for Hollis, just in case things turned bad quickly. Not that I would ever let Joe take the rap for something he didn't do. It was just that . . . well, Hollis was my sister's husband. And, for a Harper, family came first.

"He left, ma'am. Got called out on some sort of domestic disturbance." She pursed her lips and exhaled loudly. "These things always happen after the Harvest Fest Dance." At the mention of the dance, I cast a regretful glance down at my grungy dress, now paired with my field boots of all things. I sighed. Cade and I never did get our special evening together. The nurse went on. "We see all sorts of things in here after the festival and dance. Guess people drink too much, say too much and do things they shouldn't. Hangovers and jealousy are a bad combination." She emphasized this last point with a shake of her head. "Anyways, Travis said he and the sheriff would be back in a couple hours or so to talk to Mr. Puckett."

I glanced at my watch. A couple hours. That gave me some time. I thanked her and turned on my heel, determined to get ahold of Ray before things spiraled out of control . . . again. Out in the lot, I stopped short of my Jeep and punched his number into my cell. There was no answer. He was probably still en route, dropping off Cade and Hawk. I remembered him saying he might go to church before heading out of town, so I decided to try to catch up with him there.

As I neared the square, I noticed the cleanup efforts had yet to start. The streets, teeming with festivalgoers just hours before, were now empty of people but littered with reminders of them. The ground in front of the stage area was covered with empty plastic cups, discarded cotton candy tubes and red-and-white-checkered paper food boats. A few abandoned booths still remained on the courthouse lawn along with the now silent and still merry-go-round and a handful

of kiddie inflatables, scattered about the grass like a bunch
of deflated balloons. The whole town looked as if it was
suffering from a massive hangover.

I pulled into the church lot and parked near the entrance
so I could catch Ray as soon as he arrived. Wondering why
the lot was still empty, I glanced at my watch. Only a little
after nine. Services wouldn't start for another forty-five
minutes. Still, I reasoned, it would be best to stay put and
wait instead of running around town trying to locate him.
Besides, knowing Ray, he'd likely just give his thanks and
an update to Reverend Jones prior to the service and then
scoot on out. Neither of us was big on church services.

I hadn't been parked long when something caught my
attention. I sat up straighter, homing in on a man walking
by the bushes at the back of the church. I squinted. It couldn't
be, could it?

I hopped out of my Jeep and hightailed it to the back wall
of the church. Hugging the wall, I glanced around the corner
just in time to see Floyd Reeves disappear behind an overgrown winterberry hedge. So, it *was* Floyd Reeves. No wonder Hawk couldn't find him in Macon. He'd been hiding out
here all along.

I whipped out my cell and was about to call the sheriff
when I heard Floyd talking to someone. "Why meet here?"
he asked. "Church will be starting soon."

"I've got my reasons," came another voice. I flinched and
pressed myself closer to the wall, almost dropping my phone
in the process. Floyd was meeting with someone, and that
someone was Millicent!

"Just give me my money, so I can get out of here."

Millicent laughed, a low, menacing sound that sent shivers
down my spine. "Afraid that's not going to happen, Floyd."

A silence hung in the air. I assumed Floyd was caught off
guard by Millicent's remark. "What do you mean?" he finally
responded. "We agreed to an additional five thousand."

"I don't think so, Floyd."

"Like I told you on the phone, if you don't pay up, I'll go to the cops."

"Oh yeah. And what exactly is it you're going to tell them? You're in this as deep as I am."

I couldn't see their faces, but the tension was palatable, even from where I was hiding.

"Look, Millicent. This isn't about just about the arson. You told me you needed me to start that fire for the insurance money, but I've been reading the papers. I've got it figured out. You're using me to cover something bigger. Murder."

"Murder? You don't know what you're talking about, Floyd."

"Sure, I do. You see, I've got you figured out, lady. You've been playing me all along. When you first approached me, you said you'd inherited the mill and that you'd be closing it down, never lumbering these hills again. I was all for that. Then you told me about this idea to set a fire, just big enough to do some damage so you could collect insurance money. Said that if you couldn't collect the insurance money, you may have to start up the mill again. I didn't want to see that happen, so I went along with your idea, especially since you offered me part of the earnings. All I'd have to do is set the fire and hang low for a while, wait for the money to roll in." His voice wavered. "A great opportunity, I thought, to fund my anti-lumbering crusade. I was planning to head up north, take on some of the bigger mill companies." I could hear his feet shuffling against the pavement. "It didn't dawn on me until afterwards that it was weird you just wanted to burn down one woodpile, in the middle of the day, too. I mean, how much insurance are you really going to collect from such a small loss? Then, when I read the papers, it all started to click. *I* didn't put that bottle of Peach Jack up by that wood- pile. You must have done that. And your car? I bet you did that, too. You're trying to frame that Hollis fellow. You needed me because you wanted to make sure you had an alibi for the time of the fire; otherwise folks would have suspected you right away. Or maybe if your plan to frame that banker fellow failed, you'd point the finger my way. Say that I was some lunatic, stopping at nothing, including murder, to prevent the mill from continuing its operations. Well, I don't want anything to do with you or murder. So, just give me the money and I'll leave. Maybe head down to Mexico or something."

In the background, I could hear a car pull into the lot. Probably the reverend getting to church early so he could run through his sermon before the congregation arrived. I knew he wouldn't be able to see me from the front of the church, but I wondered if he might see my car and come looking for me. Or would he just assume it was left over from last night's festivities? Someone who'd had a little too much to drink and decided to ride with a friend, leaving their car to be picked up today.

"You really are such a stupid young man," Millicent said.

"Come on," Floyd pleaded. "People are starting to get here. Just give me the money."

"Sorry, Floyd. That's not how things are going to go down."

"What do you mean?" I heard a sharp shuffling of feet and a loud gasp from Floyd. I peeked around the edge of the corner to see Millicent, her back toward me, pointing a gun at Floyd's chest. He took a couple steps back, his eyes wide with fear. "What are you doing? Are you crazy?"

"I don't like to be threatened," she said, overenunciating every syllable. With her free hand, she reached up and ripped the shoulder seam on her blouse. "I'm going to tell the cops that you attacked me while I was on my way to church. I'll make it look like you were trying to kill me and I had no other choice than to defend myself. They'll believe me, too. Half the town thinks your some sort of fanatic out to ruin anyone involved in the lumber business." She reached up and ran her free hand through her hair until it looked disheveled, all the while keeping the gun carefully trained on Floyd. She laughed some more. "You were right—you've been plan B all along, Floyd. If pinning the murder on the banker doesn't work, I'll simply plant some evidence that points to you."

Floyd's eyes flicked over Millicent's shoulder and connected for a brief second with mine. I was sure the look on my face mirrored the same horror I was seeing in his. I started to duck back around the corner again, but too late. Floyd's reaction at seeing me caught Millicent's attention for a split second and she glanced over her shoulder. That single lapse in focus was enough for Floyd to make a break for it. He started for the fence, trying to climb over the top and get away. Millicent heard him scramble and turned back, raising the gun and pointing it at his back.

"No!" I screamed and then clamped both hands over my mouth. Millicent wheeled, her crazed eyes homing in on me.

I stood, paralyzed with fear as she pointed the gun at me. "You!" She quickly closed the distance between us, gun trained on me the whole time.

"Take it easy, Millicent. No need to do something crazy." Although, those were perhaps the most stupid words I'd ever uttered. Millicent's twisted expression epitomized craziness. This woman was going to kill me. No doubt about it.

We stood there, both of us frozen in place, caught between her insanity and my absolute, unequivocal terror, for what seemed like an eternity. Finally, my little voice of reason, the one I'd heard time and time again in crisis situations, cut through the fog of fear in my brain and told me to keep her talking.

"You killed your husband," I started. Out of the corner of my eye, I saw a slight movement in the back window of the church. Was someone watching right now? Calling the police? I ever so slowly started inching my way toward the church's back door. "Why'd you do it? The affair?"

"The affair?" Millicent's lips twisted upward. "I guess you could say that. I knew when I married Ben that he was a small-town guy, but . . ." Her eyes took on a strange sheen as she spoke. "But we'd worked out an arrangement. Him down here with his mill and me up in the city." She shrugged. "As long as the money was flowing, things were good. But then he got all caught up in that little hussy and started making bad decisions. I swear, his brain turned to mush."

"So, he was losing business."

She nodded, the barrel of the gun moving in rhythm with her head. "Yeah, that's right. He made one bad deal after another. Things were getting tight. We started arguing more. Then he decided he was in love with that woman. Love! Can you imagine? That girl's nothing but low-rent trash."

I blinked double time. How odd that she and Ida used the same exact words to describe Laney. "You followed him to the orchard after the party?"

"That's right. I was served with the divorce papers earlier that week. He was suing for practically all our assets, even the house. How dare he! So, I came down here to have it out with him. Only he refused to listen. I followed him to the party that night to make one last plea."

"And you found him arguing with Joe Puckett?" I raised my voice and inched a little closer to the door. Hopefully, whoever was inside had noticed us by now and called the police.

She tipped her head back and let out an evil laugh. "You mean the old man?"

I nodded.

"He set things up perfectly for me. I saw them arguing, the old man getting more heated by the second. Then Ben said something to him. Must have ticked him off real bad, because he shoved Ben back against the tree. Knocked him clean out."

"And that's when you made your move?"

"How could I not? Ben lying there unconscious. The scarf hanging in the tree branch. All I had to do was cinch it around his neck and wipe it clean of prints. Simple. Easy. Almost as if fate was calling to me, answering my prayers."

I shuddered to think of her prayers. She shoved the gun in my face, causing me to stumble backward. Over the course of the conversation, I'd worked my way toward the back door of the church, which seemed smart at the time. Only now Millicent had me pinned against the wall at gunpoint.

"You're a problem," she started. "I could have shot Floyd and called it self-defense, but no one would buy that excuse with you. So this is what we're going to do." She had the barrel of the gun pressed against my skin. "We're going to go for a little drive out to the mill." She waved her free hand toward the lot. "We'll take your car. That way, when they find your body, they'll just assume you were out there nosing around and had an accident." She chuckled. "A deadly accident."

I shook my head and pressed harder against the wall. "You're not going to get away with this, Millicent."

She shot me a wily grin. "Are you kidding? With the dim-witted sheriff y'all got?" Her grin turned to a sneer as she began to lose patience. "Now move!"

Suddenly the back door of the church flew open and Laney Burns came out screaming and wielding a can of Aqua Net. Immediately, I jumped back and covered my eyes. Millicent wasn't so quick, though. She cried out in agony and dropped the gun as Laney doused her eyes with a direct stream of the potent chemical.

"Get the gun, you idiot!" Laney yelled, still pointing the can at Millicent, who was crouching against the wall, holding her face in agony.

I bent down and scooped up the weapon, cradling it uncertainly in the palm of my hand. The steel felt surprisingly cold.

"Oh, for cryin' out loud." Laney dropped the can and ripped the gun from my hands. "Didn't your daddy teach you nothin' about guns?" I watched in amazement as she double-gripped the handle—red glossy nails gleaming in the sunlight—and spread her legs, assuming a perfect Charlie's Angel stance. She even managed to flip her hair over her shoulder in the process. "Freeze, sucker!" she barked; then her serious expression broke and she began to giggle. "I've always wanted to say that."

I pulled out my cell and started to dial. "Just hold that position, Laney. I'm calling the police."

. . .

"So, now what?" Ida asked. Almost a week had passed since the Harvest Festival and we were sitting in the rockers on the front porch, waiting for Ray to bring Mama and Daddy home. Junior was next to us, sleeping peacefully in his carrier, while Roscoe kept dutiful watch. I bent down and fingered one of the pup's long ears. At least I had a couple extra days with the little fellow. Hawk asked me to puppy sit awhile longer so he could wrap up the final details of the case. Only I knew his real reason for hanging around wore pink stilettos and had a penchant for red nail polish. I'd heard through the Cays Mill peach vine that they'd become quite the item. I was happy for them. Really, I was.

I rocked back in my chair and gazed out over the orchard where Charlotte and Savannah were walking arm in arm, their blond locks catching the sun and their heads bent together in a conspiratorial manner. I drew in my breath and started to answer Ida's question. "Well, once the cops caught up with Floyd Reeves, he turned on her. Told them all about how Millicent had hired him for arson, but how he suspected she'd planted the bottle of Peach Jack to frame Hollis to cover her own dirty deeds. His testimony pretty much solidifies the case against her. According to Ray, there's not a lawyer in the entire state who could save her from a life sentence behind bars."

Ida rocked back and dabbed at her forehead with a handkerchief. "I, for one, don't feel a bit sorry for her. When I think what that woman put me and my family through . . . Let's just say if it'd been me holding that gun instead of Laney, why, I might have pulled the trigger."

I obliged her rant with a slight nod, knowing darn well Ida could never hurt a fly.

"And I'm here to tell you," she continued, "that Laney Burns may be low-rent trash, but I'm sure as heck glad she was around when you needed her."

I chuckled. "I would have never expected to find Laney

Burns at church. Guess she was there early to get herself spiffed up for some solo she was going to sing. Who knew she was the church choir type?"

Ida pursed her lips and rolled her eyes skyward. "Oh, shoot, yes. That girl sees herself as some sort of gospel-singing diva. Takes it all very seriously. You should hear how she belts it out at church."

I shook my head in wonderment before going on to explain the rest of the news to Ida. "As for Joe . . ." I sighed. "He's doing so much better. He's back home now. The sheriff's not pursuing any charges against him."

"Thank goodness he's okay. Things could've been so much worse. . . ." She shook her head. "Hollis's drinking really got him into a heap of trouble this time. As it is, they all came to an agreement. No one's going to press charges for the shooting if Hollis agrees to work out some sort of deal to help Joe pay his back taxes and stay on his land."

"That's wonderful!" I enthused. I'd been worried about what type of trouble Hollis might face for shooting Joe.

Ida continued, "I still can't believe Hollis was mixed up in taking that poor man's land. You know, he feels real bad about all that now."

I had an inkling that his "feeling real bad" had more to do with Ida telling him how to feel and what to do about it. But, knowing Ida, she'd give credit to her husband either way. "Well, it looks like everything's going to be okay, after all."

Ida smiled. "Sure is. But getting back to my original question . . . now what?" She looked at me with a pointed expression.

"Oh, you mean with me?"

"Yes, silly. With you."

My eyes swept over the farm, from the orchards to the old barn and back again. "I'll be staying on for a while to help Mama and Daddy here at the farm. Thanks to your girls, my first foray as an entrepreneur was as success. I'll just need to convince Daddy that we can make a go of this sideline business. Thought maybe I might even look into opening a storefront somewhere down on the square. Just something small." I was trying to sound nonchalant, but lately, all I could think about was the possibility of opening such a shop—rows and rows of tasty Harper Peach products, interspersed with other peachy items. Perhaps the tangy-smelling peach-scented candles or the handmade peach soap I'd spied at the Harvest Festival. Local vendors would probably jump at a chance to consign their products in my shop. And during harvest season, I could offer crates of fresh, juicy peaches in every variety for visitors to purchase by the bagful. . . .

"Won't be easy, you know." Ida's voice cut through my daydream and brought my focus back to reality.

She was right. Dreaming of such a venture was one thing; convincing our Daddy of its legitimacy was another. I sighed. "You're right. Nothing's ever that easy with Daddy. He'll probably never go for any of my ideas."

She waved off my words. "Heck, I'll help you with him. I was talking about living back here." She bent down and shooed a fly away from the baby. "Sometimes this town's hard on a person."

Hearing a wisp of sadness in her tone, I cast a curious glance her way. The roundness of her shoulders and slight downturn of her lips hinted at the toll the past few weeks had taken on her. "How are things with you and Hollis?"

"Oh, ya know, I'm angry. Angry about a whole lot of things. But we've met with Reverend Jones a couple times this past week. Talking through our troubles. Hollis seems determined to make things up to me."

We rocked in silence for a few minutes before she finally spoke again. "You know, you could have come to me, Nola."

I stopped rocking and looked her way. "What do you mean?"

"All those years ago. When you got in trouble."

I swallowed hard and looked away.

She went on, "I put it all together the other day at the

hospital. When you were holding Junior, looking at Dane Hawkins that way."

I opened my mouth to speak, but couldn't summon any words.

"I got to thinking about that summer before you left," she continued. "I remembered how you slipped into that gawd-awful funk. It gave Mama fits." She heaved a sigh. "Plus, I'd heard a rumor that you left the prom with some boy from the next county over. Then that day you got so sick at work with those horrible cramps, Mama was so worried she took you in to see Doc Harris. Well, I didn't think much about it back then, but when Hawk showed up here, I noticed you got to actin' all strange and everything. Then at the hospital the other day"—she shrugged—"I knew. I just knew."

I unclenched my hands to swipe a tear from my cheek and sniffled. "You're right," I whispered.

She reached across the table and touched my arm. "Nola. Losing that baby wasn't your fault. It just happens sometimes."

"But I was so ashamed. I'd prayed for it to go away. And then when it did—"

"Hush, now. You know God answers prayers according to His will, not ours. And everything happens for a reason. You going away for all these years . . . all the good you did in so many places, why, honey, we've always been so proud of you. But what I'm trying to say is there was a reason for all that." She pulled back her hand and started dabbing at her own face. "Just like there's a reason for you being back here now."

I was wiping my face double time, tears freely flowing, when I heard Ray's car coming down the drive.

"They're here!" my nieces called out in unison, running pell-mell for the driveway. "They're here!"

Roscoe let out a few excited yelps and pranced around the porch, almost tripping me up as I hurried out to meet the car. Mama, the first one out, was immediately tackled by my nieces and smothered in kisses. "Nana, Nana!" Charlotte cried with excitement. "I sold all your peach preserves."

I slapped my forehead, squeezing my eyes shut, until I heard my mother respond, "Oh, that's nice, dear. Now, where's that new grandbaby of mine?"

Thank goodness for little distractions.

Daddy lumbered out of the car next. I ran to him, wrapping my arms around his neck and kissing his cheek. "I'm so glad you're home, Daddy!"

"Aw, darlin', I sure missed all you." He engulfed me in a giant bear hug, lifting my feet from the ground and twirling me the same way he did when I was a little girl. Then, putting me down, he turned his focus to the front porch, where Mama was already fussing over Junior. Savannah and Charlotte bounced around her legs, proudly showing off everything about their new baby brother, from his tiny fingers to the toes on his wrinkly pink feet. Ida looked on, beaming with joy.

Ray came up next to us and set down a couple pieces of luggage. Placing his hands on his hips, he nodded toward the porch. "Will you look at all that? Seems to me like a lot of fussing going on over there."

Daddy's grin spread from ear to ear. "Believe me, Bud. Now that there's a new baby around, the womenfolk won't pay a bit of attention to us. Why, we won't get a hot meal around here for weeks."

Ray playfully patted his belly. "I don't think you'll suffer too much, Pops."

We chuckled and started for the porch. "How was your trip, Daddy?" I asked. "Did you have fun on your cruise?"

He paused midstep and looked at me. "It was fine, darlin'. Just fine. Those white beaches and that green water were something to see. But I got to tell ya, there's really no place in the world I'd rather be than right here." He swept his arms out in front of him. "Right here on my farm with my family."

I wrapped my arm around his back and laid my head against his chest. "Me, either, Daddy. Me, either."

Recipes

Scrumptious Peach Cobbler
(Courtesy of the Baptist Church Ladies' Society)

8–10 fresh peaches
1 lemon—juiced
¼ cup white sugar
¼ cup brown sugar
¼ teaspoon cinnamon
¼ teaspoon nutmeg
2 teaspoons cornstarch

Cobbler Topping

2 cups all-purpose flour
½ cup white sugar
½ cup brown sugar
2 teaspoons baking powder
1 teaspoon salt
1 ½ sticks cold unsalted butter
½ cup hot water
2 tablespoons white sugar for sprinkling

Peach Mixture: Preheat oven to 400 degrees. Peel and slice peaches (removing the pits) into thin wedges and place inside a large bowl. Add the juice of one lemon and toss to coat evenly. In a separate bowl, combine ¼ cup white sugar, ¼ brown sugar, cinnamon, nutmeg and cornstarch. Add this mixture to the peaches and stir gently until peaches are coated. Place peach mixture into a 2 quart dish and bake for 10 minutes.

Cobbler: In a large bowl, combine flour, sugars, baking powder and salt. Cut cold butter into small pieces and mix into dry ingredients until slightly blended. The mixture should be crumbly. Add hot water, a little at a time, until a dough forms. Do not exceed ½ cup of hot water.

Remove peaches from the oven and drop spoonfuls of cobbler on top until the peaches are covered. Sprinkle the entire cobbler with extra sugar. Place the dish on a baking sheet in case it bubbles over while baking.

Bake for 30–40 minutes or until the crust is golden brown.

Ezra Sugar's Peach Scones

3 peaches
1 ¾ cup all-purpose flour
¼ cup white sugar
½ teaspoon salt
4 teaspoons baking powder
5 tablespoons unsalted cold butter
½ cup milk
¼ cup sour cream

Egg wash

1 egg
1 tablespoon milk
2 tablespoons white sugar for sprinkling

Peel, remove pits and dice peaches into small pieces and set aside. Sift flour into a large bowl and add sugar, salt and baking powder. Mix well. Cut in cold butter until the dough mixture is crumbly. Do not overwork the dough.

In a separate bowl, combine milk and sour cream. Fold this mixture into the dry ingredients just until mixed. Add peaches.

Place the dough into the refrigerator and let chill for 15 minutes.

Remove cold dough and using floured hands, roll into 3 inch balls. Place balls on a lightly greased cooking sheet and flatten slightly.

In a small bowl, whisk together 1 egg and 1 tablespoon of milk. Brush this mixture over each scone and sprinkle with extra sugar. Bake in a 400 degree oven for 10–15 minutes or until edges are golden brown.

For an extra-peachy zing, serve with Harper's Spiced Peach Preserves. Yummy!

Della Harper's Blue Ribbon Peach Chutney

20–24 peaches—slightly underripe (firm to the touch)
2 lemons—juiced
2 cups of apple cider vinegar
3 cups light brown sugar
1 cup raisins
½ cup dried cranberries
1 onion—chopped
1 clove of garlic—finely chopped
1 teaspoon finely grated ginger

1 teaspoon cinnamon
1 teaspoon salt
½ teaspoon red pepper flakes
½ teaspoon mustard seeds

Blanch peaches for easy removal of skins by placing in boiling water for thirty seconds and then immediately rinsing with cold water. Peel, pit and chop peaches into small chunks and place into large stockpot. Add the juice of two lemons and the apple cider vinegar. Stir in remaining ingredients. Bring the mixture to a boil and then reduce heat to simmer for two hours or until chutney has reached desired thickness.

Ladle into sterilized pint jars leaving ¼–inch headspace. Wipe the rim with a clean paper towel. Center sterilized lid on the jar and screw on the band until firmly in place. Place jars into boiling water bath and process for ten minutes. Remove and let cool. After twenty-four hours, check each jar for proper sealing. Properly processed chutney can be stored in the cupboard for one year.

Yield: 5–7 (16-ounce) one-pint jars.

Sweet Georgia Peach Iced Tea

4 cups boiling water
3 family-sized tea bags or 9–12 regular-sized tea bags
5 ripe peaches—peeled, pitted and sliced
2 lemons—juiced
1 cup simple syrup*
5 cups ice

*Prepare simple syrup by placing 1 cup of sugar and 1 cup of water in a microwave-safe container. Microwave on high power for 2–3 minutes or until the sugar is dissolved.

Place 4 cups of boiling water in a large, heatproof pitcher and add tea bags. Let steep approximately 10 minutes before removing tea bags.

Place prepared peaches into a blender and blend until smooth. Run liquid through a strainer to remove pulp and any leftover peach pieces. Add the juice of two lemons and the simple syrup, and stir.

Pour peach mixture into tea and add 5 cups of ice. Serve with a slice of fresh peach as garnish.

Yields approximately one gallon of peach iced tea.

Harper's Spiced Peach Preserves

4 cups fresh peaches (or 4 cups frozen peaches
    macerated in sugar*)
2 lemons—juiced
1 package powdered pectin
5 cups sugar
1 teaspoon allspice
1 teaspoon finely grated ginger

Blanch peaches for easy removal of skins by placing in boiling water for thirty seconds and then immediately rinsing with cold water. Peel, pit and chop peaches.

In a large pot, combine peaches, the juice of 2 lemons, pectin, allspice and grated ginger. Stirring continuously, bring mixture to a full rolling boil (one that cannot be stirred down) and add sugar. Bring mixture back up to a boil and cook for an additional minute. Remove from heat and skim foam from the surface.

Ladle into sterilized jelly jars leaving ¼–inch headspace. Wipe the rim with a clean paper towel. Center sterilized lid on the jar and screw on the band until firmly in place. Place jars into boiling water bath and process for 5 minutes. Remove and let cool. After twenty-four hours, check each jar for proper sealing. Properly processed preserves can be stored in the cupboard for one year.

Yield: 5–7 (8-ounce) half-pint jars.

*Frozen Peaches—If you're too busy during peach season to make preserves, freeze your fresh peaches and make preserves anytime of year! The key is to macerate the frozen peaches in sugar as they thaw. This will prevent your preserves from becoming runny.

Here's how: Place 4 cups of frozen peaches in a large bowl and cover with 2 cups of sugar (reserved from the initial 5 cups). Make sure the peaches are completely coated and allow them to thaw at room temperature. The sugar will absorb excess liquid from the thawing peaches. Proceed with the rest of the recipe as directed, remembering to add only 3 cups of sugar after fruit mixture has reached a full rolling boil.

Turn the page for a preview of
Susan Furlong's next Georgia Peach Mystery . . .

Rest in Peach

Coming soon from Berkley Prime Crime!

Any woman who's had the privilege of growing up below the Mason-Dixon Line understands the history and tradition of a debutante ball. My mother was no exception. From the time I could walk, she started grooming me for my debut to polite society. I can still remember her little bits of advice to this day—tips she called her Debutante Rules. Of course, some of them were a little offbeat; but they did encourage me to become the best woman I could be. You see, my mama's advice taught me that being a debutante is less about the long white gloves, the pageantry, and the curtsey, and more about a code of conduct that develops inner beauty, a sense of neighborly charity, and unshakable strength in character that sees us women through the good times and the bad. Later, as I traveled the world, I came to learn these rules of hers transcended borders, cultures, and economic status. In essence my mama's Debutante Rules taught me that no matter where you're from or who your people are, becoming the best person you can be is key to a happy life.

Debutante Rule #032: Like a magnolia tree, a debutante's outward beauty reflects her strong inner roots . . . and that's why we never leave the house without our makeup on.

Frances Simms's beady eyes were enough to make my skin crawl on any given day, but at that particular moment the presence of the incessantly determined owner and editor of our town's one and only newspaper was enough to frazzle my last nerve.

"Can't this wait, Frances? I'm right in the middle of something." I turned my focus back to my project. Truth was, I could have used a break, my arm was about to fall off from all the scrubbing I'd been doing in my soon-to-be new storefront. Still, I'd suffer through more scrubbing any day if it meant I could avoid dealing with the bothersome woman. And today, of all days, I didn't need her pestering presence.

Frances persisted. "Wait? I'm on a deadline. Especially if you want the ad to run in Tuesday's issue." *The Cays Mill Reporter*, the area's source of breaking news—or rather, reputation-breaking gossip—faithfully hit the hot Georgia pavement every Tuesday and Saturday. Since I was a new business owner, Frances was hoping to sign me on as a contributing advertiser. For a mere twenty-four ninety-nine a month, I could reserve a one by one inch square on the paper's back page, sure to bring in hordes of eager, peach-lovin' customers to my soon-to-open shop, Peachy Keen.

"This offer isn't going to be on the table forever," she continued. "I'm giving you a ten percent discount off my normal rate, you know."

"Oh, don't go getting all bent out of shape, Frances," my friend, Ginny, spoke up. Having a slow moment at the diner next door, which she owned with her husband Sam, Ginny had popped over to check my renovation progress. "This is only Saturday," she went on. "Besides, Peachy Keen doesn't officially open for another few weeks."

Over the past nine months since my return to Cays Mill, what started as a little sideline business to help supplement my family's failing peach farm, had grown into a successful venture. From that first jar of peach preserves sold at the local Peach Harvest Festival to a booming online business,

Harper's Peach Products had been selling like crazy. Unable to keep up with the demand, I had struck a deal with Ginny and Sam: For a reasonable percentage of profits, I'd get full use of their industrial-sized, fully-licensed kitchen after the diner closed each day, plus a couple hours daily of Ginny's time and expertise in cooking. Since the diner was only open for breakfast and lunch, we could easily be in the kitchen and cooking by late afternoon, allowing Ginny enough time to be home for supper with her family. Then, Ginny offered to rent me their small storage area, right next to the diner, for a storefront—a perfect location—which now stored much of my stock until we could open. The deal worked for both of us: I needed the extra manpower and Ginny needed the extra money. Especially with one child in college and her youngest, Emily, finishing her senior year in high school.

Frances was pacing the floor and stating her case. "That may be true, but space fills up quickly. My paper's the leading news source for the entire area."

"Oh, for Pete's sake, Frances," Ginny bantered, "it's the *only* news source in the area. Besides, that quote you gave Nola is five bucks higher than what I pay for the diner's monthly ad."

I quit scrubbing and quirked an eyebrow Frances's way. "Is that so?"

"Well, I've got expenses and—" she started to explain but was cut off mid-sentence when the back door flew open and Emily burst inside.

"Mom!" Emily cried, her freckled face beaming with excitement. She held out Ginny's purse. "The delivery truck just pulled in front of the boutique. The dresses are in!"

Ginny let out a little squeal, cast a quick glance toward the window and reached into her bag. "Okay, okay. Just give me a minute to freshen up." She pulled a compact out and started touching up her lipstick, a shocking red color that looked surprisingly fabulous with her ginger-colored hair. "Oh, I can hardly wait! Emily's cotillion dress. Can you imagine!" she gushed and glanced my way. "Come on, Nola.

You said you'd come with us, right? You've just gotta see the gown we ordered."

I peered anxiously at the stacks of wood for the unfinished shelving, the loose plaster, and the wood floors that were still only half-refinished. Knowing the renovation was too much for me to handle alone, I'd hired my friend, Cade McKenna, who owned a local contracting business, to help me transform the storage area into a quaint shop. One of the interior walls sported exposed red brick and would add the perfect touch to the country-chic look I wanted. But my vision versus reality didn't mesh easily; I'd been scrubbing loose mortar from that wall for hours already. Cade said the loose stuff really needed to be removed before he could seal the rest. I sighed and glanced out the window. I'd already known my work would be interrupted later today when the delivery truck arrived; I'd been dragged into my dear friend and her daughter's excitement since the get-go. But truth be told, I almost preferred flaking mortar to facing up to the debutante issues I knew would soon erupt into a community-wide frenzy. "I'd love to go," I said. "But I really should keep at it."

Ginny waved off my worry. "You've been at it all morning. You need a break."

"Hey!" Frances turned her palms upward in protest. "I wasn't done discussing the ad."

"Oh, shush up, Frances," Ginny shut her down. She reached back into her bag, this time pulling out a small bottle of cologne and giving herself a couple quick spritzes behind the ears.

"You're fine, Mama," Emily interrupted. "Let's get going. I'm dying to try on my dress."

Ginny finished primping and shouldered her bag. "All right, sweetie. Let's go." Her eyes glistened as she squeezed her daughter's arm. "I just know you're going to be the most beautiful debutante at the cotillion!" Then turning to me, she added with a mischievous grin. "Are ya coming with us, or do you want to stay here and discuss the ad with Frances?"

Since she put it that way, I decided I could use a little break and proceeded to rip off my apron and remove the bandana covering my cropped hair. I ran my hand through the short strands, trying to give it a little lift, the extent of my personal primping routine, as I made my way to the back door. Opening it wide, I shrugged toward Frances who was still standing in the middle of my would-be shop, a befuddled look on her face. "Sorry, Frances. Guess we'll have to talk about the ad some other time."

She opened and shut her mouth a few times but all that came out was a loud huff. Finally relenting, she threw up her hands and stormed out the door. I couldn't help but stare after her with a grin on my face. Usually I didn't take so much delight in being rude, but ever since Frances's paper ran a smear campaign on my brother-in-law last August, I'd had a hard time being civil toward her. Who could blame me? At the time, she'd relentlessly pursued, harassed and tried to intimidate information from not only me, but my then-very-pregnant sister, Ida. And when Frances found she couldn't coerce information from us, she printed libelous half-truths about Hollis—on the front page, nonetheless!— that all but landed him a lifetime prison sentence. Thank goodness all that misery was behind us now. What a relief knowing the only thing Frances could hound me about these days was a silly display ad for the back page of the paper.

Emily was right; Hattie's Boutique was already teeming with a small but enthusiastic pack of giggling debutantes and their equally excited mothers. They were pressing against the main counter like a horde of frenzied Black Friday shoppers while Hattie pulled billows of white satin and lace from long brown boxes. Carefully, she hung each dress on a rack behind the counter. "Ladies, please!" she pleaded. "Take a seat in the waiting area. I just need a few minutes to sort out the orders."

One of the mothers, Maggie Jones, the preacher's wife,

was at the head of the pack sticking out her elbows like a linebacker in hopes of deterring the other gals from skirting around her in line. "Did the dress we ordered come in? Belle would like to try it on."

Hattie smiled through gritted teeth, once again pointing across the room toward a grouping of furniture. "I'm sure it did, Mrs. Jones. If y'all would just take a seat, please, I'll be right with you." She lifted her chin and kept her finger pointing across the room, making it clear she would not unpack one more dress until we complied.

With a collective sigh, the group, including Ginny, Emily, and me, sulked to the waiting area. The mothers politely settled themselves on the flower-patterned furniture while the girls huddled off to the side to discuss the latest debutante news. It was a wonder they never tired of the topic. I, for one, could hardly take much more. For months, I'd been hearing constant chatter about our town's spin on a high society debut: the presentation, what would be served at the formal dinner and, of course, all about how elegantly Congressman Wheeler's plantation would be decorated for the Peach Cotillion. Usually the whole shindig was held up north at some ritzy country club, but this year, thanks to the generosity of Congressman Jeb Wheeler, who just happened to be up for reelection, the cotillion was staying local with the ball taking place at his family home, the historic Wheeler Plantation.

"She's awful pushy for a preacher's wife, don't you think?" Ginny whispered.

I looked over to where the other women were seated. "Maggie Jones?"

Ginny's shoulders waggled. "Uh-huh."

Leaning back against the cushion, I inwardly moaned. That's why I hadn't wanted to come; Ginny was taking this cotillion stuff way too seriously. As a matter of fact, the impending cotillion and its accompanying affairs seemed to be bringing out the worst in all the town's ladies. Like the well-dressed woman across from us who sported an expensive-looking beige leather handbag and an all-too-serious attitude. She was seated with ramrod straight posture and legs folded primly to one side, a proud tilt to her chin as she impatiently—and imperiously—glanced around the room.

"Who's Miss Proper over there?" I quietly asked Ginny.

She glanced over and quickly turned back, her face screwed with disgust. "That's Vivien Crenshaw. You know, Ms. Peach Queen's mama." She nodded toward the group of girls, where a tall blonde with dazzling white teeth stood in the center. She was gushing dramatically about her date for the dance while the rest of the girls looked on in awe. "Her name's Tara," Ginny continued. "Emily says she's the most popular girl in high school. Top in everything: lead in the school play, class president, and head cheerleader . . . you know the type."

Yeah, I knew the type. A picture of my own sister's face formed in my mind. Ida, the star of the Harper clan, always exceeded everyone's expectations; whereas I always did the unexpected, keeping my family in a continuous state of quandary. Even to this day, there were things I just couldn't bear to tell my parents, for fear it would put them over the edge. I shook my head, telling myself not to think about all that right now.

Luckily, a movement outside distracted me from my downward spiral. Adjusting my position to get a better look, I gazed curiously at the young girl washing Hattie's windows. She was dressed in sagging jeans and a too-tight T-shirt topped off with shocking black hair that shadowed her features. This must have been the girl Hattie mentioned hiring for odd jobs. She was nothing like the other girls in town. I felt an instant connection to her. As I continued to look on, the girl paused, reached into the pocket of her jeans and extracted a hair band. She pulled back her hair, exposing several silver hooped earrings running along the rim of her ear and topped off with a long silver arrow that pierced straight through to the inner cartilage. Ew. That must have hurt! I felt no connection now. But still, it was fascinating. It reminded me of some of the

extreme piercings I'd observed in remote African tribes during my days as a humanitarian aid worker.

I was about to ask Ginny if she knew the girl when Hattie
called out from the other side of the room. "Okay, ladies. I
think I've got everything straightened out. Now one at a
time . . ." She held up the first dress. "Belle Jones." The
preacher's wife and her daughter scrambled to grab the dress
before heading off toward the dressing rooms. "And, this
one's for Sophie Bearden," Hattie continued, handing out
the next dress to a squealing brown-haired girl.

Just as Hattie was reaching for the next gown, jingling
bells announced the arrival of a short, stout woman dressed
in sensible polyester slacks and a scooped-neck top. She
removed her sunglasses and unwrapped a colorful scarf
from her head. "Lawdy! Can y'all believe this humidity
today?" She patted down her tight black curls before using
the scarf to dab at her décolletage.

Hattie's face lit up. "Mrs. Busby, thanks so much for coming in early."

The woman waved off the thanks with, "So how many
girls spied that early delivery truck?"

"Just a few, but if you could pin them up, it'd save having
to make extra appointments."

"Sure enough. Just send them back to my station."

In the back corner of the shop, Hattie had utilized a lovely
folding screen with an inlaid floral motif to partition an area
for alterations. Behind the partition, a large corner table held
an industrial sewing machine, racks of thread spools, a
myriad of scissors and a divided box of pins, buttons and
clasps. To the side of the workstation, a carpeted platform
rested in front of an antique white cheval mirror.

Hattie disappeared behind the counter again, where she
continued opening boxes and checking order slips while the
rest of the girls waited impatiently. The first girls were coming out of the dressing room, proud mamas trailing after
them and holding up their gowns as they made their way to

Mrs. Busby for alterations. After a couple more girls disappeared into the dressing rooms, the Peach Queen's mother heaved a sigh and glanced disgustedly at her watch. "How much longer is this going to take? I have an appointment at the salon in about ten minutes."

Hattie was still behind the counter, tearing through packing material, her expression panicked. "Of course, Mrs. Crenshaw. I'll be right with you," she answered with a strained voice.

Next to me, Ginny shifted and rolled her eyes, quietly mimicking the woman under her breath. "Can you believe how demanding that woman is?"

Ginny's usually good-natured demeanor was being stretched thin by the overbearing woman. At the moment, she reminded me of a spark getting ready to ignite and explode. I patted her hand and mumbled under my breath, "Remember why you're here. To show your daughter the importance of social grace, right?" I shot her a sly grin and stood. "I think I'll just go over and see if Hattie needs a hand." Hattie had seemed cool and controlled before but she looked like maybe she could use a bit of help now.

Just as I reached the counter to offer my assistance, the bells above the door jingled again. This time it was a model-thin woman wearing crisp linen pants and a matching jacket. Her silky silver hair was cut at a precise angle to accentuate her strong jawline and graceful neck. Upon seeing her, Hattie stopped her work, straightened her shoulders and plastered on a huge smile. So did everyone else in the room. It was as if they were all marionettes and the puppet master had just pulled their strings.

"Mrs. Wheeler! Uh . . . you must be here to pick up your alterations." Hattie's voice was thinning even more and her eyes darted nervously between her waiting customers and a rack of clothing lining her back wall. She took a little shuffle step as if she wasn't sure which way to go first.

Mrs. Wheeler glanced over the crowded waiting area and sensing Hattie's stress, put on a gracious smile and said, "I didn't realize you were so busy. Please don't bother with my order right this minute. I've got business at the flower shop down the street. How about I stop by when I'm done there? Perhaps things will have settled down by then."

Hattie let out her breath and nodded gratefully, promising to have the order ready when she returned. But as soon as the woman left, Hattie turned back to me with an even more panicked expression. "There's a problem," she whispered.

"A problem? What?"

She nodded toward the box on the floor. "There's only one dress left."

I shrugged.

"You're not getting it," she hissed, discreetly pointing across the room. "One dress, but two girls."

My eyes grew wide. "Oh."

Joining her behind the counter, I squatted down and started ripping through the mounds of packing paper. "Are you sure?" She slid down next to me. My mind flashed back to a competitive game of hide-and-seek we once played as kids. Hattie and I crouched together behind the peach crates in my daddy's barn, suppressing giggles as her big brother, Cade, searched and searched in vain. Only this situation wasn't fun and games at all.

She chewed her lip and nodded. "I'm sure."

"Well, whose dress is it?"

"Any chance you can hurry things up a bit?" Vivien Crenshaw called out from across the room. "Like I said, I'm on a tight schedule."

Hattie raised up and peered over the counter. "Be right with ya!" Then, popping back down she started to fall apart. "I just don't know what's happened . . . neither of the numbers on the order forms match the one on the dress, but I think it's Emily's. It's just been so crazy here . . . maybe I messed up when I placed the order. What am I going to do? Of all the dresses to be missing."

"Relax. Just tell Mrs. Crenshaw there was a mistake. The cotillion is still a couple weeks away. There's plenty of time to get Tara's dress shipped and altered. Mistakes happen, right?"

She nodded, drew in a deep breath and stood up. "Mrs. Crenshaw, would you mind coming over here, please?"

I busied myself behind the counter, folding up the packing materials, revealing more of the dress that was left in the box. I couldn't help but smooth my hand over the shimmery satin of the gown. Actually, it gave me a little thrill to finally see the dress Emily had been talking about for so long. But seeing it up close also gave me a little prickle of regret. Due to a tragic, youthful mistake I didn't really want to think about at that moment, I'd missed my own cotillion, something my mama had never quite forgiven me for. Actually, thinking back on it, I was always a bit of a tomboy and never put much stock in the debutante craze anyway. Charm classes, dance lessons . . . all that was never really my thing. Of course, being raised by a mama who prided herself in her southern heritage, I understood the reasoning behind such formalities. Like many things southern, it was a ritual passed down since the days before Mr. Lincoln's war. And, we southerners lived and died by our traditions, whether it was sweet tea, SEC football, or fancy cotillions.

I ran my hand over the fine lace accents on the bodice of Emily's dress. Still, it would have been fun to wear something so elegant. . . .

"What do you mean her dress isn't in yet? That's it right there."

My head snapped up. Vivien Crenshaw was pointing at the dress I was caressing. Her daughter, Tara, stood next to her, nodding enthusiastically as they both peered over the counter.

"Oh, no. I don't think so. I believe this is Emily Wiggin's dress," Hattie responded.

At the mention of her name, Emily started for the

counter. Ginny was right behind her. Guessing by the wild look in Ginny's eye and the slight flush of her cheeks, her hackles were up. I sucked in my breath.

"Let me see that," Ginny demanded. I stood and held it upright. She took a quick look and turned to Vivien. "I'm sorry, Vivien, but you're mistaken. That's the dress Emily ordered. I'd know it anywhere." And she would, too. She and Emily had spent days scouring over the catalogs at Hattie's Boutique, searching for Emily's dream cotillion dress—special ordered all the way from Atlanta—which I'd heard described a thousand times as an off-shoulder, satin sheath that would look all so beautiful on Emily's slim figure. Why, she was going to look just like a princess in it!

"No, you're the one who's mistaken," Vivien countered. She reached across the counter and snatched the dress from my hands. "Go try it on, Tara. And hurry. We're pressed for time."

"Now wait just a minute," Ginny intercepted her, placing a hand on Vivien's arm. "That's my daughter's dress and—"

"Ladies, please!" Hattie interrupted. "There's an easier way to resolve this. Just give me a few minutes and I'll call the dress company and get this straightened out." She already had the phone in her hand and was dialing the number as she walked toward the back room for privacy.

In the meantime, a crowd was gathering. Mrs. Busby, pincushion in hand, came tooling over to see about the ruckus. Right behind her shuffled one of the debs, dragging the hem of her too-long gown. Out of one of the dressing rooms came Belle Jones and her mother, Maggie, their eyes gleaming with anticipation. Even the dark-haired, window-washing girl stopped working and came inside to gawk. I swear, the whole scene reminded me of school kids gathering on the playground to witness a smackdown.

Emily spoke up, her eyes full of concern. "That's my dress, Mrs. Crenshaw, I'm sure of it."

Vivien's eyes shifted from Ginny and homed in on Emily. "This isn't your dress, young lady, and you know it."

Ginny recoiled then sprang forward, her eyes full of venom. "Are you calling my girl a liar?"

"Just calm down, Ginny," I pleaded, dashing out from behind the counter and grabbing ahold of my friend. "We'll get this figured out."

Under my grip, I could feel Ginny's muscles tensing. She was ready to fight for this dress. Thank goodness Hattie finally came out of the back room. She was carrying a large binder, her hands trembling as she flipped through the pages. "I'm afraid I've made a horrible mistake," she started to confess.

Vivien raised a brow. "A mistake?"

Hattie nodded. "Yes, you see, I would never order two of the same style dress for a cotillion. Y'all know how embarrassing it would be for two girls have the same one." She choked out a nervous little laugh before continuing. "But it seems both Tara and Emily picked the same dress from the catalog but I somehow got the numbers on one of them mixed up, so I didn't know there were two of the same. So when I ordered it, the company called for clarification on a number, and . . . well, the right catalog number was already ordered, even in the right size . . . so I thought I had everyone covered . . ." She swallowed hard, unable to dredge up her usual shopkeeper's smile.

Ginny lifted her chin. "Well, it's simple enough. Which one of us placed the order first?"

Hattie turned back a couple pages in the binder. "It looks like Emily did."

Vivien clutched the dress tighter. "Why does it matter who ordered first? We picked it up first. Besides, I'm sure Emily can find something else to suit her."

Two bright crimson circles suddenly appeared on Ginny's cheeks. "No way! You heard Hattie. That's our dress."

"I don't think so," Vivien countered.

Ginny reached for the gown, but Emily stopped her. "Don't, Mama. Please. It's alright. I'll pick out another." Tears welled in her eyes and her cheeks flushed with embarrassment as she scanned the room, taking in the reactions of the other girls.

Ginny wheeled and glared at her daughter. "Why should you? They're just trying to bully us."

Emily didn't respond. Instead, she pleaded silently with the most heartbreaking expression I'd ever witnessed. I knew exactly how she was feeling. If Tara Crenshaw was the most popular girl in school, crossing her would mean social suicide. The same thing must have dawned on Ginny too, because instantly her expression softened and she backed away from Vivien and the coveted dress.

Taking the change in Ginny's demeanor as a sign of surrender, Vivien triumphantly marched over to Mrs. Busby and shoved the dress into her hands. "Like I said, Tara and I are on a tight schedule. I'm afraid we won't be able to be fitted for alterations until later this evening. Let's say, six-thirty."

Mrs. Busby looked shell-shocked. "Six-thirty?"

Hattie piped up. "I'm afraid we close at six tonight, Mrs. Crenshaw. You'll have to—"

Mrs. Busby held up her hand. "It's alright. I don't mind staying a little longer."

"But, Mama!" Vivien's daughter cut in. "I'm supposed to meet my friends at the library. We won't be done by six-thirty."

"Don't interrupt," Vivien admonished, then turned back to Mrs. Busby with a slight nod. "It's all settled then." She turned on her heel and headed for the door, Tara following behind and whining all the way about the appointment messing up her plans.

As soon as the door shut behind them, Ginny's hands shot to her hips and her chest heaved as she drew in a deep breath.

Emily tried to intercept her. "It's okay, Mama. Let's just go. We'll come back tomorrow and look for another dress."

But my fiery friend was never one to simply back down from a fight. With an exaggerated harrumph and a waggle of her shoulders, she started in with, "Well, I never . . . !" and

continued on describing Vivien Crenshaw with a list of colorful adjectives that would threaten anyone's good standing
with the local Baptists, finally finishing the tirade with something like, " . . . I sure hope that nasty, dress-stealing, back-
stabbing snob gets hers one day!"

A collective gasp sounded around the room followed by
a moment of stunned silence. Emily looked like she wanted
to crawl under a rock. This was definitely not social grace.
"It's okay, everyone!" I assured the ladies, while trying to
pull Ginny aside for a little chill time. "She's just been under
a lot of pressure, that's all."

But Ginny shook me off and stomped toward the door,
turning back at the last minute. "I meant what I said," she
spat. Then, she lifted her chin and announced with a murderous gleam in her eye, "That witch stole my girl's cotillion
dress. And don't y'all think for one second that I'm going
to stand for it, neither. You mark my words, I'll make sure
that woman gets her due!"

The delicious mysteries of Berkley Prime Crime for gourmet detectives

Julie Hyzy
WHITE HOUSE CHEF MYSTERIES

B. B. Haywood
CANDY HOLLIDAY MURDER MYSTERIES

Jenn McKinlay
CUPCAKE BAKERY MYSTERIES

Laura Childs
TEA SHOP MYSTERIES

Claudia Bishop
HEMLOCK FALLS MYSTERIES

Nancy Fairbanks
CULINARY MYSTERIES

Cleo
COFFEEHOUS

Solving crime

pengu